THE LAIRD OF BLACKLOCH

HIGHLAND ROGUE
BOOK TWO

AMY ROSE BENNETT

DEDICATION

To my very own romantic hero, Richard. Your love, support, and unwavering belief in me mean the world to me. I love you, always.

PROLOGUE

Loch Arkaig, the Highlands, Scotland
July 1746

After stumbling through a hellish wilderness for months, Alexander Ewan MacIvor, Jacobite on the run and the last claimant to the attainted title, Baron Rannoch, felt his heart twitch with something akin to interest.

Lying low in the cool green shadows of a dense pine forest, a lichen-covered tree trunk and clump of bracken his only cover, he watched the group of braw Highlanders—Cameron men, by the look of their plaids—lug casket after heavy casket up the mossy slope below him. Seven wooden boxes in total.

He should be exercising extreme caution given the size of the party—a dozen men, all heavily armed with muskets, broad swords, dirks, and shovels—but burning curiosity urged Alex to inch closer and push a frond of bracken farther aside. Come hell or high water, he had to know what was in those chests.

Snatches of disjointed conversation and gruffly issued orders reached his ears. A mixture of Gaelic, French, and English thickened with a strong Scots burr not unlike his own.

Greas ort! Hurry. No, dig here. We have tae bury it afore night sets in. The Lochiel. Louis d'Or. Watch oot, ye daft prick.
Mr. Secretary "Traitor" Murray, damn him to hell.
Bloody Sassenachs...

And then there was the sweet musical chink of coins as one man prized open a box and thrust his hand inside.

Alex's heart kicked into a full gallop, hurtling against his ribs. *Sweet Jesus.* He'd stumbled across an absolute fortune. A king's ransom. Or a prince's...

One prince in particular. Prince Charles Edward Stuart. The Young Pretender. What a foolish, selfish, trumped-up cock the man had turned out to be. A pathetic leader and a sorry excuse for a soldier.

The memory of the slaughter on Drumossie Moor at the hands of the Hanoverian troops and everything that happened afterwards at his home, Blackloch Castle, chilled Alex to the marrow of his bones. Made him sick to the pit of his stomach. Even though almost three months had passed, the memory of nightmarish screams and the acrid smell of smoke swirled through his mind. His ears rang with the echoes of raucous laughter and whoops of men—the Earl of Tay and his clansmen —rampaging and rutting.

His fingers curled into fists so tight his knuckles cracked.

A masculine guffaw dragged Alex back from the hellscape in his mind. It served the Young Pretender right if these Cameron clansmen had taken possession of the lost gold—Louis d'or in fact—that the Spanish had promised to send during the Rebellion. Alex had once heard the Prince's secretary, Murray of Broughton, complain that the "Spanish gold" hadn't arrived when expected, along with other desperately needed supplies to sustain the Jacobite cause. *A failed cause.* The Prince didn't deserve this gold, just as he no longer deserved Alex's, or any Highlander's loyalty.

But from whence the gold came or who it really belonged to, Alex didn't much care right at this moment. All that mattered was that these clansmen were burying a veritable treasure right before his very eyes. And he meant to have his share. Indeed, the rays of the setting sun glinting off the waters of the loch suddenly penetrated the heavy gloom of the woods and glanced off the pile of coins in the open casket, making them wink at him. *Tempting him.*

Alex's mouth almost watered. Long forgotten emotions—not happiness nor hope but something darker and colder—stirred in his leaden heart. Determination, perhaps. And the desire for vengeance.

Sweet, sweet vengeance.

At long last, fate had meted out a chance for him to reclaim a little of what he'd lost. He certainly didn't think God was responsible. More likely the Devil.

Either way, he sure as hell wasn't going to miss this precious opportunity to take charge of his destiny again. After all, he was only two and twenty. When the time was right, that evil bastard Malcolm Campbell, the Earl of Tay, would know his wrath.

As Alex carefully inched forward on his belly to get a better view of the Cameron men's activities, he grimaced as his damaged thigh and shoulder protested. After Culloden, he hadn't been able to dig out all the shrapnel embedded within the muscles, but at least the wounds hadn't turned purulent. He might be sufficiently able-bodied to best one, perhaps two men, but certainly not a dozen fighting-fit Highlanders armed to the teeth.

Logic dictated subterfuge and patience were his only real weapons.

Once the gloaming had fully descended, and while the men were still fully engrossed in digging up the damp, dark earth, Alexander silently retreated up the brae to the ridge and the isolated corrie beyond where he'd tethered his stoic horse.

For weeks, it had been his custom to travel around remote and inhospitable countryside at night to avoid patrolling dragoons. But tonight he wasn't going anywhere. When the moment came—perhaps tomorrow or the next night, when Cameron of Lochiel's men were truly gone—he'd return to claim what he could.

In the end, Alex waited two nights before returning to the woods. With only a tin mug, his sturdy dirk and his bare hands, and barely any light save for the moonlight filtering through the pine canopy, it had taken him several hours to dig up one of the caskets. It had taken another few hours to transport the hefty bags of gold coin, five and thirty in total, to the upland cave he'd chosen as a hiding place. He'd made three trips to make it easier on his poor mount, so by the time he'd reburied the empty chest and covered it over with moss and spent bracken leaves, then returned to his mountain lair, the sun was beginning to rise.

After rinsing his filthy, torn hands in a tumbling burn, Alex took a long draft of sweet Highland water. For the first time in such a long time, he felt a small measure of satisfaction somewhere deep in his soul.

He was as rich as Solomon.

But the gold he'd taken wasn't just for him. He would use it to deliver justice to his clan and kin—all those who had been displaced, murdered and worse. His dead brothers-in-arms, the staff of Blackloch Castle, all the Clan MacIvor tenants and families who'd lived upon the estate. His slaughtered parents, Lord and Lady Rannoch, his younger sister, and his sweetheart, Maggie Stewart. The first lass he'd kissed. The *only* lass he'd kissed.

The only lass he'd wanted to wed.

Oh God, what they'd done to the women he'd loved. Still loved... Hot tears scalded his eyes. He couldn't bear it.

But bear it he must.

Gritting his teeth against the pain in both his aching heart and wounded body, Alex rose from the rocky bank of the burn and gazed out over the beloved land he would soon be leaving: rugged mountain peaks, the dark still waters of Loch Arkaig, the rosy sky streaked with gold. With ready coin in his pockets for bribes, he was sure he could buy a passage to anywhere, anywhere at all. Perhaps France. Better still, the New World: the Caribbean or the Americas. It really didn't matter.

As soon as he was able, and when the stars aligned, he would return, remade. His will would be like forged steel, honed to lethal sharpness. The Earl of Tay would be held to account for every foul act he'd committed. Indeed, the man would rue the day he was born.

Alex slid his hand into his pocket and retrieved the precious tattered blue ribbon holding together a tiny braid containing three locks of hair —one bright red, one black, and one brown—and he kissed it. He returned it to his coat then drew his dirk, relishing the hot sting as he made a shallow slice across his palm. The pain reminded him he was still alive, even though he was all but dead inside. For a few moments he watched the blood drip into the stones and the icy water at his feet.

"*Nunquam obliviscar,*" he whispered. "I, Alexander Ewan MacIvor, will never forget what you did, Malcolm Campbell. One day, you will pay."

CHAPTER I

Kenmuir House, Edinburgh, Scotland
Saint Valentine's Day, February 1757
Eleven years later...

"More champagne, my dear Miss Burns?" Alex turned to his paid companion for the evening, a young woman named Nell, and offered her a glass along with his most charming smile.

The prostitute fluttered her eyelashes and murmured a coy "thank you" in return, but it was all for show, of course. Not for a moment did Alex entertain the thought that she truly blushed beneath her scarlet half-mask and face powder; not when her ample bosom all but spilled from her red and gold brocade ball gown. Indeed, Alex imagined nothing much at all made a woman of her profession blush. He wasn't even sure if Nell Burns was the lass's true name...but then, it didn't really matter.

He certainly couldn't pass judgment, not when the world now knew him as Alexander Price, an indecently wealthy gentleman—half English and half Scots—who hailed from the English town of Berwick. A ruthless man of business who received invitations to Society's best dinner parties and balls wherever he went, be that London, Glasgow, Edinburgh, or even Jamaica.

It seemed money *could* buy Alex just about anything he wanted. A new identity. A mercantile and insurance company. Land, commercial properties, and a logging business. Even his own forfeited estate and ruined castle.

And at long last, Lord Tay's demise.

Alex smiled behind his black domino mask. It wouldn't be long before he hammered the last nail in the bastard's coffin and consigned him to Hades. Though it had taken him over a decade to get to this point, the wait had been worth it. Success would be headier than the Marquess of Kenmuir's very fine French champagne.

Nell touched the sleeve of his black velvet frockcoat and gave him a smile just as practiced as his own. "Just say the word, sir, and I will seek out his lordship. Ye mentioned afore that he is verra partial to fair-haired lasses." She tossed her guinea-gold ringlets over her shoulder as if to emphasize her desirability.

"Aye. He is." Alex scanned the throng gathered in Lord and Lady Kenmuir's ballroom. Thanks to his height, he could see Malcolm Campbell, Lord Tay, above the heads of the other guests. The brute was presently prancing about the dance floor with his sister, Damaris, the widowed Countess of Glenleven, as though he hadn't a care in the world. A powdered peruke covered his dark red hair but his distinctive *Medico della Peste* mask and elaborate blood-red cape made him an easy mark. "Actually, see if you can claim Lord Tay's attention when the minuet is over." He slid a key into Nell's slim hand and added sotto voce, "Here's the key to the private parlor you can use. As we've discussed, I trust you'll be able to keep Tay busy—shall we say?—for a good half hour or more. Remember to leave the curtains open."

Nell's eyes sparkled as brightly as the cut-crystal chandelier above the ballroom floor as she slipped the key between her plumped-up breasts. "Och aye, sir. 'Twill be my pleasure."

Alex inclined his head before returning to study his nemesis. The last time he'd spied Lord Tay, it had been over a year ago in London at another masquerade ball. He doubted Tay would recognize him after all this time—it was almost eleven years since they'd truly crossed paths.

And of course, it had been quite easy to orchestrate his schemes from the wings when he employed a network of spies who kept him well informed and carried out his dirty work when necessary.

Even so, while Alex's features were partially obscured by his mask this evening, it wouldn't hurt to keep to the shadows. Why risk discovery when he was so close to achieving his goal?

Ah, if you only knew what I have planned, Tay, you'd be shaking in your silk-covered pumps.

Alex's blood practically hummed with anticipation.

The minuet at last drew to a close and the delectable Nell sashayed away, heading toward the dance floor. If she could keep the cur suitably occupied, Alex should have ample time to seek out his intended quarry for the night—a Miss Sarah Lambert, a decidedly pretty, extremely wealthy English heiress.

Lord Tay's betrothed.

But not for long. Not if Alex had his way.

Thanks to a well-mapped out and painstakingly executed campaign enacted over the best part of a decade, the Earl of Tay was on the brink of utter financial and social ruin. And there was no way on earth that Alex was going to let the man marry his way out of penury.

Alex circumnavigated the perimeter of the dance floor, heading for the main hall. He'd observed Miss Lambert exiting the ballroom a few minutes earlier, but he didn't think it would take long to locate her. Earlier in the evening, when he'd first laid eyes upon her, he'd discovered she was the sort of young woman who most definitely stood out from the crowd.

Watching her stand beside an arrogantly smiling Lord Tay at the head of the reception line, one small, elegant hand resting on her *fiancé's* arm, Alex had grudgingly conceded that Sarah Lambert was as exquisite as an English rose. Her rich satin gown, a confection of rose pink, cream and soft apricot, was the perfect foil for her bright gold hair and peaches-and-cream complexion. Even her gold half-mask couldn't hide her glowing beauty. She appeared to be quite the catch.

What a pity she has such poor taste, Alex had thought. *And clearly no scruples.* But then she wouldn't be the first woman who'd prostituted herself for a title. Unless she was an innocent Tay had duped into marriage with false protestations of love and fidelity. That was definitely another possibility.

Nevertheless, whether Miss Lambert lacked taste, was unscrupulous, or merely easily duped hardly mattered. What mattered was the fact that she was a convenient pawn he could use to hasten Tay's downfall.

Considering the pair were due to wed in less than a month, the sooner he removed the heiress from the earl's greedy grasp, the better.

Sarah wasn't sure when she first noticed the mysterious man dressed in black watching her. Perhaps it was when Malcolm had escorted Damaris out onto the ballroom floor for a minuet. Perhaps it was before.

Movement and noise surrounded her: laughter and chatter and the elegant strains of the small orchestra filled the air; the swirl of opulent silks and satins and velvets, and the flash of jewels dazzled the eye as dancing couples floated by. But lingering in the shadows on the other side of the room was a tall, dark stranger. He stood perfectly still, his attention focused solely on her. Sarah could feel the weight of his gaze like a physical, intimate touch upon her—or so she imagined—and her cheeks grew hot, first with embarrassment and then silent indignation.

How rude. Where were his manners?

With a lift of her chin, Sarah turned her head away and directed her attention back to Malcolm and his sister. But it was all for naught; her gaze kept straying to the man in black. There was something inexplicably compelling about him. Even though he was some distance away, she could tell he was handsome beneath his black half-mask. Unlike many of the other gentlemen of the party, including Malcolm, he was sans peruke. His raven black hair was clubbed at the nape, revealing the sharp cut of his square jaw above the frothy white lace of his jabot. Aside from white silk stockings, and a touch of white lace at his cuffs, everything else he wore, including his cloak, was as dark as midnight.

Who was he? And why was he so interested in her? Since her father's passing six months ago, Sarah had been in mourning and hadn't been out and about all that much. Considering she'd only been in Scotland since Hogmanay, she wasn't all that well acquainted with Edinburgh's polite society yet.

She was about to ask Aunt Judith, her chaperone, if she'd noticed the stranger's pointed interest when a young, fair-haired woman in a scandalously low-cut gown of scarlet and gold brocade claimed the man's attention. She touched his arm in a familiar fashion before murmuring something in his ear. The enigmatic stranger's wide, well-shaped mouth curved into a slight smile and his gaze shifted to the dancers. *Was he studying Malcolm now? How peculiar.* Sarah's nape prickled with unease.

Something odd was going on, she was sure of it. She would discreetly mention the stranger to Malcolm when he returned to her. Then again, there *could* be a simple explanation for the stranger's interest. Perhaps they were just old acquaintances...

"Sarah, my dear, I...I'm afraid I'm feeling rather poorly."

Aunt Judith grasped her hand and when Sarah turned to examine her, alarm spiked through her. Lines of tension bracketed her aunt's mouth and eyes, and her cheeks were ashen. Although she was only three-and-fifty, this was the third social event she'd attended this week. The hustle and bustle of large group gatherings and the late nights were clearly taking their toll.

"You have a megrim again, don't you?" Sarah said gently. "Let me find you somewhere quiet to rest."

Aunt Judith gave her a weak smile. "I'm so sorry, dear child. But yes, I think that would be best."

Sarah glanced back toward the ballroom floor but Malcolm and Damaris were now too far away; she doubted she'd be able to catch their attention. But she wouldn't be long. She'd install her aunt in the ladies' retiring room or somewhere else nearby, then return.

Although, as she took Aunt Judith's arm and carefully steered her through the crowd toward their destination, Sarah couldn't suppress a small unladylike sigh. Malcolm probably wouldn't even notice her absence...

She'd been reluctant to acknowledge how mercurial her *fiancé* had become of late. Their nuptials were only three weeks away—even though it would be Lent, Malcolm had insisted it didn't matter—and as she herself was feeling nervous, she reasoned it was only natural for Malcolm to be out of sorts too. One moment he was sweetly attentive and eager to be in her company—perhaps too eager, considering how ardent his kisses had become whenever they happened to be alone. Then there were times when Malcolm was hopelessly distracted and irritable, even distant. Sarah didn't like it when he snapped at her about the most trivial things. Of course, he would always apologize afterwards for his ill-mannered behavior and ask for her forgiveness, which she freely gave. How could she not?

She'd trusted her father's judgment in choosing a suitable husband for her, and in his last moments on earth, she'd promised him she would wed the Earl of Tay, an honorable peer of the realm who would protect and provide for her. She would never go back on her word.

Besides, for all Malcolm's faults, Sarah had grown to care for him—deeply—since they'd become engaged nine months ago. Perhaps even love was beginning to stir in her breast. Even though Malcolm hadn't professed any deep and abiding affection for her yet, she was certain he cared for her, too. After all, he'd been patiently waiting to wed her for so long.

They would be happy together, she was certain of it.

"Are you quite all right, my dear?" Aunt Judith asked as she lowered herself onto a small tapestry-covered settee. They'd found a vacant parlor only a few doors away from the ladies' retiring room. "You seem... not quite yourself. Perhaps you could call round the carriage and we might both return to Tay House. I'm sure his lordship wouldn't mind—"

"No, no." Sarah waved away her aunt's concern with a forced smile. "I'm perfectly fine."

She was not going to admit to Aunt Judith that she was worried Malcolm would be cross with her if she left early. He was always so concerned about appearances and of course, she understood. She might be an heiress in her own right now she'd recently come of age, but in the eyes of Society, she was the daughter of a mere merchant. A nobody who'd been lucky enough to ensnare a nobleman. She must never put a foot wrong. Ever.

Besides, she wanted to speak to Malcolm about the curious stranger.

"If you are sure, then…" Aunt Judith pressed a hand to her forehead. "Perhaps you could arrange some refreshments for me? Some elderflower cordial or barley water would be nice. And a cold compress for my forehead. It aches so. And if it's not too much bother, perhaps you could procure a book for me to read while I wait for you? I'm sure Lord and Lady Kenmuir wouldn't mind if you borrowed something from their library. Oh, I am such a bother—"

Sarah patted her aunt's shoulder. "Of course. And it's no bother at all. I will even polish your spectacles as well." In fact, she'd do anything for her aunt. After Sarah's mother had tragically passed away not long after Sarah's birth, Judith had stepped in to raise her. Her aunt was the only mother she'd ever known and Sarah loved her dearly.

On exiting the parlor, Sarah found a maid, requested the items her aunt wanted, and obtained directions to the library. Thankfully it wasn't too far from the ballroom. Malcolm was probably looking for her by now. She might see him along the way.

But she didn't. Scanning the sea of people gathered in the ballroom as she passed by, she saw neither hide nor hair of her *fiancé*, or her sister-to-be for that matter. Perhaps they were in the card room; both were partial to faro, a game she had little time for.

She was also relieved that she didn't spot the man in black again. Determined to push away all thoughts of the mysterious stranger, Sarah swiftly traversed the marble floor in the main hall and followed the long, oak-paneled gallery until she reached the Kenmuir's library.

To her surprise—and relief—it was vacant when she entered. Aunt Judith had often warned her about poking her nose into out-of-the-way rooms at affairs like this, as one was liable to come across courting couples or even worse, have one's reputation ruined if caught alone with a gentleman. But perhaps her aunt was no longer concerned about such things because her betrothal to Malcolm was common knowledge. A man would be foolish indeed to attempt a dalliance with the Earl of Tay's *fiancée*.

Closing the door behind her, Sarah advanced into an impressively appointed room; a blazing fire and several large branches of candles revealed towering oak bookcases, beautifully polished occasional tables, and fine leather chairs. The comforting scents of wood smoke, beeswax polish, and leather permeated the air, reminding her of her father's study in their old Northumbrian home by the sea, Linden Hall—a home she would have to give up once she and Malcolm were married. Instead, she would be the mistress of Taymoor Castle.

A countess. She could scarcely fathom it.

Oh, Papa... I wish you were still here to see me wed. Here to walk me down the aisle into my new life.

Blinking away a rush of bittersweet tears, Sarah crossed to one of the bookcases and pulled a random volume from the shelf; she had no idea what the title was as the letters on the cover were nothing but a blur. With a sigh she tugged off her gold half-mask, placed it on the shelf, then dabbed at her eyes with her satin and fine lace sleeve. She could almost hear Aunt Judith admonishing her for being so unladylike, but she hadn't a kerchief to hand. Besides, it was not as though anyone could see—

"Looking for something?"

Sarah jumped like a startled rabbit and dropped the book at the unexpected question—one spoken by a man. Her pulse skittering, she whirled around to find her mystery stalker from the ballroom standing only a few feet away.

Before she could even think or utter a word, the gentleman stepped forward and retrieved the book from the rug near her feet.

"Ah, *Clarissa*," he said in a soft Scottish burr, offering her the leather-bound volume with a smile. "I've been told it is quite a good read, if one likes weighty tomes about virtuous maidens. And then of course there is *Pamela*." He nodded toward the shelves behind her. "Although I hear it is a little more scandalous. I suppose it depends on what sort of mood you are in." His deep, smoky voice was just as potent as his gaze, his words heavy with secret meaning. It was as though he'd uttered a jest she didn't quite understand.

Sarah took the book with a shaking hand and held it against her chest. Now the man was closer, she could see his eyes were dark too—storm-cloud gray fringed with long sooty lashes that would make any woman green with envy. He was much taller and more physically imposing than she'd previously thought. His black velvet frockcoat and brocade waistcoat were perfectly tailored to show off his muscular frame, and the snug fit of his black silk breeches did nothing to hide his long powerful thighs. Indeed, his masculine presence seemed to dominate the large room. And to her great shame, despite her suspicions that this man was up to no good, she couldn't look away.

He was, in a word, enthralling.

"Wh-Who are you? What do you want?" Sarah managed to stammer when she found her voice.

He shrugged and his chiseled mouth tipped into a half-smile as he leaned a wide shoulder negligently against the bookcase. "I thought it was rather obvious, my dear Miss Lambert," he drawled as he slid a book from the shelf then flipped nonchalantly through its pages. In the muted fire and candlelight, she noticed the gleam of a large onyx and gold ring upon the ring finger of his right hand. "Like you, I thought I'd seek another diversion." He grimaced and put the book back before catching her gaze again, regarding her from beneath half-lowered lids. It was a sensual look, lazy but watchful at the same time. The look of a predator feigning disinterest, right before it pounced. "These affairs can be frightfully dull sometimes, wouldn't you agree?"

"How...how do you know my name?" she asked, breathless with nerves. The stranger was standing far too close but Sarah couldn't seem to summon the urge to step away. Her cheeks felt hot and she had the awful feeling she was blushing.

The man's mask didn't hide the amused quirk of one slashing black brow. "Why, everyone knows your name. I was in the ballroom when you and your gallant *fiancé* were formally introduced. Lord Tay is a lucky man."

Good, thought Sarah and the tension thrumming through her body began to ebb. *He knows who I'm betrothed to.* That should provide her with some measure of protection. Only a fool would cross a nobleman of Malcolm's stature.

Aloud she simply said, "Thank you," with an incline of her head. "Which reminds me, I should be getting back to my aunt." She picked up her discarded mask from the shelf. "She's expecting me. As is Lord Tay."

The stranger smiled as he gave a small bow. "I'm sure he is, so don't let me keep you. Good evening to you, Miss Lambert."

"Good evening." With her mask and *Clarissa* in hand, Sarah turned and left the library. Even though she didn't look back, she swore she could feel the enigmatic stranger's eyes upon her. It was only as the door shut behind her that she realized the man had never actually given her his name.

~

Damn, bloody damn.

Leaning an arm along the bookshelf, Alex rubbed his jaw as he scowled at the closing library door. Why did Miss Sarah Lambert have to be so...so damned lovely? A young woman who, on first meeting, seemed completely free of artifice. *Likeable.* His informants had reported she was from a good family and that despite her questionable choice in men—or one man in particular—there was no hint of scandal attached to her name. He hadn't wanted to believe Miss Lambert might actually be agreeable. But then, all things considered, his scheme would be much easier to carry out if she *was* actually amiable and not the social climbing, conniving bitch he'd supposed her to be.

Though their meeting had been brief, his gut instincts told Alex he was right about her. When she'd regarded him with wide, innocent blue eyes and had taken a book from him with a trembling hand, he'd been quite disarmed. Good Lord, she'd even blushed at his innocuous attempts at flirtation.

Alex heaved a sigh as he pushed away from the bookcase and crossed to a cabinet, where he helped himself to a liberal glass of Lord Kenmuir's cognac. After observing Miss Lambert from afar in the ballroom, he'd thought it would be a good idea to assess her firsthand before he made his next move. To take her measure, so he'd have an idea of what sort of woman he would be dealing with, and how she would react to what he had planned for her.

How inconvenient that he should be afflicted by a sudden pang of conscience.

He hadn't expected that.

Alex downed the cognac in one savage gulp then released the catch on the onyx ring he always wore on his right hand. A tiny tri-colored braid and a snippet of blue ribbon lay curled beneath the glass. His jaw clenched. He wasn't going to alter his plans even though Miss Lambert appeared to be a proper young lady who'd stammered breathlessly when he'd stood too close to her. A woman who, in some respects, reminded him of his sweet Maggie when he'd first courted her...

He might feel a little sorry for Miss Sarah Lambert, but the emotion paled into insignificance when he recalled why he was doing this. *He would not be swayed.*

Alex flipped the ring closed. As planned, Tay was currently busy with Nell. Lady Glenleven, his sister, was shamelessly flirting with whomever she could in the card room, and Miss Lambert's chaperone appeared to be conveniently indisposed.

Now to set the rest of his scheme in motion... Alex slipped his hand beneath his frockcoat and withdrew a silver flask from the satin-lined breast pocket. He uncapped it and carefully topped up the bitter contents with Lord Kenmuir's cognac.

As he repocketed the flask, Alex's lips curled into a mirthless smile. It seemed there was no time like the present to exact his revenge...

CHAPTER 2

After she'd seen Aunt Judith settled with *Clarissa*, a compress, and a cut-glass tumbler filled with elderflower cordial, Sarah donned her gold domino mask again and returned to the ballroom to look for Malcolm. Even though she'd only been gone a short time, the atmosphere had changed—the laughter had grown raucous, the chatter louder, the dancing wilder. She wrinkled her nose a little as she carefully wove her way between the tight clusters of masked guests. The candles in the chandeliers had burned low and the air was heavy with the smell of melted wax, smoke, and perspiration barely masked by the scent of stale perfume. Pausing at the edge of the dance floor where a lively gavotte was taking place, she searched for Malcolm's tall, broad-shouldered form, but despite the fact that he was shrouded in a crimson cape, she failed to spot him anywhere. But then, perhaps he was playing cards with his sister as she'd earlier surmised.

On entering the card room, Sarah spied Damaris playing faro with an older, bewigged gentleman in a leering *Pulcinello* mask, his cheeks ruddy with drink. However, her sister-in-law-to-be wasn't much help. She tossed her dark auburn curls over one slender shoulder, barely looking up from the cards in her hand as she answered Sarah's query about Malcolm. "I have no idea where he is, my dear. I'm not my brother's keeper. Why don't you try the supper room? Or Lord Kenmuir's private study. He's probably sampling our host's cognac."

Sarah pressed her lips together but she was unable to suppress a small sigh of frustration. Damaris could be annoyingly self-centered at times. She was a young widow—only six-and-twenty—and like Malcolm, quite beautiful with a high forehead and sculpted cheekbones, and eyes the color of golden-brown topaz. She certainly received a lot of attention from men, both young and old. Her faro opponent was a case in point; he was quite transfixed with Damaris's décolletage rather than what was in his hand—and Damaris did not seem to mind his unseemly interest. In fact, she seemed to be deliberately drawing attention to her bosom. One of her fingertips trailed lazily back and forth along the low sweeping neckline of her turquoise silk bodice. Bewitching her card-playing partner was clearly more of a priority than helping her find Malcolm.

"Well, if you see your brother before I do, please tell him I'm looking for him," Sarah murmured as she began to turn away. She wasn't surprised in the least when Damaris simply waved a dismissive hand by way of a reply.

A brief search of the supper room proved futile as well. Sarah hovered by a glass-paneled set of doors leading to the empty, snow-dusted terrace. She was wondering whether she should give up her quest and take a plate of sugared sweetmeats and dainty cakes to her poor aunt when she sensed the presence of another guest by her shoulder. A particular guest she could not ignore.

"Still looking for something, or should I say, someone? Lord Tay perhaps?"

Sarah's brows snapped together as she whirled around to face her enigmatic stalker. "Why are you following me?" she demanded, not caring if others in their vicinity overheard. *What on earth was this man up to?* Surely he wasn't attempting to seduce her... He'd be mad to attempt such a thing. Malcolm would kill him.

Clearly unperturbed by her brusque tone, the stranger simply smiled, ignoring her question just as she'd ignored his. He tilted his head toward the doors leading to the terrace and the enclosed garden beyond. "Have you looked outside?"

"For Lord Tay? I seriously doubt he would be taking a turn about the terrace on a night like this."

The man in black shrugged. "It was just a thought," he said softly in that rich, deep voice of his that seemed to wrap around her like smoke. "I'd be willing to escort you. It is rather dark out there."

"I don't think so," replied Sarah, steadfastly turning her head away. "I don't even know your name. We've not been formally introduced."

"No, we haven't," he agreed. "But then, isn't one supposed to be in disguise at a masquerade ball? It's a night designed for all manner of clandestine activities, don't you think? Who knows what might happen."

"You're incorrigible, Mr...Mr. Whoever-you-are."

Mr. Whoever-you-are laughed. "True." He took a step back and affected a courtly bow. "Allow me to introduce myself then. My name is Alexander Black."

"Mr. Black." Sarah arched a disdainful eyebrow. "How clever of you to match your attire to your name. And possibly your nature."

Alexander Black grimaced. "You wound me, Miss Lambert. We've only just met."

"I know a rogue when I see one."

Mr. Black, or whatever-his-name-was, flashed a grin. "Do you now? Have you met many?"

"Enough. Now, if you'll excuse me, I must be getting back to my aunt."

"What about your *fiancé*?"

"Yes, of course. Lord Tay too."

"Well then, I bid you adieu yet again, Miss Lambert."

Sarah stepped away but turned back, her satin skirts brushing the tops of Mr. Black's silver-buckled shoes. Something was still bothering her. "You...you know something about Lord Tay's whereabouts, don't you? You keep alluding to it."

She narrowed her eyes, studying Mr. Black's countenance, but his expression was inscrutable behind his black domino. "You're toying with me. I saw you watching my *fiancé* as he danced with his sister, Lady Glenleven, earlier this evening. You were watching me too. I want to know why."

He didn't deny her assertions. Instead, Black's mouth tipped into a grin that was both maddening and appealing in equal measure. "You are a very lovely young woman, Miss Lambert. I'm sure I'm not the first man to have admired your"—his gaze blatantly raked over her bosom—"person."

A blush scalded Sarah's cheeks. "What rot. There are countless beautiful women here tonight that you could ogle. Indeed, there was an attractive young woman dressed in red flirting with you earlier this evening. Why should I, in particular, catch your interest?" She folded her arms. "What do you want from me? And do you know where Lord Tay is or not?"

Even though the lighting by the doors to the terrace was muted, Sarah caught the flicker of a muscle in Black's lean cheek. She was convinced more than ever that something was afoot.

"He's outside, isn't he?" Sarah pushed past Black and reached for the handle of the doors. But then Black placed his large hand over hers. A strange tingling sensation spread from Sarah's fingers, up her arm, all the way to her chest, and her heart began to race. Heat rushed up her neck and washed over her face.

Thankfully Black didn't seem to notice her foolish reaction to his touch.

"Miss Lambert..." he murmured, his warm breath brushing her temple. Was there a tinge of regret lacing his tone? "I'm not sure—"

"Well, I am. Unhand me, sir."

Black immediately released her and Sarah opened the door and marched out to the terrace.

The biting cold stole her breath. The moon's pale orb was partly obscured by a shredded veil of silver-gray clouds and Sarah halted by the white marble balustrade, waiting for her eyes to adjust to the inky darkness.

Then something slid over her shoulders—a black wool cloak lined with silk that smelled like warm male and some kind of exotic scent or soap. A blend of sandalwood and citrus—bergamot or citron, perhaps.

"If you are going to come out here, at least wear something to protect you from the cold," murmured a dark velvet voice close to her ear.

Black. Drat the man.

Sarah made a half-hearted attempt to shrug off the garment even though it was deliciously warm and her natural instinct was to wrap it around herself. "Mr. Black," she said frostily, "I hardly think it is appropriate—"

"Just humor me, Miss Lambert. You may think me a rogue, but a gentleman would never let a woman catch her death."

"Very well." At Sarah's words, Black gently turned her around and fastened his cloak beneath her chin. His warm fingers brushed her jaw, making her shiver for a reason which had nothing to do with the cold; whether his intimate touch was by accident or design, Sarah wasn't certain. She should rebuke him for his overfamiliarity but it seemed, for the moment, her tongue and lips wouldn't work.

"Shall we?" Black offered her his arm with such an air of presumed intimacy that Sarah at last found her voice.

"I'm neither an imbecile nor an invalid, Mr. Black," she remarked in a clipped tone, annoyed at herself for almost succumbing to the black-guard's charm. "I thank you for the loan of your cloak but pray, do not follow me. If Lord Tay is out here, I will find him. On my own."

She turned and stalked away, relieved that Black appeared to heed her pronouncement.

At first glance the terrace seemed deserted, although there were so many deep shadows between the pools of light cast from the occasional uncurtained window, it was difficult to tell for certain. Marble statues— nymphs and satyrs and other mythical creatures—had been placed at regular intervals along the gray brick, ivy-clad walls and more than once, Sarah started when she mistook a statue for an actual person.

Upon reaching the end of the terrace, Sarah discovered it continued around the corner of Kenmuir House. A denuded arbor and stone bench stood about halfway along, and a set of stairs led down to a gravel path that appeared to wind back to the main garden. This was surely a fool's errand, but she should at least satisfy herself that Malcolm wasn't out here taking the fresh air or conversing with a male acquaintance about some private matter of business.

Pausing, Sarah glanced back toward the doors leading to the supper room. Alexander Black was where she'd left him and he raised a hand in greeting when he saw her looking his way. Steadfastly resisting the urge to wave back, she turned the corner and approached the rectangle of golden light spilling from the first set of windows.

Malcolm was nowhere in sight. Inwardly cursing herself for being so easily gulled by Black and his not-so-subtle intimations, Sarah was about to retrace her steps when something—a movement or perhaps it was a sound—made her pause and look through the window into the illuminated room beyond.

And her heart stopped. There, in the center of a lavishly appointed private parlor, was Malcolm.

But he wasn't alone.

The blond woman in scarlet and gold brocade—the woman she'd seen flirting with Alexander Black—was with him. At least, Sarah thought it was the same woman. It was difficult to tell, considering she was bent over the side of a silk-covered settee, head down with her voluminous skirts bunched up around her waist, her bare derrière and legs exposed. Malcolm, his mask still in place, was also in a state of dishabille. The fall of his satin breeches was undone and the slit in his smallclothes gaped open. His hands grasped the woman's hips, holding her in place as he pumped his—oh heavens, his *member*—in and out of her in the manner of a wild, rutting beast.

Oh, God. Oh, dear God. Sarah stumbled backward into the terrace's balustrade. The man she was supposed to marry, the man she was falling in love with, was *fornicating* with another woman.

The depth of Malcolm's betrayal struck her with sickening force and Sarah spun around and gripped the hard marble handrail, willing herself not to cast up the contents of her stomach into the dead, frozen garden bed below. With a shaking hand, she pulled off her mask before tipping back her head to suck in great lungfuls of frigid air. It felt as though she couldn't breathe. Like she was drowning. Her head began to spin and she closed her eyes, dropping her head forward again. A strange shuddering sound, somewhere between a low moan and a sob escaped her lips. *Why would you do this, Malcolm? I don't understand. I thought you cared for me...*

Dear Lord, what am I to do?

"Miss Lambert? Miss Lambert. Here, sit down." Black was at her side, steering her toward the stone bench.

Too weak to question or resist, her vision blurred by stinging tears, Sarah complied. Black's arm enveloped her heaving shoulders and she subsided against him. Without thinking, she curled a hand into the silk lapel of his velvet frockcoat and pressed her wet cheek into his wide chest, grateful for the comfort he offered. She couldn't stop shivering.

She wanted to close her eyes but every time she did, all she saw was Malcolm and the vile act he'd been engaged in. She had no idea what to do next. With her heart torn to shreds and her mind in whirling chaos, it hurt too much to think. Instead, she tried to focus on the sights and sounds of the night—the clouds scudding across the moon, the muted laughter and chatter emanating from the supper room, and the steady beat of Alexander Black's heart beneath her ear.

They sat that way for several minutes, until Black reached into his coat and pulled out something. She'd expected a kerchief to dry her tears, but it was a small silver flask. It gleamed and winked at her in the moonlight as he uncorked it.

"You've had a terrible shock, Miss Lambert," Black murmured, his tone low and soft with compassion. "I suggest you take a sip or two of this before we go back inside. Then I'll escort you back to your aunt."

Sarah nodded and straightened. That sounded eminently sensible. She took the offered flask with trembling fingers and sniffed. "What is it?"

Black's mouth curved into a reassuring smile. "Brandy. Cognac, actually. It will stop the shaking. But if it's not to your taste..."

"No, it's quite all right." She really should stop being so suspicious of Black. After all, he was only trying to help.

Sarah closed her eyes and took a long sip from the flask, then coughed and gasped. The concoction tasted overly sweet yet bitter and nothing like any brandy she'd ever had before. "What...on earth...*is* that?" Sarah's vision swam and the world began to spin again. Horror gripped her heart as she tried but failed to wrench herself away from Black's suddenly tight hold. Why was she so...so weak? Her body was a lead weight. Her limbs were as limp as wet rags, yet her thoughts were scattering, drifting...as insubstantial as snowflakes in the wind.

Had she been drugged? Poisoned?

Oh, God!

"Just a few more sips, sweeting," whispered Black as he tipped more of the foul-tasting liquid into Sarah's mouth. His hand covered her lips so she couldn't spit it out.

Terrified she might choke, unable to summon the strength to struggle, or even utter more than a faint and completely ineffectual murmur of protest, Sarah swallowed down the drug-laced alcohol before plummeting headlong into darkness...

~

Alex sighed heavily as Sarah Lambert slumped in his arms. If his circumstances had been different—if his history were different—he wouldn't be doing any of this: drugging then kidnapping an apparently innocent young woman so he could turn her against her evil cur of a *fiancé*.

Considering how readily Malcolm Campbell took the bait offered to him in the form of Miss Nell Burns, perhaps he was actually saving Miss Lambert from making the worst mistake of her life. Did the lass know her prospective husband was not only faithless, but a rapist and murderer?

He rather doubted it. Perhaps, in the future, she'd even thank him for what he was about to do.

At least, that's what Alex tried to tell himself as he pocketed his recorked flask then stood and carefully lifted Sarah, still clothed in his wool cloak, into his arms. She was surprisingly light and he had no trouble at all carrying her down the terrace stairs and along a short gravel path to a gate that led out to a narrow laneway between Kenmuir House and the neighboring residence. One of his trusted staff had forced the lock earlier in the evening.

So far, his plan had worked perfectly.

After closing the gate behind him with a small kick, Alex followed the lane to the end where his carriage waited. One of his footmen—plainly attired for the sake of subterfuge—opened the door and let down the step, and within moments, Alex and his hostage were safely inside. Once he'd settled Miss Lambert onto the blanket-lined bench, he rapped on the roof and took a seat next to her to ensure she wouldn't fall when the carriage rolled forward.

His own residence was only a short distance away, a bit farther along the Royal Mile. All going well, he'd be back at Kenmuir House within the space of half an hour, entirely unmissed. With any luck, he'd also return in time to witness Malcolm Campbell's reaction to finding out his very wealthy *fiancée* had disappeared into the night without a trace.

Alex's mouth curled into a grim smile. The next few hours were going to be entertaining indeed.

CHAPTER 3

"Where in *Hades* is Sarah? Why don't either of you know? Miss Lambert, you're her chaperone for Christ's sake!"

Malcolm scowled at Sarah's maiden aunt as she cowered upon a settee with her face in her hands before shooting a glance at his sister. Damaris stood by the private parlor's small fireplace, watching her mask twirl at the end of its ribbons. She might be feigning boredom, but Malcolm could tell she was vexed by the way she pursed her lips. No doubt her irritation was related to the fact he was keeping her from pursuing her latest conquest, not because Sarah was missing.

Neither woman was immediately forthcoming with a response to his repeated questions, which didn't really surprise him. They'd already recounted Sarah's last known movements several times and, damn it, he was still none the wiser. His *fiancée* clearly wasn't in any of the places one might expect her to be. They'd all searched the ballroom, card room, supper room, ladies' retiring room, the library, even the terrace. No one he'd discreetly questioned—their hosts, the footmen at the front door, nor any of the other staff at Kenmuir House—had seen Sarah leave. Besides, her pelisse was still in the cloakroom.

She'd all but vanished into thin air.

"My lord," began Judith Lambert in a thin, quavering voice. "I'm afraid I have nothing else to add. As I told you before, when Sarah left me here to rest, she intended to return to the ballroom to seek you out. When we departed, you were dancing with Lady Glenleven. I wish I knew more but I do not. Believe me, I'm just as worried as you."

I seriously fucking doubt it. Malcolm ground his teeth together to stop himself snapping at the foolish woman.

He needed funds. Desperately. Ergo, he needed Sarah.

Only today, his man of business had been forced to placate a creditor by arranging the sale of his second-last carriage and half his town stable. Taymoor Castle had already been stripped of most of its artwork, tapestries, carpets, any furniture that was decent—thank God Sarah and her aunt hadn't visited yet. He had no more unentailed properties, land, nor any other business assets to sell. He was up to his ears in unpaid debts and overdrawn at the Royal Bank of Scotland. Even the jewels Damaris wore were paste. The contents of Tay House here in Edinburgh would be the next to go to auction. He'd already dismissed a good deal of his staff. Whoever remained was for show alone...

If he didn't wed the Lambert chit, he would be utterly ruined—financially and socially.

He *had* to find her.

Malcolm removed his silver snuffbox from his coat pocket and inhaled a good pinch to loosen the tight knot of panic in his chest. He'd love to down a glass or two of Kenmuir's cognac, but he needed a clear head so the snuff would have to do.

As his pulse slowed, he considered what action to take next.

He was about to quit the parlor with the intention of checking every single room in Kenmuir House from attic to cellar, when Judith spoke again. "I didn't mention it before, but Sarah did not seem herself earlier on. She denied feeling unwell, but now I wonder..."

"Wonder what?"

"If something was wrong. She seemed distracted. Bothered."

Damaris yawned. "Oh, for heaven's sake, Malcolm. Sarah probably grew tired of looking for you and went back to Tay House. It's easy enough to hire a sedan chair along the Canongate. Don't fuss so."

Suddenly the pieces fell into place in Malcolm's mind. *Oh, Christ.* Sarah had been looking for him...and she'd been troubled.

What if...what if she'd discovered he'd been fucking that blond chit, Nell or Nelly, or whatever her bloody name was?

Malcolm clenched his fists and somehow swallowed down the urge to slap Judith Lambert for not mentioning such a pertinent detail earlier. Then he squared his shoulders. If Sarah hadn't been such a cold fish, he wouldn't have had to slake his lust elsewhere. Not wanting to scare her off before they were married, he'd been the epitome of a gentleman—aside from pressing a few kisses on her—during their tedious, drawn-out engagement. If only her fucking father hadn't died, they'd already be wed and he'd have taken over her entire fortune months ago.

After he'd drawn a few deep breaths to calm the rage pounding through his veins, Malcolm redonned his mask. "Damaris, scour the ballroom and card room again. Miss Lambert, check the ladies' retiring room once more. And the library for good measure. Make sure your inquiries are discreet—I won't have either of you stirring up a scandal. I'll question the footmen at the front door again about guests who've taken sedan chairs. I'll also send word to Tay House to check if Sarah has slipped out undetected and gone home on her own. Meet me back here when you're done."

Of course, the Kenmuir's footmen had no further information that was of help. A few guests had arrived in private sedan chairs, but no one had asked for a public chair to be summoned. Indeed, only a handful of guests had left all evening, and none at all fitting Sarah's description.

His guts roiling with frustration, Malcolm returned to the supper room. He'd made a quick sweep of the terrace earlier, but not the walled garden. He doubted Sarah would be out there—it was freezing and a light snow had begun to fall—but at this point, he couldn't afford to leave any stone unturned.

Turning up the collar of his cape, Malcolm pushed through the door and strode along the length of the deserted terrace until he reached the very end—or what he'd thought was the end, until he realized it extended around the side of Kenmuir House. Pulse hammering, he turned the corner...then swore. There, lying on the marble balustrade, gleaming in the light emanating from the nearest window, was a gold domino dusted with snow. *Sarah's?*

Malcolm seized it with shaking hands. It *had* to be Sarah's. A strand of fair hair was caught in the silk ribbons. He spun around, searching for any other clues that might help him locate his *fiancée*, then he cursed again. *Bloody, bloody hell.*

The nearby window gave him a clear view of the parlor Nell had taken him to. The fireside where she'd fellated him and the settee she'd bent over so he could take her from behind.

Fuck. Malcolm sank onto the balustrade. He'd been so consumed with lust, he hadn't noticed the curtains hadn't been drawn. *Shit.* His fist crushed the mask and it snapped in two.

As much as it rankled, he was going to have to do some serious groveling when he found Sarah. She must have fled when she'd seen him. Perhaps Damaris had been right. If Sarah had been upset, she might have slipped away and returned to Tay House on her own. There was probably a garden gate out here somewhere. Or she might have used an out-of-the-way servants' entrance. That *had* to be it.

If she takes against me... If she leaves me... Sheer panic shot through Malcolm, turning his blood to ice and freezing his heart.

He had to catch up to Sarah to stop her from doing anything drastic like breaking off their engagement.

When Malcolm Campbell, the Earl of Tay, stormed back through the terrace doors into the supper room, Alex's lips curled into a smile of deep satisfaction. By now the cur would have realized that Sarah was no longer within Kenmuir House or its grounds. He might even have guessed that she'd accidentally stumbled upon him rutting with Nell. But the blackguard was yet to learn how dire the situation really was.

Oh, how I'd love to be a fly on the wall when that happens.

Lady Kenmuir touched Alex's sleeve, drawing his attention. "My dear Mr. Price, would you like more champagne?" She leaned closer and her plump breasts pressed against his bicep as she murmured into his ear, "Of course, if nothing here is to your taste, I'm sure I could find something else to whet your appetite."

Alex donned a rake's smile. "As tempting as your offer sounds, my lady, I'm afraid I must depart." Now he'd had the pleasure of witnessing Lord Tay's descent into full-blown panic, and had established an alibi by flirting with his rather attractive hostess, he needed to return to his townhouse. Sarah Lambert would probably sleep for hours but he wanted to be at home when she woke. He bowed over Lady Kenmuir's hand and glanced a kiss across her knuckles. "You and your husband have been wonderful hosts and I thank you for your most generous hospitality."

Lady Kenmuir's other hand slipped to the small of his back...and then lower. "Oh, that's such a shame," she said before whispering, "Lord Kenmuir departs for London in a sennight. If you need a diversion..." She squeezed his buttock.

"I will know your door is open," he murmured.

Lady Kenmuir threw him a coquettish smile. "Most definitely. *Wide* open."

Alex kissed his hostess's hand again for good measure—if he hadn't embarked on the course he was currently on, he might have considered the marchioness's scandalous invitation—then quit the room and Kenmuir House without a backward glance.

As his carriage clattered along the Royal Mile, he toyed with his onyx ring and mentally steeled himself for the long night and journey ahead.

CHAPTER 4

Something was wrong... Very wrong...

Cold foreboding slid down Sarah's spine as she forced her heavy eyelids apart. Her vision blurry, she blinked and squinted, trying to focus on her surroundings, but everything was cast in shadow, the edges of everything hazy. A dark memory hovered at the edge of her mind... *Something terrible had happened...*

There'd been a man...

A blond-haired woman in a red dress...

And Malcolm.

Oh, God. Malcolm.

The stab of her *fiancé's* betrayal pierced Sarah's heart anew and hot tears pricked her eyes. Dashing them away with the heel of her hand, she clumsily pushed herself upright. For a moment the room swam horribly and then panic flared as she took in her surroundings—she was in an unfamiliar tester bed...dressed only in her shift.

Dear Lord above! Whose bed? she thought as apprehension tightened her lungs. How long had she been asleep? Was she still at Kenmuir House? She certainly wasn't in the guest room of Tay House. In fact, this room was far finer...

The glow from the fireplace revealed that the bedchamber was well appointed: swathes of plush golden velvet adorned the windows and the bed; an ornate walnut armoire and matching washstand stood against one wall; and her ball gown was spread neatly upon a nearby settee.

Sarah's hand fluttered to her throat as her pulse bolted clean away. She had no recollection of undressing.

Who had *dared* to remove her clothes?

Then all at once the fog cleared—the man at the masquerade ball, Alexander Black, had forced her to drink something vile. Something that had made her lose consciousness. Laudanum perhaps.

Terror gripped Sarah's insides and nausea roiled. *I've been drugged and kidnapped. Stripped.* With a shaking hand, she reached below the fine linen sheets and touched between her thighs, but mercifully, every-thing *down there* felt as it should. Although, as she moved her legs together, something tightened around her right ankle.

What on earth? Sarah threw off the covers and shrieked. She'd been tethered—*tethered* to the bedpost with a gold silk rope. Like a prisoner. *An animal.*

Pushing herself down the bed, she began to frantically tug at the knots at her ankle and at the bedpost, but they were tight and the silk was slippery. Tears of frustration blurred her vision as her trembling fingers failed to loosen her bonds even a fraction.

"Ah, ye're awake, lassie."

Sarah jumped and her gaze darted to the door. A stout, middle-aged woman dressed in a plain gray gown and white cap entered the room and placed a large china ewer on the washstand. She returned to the door and locked it with a key that hung from a large iron keyring tied at her waist. Was she the housekeeper?

A spark of hope leapt in Sarah's heart. *A woman could be reasoned with, surely.* "Where is Mr. Black?" she said in the most authoritative tone she could muster. "I demand you untie me, help me dress, then take me to him. Or better yet, let me go. He cannot keep me here."

The woman clucked her tongue as she crossed to the washstand again and rummaged in a drawer. "Aye, the master did warn me that ye may be a wee bit feisty."

"I don't much care what your master said about me," returned Sarah firmly. "What he's done... What he's doing is wrong. If you release me, I will make sure you shan't be prosecuted." She lifted her chin. She wouldn't plead or beg. If she acted like a victim, she suspected she wouldn't get anywhere with this woman. "My *fiancé—*"

She broke off. *Was* Malcolm still her *fiancé*? Did she want him to be?

Sarah swallowed past the tight ache in her throat and started again. "My *fiancé*, the Earl of Tay, is a most powerful man. He may even reward you for your assistance. In fact, I shall reward you myself. I have the means."

The woman steadfastly ignored her. She turned her back and placed a white linen towel and a washcloth beside the ewer and a bowl. Then, without so much as a glance toward the bed, she crossed to the fireplace and poked at the coals before throwing another lump of wood into the fire.

Frustration as bright and angry as the embers in the grate stirred inside Sarah. "Why won't you answer me?" she demanded. "I'll scream my lungs out. Someone will hear me. Then you'll-you'll be sorry."

The woman heaved a weary sigh and at last turned to face her. "Now, now, miss. I ken ye've had a verra nasty shock. But no harm will come to ye."

"No harm will come to me?" snapped Sarah. "Your wicked scoundrel of a master forced me to drink laudanum and has locked me up"—she tugged on the silk rope—"nay, tied me up in a bed, against my will, for God knows what purpose. And considering I'm wearing naught but my shift, it's quite obvious his intentions are nefarious!"

The woman crossed her arms over her ample chest and humphed. "Ye can scream all ye like, lassie. No one'll hear ye. But you dinna have to worry. The master willna hurt ye, so long as ye go along with what he wants."

"But what *does* he want?" Sarah's voice broke as a sob clogged her throat. "I don't understand any of this. I just want to go home. P-Please let me go." To her mortification, tears began to run down her cheeks.

"Crying willna help either, lassie, and we are wastin' time. The master says we will be leaving in a half hour."

"Leaving?" Sarah narrowed her eyes, struggling to understand. If she had any hope of escaping, she needed to gather more information. "But where am I now? And where are we going?"

The servant huffed and poured steaming water into the bowl. "It's no' for me to say. It's time to wash and get dressed."

Was she even still in Edinburgh? Sarah couldn't hear any of the usual noises she associated with the city at night. Nor did she have any idea how long she'd been unconscious. Her throat was dry and her head felt like it was stuffed with feathers. Her gaze traveled to the windows and icy fear shivered over her skin. The pale light of morning was beginning to seep in around the edges of the curtains. She'd clearly been asleep for hours and hours.

Was Malcolm looking for her? Had he even noticed she'd gone? If he hadn't, Aunt Judith certainly would have. Yes, Aunt Judith would be looking for her. If she *were* in Edinburgh, her aunt would surely go to the Town Guard to enlist their help. They would find her. She had to believe that.

When the serving woman approached with the washcloth, a towel, and the bowl, Sarah ventured a question. "May I ask your name?" she asked in a mild tone. After all, one could catch more flies with honey rather than vinegar. And clearly vinegar wasn't working... "If you are to act as my lady's maid, I should like to know what to call you. I'm Sarah Lambert, by the way." Yes, if she could distract the woman and wrest the bowl from her, perhaps she could use it to knock her unconscious. She didn't want to hurt the servant, but if this was her only chance to get away...

But the woman was wilier than Sarah had anticipated. She deposited the bowl on a small bureau well out of reach, soaked the washcloth, wrung it out with her red, work-roughened hands then passed it to Sarah. "My name is Aileen," she said gruffly, "and I ken yer name, lass."

"Oh..." Sarah took the cloth and wiped her face, neck, and hands before handing it back to Aileen. "Then maybe you've also heard how wealthy I am. I could pay you whatever sum you asked for if—"

The woman grunted. "Money doesna matter to me. I dinna want yer coin, lassie. Ye canna bribe me." She gave Sarah the towel then nodded at the floor. "If ye need the chamber pot, it's beneath the bed. There's enough length in the rope for ye to stand and use it. Then I shall help ye with yer gown." Aileen picked up the basin but turned back, her expression grim. "But mind ye dinna try anythin'. I'm a braw woman and I'll best ye in a struggle. And if ye think to try and brain me with the chamber pot, I'll be forced to call the master, and he'll make ye take the laudanum again. I dinna think ye'd want to be leaving here in only yer shift. It's a wee bit cold outside." As she headed for the door, she called over her shoulder. "I'll give ye some privacy for a few minutes. But that's all, mind ye. Dinna dillydally."

Gah! Sarah poked her tongue at the door as it shut firmly. Of course, the odious woman locked it behind her. Aileen was far too canny for Sarah's liking. As for her master, braining him with a chamber pot would be *immensely* satisfying.

But must needs when the call of nature was upon one... Sarah slid carefully to the floor and held onto the side of the bed for a moment. When her head stopped spinning—the effects of the laudanum hadn't totally dissipated—she reached for the chamber pot. Made of heavy porcelain, it *would* make a decent weapon. But if she failed to knock Aileen out, the consequences did not bear thinking about. The last thing she wanted was Alexander Black arriving on the scene whilst she was in this state of undress. And she most certainly didn't want to be drugged again.

True to her word, Aileen returned within a handful of minutes, locking the door behind her then pocketing the key in her skirts.

"You still haven't told me where we're going," Sarah remarked as the serving woman approached the bed with a pile of garments in her arms. Was that a riding habit or traveling gown of claret-red wool? Sarah eyed the items with suspicion as Aileen laid them upon the bed. "Those are not mine. I wish to wear my own gown, stockings, and stays."

The glowering servant crossed her arms. "Lassie, we can do this the easy way or the hard way. Ye can get dressed in these"—she thrust her chin toward the bed—"or you can freeze yer bonnie wee arse off in yer shift. Whilst yer ball gown is verra fine, it isna fit for traveling. Nor yer boned stays. They are far too tight."

Sarah pressed her lips together. *Was everything to be so difficult?* "Very well," she gritted out from between clenched teeth. "But I don't see how this is going to work whilst I'm tied up like...like someone's dog."

Aileen tutted as she held out jumps—soft stays—for Sarah to slip her arms through. "Weel, I shall untie ye when ye need to don yer stockings and skirts. But I'm trustin' ye to behave yerself, now that ye ken what will happen if you do no'."

As Sarah submitted to Aileen's ministrations, her mind worked feverishly to come up with another escape plan. Once she was untied, perhaps she could flee the room and find a door leading outside. Aileen might be stronger than her but she surmised the older woman wasn't as agile.

Once Sarah's stays were laced, Aileen bade her to sit on the bed so she could untie the rope from her ankle. The servant's large, strong fingers deftly loosened the tight knots and the silk noose slipped free.

When Aileen bent down to slide an ivory wool stocking over her foot, Sarah took the opportunity to strike. *Now.* Leaning back on her hands for purchase, she lifted her other foot and kicked at Aileen's shoulder with all her might. The serving woman flew backward onto her rump with a grunt and Sarah dashed to the bedchamber door. Her heart hurtling against her ribs, she grasped the handle with shaking hands, but it wouldn't budge.

Damn, damn, damn. In her desperation, she'd forgotten Aileen had locked it and still had the key.

Tears of frustration flooded Sarah's eyes as she leaned her forehead against the unyielding wood paneling of the door. *This cannot be happening. I must be in some sort of nightmare.*

The unexpected sound of a key scraping in the lock made Sarah jump and back away from the door with faltering steps...and then the devil himself, Alexander Black, walked in, as bold as you please.

Oh, Lord help her...

CHAPTER 5

Anger warring with trepidation, Sarah stumbled to a halt and wrapped her arms about herself, as though that would be enough to ward off the blackguard who'd treated her so abysmally. Although her insides were quivering like a barely set blancmange, she would *not* be cowed...

Well, truth to tell, she might be cowed a little bit, considering she'd just attacked a woman in her kidnapper's employ...

Alexander Black was a formidable sight indeed in the cold light of day. He'd changed out of his evening finery into plainer garb and of course, he no longer wore a mask. It didn't matter one jot that he was as darkly handsome as a fallen angel—perhaps even Lucifer himself. To Sarah he was detestable, from the top of his raven locks to the tips of his shiny black boots.

When his wide mouth climbed into a wicked grin by way of a greeting, her fear fled. Pure rage washed through Sarah, lending her a fiery boldness she hadn't known she possessed. "You! You despicable rogue," she cried, starting forward and poking his hard-as-a-rock chest through the ruffles of his cambric jabot. "How dare you drug me and hold me prisoner? I knew you were up to no good as soon as I laid eyes on you, but I never imagined you'd...you'd go to these lengths. What do you think you're about?" Bristling with indignation, chest heaving, she planted her hands on her hips. "Actually, I do not want to know. Just let me leave."

Black pushed the door closed, then leaned back against it with his arms crossed. His shoulders seemed to take up the whole doorway. "Dressed like that, Miss Lambert?" he asked, cocking a black winged brow. Sardonic amusement danced in his dark gray eyes as they insolently raked over her scantily clad body.

Sarah felt a furious blush scorch her entire face. She might be dressed in only a thin shift and stays but she wasn't backing down. "Of course not. I'm not some doxy even though you are treating me like one. Worse, actually. Incapacitating a woman and then tying her up, it's appalling."

Black's attention slid past her and his expression softened. "Are you all right, Aileen?" he asked.

"Aye, sir, I'm verra sorry aboot this. The lass caught me off guard. Ye were right. She is a wee bit feisty. And cunning."

"Stop talking about me like I am not here," fumed Sarah, anger burning through her chest. "I want my clothes and I want to go back to Tay House."

Black's gaze narrowed in judgment as he looked down the strong blade of his nose at her. "You really want to go back there? After what you witnessed last night?"

Sarah bit her lip so it wouldn't quiver. *Don't think about it.* "My aunt and my possessions are there," she managed even though it felt like a boulder was lodged in her throat. "Besides, it's none of your business what I do."

Black uncrossed his arms and stepped forward, his flint-like gaze locking with hers. "I'm afraid it is my business, my dear Miss Lambert. You are *not* going back to Tay House. You are going to get dressed in the garments I have provided and you are coming with me."

"No." Sarah resisted the urge to step away from him. She wouldn't be bullied and abused. "I won't."

Oh dear, now I've done it.

The expression in Black's eyes grew colder and a muscle twitched in his lean jaw. He reached into the pocket of his navy wool frockcoat. "I didn't want to make you take this again," he said, withdrawing a familiar silver pocket flask. "But if we have reached an impasse…" He shrugged.

"No." Sarah stepped back. "I won't drink it, you—you wicked devil. You cannot make me."

"I can and I will," said Black darkly. But then he spread his hands in a placatory gesture and added in a gentler tone, "Look, we can avoid all of this unpleasantness if you would just do as I ask and get dressed."

Sarah scowled at him. It seemed she had no choice but to comply. She could hardly resist him *and* Aileen. And part of her really did want to put some clothes on. Facing down Black was difficult to do in a state of dishabille. She'd never felt so naked and vulnerable in her entire life.

Nevertheless, the stubborn side of her insisted she make a last-ditch effort at trying to extricate herself from this intolerable situation. "Why are you doing this?" she demanded hotly. "Are you a fortune hunter trying to compromise me? To extort money from me? Socially ruin me to force me into marrying you? Because if you are, I can offer you—"

Black snorted. "I know exactly how much you're worth, but I don't want or need your money, my dear. Although"—he reached forward and wound one of her disheveled locks around his finger—"now I've seen you in next to nothing"—his gaze dropped pointedly to the low, scooped neckline of her shift—"ruining you does seem rather appealing."

Her pulse racing faster than a startled hare, Sarah batted his hand away. "Don't jest so."

"What makes you think I'm jesting?" Black's gaze was intense. "You are a very beautiful woman, Sarah Lambert."

Oh no, she'd woken the predator. Sarah swallowed. Surely he wouldn't really take her by force. But what if he tried to? She wouldn't be able to stop him. She'd been tethered to the bed before and he could easily tie her up again. Cold dread trickled down her spine as visions of Black taking her just like Malcolm had taken the blond woman at the ball filled her head.

A loud "ahem" came from somewhere close behind her and Sarah released a shaky breath.

"Let me help you with yer gown, lassie. Here are the petticoats."

"You're despicable," Sarah shot at Black, before turning to Aileen.

"You said that before," he returned dryly.

"When Lord Tay finds me—" Her throat convulsed. Why did she keep forgetting that Malcolm was not the man she thought he'd been? "Never mind," she murmured in a voice that was noticeably husky.

Closing her eyes, Sarah submitted to Aileen, letting the woman fuss over all the tapes and hooks and ribbons that needed to be done up as she got dressed. When she was suitably attired in the claret-red riding coat and matching skirts, with her hair brushed and tied at the nape with a black velvet ribbon, she slid on her own cream satin pumps then turned back to Black. "Are you happy now?" she asked with an arch of her brow. She was surprised to find the clothes fit so well. It was as if they'd been made just for her. Another bizarre occurrence she'd rather not dwell on at this point.

Black had moved to the fireplace whilst she'd dressed, but at her words, he ceased twisting his distinctive gold and onyx ring around his finger and lifted his gaze from the dancing flames. His face was in shadow, his expression inscrutable as he ignored her question and said, "You look well, Miss Lambert." He approached and offered his arm as a gentleman would. "It's time to go."

Sarah glared at him, bunching her fists in the riding habit's woolen skirts to stop herself slapping his arrogant, deceitful, too-handsome face. "I cannot believe you are acting so when there is nothing remotely *civilized* about this entire situation." She couldn't hide the bitterness in her voice. "By rights I should be screaming and hammering at the windows, entreating someone to rescue me from whatever *this* is. But I rather suspect you would try to subdue me in whatever reprehensible manner you saw fit."

Black's mouth twisted into a mirthless smile. "You are correct. Don't try me, Miss Lambert. Because you will not like the consequences."

CHAPTER 6

Alex unlocked the door and ushered Aileen through, followed by a seething Sarah Lambert. She swept past him, claret-red skirts swaying around her slender hips, her blue eyes darting fire. He could hardly blame her for feeling both outraged and terrified, and a better man would let her go. Indeed, a better man wouldn't have abducted her in the first place. But needs must when the Devil drives, and Miss Lambert was a pawn he had to play in order to best Malcolm Campbell.

Even though the final stage of this game was only just beginning, Alex was determined to win.

Lifting her skirts with one hand, Sarah held onto the carved mahogany railing with the other as she began to descend the stairs to the lower floor. Alex followed close behind, not at all certain that she wouldn't try to make a break for it. Not that it would do her any good. There was a loyal footman standing guard at every door.

They'd just gained the landing before the descent to the main hall when Sarah tripped on the edge of the Turkish runner. She let out a terrified squeal as she stumbled and pitched forward toward the stairs and Alex only just caught her in the nick of time.

"Careful, lass," he murmured as he pulled her backward and she sagged against him. He could feel the frantic rise and fall of her chest, the pounding of her heart, and a small part of him *almost* regretted what he was putting her through. "Trying to break your neck to escape me seems a trifle drastic."

Aileen, several steps below them, turned back. "Perhaps it is the laudanum, sir."

Sarah put a shaking hand to her head. "I do feel a little dizzy."

"Well, that won't do, lass." Alex swept Sarah up into his arms and began to descend the stairs again.

She immediately began to wriggle and push at his chest. "Put me down. I can manage."

"I don't think so. I need you alive and well, Miss Lambert."

"For what?" Sarah's blue eyes were bright with anger, the color high in her cheeks. "I still don't understand what is going on. Why are you abducting me? You say you don't want my money." Her cheeks grew beet red as she added, "And I won't become your whore."

God, if she knew what he ultimately had in mind for her, she'd be horrified. Instead, Alex simply said, "As lovely as you are, I don't want you for that reason either." They'd gained the main hall and Alex followed Aileen toward the servants' entrance at the rear of the townhouse.

"Then why—?" Sarah's dark blond eyebrows drew together in a deep frown. "Has this got something to do with Lord Tay and the woman at the ball? The one he was...he was with...?" Her voice cracked and she swallowed. "Was she someone you cared for? Are you stealing me away because of what Malcolm did? Because if you are—"

"It's complicated. And yes, this is about Lord Tay. But not the other woman. Or you."

Sarah's pretty pink mouth flattened into a disapproving line. "It's hardly fair to involve me in your diabolical scheme then."

"I know."

"Surely there's some other way."

"There isn't."

"If we could just talk—"

"Trust me, it won't make any difference."

They'd reached the servants' entrance where Aileen stood by the door with a footman; both waited for his directions.

"My carriage is outside, Miss Lambert. I'm going to put you down." Alex set her on her feet, facing Aileen, then surreptitiously drew a silk rope from the pocket of his coat. "And I hope you'll accept my apology in advance for what I'm about to do..."

~

Before Sarah could draw breath to question the reason for Black's apology, he was deftly lashing her wrists together behind her back and Aileen was pushing a silk gag into her mouth.

Unbridled anger and panic coursing through her veins, Sarah attempted to scream as she struggled and writhed, but her efforts to escape were to no avail. Black had tied her in such a way that each movement seemed to pull the bonds tighter, and her cries were nothing more than muffled moans. Tears stung her eyes as she slumped to the ground, refusing to walk, but Black simply picked her up and unceremoniously slung her over his shoulder so that she was upside down, her derrière in the air.

Even though she kicked and twisted, it made no difference whatsoever—Black held her easily as though she weighed nothing more than a child. Within moments, the door had been unbolted and Black was carrying her outside into a cobbled close—at least Sarah thought it was a close, considering her view of the world was topsy-turvy. As she was deposited onto a leather bench inside a carriage, she caught a brief glimpse of gray bricks and whirling snowflakes before Black climbed in after her. And then the door slammed shut against the frigid morning air and any hope she had of freedom.

Sarah glared at Black as he claimed the spot beside her. His long, powerful legs were canted across the space between her and the door and she knew if she tried to launch herself toward it, it would be no effort at all for him to restrain her.

"I will remove the gag and untie you as soon as we leave the city," he said gruffly, before lifting the black velvet curtain covering the window to peer outside.

Was that a note of remorse in his voice?

The carriage rolled off and Sarah closed her eyes as the tears she'd been trying to keep at bay slid down her cheeks. It seemed she was still in Edinburgh. Not that it mattered. For the moment, she was trapped with no obvious way out. And after last night, she clearly couldn't count on Malcolm to mount any sort of search and rescue attempt.

But somehow, some way, she would get out of this mess. She was intelligent and she was capable. And Alexander Black, for all his power and ruthless machinations, must have a chink in his armor. She would find it, and when the time was right, she would exploit his weakness and escape.

She had to.

~

"Milord, my apologies for disturbing ye…"

Malcolm groaned and prized open his eyelids. "Fuck, Drysdale," he growled at his old-as-Methuselah butler. "What is it?" He straightened in his wingchair and cracked his neck. His head pounded and his mouth felt as dry and dusty as the ash-strewn grate. Why, in the Devil's name, had he drunk so much last night after he'd returned to Tay House after the Kenmuir's ball? He couldn't believe he'd fallen asleep by the fire in his private sitting room instead of crawling into bed. It was moments like these that he really wished he hadn't dismissed his valet. "What time is it?"

The wizened butler hovered by the heavy oak door, nervously shifting his ill-attired weight from one foot to the other. "Eight of the clock, milord. Again, I apologize but—"

"Eight o'clock? You useless cock, why are you waking me at such a godforsaken—"

Malcolm froze. *Shit, Sarah. Sarah's gone.*

He swallowed and rubbed his face with a shaking hand as reality dashed over him like a bucket of cold water. Sarah hadn't returned to Tay House last night, and he hadn't a clue where she'd gone. All his discreet inquiries and a search of the streets between here and Kenmuir House had proved fruitless.

He cast a narrow-eyed look at Drysdale, not daring to hope he had any news. "Well, out with it, man. Is this about Miss Lambert?"

The elderly butler hobbled toward the fireside and proffered a folded piece of cream parchment upon a tarnished silver tray. "A message was delivered verra early this morning, milord, and ye said that if there should be any word aboot Miss Lambert..." The butler swallowed audibly. "Weel, MacThomas, the night footman, says that someone pushed this letter under the front door some time afore dawn. Whilst we dinna know if it *is* aboot yer betrothed—"

"Christ, just give it to me." Malcolm snatched the parchment from Drysdale and cracked the plain red wax seal.

Tay,

Your pretty little heiress is now in my possession. To ensure her safe return, a substantial sum is required. Further directions shall be delivered at my convenience in the coming days. But harbor no illusions, if you do not provide what *I ask for,* when *I ask for it, Miss Lambert will be no more.*

Janus.

"Fuck!" Malcolm stared at the paper in his hand. *How could this be?* Surely this had to be some sort of mad prank or sick joke.

But of course, it wasn't.

Someone had kidnapped Sarah.

How in the Devil's name was he to pay the ransom? He couldn't even afford to pay his bloody servants properly.

Malcolm sent Drysdale for coffee then tossed the paper onto a nearby table where his silver snuffbox and an almost empty bottle of brandy sat. The kidnapper—this Janus, whoever he was—hadn't stated how much money he wanted exactly. "Substantial" could mean anything, depending on who was making the demand. It could be one hundred pounds, a thousand, or ten thousand. Even the King's bloody Crown Jewels.

Malcolm picked up the brandy and sloshed what remained into a sticky tumbler before taking a sizable swig. The problem was, he had virtually nothing left to give. Marrying Sarah should've been the solution to all his woes. She was worth an absolute fortune. But now the stupid bitch had allowed herself to be kidnapped from under his very nose by some prick calling himself Janus.

Who the bloody hell was he? Malcolm ran a hand through his hair, racking his brains for some kind of answer. Who did he know who was both short of funds and desperate enough to carry out such a brazen attack?

He grimaced. No one except himself.

One thing was certain: he had to get his hands on more money, and discreetly. It was a predicament like no other. He couldn't afford to lose Sarah, but he also couldn't afford to let it be known that she'd been kidnapped. The resultant scandal would kill him. If Society learned the mighty Earl of Tay was in dire financial straits, and he couldn't pay the ransom, he'd be well and truly fucked, and for all time. He'd wouldn't have a hope in Hades of finding another gullible heiress.

Malcolm supposed he could always approach Sarah's former legal guardian and executor of the late Edwin Lambert's will, Charles Swindon, as a last-ditch plan. Sarah had only recently come of age, so perhaps Swindon still had access to her fortune... It meant he would have to travel to Newcastle—another expense if he were to stay at an inn rather than sleeping in his last remaining carriage at the side of the road. There was also no guarantee the journey would be worth it.

He'd only met Charles Swindon on a few occasions, and he'd come across as a stuffy tight-arse. Of course, Sarah's bird-witted Aunt Judith might prove useful in convincing Swindon to cough up the funds. The biddy would undoubtedly be desperate to get her niece back, too.

Then again, if the woman suspected he was penniless, she might use the information against him. She might go to Swindon on her own and *they* might arrange to pay Sarah's ransom. Then turn Sarah against him, which wouldn't be hard considering she'd undoubtedly come upon him screwing that woman, Nell. No doubt there'd be a massive to-do. And the Earl of Tay's name would be mud.

Malcolm downed the last of the brandy then took a pinch of snuff. Perhaps all was not lost. The wait for the next lot of instructions would be excruciating, but in the meantime, he could approach a friend or two to see if he could acquire some extra funds. And of course, Damaris would probably be willing to fuck a few more noblemen in exchange for jewels, which he could then pawn. It wasn't as though they hadn't done it before.

He'd best stay away from the gaming tables...

One way or another, he would get Sarah back and her fortune would be his. Anything else was unthinkable.

CHAPTER 7

To Sarah's immense relief, Black removed her gag and bonds as soon as the carriage began to bowl along the open road just outside of Edinburgh.

"Thank—" Sarah bit her lip, swallowing back the words as she rubbed her wrists and rolled her stiff shoulders. *Why, in God's name, was she thanking her captor?* He was a brute. A monster. He'd ripped her away from her aunt and her life. It didn't matter one little bit that her life was in tatters right now. She was being denied her liberty and the right to sort through and reorder the remaining pieces. She wanted to confront Malcolm about his betrayal and decide what to do next.

She wanted to go home to Linden Hall.

Black had acknowledged he was being unfair, but it was worse than that. What he was doing was undeserved and unjust, especially since he'd hinted her kidnapping had ostensibly nothing to do with *her* per se.

But considering she was the one being held captive, it most certainly did.

Angry tears scalded her eyes but Sarah blinked them away and swallowed hard. She wouldn't cry again. At least, not in front of Black.

"Miss Lambert, I know this is difficult for you, but I will do my utmost to make this situation as painless as possible," said Black carefully. After he'd released her, he'd moved to the opposite bench seat. His long muscular legs, encased in form-fitting buckskin breeches and top boots, stretched out before him as he lounged negligently back against the squabs. Regarding her through half-closed eyes, he reminded Sarah of the lions she'd once seen prowling around the Royal Menagerie at the Tower of London. His pose might be casual, but Sarah sensed the coiled, leashed power within him. She had no doubt he'd stop her if she made any move to try and escape.

"How considerate of you," she replied, not bothering to hide the sarcasm in her voice. Taking a chance that Black wouldn't complain, she drew back one of the curtains to study the countryside. "I'm still trying to work out what this *situation* actually is. I don't even know how long you intend to *keep* me. Or where you are taking me." She didn't recognize the road or the snow-dusted landscape beyond, so perhaps they were heading westward rather than south toward England. Or north? Lord, it could be any direction.

"Somewhere safe," said Black. "That's all you need to know."

Sarah shot him a withering look. "You'll forgive me if I don't believe you."

Black inclined his head. "Fair enough. But I hope you'll soon see I'm a man of my word."

"Yes, it's already very clear to me how *noble* you are." Sarah turned her head away again and tried to focus on the passing scenery instead of Black. His steady scrutiny was making her blush so she added, "And by the way, has no one ever taught you it's rude to stare?"

"I like the view."

Before Sarah could scold him again, he opened a compartment beneath his seat and withdrew a wicker basket.

She swallowed. "What's in there?"

Black opened the lid and looked at her over the top of it. "There's no need to be nervous. It's just food and drink for the journey. I imagine it's been some time since you last had a meal."

Oh. Sarah swallowed again. Her mouth *was* incredibly dry and she'd been trying and failing to ignore the hollow feeling in her stomach since she'd woken up. "Yes, it has been a while."

"I promise you that everything is safe," Black said, turning the basket toward her. "Choose anything you like."

Sarah leaned forward and peered into the napkin-lined basket. Aside from a bottle of what appeared to be wine or ale or even cider, there were several small pies, some bread rolls, a hunk of cheese, and fruit—apples and pears. Her mouth watered. She selected a pear then sat back in the corner.

Black raised a quizzical brow as if questioning her choice, then took out a pie. "I'm glad you didn't try to knock me out with the bottle," he said, before biting into the golden flaky pastry with relish.

"The thought did cross my mind," admitted Sarah, and when Black smiled, she dropped her gaze to examine the pear. The fruit looked completely ordinary—the pale golden skin was unblemished. Besides, it appeared Black had chosen his pie without hesitation. She risked another glance at him and he was still chewing with gusto. Surely he wouldn't be doing so if everything was tainted with laudanum...or something worse. Would he?

Taking a deep breath, she bit into the flesh and closed her eyes as the sweet juices hit her tongue. Had a pear ever tasted so good?

When she looked up again, it was to discover Black was still watching her. His gray eyes were alight with amusement as he handed her a napkin. "You may need this, Miss Lambert."

Oh, my goodness, she did. To her dismay, sticky pear juices had run down her chin and she quickly dabbed them away. "Thank you," she murmured, before wiping her fingers and then wrapping the pear core in the linen.

"Would you like some apple cider as well?"

"Yes, please."

Black uncorked the bottle and offered it to her. "I'm afraid there aren't any glasses," he said with an apologetic smile.

Sarah shook her head. "You first, Mr. Black."

He shrugged and took a good swig from the bottle before passing it to her. His long fingers brushed hers, and to Sarah's great consternation she blushed again. The idea of putting her lips where his had been only moments before was too odd, too intimate, but what else could she do? She was well and truly parched. Thankfully, Black began to rummage around the basket again, so while he was distracted—whether by accident or design—she took the opportunity to take a few long sips of the cider before handing the bottle back.

When Black had polished off another pie, she ventured another question. "So...so how is *this*"—she gestured around the carriage—"all going to work?"

He frowned as he brushed a pastry crumb from the snowy cuff of his shirtsleeve. "In what sense?"

Sarah nodded toward the basket. "We clearly have quite a way to travel. How...what if I need...?" How could she possibly talk to this man about the call of nature? Her face burned with embarrassment.

Black seemed to recognize the reason for her discomfort as he stated matter-of-factly, "Aileen has accompanied us. She's sitting atop with the coachman, Dobson. She will continue to assist you when necessary."

Sarah's mouth twisted. "And I'm sure she'll try to stop me escaping. This traveling ensemble is red for a reason, isn't it? And it's not because red is your favorite color." She'd stand out like a hunted fox in the snow if she tried to run, curse him.

Black's gaze drifted lazily over her before returning to her eyes. "I stand by my assertion that you look well in it."

Why did it feel like Alexander Black was always trying to *flirt* with her?

Ignoring the fact that her pulse was racing and her face was probably as red as her gown, Sarah squared her shoulders and firmed her resolve; she was determined not to let the scoundrel's charm affect her. He was a rogue with a black heart. He'd drugged and kidnapped her. Tied her up and gagged her. And she *still* had no clue as to what his intentions were, or what would become of her. Even though she didn't seem to be in any immediate physical danger, Black was a stranger and she had no idea what he might be capable of.

It was beyond frustrating. And terrifying. Like fumbling about on a precipice in the dark.

If she couldn't get away from him, Sarah needed to talk her way out of this situation. And she couldn't do that until she'd worked out Black's motivation for kidnapping her. "I don't understand you," she said as evenly as she could. "You said you don't want my money, that you need me alive and well..." She trailed off as another thought struck her. "You're going to demand a ransom, aren't you? That Malcolm must pay."

Black didn't answer. However, a muscle twitched in his lean jaw.

Why? Black says he doesn't need money. This doesn't make any sense. Unless... Sarah's brow knitted as she turned over all the possibilities, examined them, then rearranged them again. *Maybe it does make sense, if Black wants to hurt Malcolm.*

Sarah met Black's gaze. The expression in his gray eyes had grown steadily cooler as she'd questioned him, and she knew she was getting closer to discovering the truth. A cold wave of foreboding washed over her. "This is about revenge, isn't it? What terrible thing has Malcolm done to you, Mr. Black? Tell me."

~

If you only knew...

Alex pushed the dark memories that haunted him to the back of his mind as he fought to keep a neutral expression. "I don't wish to discuss it."

Sarah's blue eyes sparked with determined fire. "Well, I do. I offered you money—"

"And I already told you I know how wealthy you are."

"Then you know very well that I can pay you handsomely."

"It doesn't matter one jot what you say, or what you offer. I don't want or need anything from you, Miss Lambert."

She arched a fine brow. "But of course you do," she returned hotly. "You're using *me* to punish Malcolm. I'll ask you again, what did he do—"

"Enough!" Alex growled. "I do not wish to talk about it anymore." *Stubborn chit.* He crossed his arms and turned his gaze to the window. Sarah Lambert was clever and she was clearly trying to negotiate her way out of this situation. But there was nothing she could say that would move him. He'd charted his course and he wouldn't deviate from it until the Earl of Tay was utterly destroyed.

If he were lucky, the bastard might end it all and send himself to purgatory. Or better yet, hell.

Out of the corner of his eye, Alex watched Sarah subside into her corner and rest her fair head against the leather squabs. Her pale brow was furrowed and he had no doubt her mind was working furiously to come up with various escape plans. He had to ensure that didn't happen. That would be an utter disaster, especially if she went straight back to Tay and they both worked out who he really was.

Then he would be the one who'd be ruined.

The journey was interminable. As Sarah watched the snow-blanketed fields and drear woodlands slip by, her eyelids eventually grew heavy and she dozed. Sometime during the afternoon, Black bade the carriage stop in the middle of nowhere for a comfort break. Sarah guessed they must be heading north as the snowfall had become heavier, and the drifts deeper. When she stepped down from the carriage into a freezing mizzle, her thin satin shoes had immediately become soaked right through.

Aileen, her face red and pinched with cold, had tied a rope tightly around Sarah's wrist before leading her off the road to a small copse of fir trees. Sarah had briefly thought about trying to undo her bonds, but even if she did manage to untie the knots with her frozen, gloveless fingers, then tried to make a run for it, there was nowhere to go, nowhere to hide. All around was only open ground, sparse woodland, and fog-blanketed hills in the distance.

And Alexander Black would be sure to catch her before she'd even managed to run fifty yards across the snow-covered field.

And then he'd probably drug her again. A frisson of fear tripped down Sarah's spine at the thought.

No, she'd best bide her time and wait until a better opportunity arose. If they were to maintain the cracking pace they'd been traveling at, at some point they'd need to change horses at a coaching inn. So she would watch and wait, and when the right time came, she would act.

By the time she'd taken her seat in the carriage again, she was shivering violently, toes and fingers numb, teeth chattering.

Black flicked a wing of dark, damp hair out of his eyes, revealing a frown as he sat down. "Miss Lambert, you look half frozen," he said, tugging off his black kid gloves. His onyx and gold ring winked at her in the uncertain light as though mocking her.

"I'm f-f-fine," she said, pushing her hands into the sleeves of her woolen jacket. She was hardly going to give him the satisfaction of knowing just how discomforted she was. "T-T-Truly."

"No, you are not. You're blue with cold." Black's gaze raked over her then he cursed beneath his breath. "Damn it, lass, what are you wearing on your feet?" He leaned forward and flipped up the hem of her skirts. "Sweet Jesus," he muttered when he saw Sarah's wet, mud-stained satin ball shoes. Scowling, he got up and threw open the carriage door. "Aileen, Dobson. I need Miss Lambert's trunk. Now."

Sarah blinked in confusion. "Wh-What trunk?"

Black ignored her and jumped down from the carriage. The man barked a few more orders and then after a minute, he climbed back inside. In his arms he carried a large bundle of woolen items which he tossed onto his seat. He draped a large black cloak around her shoulders—it smelled of sandalwood and citrus, and Sarah suspected it was the same cloak she'd worn last night on the terrace at Kenmuir House.

As the carriage rolled off, Black sat on the edge of his own seat, his knees almost bumping hers. "I'm sorry, Sarah," he said gravely as he draped a blanket across his lap. "It was thoughtless of me not to make sure you were dressed for the conditions." Before she knew what he was about, he'd lifted her legs up, flipped off her pumps, and had placed her stocking-clad feet onto the blanket.

"Wh-What are y-you d-doing?" she demanded, trying to pull away from his firm grasp.

"Your feet are frozen. I won't have your toes falling off because of frostbite."

Before Sarah could draw breath to protest, Black had reached beneath her skirts and had peeled off one of her wet stockings.

"Stop," she cried, but she didn't pull her foot away. His bare hand upon her ankle felt deliciously warm. "Please, let go."

Black cocked an eyebrow. "Miss Lambert, I've seen you in practically nothing but your shift. Upon my honor, all I'm going to do is attempt to restore your circulation."

Sarah eyed him for a moment but couldn't detect any insincerity in his tone or manner. "Very well," she said. "But don't dillydally about it."

"I won't." After he'd removed her other stocking, Black used the blanket to gently chafe and rub her frozen feet back to life.

Sarah bit her lip as the blood began to flow again. A burning, tingling sensation spread through her tissues but the pain soon abated and it wasn't long before she closed her eyes and relaxed against the squabs. Somewhere at the back of her mind, warning bells sounded. She really shouldn't let herself succumb to the illicit pleasure of having Black's large warm hands massage her toes and the soles of her feet...but another part of her was melting. His ministrations felt so very good. If she were a cat, she would have purred.

When Black gently placed her feet on the floor, she discovered he was smiling. "Better?" he asked.

"Yes. I suppose I should thank you," she said stiffly while her mind whispered a warning. *Be honest. You liked it* too *much, Sarah Lambert, you contrary ninnyhammer.* Malcolm had never touched her so intimately or with such tenderness. It was befuddling, not to mention vexing, that her kidnapper's touch could turn her into a mindless syrupy puddle.

Black's gray eyes darkened and his smile developed a sensual edge. "It was my pleasure."

Oh, blast. Somehow he *knew* what affect he'd had on her. Sarah blushed and set about straightening her skirts so her bare feet were tucked away.

"These are for you." Black passed her a fresh set of wool stockings and a pair of shiny black leather ankle boots with neat little buttons up the sides. "Aileen should have given them to you earlier."

Sarah narrowed her eyes in suspicion as she examined them. Her kidnapping was clearly well planned—remarkably so. Black hadn't done this on a whim. "Why... How did you manage to arrange all this? You asked for my trunk just before. This habit"—she gestured at herself— "fits remarkably well and these boots also look like they will be the perfect size."

Black shrugged. "What can I say? I like to be prepared. Despite what you may think of me, I'm not a monster. It has never been my intention to treat you badly."

Resentment flared to life within Sarah. "Yet you are," she countered hotly. "If you had any decency, you'd let me go. When we stop to change horses at an inn, I could easily hire another carriage—"

Black's gaze was stony. "No."

"But what if Malcolm won't pay the ransom?" Sarah demanded, desperation sharpening her tone. "After last night, after what I saw—"

"He wants you back."

"How can you be so sure?" To Sarah's mortification, her lower lip trembled. "I'm certainly not."

"Sarah—" Black reached for her hand but she snatched it away.

"Leave me be," she spat, angry at herself for momentarily falling under Black's spell. "Trying to mollify me with pretty clothes, flirtatious words, and gestures of kindness won't help. No matter how much you deny it, you are a selfish, dishonorable beast. I detest you. Now turn around. I wish to put my stockings and boots on without you leering at me."

Black's smile was tight as he turned away. "Of course, Miss Lambert."

Alex turned his gaze to the window to give Sarah the privacy she'd asked for.

Although, little did she know he could see tantalizing glimpses of what she was doing in the reflection caught by the carriage's windowpane. No matter how hard he tried to focus on the passing scenery, his attention was hopelessly drawn to the much more appealing sight of Miss Lambert rolling on her stockings and fastening the ribbon garters about her slender legs.

There was no denying the fact she was unaccountably pretty. More than that, she appeared highly intelligent and he had nothing but admiration for how brave she was, how she fought back and scolded him rather than dissolving into a blithering wreck or becoming hysterical.

Indeed, if he weren't an attainted Jacobite, she was exactly the sort of woman he'd be tempted to formally pay court to. A woman who'd make a fine Lady Rannoch... If he were ever pardoned and his title was reinstated.

Lord Tay certainly didn't deserve her.

Of course, a part of Alex did regret the mental and emotional suffering he was putting her through. A beast and a scoundrel he might be, but he would never, ever subject her to the vile, depraved, unspeakable things Tay had done to his mother and sister.

And his sweetheart, Maggie.

Alex clenched his jaw and closed his eyes as the anguish of eleven years ago burned through him. He could still feel the scar on his left palm. Could still recall the deep, satisfying sting as he'd made his blood vow to avenge those he'd loved and lost.

No matter how wronged Sarah Lambert felt, her discomfort paled into insignificance whenever he remembered that long ago day at Blackloch Castle.

He wouldn't stop until Lord Tay was rotting in hell.

CHAPTER 8

Tay House, Edinburgh
February 16, 1757

"For heaven's sake, Malcolm, how do you know these silly little letters are genuine ransom demands?" asked Damaris, tossing both pieces of parchment onto the gilt-edged table beside her.

She was lounging on a rose-patterned chaise longue in her morning room with her white terrier, Bonnie, on her lap. The remains of her breakfast, congealing on another nearby table, made Malcolm's stomach turn in an uneasy somersault. He really shouldn't have had so much claret last night, but drinking himself into a stupor seemed to be the only way he could get any sleep.

Oblivious to his foul mood or the impending crisis, Damaris continued on with irritating blitheness. "Sarah's probably run off with some other man she likes better than you. She always struck me as the flighty type. Good riddance to her, I say. I'll be glad to see the back of her miserable aunt too."

Malcolm snatched the papers up and Damaris winced as her terrier growled. "Of course these are bloody real, Damaris."

The second letter had arrived before dawn this morning, pushed beneath the door just like the first. This time, a torn piece of heavily embroidered apricot-pink satin, edged with gold lace, had been enfolded within. "Even you agree that this"—he waved the scrap in Damaris's face—"belongs to Sarah." Although he generally didn't pay much attention to women's attire, Malcolm knew the distinctive fabric came from the gown Sarah had worn to the Saint Valentine's ball at Kenmuir House.

Damaris sighed and tickled Bonnie's ears. "Even if the demand *is* genuine, I don't see that railing about it will help." She popped a sugared sweetmeat into her mouth before feeding one to the terrier. "I'm well aware that you would have considerable difficulty paying any sort of sizable ransom. I say let this Janus—whoever he is—have her. If we go to London straightaway, I'm sure you'll find another wealthy, gullible lass who'd be willing to trade her fortune for a title. How long could it possibly take?"

Malcolm grabbed Damaris by the chin, forcing her to look at him. "Now listen here, my very pretty but very dim-witted sister. I've just sold off all but one of our carriages. The horses are gone too, and I've precious little coin to hire any. Not only that, but I can't afford to rent a townhouse once we arrive."

Fear flickered in Damaris's golden-brown eyes. "Wh-What? You must be joking," she breathed.

"Well, I'm not," he snapped. "We can't afford to go to London, and the only one who's going to be whoring herself at the moment is you. Why don't you go and visit Lord Arbelour and let him screw you in exchange for some jewelry which we can then sell off? You told me he was quite taken with you at the Kenmuir's ball."

"Yes, he was." Damaris jerked her chin away and pouted. "Do we really have so little money?"

"Yes, dear sister. I'm afraid so."

"And how much is this ransom again?"

"Ten thousand pounds. I'm to pay it by the first of March, which only gives me two bloody weeks to find the money."

The color drained from Damaris's cheeks as she swallowed audibly. "Oh."

"Yes, *oh*." The ransom date was only a week prior to the day he was supposed to marry Sarah at Taymoor Castle. It made Malcolm wonder again who Janus actually was. The timing seemed rather pointed, the message clear—pay the ransom or you won't have the chance to wed your wealthy *fiancée*.

"Do you think..." Damaris drew a shaky breath. "Do you think you could go to the bank and arrange another loan? If the bank manager knows you are due to wed Sarah in less than a month, perhaps—"

"Don't you think I haven't already thought of that?" Malcolm growled. "The bank won't let me in the damn door let alone lend me another penny."

"Perhaps if Judith knew—"

"Christ, no. If Judith found out that I can't pay the ransom, she'd be off to Newcastle to tattle to that pompous ass Swindon that I'm all but financially ruined. Between the two of them, they'd probably bloody pay the demand, and Sarah would be sure to call off the engagement as soon as she found out I hadn't been the one to save her."

"But if Sarah loves you, as you believe she does, surely she wouldn't care that you are not as wealthy as she thought," rejoined his sister.

Malcolm paced the threadbare Aubusson rug. Until recently, perhaps Sarah would have overlooked such a thing—but he was certain she'd caught him fucking the blond chit. She wouldn't willingly marry him if she believed he was faithless as well as penniless.

Unlike Damaris, she wouldn't do anything to get what she wanted.

But what if Sarah had no other choice but *to marry him?*

Malcolm stopped by the window and studied the fog-shrouded view of Calton Hill through the grimy panes. This Janus, whoever he was, might just dip his wick whilst he had Sarah in his possession. God knows, he'd wanted to. She was pretty enough. If she were ruined— perhaps even with child—she'd have to marry him, Malcolm, to save herself from disgrace.

Malcolm's lip curled. Yes, he rather fancied playing the part of Sarah's knight in shining armor. Of course, he also couldn't afford to be fussy. He could stomach another man's leavings—even pretend Sarah's by-blow was his—for a chance to acquire the Lambert family fortune.

But first things first. He had to pay the ransom.

"What shall we tell Judith?" asked Damaris. "She's been talking about going to the Town Guard to enlist their aid, to see if they can find her niece. I've told her you've sent out men to search for Sarah. But if the old tabby makes a fuss, and then others find out what's really happened...and that we have no money..."

"Yes, keeping Judith quiet is a priority," agreed Malcolm. "She mustn't suspect, even for a moment, that Sarah has been kidnapped. The one thing we *cannot* afford, if we can afford anything at all, is a scandal." He turned away from the window to eye Damaris. Aside from fucking men well, his sister had other talents. "Do you think you can forge Sarah's handwriting? Could you fool her aunt?"

Damaris cast him an arch smile. "You know I can. Just tell me what to write and I will do it."

"Good."

Damaris plucked at the lace edging of her pink silk peignoir. Her brow was furrowed in thought. "So who do you think Janus is? This whole scheme seems very...personal."

"I wish I knew." Malcolm's hands curled into fists as he contemplated what he'd do to the dog who was doing this to him. Making his life even more of a hell than it already was. "But if I ever discover his identity, make no mistake, he'll regret the day he ever fucking dared to cross me."

CHAPTER 9

Somewhere in Scotland...

Sarah lay in a lumpy tester bed with a sagging blue canopy, listening to rain squalls viciously lashing the window of her bedchamber at some godforsaken inn—the Stag's Head—in the middle of nowhere. *Her prison cell...*

She was utterly spent yet taut as a bowstring. Her eyes were gritty with fatigue and she would love nothing more than to go to sleep—but she mustn't.

Because tonight she was going to escape.

To her relief, Black had taken the chamber adjoining hers and Aileen's. Even though he'd closed the connecting door when he'd bid her goodnight, she still needed to exercise extreme caution—she hadn't heard the lock tumble and Black could enter the room at any time. She prayed he was weary too and wouldn't come to check on her in the next hour or so. Her plan, such as it was, depended upon it.

Aileen was currently tucked into a pallet bed to one side of the fireplace, and judging by the woman's gentle snores, she was sound asleep. She had to be exhausted. They'd traveled through much of the night on the first day of their journey north, bumping along inferior roads in foul weather. Sarah, who'd been half-frozen in the relative shelter of the carriage, imagined that Aileen, sitting atop with the driver, would have turned into a block of ice if they'd continued on for a second night in such a fashion. She *almost* felt sorry for the woman. But considering the servant had helped Black to smuggle her into the inn, and then tether her to the tester bed, it was hard to summon much sympathy.

Of course, Sarah's heart had pounded with excitement when Black had first announced they would be stopping for the night. However, all her hopes of entreating someone to help her were dashed when Black had also informed her that he'd made arrangements to hire not just two, but every single room at the inn. On their arrival, well after dark, he'd apparently instructed the staff to keep to the public rooms during their stay, so if she screamed, no one would hear her. To Sarah's frustration, he also bound and gagged her again before taking her to her room—her cell, she reminded herself—via a side entrance, most likely one used by the staff. Aside from Aileen and Black, Sarah hadn't encountered a single soul.

As Black had tied her to the bed, Sarah had decided then and there to do what she must in order to free herself. This was perhaps her very best chance. If she could break her bonds, get dressed, then procure the room key without waking Aileen, she'd make her way to the stables and take a horse. She was an able rider, and despite the fact the weather was abysmal, she'd rather brave the elements—even risk being turned into an icicle—than endure another minute as Black's hostage.

The man was hell-bent on seeking vengeance against Malcolm, and Sarah had no idea how far he would go to exact it. Black had assured her he wouldn't hurt her, but she didn't trust him. Not at all.

From what she'd seen so far, Alexander Black had been plotting to kidnap her for some time—she shuddered every time she thought about how well orchestrated this whole scheme was. From the way he'd stalked her at Kenmuir House, then offered her false comfort. Drugged her and spirited her away. Provided her with a wardrobe that appeared to be tailor-made. Hired out every room at this inn. The man was as meticulous as he was diabolical and she must never, *ever* forget that.

Malcolm had already betrayed her, so she'd be foolish indeed to think she could rely on him to pay the ransom. And since early evening, as the light was fading, Sarah's hope of negotiating her release with Black had faded too. Pleading with him to free her was a lost cause. Reasoning, honeyed words of persuasion, hurled insults, tears, nothing worked. The odious man was as implacable as the granite peaks they'd been heading toward this afternoon.

No, it was up to her and her alone to escape Black's clutches. Somehow, she would get back to Edinburgh and Aunt Judith. Only then would she have the freedom to decide what she would do with her life.

Her heart hammering an erratic tattoo, Sarah sat up and pushed the bedcovers aside as quietly as she could. Thankfully, Aileen continued to snore steadily. Even though the dying fire was the only source of light in the room, it would be sufficient to allow her to do what she must.

Black had tethered her right ankle to the bedpost with another silk rope; she already knew the knots would be impossible to untie so she'd made a plan. When Aileen had left her alone to fetch their supper from the taproom, Sarah had broken a small spill vase that had sat on the nearby bedside table. She'd then hidden the tapers and all the vase's pieces, bar the biggest and sharpest one, beneath the bed in the farthest, darkest corner; the largest shard was secreted within easy reach beneath the mattress.

With a shaking hand, Sarah pulled out her makeshift knife, then drew her right knee up so she could reach her ankle. Fortunately, Black had left enough length in the rope to enable her to move about a little. Gritting her teeth against the bite of jagged edges pressing into her palm, she began to saw feverishly at the silk rope. It was a tight bond and more than once her grip slipped and she cut her ankle, then two fingers, but the pain mattered little. She was determined to free herself as quickly as possible. If Aileen awoke, or worse still, Black came in... She really didn't want to think about what he would do.

At last, the silk began to fray and unravel and Sarah choked down a sob of relief. She tugged off the rope and ignoring the sting of her cuts, slipped from the bed. The floorboards were icy-cold beneath her bare feet and she shivered in her thin shift. Outside, the wind howled like a wild animal; it rattled the windows and every now and again a flurry of hail dashed the mullioned panes. Although she was loath to waste time dressing, she couldn't leave here in next to nothing. She would need to dress warmly if she were to avoid freezing to death.

She was lucky Aileen had been too tired to put her clothes away; the servant had left everything lying on a worn damask armchair by the bed. Working swiftly, Sarah donned her stockings and stays, then the petticoats, undershirt, and red riding habit as quietly as she could. Her hands trembled so much, it was difficult to do up all the tapes and ribbons and buttons, especially with bleeding fingers, but in the end she managed everything.

Last of all, she threw on Black's own woolen cloak, tugged on her new boots, and then a pair of leather gloves—Black had provided them the day before when they'd stopped in the middle of nowhere for another comfort break.

Sarah released a shaky breath as she tucked her loose hair behind her ears. Now she was dressed, God willing, she'd make it outside.

Picking up her skirts, she tiptoed across the chamber to the fireplace. Aileen had placed the key on the mantelpiece before she'd climbed into bed. Not daring to breathe, Sarah snatched it up then crept back to the door. When the key scraped inside the old iron lock, and Aileen turned over and mumbled in her sleep, Sarah's heart stopped and she willed herself not to faint.

Frozen, too terrified to draw another breath, she waited for Aileen to settle again. *Please, God...*

Several taut seconds passed but when it was clear the servant was still fast asleep, Sarah lifted the latch with painstaking slowness. She almost cried with relief when the door eased open without so much as a creak.

As she'd expected, the hallway was deserted and dark, save for a faint strip of light escaping from the bottom of Black's door. Praying the blackguard wouldn't hear her, Sarah walked as swiftly and silently as she could on her tiptoes, past his room, heading toward the set of servants' stairs that Black and Aileen had used to smuggle her up to her room a few hours ago.

Sarah offered another silent prayer of thanks to heaven when she discovered the door at the bottom of the stairs was only bolted rather than locked with a key. But when she drew back the bolt and inched open the door, she cursed beneath her breath.

The stable yard was awash, the rain coming down in sheets, and the stables were as black as Hades.

It's only rain. It won't kill you, Sarah. And you'll never get another chance like this.

It's now or never.

Inhaling a lungful of frigid air, Sarah raised her skirts, then dashed toward the shelter of the stables.

By the time she reached the other side of the yard, she was half soaked and shivering, but it seemed she hadn't been detected. Wiping the raindrops from her eyes, she squinted through the darkness at the back of the inn. It was quiet as the grave and all the windows—bar the one she suspected was Black's—were dark. *So far so good.*

On entering the stables, she noticed that somewhere toward the back, near the tack room, was a glimmer of light. It seemed someone— perhaps the ostler—had left a lantern burning. She waited in the shadows by the door, listening for any sounds of human activity, but all she could hear above the pounding of her heart was the rain drumming on the roof and the occasional equine snuffle.

There were a dozen or so stalls, at least half of them occupied. But she only needed one mount. And a saddle and a bridle. Thankfully, she knew how to ready a horse. Her dear father had taught her to ride when she was only eight years old, and by the time she was twelve, riding was a part of her morning routine whenever they stayed at Linden Hall.

However, her good fortune appeared to run out when Sarah tried the door to the tack room and discovered it was locked. *Hell and damnation.* Why hadn't she anticipated such a possibility? Tears pricked but she blinked them away. She wouldn't be defeated. She would ride bareback all the way to Edinburgh if she had to—

"Weel, what do we have here?" demanded a gruff male voice from the shadowy darkness.

Oh, no. Sarah spun around and her stomach plunged to the hay-strewn floor. A middle-aged man with a wild mane of red hair and a bush of a beard was descending a ladder that appeared to lead to an overhead loft. She'd obviously woken the ostler or one of the stablehands.

Before she could formulate some sort of plausible reason for being in the stables—it would be foolish of her to admit she'd been trying to steal a horse—another man peeked over the edge of the loft. "Looks like a bonnie wee lassie to me, MacMunn."

The redheaded man, MacMunn, smirked and pulled at the crotch of his breeches beneath his filthy shirt. Even though the light was dim, Sarah could detect the glint of lust in his small, pale eyes. "Aye, she's verra bonnie, Angus. Is there summat in particular that ye wanted, miss?" He emitted a low rough chuckle. "Seekin' some male company, perhaps?"

Sarah shook her head and stumbled backward toward the stalls. This could *not* be happening. "N-No. I d-don't need anything," she stammered as sharp fear spiked through her. It seemed she'd unwittingly jumped from the frying pan straight into a blazing inferno. "I'll just g-go back to the inn. M-My traveling companions are expecting me."

Angus, a tall and gangly youth dressed in a rough cambric shirt and patched breeches descended the ladder. "Mayhap she *is* after a tumble in the hay, MacMunn?"

MacMunn's smirk widened to a grin as he stepped closer. "Aye. I ken ye might be right, m'lad."

Oh, dear God, no. Bile burned the back of Sarah's throat. The servants' entrance wasn't far and the door would still be unlocked. She was sure she could outrun them.

She turned to flee, but faster than a striking adder, MacMunn lunged and grabbed her by the arm. When she sucked in a breath to scream, he clapped one dirty hand over her mouth and hauled her against his bony chest. "Whisht. Keep the heid, lassie." His voice was a low growl and his breath stank of stale ale. "The three of us will have a braw time. Just you wait and see."

Thought-obliterating terror turned Sarah's legs to water as MacMunn and Angus dragged her into the nearest vacant stall and threw her face down onto the floor. The stench of dirty, damp hay and unwashed male assaulted her senses and her stomach rolled. Tears scalded her eyelids. *Oh, dear Lord, please help me.*

But it seemed no help was at hand. MacMunn roughly gripped her by the head and pressed his knee into her shoulder at the same time Angus threw up her skirts and cloak. She dragged in another breath and managed a short scream before MacMunn pushed her face into the hay again. Anger and despair clogged her throat as Angus forced her legs apart. She twisted and bucked but he grabbed her hips and pinned her down with his weight. She couldn't move. Couldn't breathe. *Oh, no. No, no, no!*

And then MacMunn swore and let go of her at precisely the same moment Angus rolled away, howling in pain. Startled by the unexpected reprieve, Sarah turned over and pushed herself against the side of the stall, scrabbling to pull down her skirts...and gasped.

Black. She'd never thought she'd welcome the sight of him but at this precise moment, she most certainly did.

A vicious snarl contorting his handsome features, he advanced farther into the stall and felled MacMunn with two swift punches—one to the stomach and then another bone-crunching blow to the man's face. The ostler crumpled to the floor where Angus still lay, moaning and clutching his groin.

"Sarah." Black stepped around her assailants and pulled her to her feet. His hand touched her cheek. "Can you walk, lass?"

"Yes..." Her voice caught and she had to clear her throat before she added, "I believe so."

"Good girl." Black's brow was furrowed with an emotion which might have been concern. *Yet how could it be? He was her kidnapper after all.* "Go and wait by the door for a minute whilst I deal with these two disgusting dogs."

More than happy to oblige, Sarah nodded, and on shaky legs made her way to the entrance. It was still pouring and an icy wind swept gusts of rain inside. Leaning against the stone wall behind the shelter of the door, Sarah wrapped her arms around herself. She was shivering uncontrollably and despite her best efforts not to cry, tears kept slipping from her eyes.

How low she had fallen. To think that only two days ago—on Saint Valentine's Day—she'd been counting the days until she wed Malcolm.

And now...now she was Black's hostage again and she'd been physically assaulted and almost raped. Not only that, but she couldn't be certain of Malcolm's commitment to her. Truth to tell, the idea of marrying such a faithless, despicable, lying rogue made her stomach turn.

A sob rose in Sarah's throat and she swallowed hard to stop it escaping. She felt as hopelessly crushed as the sodden straw beneath her feet.

"Sarah?"

She looked up to find Black standing beside her, but she didn't say anything. Weariness and despair weighed so heavily upon her, she couldn't summon the will to speak.

"I've contained the bastards that hurt you, Sarah. I know the innkeeper, and they will be dealt with." He raked a hand through his wet, disheveled hair then blew out a heavy sigh. "We need to go back inside."

"I know." Even to Sarah's own ears, her voice sounded dull with defeat. She supposed, if the circumstances were different, she might have thanked Alexander Black for coming to her aid. But he was going to take her back up to her room and tie her up again.

Her life had become a nightmare that seemed never-ending.

Guilt crushed Alex's chest as he escorted Sarah through the driving rain, back to the inn. He couldn't blame the lass for wanting to escape. It was only natural; he would do the same thing if their positions were reversed.

Of course, it was well and truly his fault that she'd grown so desperate she was willing to take such wild risks. When he pictured what the ostler and stablehand had been doing to her, incandescent anger flared to life inside him. The Stag's Head was one of his commercial property acquisitions and he couldn't believe the innkeeper had hired such disreputable staff. Taking a woman by force, it was an unconscionable act. Those two curs were lucky they were still breathing.

But aren't you hurting her, Alexander MacIvor? Kidnapping and manipulating an innocent woman are unconscionable acts too.

Sarah tripped on the threshold as they entered the servants' entrance and she gripped Alex's arm to steady herself. That she would voluntarily touch him—her captor—spoke volumes about her mental state. She was clearly still shaken. Indeed, the lass was as docile as a lamb as he guided her up the stairs and back to her room.

Aileen scowled when she saw Sarah. "Ye're a crafty lass, I'll give ye—"

"Now, now, Aileen. We'll have none of that," chided Alex as he closed the door. "Miss Lambert has been through a terrible ordeal—"

"T-Two m-men attacked me and tried to...tried to *use* me." Sarah's voice was flat, her lovely blue eyes unusually dull as she stared at the floorboards. Pieces of straw were caught in her tangled, dripping blond hair, and her red habit and his cloak were sodden and streaked with mud.

"Och, weel, that's truly dreadful." Aileen crossed her arms and gave Sarah a stern, narrow-eyed look that reminded Alex of a nursemaid who was scolding a naughty child. "But really, ye only have yerself to—"

"That's enough, Aileen," snapped Alex. "She is *not* to blame for the actions of those sorry excuses for men." He drew a measured breath then added in a gentler tone, "Miss Lambert needs to get into dry clothes." Without thinking, he touched Sarah's arm, and when she flinched, guilt stabbed him anew. "Sarah, I must change then talk to the innkeeper, but after that, I will bring something back from the kitchen. Tea, perhaps?" He'd also speak with the local magistrate in Dunkeld first thing in the morning. He couldn't afford to officially report the attempted rape upon Sarah, given he'd kidnapped her, but he sure as hell wasn't going to let the men get away with what they'd tried to do. Between the innkeeper and himself, he'd make sure the contemptible maggots paid.

Sarah nodded without looking at him and it made Alex wonder how far the assault had gone. In the firelight he could easily see an abrasion on her ashen cheek.

He caught Aileen's attention on the way to the door. "Please treat her with care," he murmured. "She may have been injured in ways that are not obvious to the eye."

Aileen's expression was grave. "Aye, sir."

When Alex returned to the room a half hour later, he found Sarah seated by the fire in an armchair with a rug across her lap. Dressed in a simple flannel night rail and a pale blue shawl, she looked a little better.

Her hair was brushed and braided and there was more color in her cheeks.

Aileen grunted with approval when she saw the tray he carried, but Sarah ignored the cup of tea and piece of almond-studded fruitcake Alex placed on the table beside her. She stared into the fire and gripped her shawl about her chest so tightly, her knuckles were white. Alex suspected she would need something stronger than tea. It was a good thing he'd also procured a bottle of whisky from the innkeeper's illicit stash.

"Aileen, I would like to talk with Miss Lambert. Privately," he said quietly, nodding toward his chamber.

The servant glanced at Sarah then drew close. "She has a few minor cuts and bruises and grazes, but I...weel. I ken she's still a maid," she whispered.

Alex nodded. "Thank you. After everything that's happened, I think it would be best if I stayed here and you took my room. Get some rest."

When the door shut, Alex poured two drams of whisky then pulled a straight-backed wooden chair closer to the fireside. He offered Sarah the drink and she took it from him with a trembling hand. He noted two of her fingers were bandaged, and considering there was blood on the bedsheets and the silk rope, he suspected she'd injured herself when she'd cut through her bonds.

He'd clearly underestimated how determined she could be. And wily.

"What's this?" Sarah asked after she'd sniffed the contents of the glass.

Relieved the lass wasn't entirely uncommunicative, Alex gave her an encouraging smile. "Whisky. I think it will make you feel a wee bit better."

She cast him a suspicious look through her eyelashes. "I'm sure."

He tossed back a large mouthful of his own drink—partly to show her it was safe and partly because he was in desperate need of it—then Sarah sipped hers. She gasped and coughed and somehow managed to glare at him even though her eyes watered. "It's terrible. It's like swallowing fire."

Alex's smile widened. "Ah, but it's sure to warm you up."

"Or burn a hole in my stomach," she grumbled, putting the glass aside. "I'd rather drink laudanum."

Alex sighed. "Sarah, I'm sorry about that—"

"No, you're not. And I don't want a hollow apology from you," she flashed back at him. "I just want you to let me go."

"I cannot."

"Cannot, or *will* not?" Sarah's blue eyes were bright with anger.

"Both." Alex put down his whisky and rested his elbows on his thighs. "Sarah, what those men tried to do to you was despicable. Loathsome. In Edinburgh, I threatened to ruin you and I...I truly regret what I said. I would never force myself on you, or indeed, any woman. I think it's important you know that."

"But by holding me captive, I'm already as good as ruined," she rejoined. "In Malcolm's eyes and in the eyes of Society, if anyone finds out. Besides, how can I trust you...?" Sarah's voice cracked and a tear slipped onto her cheek. "You are mistreating me too. Let me go. I implore you."

Ignoring the pain in his chest, Alex straightened in his chair. "No."

Sarah dragged in a shuddering breath and lifted her chin. The expression in her eyes was colder. Harder. "Why won't you tell me what Malcolm did to you?" she demanded. "I keep thinking about the blond woman, at the ball. Who was she to you? You say this isn't about her and what she did with Malcolm, but surely it is." Her eyes narrowed and her gaze grew fiercer. "Was she your lover and you've decided to retaliate by taking an eye for an eye?"

"She is no one of consequence."

"Well, she is of consequence to me. Malcolm's not going to pay your ransom. I thought he cared for me, but he was with that other woman —" Sarah turned her face away and stared into the fire, her lower lip trembling.

Alex fought the urge to touch her, to offer comfort. *Christ, this was hard.* Harder than he'd thought it would be. He'd never bargained on feeling anything for Sarah Lambert.

Of course, he'd harbored carnal thoughts about her since their very first meeting—what man wouldn't? She was beautiful, after all. But now...now he was beginning to admire her in more ways than he cared to think about. Even worse, he was beginning to care about how she felt. He didn't like seeing her so upset.

He was off balance and shaken. Off kilter. Like the rug beneath his feet had been yanked away and he was teetering on the edge of the unknown.

Alex's heart had been as cold and hard as a lump of lead for so long, he didn't know how to deal with the tender emotions stirring within his chest. Part of him wished he could tell Sarah the real reason behind his plan for revenge. But then she would learn who he was. And he couldn't risk giving her that sort of information. Too much was at stake.

His life and his legacy, his leaderless clan, were at stake.

But the way she was looking at him—the despair in her gaze... He hated himself for engineering the situation between Malcolm and Nell. For every hurt he'd caused. He'd made Sarah Lambert feel worthless. But she wasn't.

"Sarah..." He wanted to say something to make her feel better but didn't know what.

She brushed another tear from her cheek as she turned to look at him, a question in her sad blue eyes.

And then the words fell from Alex's lips before he could stop them. "If you were mine, you'd never have cause to doubt me."

Sarah stared at Black, searching the turbulent gray of his eyes. For a moment, confusion clouded her mind. He looked so *sincere*. If she weren't his prisoner, she might be tempted to believe him. "I don't understand you," she said, furrowing her brow. "At all. Why would you say such a thing?"

She dare not think that Black might actually have a flesh and blood heart rather than one made of obsidian. She would be a fool indeed to entertain such an outlandish idea about her captor.

Yet he'd saved her from MacMunn and his vile companion... In the stables, Alexander Black had been angry. No, it was more than that.

She'd seen murder in his eyes. He'd looked like a man who'd wanted to rip her assailants apart with his bare hands.

Black looked away from her and picked up his whisky. Took a sip then poured himself another dram, all the while avoiding her gaze as if he regretted what he'd just said. "I simply meant you deserve a man better than Lord Tay."

"Really? That's rich coming from someone like you," Sarah scoffed. "I deserve better than this too"—she gestured about the room—"yet here I am."

"Sarah, I understand you are angry—"

"I'm more than angry. I'm livid," she retorted. "And stop using my Christian name. I've never given you permission to use it."

Black's mouth flattened as he rose to his feet. "Very well, *Miss Lambert*," he said with a mocking bow. "The hour grows late so I think it's time for both of us to get some sleep. We have another long journey ahead of us tomorrow."

He shrugged off his coat then tossed it onto the back of the chair before crossing to the pallet bed.

"Wait. Wh-What are you doing?" Sarah's heart pounded with panic as Black began to unfasten his black waistcoat. In the firelight, his distinctive onyx and gold ring seemed to glint impudently at her as he worked at the buttons.

He cocked an eyebrow and dropped the garment on the end of the pallet. "Getting ready for bed."

"But...but what about Aileen? You staying here with me... It's...it's not appropriate."

"Miss Lambert, we've already spent countless hours alone in each other's company," Black said as he tugged off one boot and stocking, revealing a muscular calf and a long, rather elegant foot. "So I hardly think it is a breach of etiquette when the inn is all but empty." The other boot and stocking followed. "And I rather thought you would prefer it if I didn't tie you to the bed again." He unfastened his jabot and quirked an eyebrow again. "If that's all right with you."

Sarah tried not to stare at Black's naked lower legs and the triangle of bare throat and chest revealed by the open neck of his shirt as she contemplated what he'd just said. Of course she didn't want to be tied up. And she also didn't want Black to leave. Despite everything he'd done, tonight she would feel a little safer with him in the room. What had happened in the stables had shaken her. Badly.

She gave a hesitant nod. "Very well. You may stay, Mr. Black. On that side of the room in that pallet bed."

"Of course. I'm glad you agree," he said with a wry smile. He crossed to the door, locked it, then with a waggle of his eyebrows, slipped the key into the pocket of his breeches. "It's not that I don't trust you, Miss Lambert, but..." He shrugged as though she had given him no choice.

"Perhaps you should stash the poker away too," said Sarah dryly as she rose from her chair. "On second thoughts..." She took a step toward the hearth and grasped the fireiron, preparing to remove it from its wrought-iron stand. "Perhaps I should take it to bed with me. It's not that I don't trust you... Oh, wait a moment"—she shot him a narrow look over her shoulder—"I don't."

Black prowled across the room and she would have retreated except she had nowhere to go. His fingers gently curled over hers so he was holding the poker as well. "I don't think so, Miss Lambert," he said, his voice a low, seductive purr. His gaze trapped hers. "You won't need to arm yourself against me. I meant what I said before. I would never force myself upon you."

Sarah swallowed. Black's hand was large and hot and a strange flickering warmth spread from her fingers, all the way up her arm and through her body, setting her nerves alight and tightening her nipples. Whilst her heart and mind railed against Black, it seemed her traitorous body had other ideas. She was acutely aware that she wore only a night rail and shawl, and Black was only half-dressed as well.

And they were quite alone.

Whilst Sarah was inclined to believe his assertion, that didn't mean he wouldn't try to seduce her. He was a handsome devil and charm was one of the many weapons in his arsenal. Indeed, right at this very moment, his smoldering gray gaze was fixed intently on her mouth, and to her dismay, she suddenly wondered what it would feel like to be kissed by someone other than Malcolm. Black smelled wonderful—both clean and masculine, like whisky and rainwater and citron. Her breath quickened and she had to resist the insane urge to press herself against his lean, muscular body. If she closed her eyes, would he lower his mouth to hers? Would he be gentle or would he kiss her with ruthless purpose? How would he taste?

Sarah, stop it. You are clearly mad. He's kidnapped you. You should hate him, not be in his thrall.

Drawing a shaky breath, she pulled her hand away, breaking the bizarre spell he'd cast over her. "I'm sure you'll understand if I don't believe you, Mr. Black," she said in a voice that was far too breathless for her liking. Her heart racing, she stalked over to the tester bed. As she climbed in, Black snuffed out the candles on the mantel with a pinch of his fingertips.

"Good night, Miss Lambert," he said softly. "I hope you sleep well." He lay down on the pallet bed and pulled the quilt over his long body before turning toward the fire.

Sarah didn't know what to say so she simply lay down as well. In the uncertain light of the fire, she noticed the poker was still in its stand on the hearth. *Interesting.* Black was a cocky devil to be sure. He obviously didn't think she had the courage to strike him whilst he slept.

If she were honest with herself, she wasn't certain she could do it either.

She briefly considered then discarded the idea of making a second escape bid. She could always try to sneak out of the room where Aileen now slept—she was sure the interconnecting door wasn't locked. But that would mean she'd have to get dressed again, without waking Black. Even now, fatigue weighted her eyelids and her bruised body ached. She didn't think she'd be able to stay awake until he was sound asleep. As much as she longed for freedom, she knew she couldn't possibly manage another attempt tonight.

She'd also have to brave the stables again and she couldn't bear the thought of catching sight of the ostler and stablehand, even if Black had tied them up. Sarah shivered and pulled the quilt and blankets up to her chin.

No, she would sleep and regain her strength. There would be another chance, another day.

And next time, she would not fail.

CHAPTER 10

Tay House, Edinburgh
February 17, 1757

My Dearest Malcolm,

*I hope you can find it in your heart to forgive me for my sudden
desertion, but as the day of our nuptials draws ever closer, I have
become plagued with self-doubt and I wonder if I can truly be the
wife you deserve. You are in your element here in Edinburgh,
whilst I...I must confess that I feel like a fish out of water. It
became abundantly clear to me during the Saint Valentine's ball
at Kenmuir House that I am but a Society novice. I have so much
to learn, and the weight of my inadequacy is almost too much to
bear. Indeed, I am in such a state of disquiet, I have decided that I
must remove myself from your world. But only for a little while.*

*Whatever you do, do not blame yourself, my dearest heart. You
have been nothing but kindness and patience itself throughout our
engagement. When I no longer feel at sixes and sevens, I promise I
shall return to your side. If you will still have me.*

Your undeserving but ever constant fiancée,

Sarah

*P.S. Please tell Aunt Judith not to worry. I will be back before she's
even had time to miss me.*

*P.P.S. Tell darling Damaris that I most certainly do owe her
fifteen pounds from the card table.*

"You say you only received this letter early this morning, Lord
Tay?"

Malcom watched Judith Lambert closely as she frowned down at
the note her niece had supposedly penned. The middle-aged woman's
cheeks were paler than the ivory lace edging her mobcap, and her hand
trembled as she carefully placed the piece of paper on the occasional
table by her fireside armchair.

"Yes," lied Malcolm, draping his arm along the drawing room
mantelpiece, feigning a nonchalance he in no way felt. "The night
footman believes it was pushed under the door sometime during the
night."

"I don't understand. Why would Sarah dash off like this? It's most
perplexing, and entirely out of character." Judith removed her spectacles
and her worried gaze shifted to Malcom's face. "She's never mentioned
feeling this way before. If she were having second thoughts about
becoming your countess, Lord Tay, I'm sure she would have spoken to
me. Leaving like this...so abruptly, with no indication as to where she
has gone..." She shook her head. "I cannot help but feel something is
very wrong."

Malcolm clasped his hands tightly behind his back, fighting the urge
to slap Sarah's aunt across the face. *Silly old bat.* But at least she
appeared to believe that her niece had written the note, even if she
hadn't expected her to behave in such a way.

Swallowing his ire and summoning a suitably concerned expression, he crossed the drawing room rug and picked up the letter.
Damaris's forgery seemed to have worked thus far, but he didn't want

Judith to examine the handwriting for *too* long. "I don't quite understand it myself, Miss Lambert. I thought Sarah's eagerness to wed matched my own. And I'm not ashamed to admit that I feel somewhat hurt by her need to spend time alone rather than confide in me. I'm sure I could ease her fears. But I trust that she will come to her senses and return in due course. She must know how much I adore her."

"Yes. Well..." Judith pursed her lips as if she doubted the veracity of his declaration.

Perhaps the old bird was cannier than he'd thought. He'd have to play the part of 'devoted *fiancé*' with more alacrity if that were the case.

The woman rose from her seat and crossed to the nearest window. She was as slight as a sparrow in her gown of plain black silk, and Malcolm didn't think it would take much effort to wring her scrawny neck. His fingers twitched. If she became too nosy, he might be tempted to do just that.

Oblivious to his dark thoughts, Judith pushed back the faded velvet curtains and examined the gray, rainy day. "I wonder where she is. It really does puzzle me that she didn't mention her destination. She hasn't taken any of her things, or our carriage..."

"The note only arrived during the night"—a lie of course—"so perhaps she is close by," said Malcolm. "And we both know she has the means to look after herself."

"Yes, she does," agreed Judith. "If we were still in Newcastle, I'd be inclined to believe she was staying with friends. But she knows no one here, not intimately, aside from you and your sister..." In a low voice she added as though she were speaking to herself, "You know, I'm actually beginning to wonder if something terrible happened at the ball."

Malcolm's interest immediately stirred. "Terrible? Like what?"

"That's just it. I don't know." Judith turned back to face him, her brow creased with concern. She pressed a hand to her stomach as though it pained her. "Perhaps someone insulted her, or her background. Made her feel unwelcome or not good enough. Her father was in trade, after all."

Malcolm cast his features in an expression he hoped would approximate 'concerned yet reassuring' as he said, "I should hate to think so.

But yes, perhaps you are right. You said yourself, she was a little distracted and not quite herself that night."

Judith sighed heavily. "Yes…"

"The most important thing, at this stage, is to ensure there is not a breath of scandal about this. I'm sure Sarah would hate to be the main topic of the town gossipmongers."

"I'm sure you and Lady Glenleven would loathe that too, my lord," remarked Judith dryly.

A spark of irritation leapt in his chest, but somehow Malcolm kept his voice in neutral territory as he remarked, "Yes. And quite rightly so. I will do my utmost to protect Sarah's reputation."

Judith lifted her chin. "As will I."

"So we are in agreeance?"

The old tabby nodded. "Yes."

"Good." Malcolm adopted another expression of deep concern. "One thing I am sure of, Miss Lambert, is that I want Sarah for my wife. If she needs time, she may have it. I will wait for her and always stand by her, come what may."

"I'm glad to hear it." Judith turned back to the window. "You know, I'm tempted to ready our coach and journey back to Linden Hall. Sarah loves that house. I suspect she has been pining for it these last few weeks. She would see it as a sanctuary. A place to regroup."

Malcolm scowled at the woman's back. No doubt Judith would also travel to Newcastle and speak with Edwin Lambert's former solicitor and Sarah's erstwhile guardian, Charles Swindon, about all of this. And if the man's suspicions were aroused, and he alerted Sarah's London-based bank, Campbell & Coutts, that she was missing, it would make it even harder for him to secure some of Sarah's funds to pay the ransom.

But then again, if Judith were out of the way, he would have greater freedom. He wouldn't have to take care whenever he spoke to Damaris or be careful of his movements. If he could work out who Janus was, he could retrieve Sarah. Which meant he wouldn't have to pay the ransom at all.

In the meantime, his man of business would be able to sell off more of Tay House's assets—the marble busts from the entry hall and the mahogany longcase clock in the library, perhaps.

"By all means, return to Northumberland, my dear Miss Lambert," he said as genially as he could manage. "And if Sarah is there, I will be much relieved to hear it."

"I shall leave at once then." Judith retrieved her spectacles from the table where she'd left them. "Please make my farewells to Lady Glenleven. I do not wish to disturb her."

"Yes, of course." Damaris was generally a late riser but, unbeknownst to Judith, his sister had spent the night at Lord Arbelour's residence. With any luck, it wouldn't be long before the old goat was showering her with jewels.

"Farewell then, my lord." Judith dipped into a cursory curtsy. "If Sarah is at Linden Hall or staying with friends in Newcastle, I shall send word to you straightaway."

Malcolm inclined his head. "Thank you." Another thought struck him as Judith opened the door. He really didn't know why he hadn't thought of it sooner. "Miss Lambert," he called.

"Yes, my lord?"

"I think it would be wise to leave all of Sarah's belongings here. Just in case she returns before you do. She did say she would only be gone a little while."

Judith bobbed another curtsy. "Yes, of course. A most sensible idea."

As the door shut, Malcolm smiled to himself. The situation wasn't as dire as he'd thought. Sarah had a lovely sapphire and pearl parure that had once belonged to her mother; he'd secured it in a hidden compartment in his private study to 'keep it safe' when she'd first arrived at Tay House. It would definitely fetch a pretty penny. A soon as Judith was gone, he'd search the chit's room and sell anything else of value he could lay his hands on—there had to be numerous jewels, did there not? Perhaps there were some spare blank bank notes in her personal papers. Damaris could easily forge Sarah's signature again.

He might even be able to afford the expense of hiring an inquiry agent.

Yes, when Damaris returned, they'd celebrate with a late breakfast of champagne. After that, he might just pay a visit to his favorite brothel. And one of the gaming hells along the Cowgate.

Anticipation thrumming through his veins, Malcolm called for Drysdale. He'd have him powder his best peruke and brush down one of his brocade frockcoats. Perhaps the one in teal blue.

Yes, penury and Janus be damned. All was not lost, yet.

CHAPTER II

Somewhere in Perthshire...

The rain gave way to sleet then thick snow as Black's carriage continued its journey along the road leading into the wild, desolate depths of Scotland. The hot bricks at Sarah's feet had grown cold long ago and she'd given up trying to discern the features of the passing landscape. Whatever slid by, mountains and moorland, or forest and river, it was all obscured by a swirling white cloud. Even though spring was only a month away, it seemed this part of the world was still firmly in the icy clutches of winter.

Sometime during the afternoon—Sarah suspected they'd been on the road for at least five hours, if not more since they'd left the Stag's Head—the carriage halted at a cluster of small, whitewashed dwellings beside a stone bridge that spanned a black rushing river; a hamlet in the middle of nowhere.

Black helped Sarah down from the carriage, and with his hand firmly on her arm, escorted her toward a low stone building that appeared to be a stable. Sarah had already decided it would be useless to try and run when there were only snow-shrouded braes as far as the eye could see. And no doubt, anyone hereabouts could surely be silenced by a handful of Black's coin.

A freezing wind tore at her riding habit of royal-blue wool and thick navy cloak with a hood—it was another bespoke ensemble that had been pulled from the traveling trunk that was supposedly hers. Sarah still had no idea how Black had managed to procure so many clothes which appeared to have been made just for her, but right now, she set aside her questions and welcomed the warmth.

A stableboy stepped out as they approached, and Black greeted the lad in a tongue Sarah didn't understand. Was it Gaelic? The youth responded, his words an incomprehensible string, and Black nodded.

The mystery of Alexander Black deepened. Not only did he speak with a soft Scots accent, but he knew Gaelic as well. But his surname didn't seem Scottish—Sarah had always suspected it was a false name and the more she learned about the man, the more she was convinced he was hiding who he truly was.

Black issued a few more instructions to the boy, and after the lad disappeared, he turned back to Sarah. "I'm afraid we're going to have to continue our journey on horseback from here. I know you are probably sore after last night, but I take it you can ride?"

Sarah tried to keep her expression neutral. "Yes." If she could break away from Black—

As if reading her thoughts, Black leaned close and murmured in her ear, "I know your mind is still working feverishly to hatch an escape plan, Miss Lambert. But I am not a fool. Your horse will be tethered to mine, and Aileen and Dobson will follow behind. You don't know the area and this hamlet"—Black gestured to the buildings behind them—"well, the inhabitants are in my employ and barely speak a word of English. So fair warning, you'll not find much support here if you decide to kick up a fuss."

Damn and blast. Why could he read her so easily?

Sarah couldn't suppress her scowl and Black's mouth twitched with a smile. "You'll be pleased to hear we only have a few more hours to travel before we reach our destination."

"Which is?" Sarah asked with false sweetness.

"You'll find out soon enough." Black's gaze moved to the stables.

The stableboy and another young man were leading out four well-groomed mounts.

"I suppose everyone in *that* corner of Scotland is in your employ as well."

"More or less."

Sarah frowned. Black's influence was wide indeed. *Who was this man?*

From what Sarah had seen, he wasn't short of funds by any means, and he clearly inspired loyalty wherever he went. Their early morning departure from the Stag's Head Inn had been delayed as Black had sought an audience with the local magistrate in Dunkeld. He'd later informed her that the ostler and groom would be charged with assault and theft. Apparently the innkeeper had suspected the recently employed men of pilfering ale and other stock from the Stag's Head for some weeks, and he was more than happy to support Black's claim that the men attacked him and attempted to steal his coin last night.

Black hadn't reported the attack on her and had sincerely apologized for the omission. Sarah didn't quite know what to make of it all. Of course, the true crime which had occurred at the Stag's Head had been hidden by Black because he was in the process of committing a crime himself—her abduction. She was his hostage and for that reason, she could hardly regard him as a champion.

The man was certainly a conundrum. On one hand, he appeared to have no scruples whatsoever. Yet he'd gone out of his way to make sure the ostler and the groom would receive some sort of punishment for what they'd done to her. And though he'd flirted with her on occasion, Sarah sensed that was all he would do. If he were going to take her by force, he'd had ample opportunity to do so over the last few days.

The man possessed a strange, warped sense of honor and Sarah couldn't help but wonder why. What events in his life had shaped him? For much of the morning, she'd puzzled over the enigma of Alexander Black. There was one particular question, louder than all the others, that buzzed around her mind, demanding to be answered: what had Malcolm done to him?

If she could discover the truth, perhaps she could use it to free herself.

~

Night was falling by the time Black called a halt to their journey. Sarah was half-frozen and ached all over as her exhausted mount, which had been tethered to Black's, drew to a stop too. Aileen and the gray-haired poker-faced coachman, Dobson, reined in a few yards behind them.

They were in a copse of pines on the edge of a loch. Sarah could hear the water lapping against the stony shingle and through the trees she caught a glimpse of dark water. Over the snow-covered peaks on the opposite shore, a full moon was rising in the dusky blue and lavender hued sky. The snow had mercifully ceased to fall and the wind had dropped so there was barely a rustle in the surrounding woodland.

Sarah surreptitiously scanned the trees. If she tried to run once Black untied her from her horse, how far would she get before he caught her? She was stiff with cold and even if she could lose Black in the fading light, she had no idea where she was or which way she should go in order to reach help. And if it snowed before she reached shelter... She shivered. She didn't fancy spending the night in the open. She would surely perish.

Black dismounted with ease and placed a gloved hand on hers as she gripped the reins. "It won't be long before you're before a roaring fire with supper in your belly," he said gently.

Sarah wanted to kick him. "Is that supposed to comfort me?" she snapped, her breath misting in the frigid evening air.

"No. But it's the best I can offer you at the moment. It's been a trying few days and I thought you would be pleased to know the journey is almost over."

"How wonderful. It's a shame this nightmare isn't."

Black's mouth flattened. "I won't disagree with you. For me, it's been unending." He swiftly untied her ankle, which had been lashed to one of the stirrups, before gripping her about the waist and lifting her down from her horse. "I wouldn't bother trying to run. There's nowhere for you to go."

"Well, that's hardly a surprise," grumbled Sarah. "And I'm sure if I scream, no one other than you and your stubbornly loyal servants will hear me?"

Black took her arm. "Aye."

Fiery resentment melded with icy trepidation and a small dose of sharp curiosity as Sarah reluctantly followed Black through the trees toward the water's edge. Dobson had gone on ahead of them and she could hear a crunching, sliding sound as if he were moving something heavy. When they emerged onto the shore, she could just discern the manservant pushing a rowboat out of a stone and wooden boathouse onto the shingle...and several hundred yards away, across the water, loomed a rectangular tower on a small island.

Oh, no.

Sarah stopped and her stomach plummeted to the gray stones beneath her feet. Alexander Black was going to hold her prisoner on an island. And she couldn't swim. Once he took her across, there was no way on earth she would be able to escape. She'd be trapped, well and truly.

"I cannot... You cannot..." Panic tied Sarah's tongue in knots as she tried to wrench her arm free. "I will not go."

Black's grip grew firmer. "You must."

"No." Sarah pulled with all her might and her feet skidded across the stones.

"Sarah." Black grasped her tightly by the upper arms. "Stop. No harm will come to you if you do as I say."

A bitter laugh that was more like a sob escaped her. "No harm? I've already been harmed. Drugged and kidnapped and threatened and abused. How do I know you're not going to throw me in the loch to drown, or abandon me to rot in your island jail?"

Black's mouth was set in an obdurate line. "Miss Lambert, I give you my word. I will not hurt you. You'll be perfectly safe."

"I don't believe you! No!" Sarah pushed at Black's far-too-solid chest and kicked at his legs, but her efforts proved futile. He simply picked her up and slung her over his shoulder like he had in Edinburgh.

As Sarah screamed and twisted and beat her fists against his back, Dobson tethered her ankles with rough rope. When Black lowered her onto the shingle, he held her wrists so Dobson could lash them tightly together as well.

Her struggles against her bonds were completely ineffectual. Her cries and frantic pleas fell on deaf ears. Black was resolute. Relentless.

The wicked rogue swept her up and unceremoniously deposited her in the bottom of the rowboat. Before she could sit up, Dobson and Black had pushed the small craft out onto the water and then Black climbed in.

Tears streaming down her cheeks, Sarah pushed herself up and skewered Black with a fulminating glare. "You have no pity. No soul. I hate you."

"So you should," he replied calmly as he gripped the oars and began to row. His strokes were long and sure and within moments, they were pulling away from the shore.

The last vestiges of Sarah's hope slipped away too, and she laid her head on the side of the boat and closed her eyes. Fear and anguish rolled through her, making her stomach churn. She didn't want to look out across the dark still water or watch the grim tower draw closer. She especially didn't want to see Black's hateful face. His hard, determined expression.

For the first time since Black had taken her, she contemplated the possibility that she might never see Linden Hall, Aunt Judith, or any of her friends ever again. She might never see Malcolm again. Even though she didn't think she could forgive him, she deserved the chance to confront him about his transgression and end things properly.

But Black had taken all these things away. And despite his assurances that no harm would come to her, she had no way of knowing if he would ever let her go. His thirst for vengeance seemed unquenchable.

And she had nothing to offer him—he'd told her that over and over again, but it was only now that she truly believed him. She was nothing but a piece to play in his wicked, selfish game.

Yes, she hated him. As far as she was concerned, Alexander Black could go to Hades.

A jolt and the scrape of the boat against rocks startled Sarah and she opened her eyes.

"Welcome to Eilean Dubh," said Black. He leapt into the shallows and pushed the boat farther up the shingle.

Eilean Dubh? It sounded like a Gaelic name. Sarah wanted to ask what it meant but she was so angry with Black, she had no wish to speak to him. Instead, she straightened and tried to make out her surroundings. The moonlight revealed a squat rectangular tower surrounded by a dense copse—a mixture of snow-shrouded pines and firs and the skeletal forms of denuded trees. Aside from the lap of the water and the distant hoot of an owl, all was silent. The tower itself was in total darkness and had a desolate, abandoned air about it. Sarah shivered as an icy gust of wind swept by, tossing the tree branches and whipping her unbound hair into her eyes.

Black knelt beside the prow of the boat. "I'm going to free your legs, Sarah."

She didn't bother to reply but he appeared to take her silence as consent. The bonds were tight, and after a minute of trying and failing to loosen the knots, Black withdrew a wicked-looking knife from his belt. The silver blade flashed in the moonlight and Sarah swallowed to moisten her suddenly dry mouth. She hadn't realized Black was armed. However, she didn't have time to dwell on this disturbing fact as with a few deft cuts, Black sliced through the rough rope and it fell away.

Sarah held out her hands but Black shook his head.

"Not yet," he said, resheathing his knife. "When we are safely inside I'll release you. Can you hop out?"

"Yes." Sarah stood carefully and Black steadied her at the elbows as she climbed over the side of the boat.

"This way." His hand at her back, Black steered her across the rocky shore toward the trees.

It was too dark and there was too much snow underfoot for Sarah to note if there was a path, but it wasn't long before they reached an ornate, wrought-iron gate set in a high stone wall. Black pulled a key from the folds of his greatcoat and unlocked it. The gate's hinges were well oiled and it opened without a sound.

Despite her antipathy and despair, a question burned on the tip of Sarah's tongue. "Is there anyone else here?" she whispered.

Black's face was in darkness, but Sarah sensed his reticence to respond as he hesitated before replying. "No. But Aileen will return tomorrow."

A shiver of apprehension washed over Sarah. She'd been alone with

Black for hours on end over the past few days, but never in such isolated circumstances. And there was not a thing she could do. She was entirely at his mercy. She just prayed to God he'd meant what he'd said—that he wouldn't hurt her.

Well, more than he had already.

Too exhausted, defeated, and heartsore to make a protest, she allowed Black to lead her through the gate toward an archway in yet another stone wall. Stepping through, she stopped and sucked in a startled breath. The light of the moon glanced off a deep snowdrift piled up against a section of crumbled wall and through a second archway, she glimpsed well-worn stairs. "You intend to keep me locked up in a ruin?"

"Eilean Dubh is very old, I'll give you that, but the main tower is structurally sound." Black clasped her arm. "Come and see."

Sarah shook her head and wrenched herself away, stumbling back a few paces. Her throat constricted and her voice, when it emerged, was hoarse with terror. "N-No. I-I don't want to."

It suddenly struck her that Black might have a very good reason for bringing her to such an out-of-the-way, derelict place. He kept claiming she was safe, but perhaps he thought to lull her into a false sense of security. He could have freed her hands, but he hadn't.

Why not?

She didn't feel safe. Every little piece of her screamed she was in danger.

And there was a large knife at Black's waist...

"Sarah." Black closed the distance between them and gently framed her all but numb face with his gloved hands. "Good God, lass, you're trembling."

Sarah didn't know what to say. Indeed, she was incapable of speech. Her lungs had frozen while her galloping heart stuttered madly as though it might stop at any moment. Black's large hands were warm and gentle, but...but what if he slid them to her neck? He was so strong and her hands were bound. She wouldn't be able to defend herself.

"Sarah. I swear to you, with God as my witness, I will not hurt you," he persisted, his tone urgent. "I'm not the monster you think I am. You must believe me. Say you believe me."

She nodded weakly. What other choice did she have?

"Good girl. I'd untie your hands right now, but if the knots are too tight, I'll have to cut through the rope. And that's far too risky in this poor light."

Again Sarah nodded, a stiff jerky movement, but it seemed to satisfy Black. He took her arm, gently this time, and led her to the stairs. The shadows were black as pitch and she couldn't see a thing.

"You go first," he urged. "I'll be right behind you. The stairs curve to the right and there are twenty."

"I-I can't," she whispered hoarsely. "I cannot p-pick up my skirts properly. I'll trip."

Black cursed beneath his breath. "Hold on," he said and before Sarah knew what he was about, he'd swept her up into his arms and had started up the stairs.

Oh, God. Sarah closed her eyes and gripped the lapels of Black's coat with her bound hands, praying he wouldn't stumble. She needn't have worried as within the space of several heartbeats, she found they were at the top of the staircase. Moonlight streamed through a narrow window aperture, and she could see they were on a small stone landing. Before her was a sturdy-looking wooden door.

Black put her down, ensured she was steady, then pulled his keys from his coat again. Reaching around her, he unlocked the door and pushed it open. "Here we are."

A pair of windows with diamond panes let in just enough light for Sarah to discern a large rectangular chamber furnished with a table and chairs and a dresser. A floor-to-ceiling tapestry adorned one wall, obscuring the stonework. A massive stone fireplace yawned darkly on the opposite side of the room.

At least Black hadn't lied to her about the state of the building. On stiff and sore legs—it had been a long time since she'd ridden such a significant distance on horseback—Sarah crossed the room to one of the windows. A cushioned window seat beckoned but she was too on edge to sit down. Black was locking the door so she turned away to study the view from her island prison.

Night had rendered everything in shades of silver, gray, and black. The moon shone across the dark waters of the loch and the snow upon the distant mountains glowed with a faint pearlescence. There wasn't a light anywhere on the far shore. Like the hamlet they'd passed through earlier in the day, Eilean Dubh was clearly in the middle of nowhere, too.

The glass panes reflected a sudden flare of light and Sarah's gaze was drawn to Black. He'd lit a candle on the sturdy square table and was in the process of lighting several more in an iron candelabra upon the mantelpiece. When he was done, he crossed over to her and unsheathed his knife.

"Here, let me untie you."

Sarah lifted her painfully bound hands and watched Black's face as he set about cutting through the rope. His eyes were hidden by the sweep of his black lashes and his stubbled jaw was as hard as granite.

When the rope fell away, he swore. "Sweet Jesus, I should flog Dobson for this."

"What? Why?"

"Look at your wrists, Sarah. The fool tied the ropes too tightly. You're hurt."

Sarah glanced down and winced. Her wrists had begun to sting and burn, now Black had drawn attention to them. Between the lace cuff of her sleeve and her gloves, her flesh was marked with angry red weals. Strange how she hadn't noticed the pain until now. But then, she'd been so miserable and frightened, the irritation caused by her bonds had been the least of her woes.

"I'll be fine," Sarah murmured. She pulled off her gloves but had to bite her lip to stifle a gasp as the lace of her sleeve brushed over the fresh abrasions.

Black removed his black wool greatcoat and tossed it onto the window seat. "I'll start a fire. Then after we've bandaged those burns, how about some supper and a cup of tea?"

Sarah nodded then asked haltingly, "Is there...? What about...?" Her cheeks heated. "Where is the necessary?" It seemed like an age since she'd attended to the call of nature, and Aileen wasn't here to assist her.

Black didn't seem perturbed. His expression a study in neutrality, he nodded at a door to the left of the fireplace. "If you go through there, you'll find a garderobe before you reach the bedchamber."

The bedchamber? Sarah really hoped there was more than one in this tower.

Thrusting all thoughts of Black in any kind of bed aside, she took one of the candles and found the medieval privy. After she'd attended to her needs, she decided to investigate the bedchamber beyond.

Raising the candle, Sarah scanned the room: a wide oak canopy bed with sage green hangings and a matching counterpane dominated the center of the chamber; a washstand, matching armoire, and a screen covered in Chinoiserie-patterned silk occupied the far corner; a large carved oaken chest stood at the end of the bed; and two oak wingback chairs upholstered in pale gray damask graced a plush Aubusson hearthrug in front of the massive stone fireplace.

It was a graceful, feminine room. And not what she'd expected.

Black continued to confound her. He clearly didn't wish to mistreat her whilst he held her captive at Eilean Dubh...but there was the rub.

She *was* his captive.

Sarah Elizabeth Lambert, she admonished herself as she returned to the main chamber. *Even if Alexander Black gifted you the Crown Jewels, it shouldn't make one iota of difference to how you see him. He's abducted you and you do not know his endgame. You cannot trust him. Don't* ever *forget that.*

CHAPTER 12

When Sarah disappeared into the main bedchamber, Alex blew out a heavy sigh and ran a hand down his face. He knew the lass was still angry, and wary of him—and rightly so—and part of him deeply regretted that. But he hoped that over the coming days, she would discover she really did have nothing to fear from him in a physical sense. That the worst was over until he released her.

If I release her, he mentally amended. How and when that would happen depended on how well the next and riskiest part of his scheme played out. Whether Tay paid the ransom to secure Sarah's release, or not, was immaterial at this point.

Indeed, it had always been immaterial.

As Alex set about lighting the fire and gathering the items he would need to attend to Sarah's rope burns, his thoughts turned to the challenges that lay ahead. The final stage of his plot for revenge had seemed simple when he'd envisaged it half a year ago, when he'd first learned of Tay's betrothal to the heiress Miss Sarah Lambert: steal the woman and somehow drive a wedge between her and Tay so she would never want to marry him. So far—considering she'd witnessed Tay's act of infidelity at Kenmuir House—he appeared to have succeeded, at least at a superficial level. However, he needed to take things further.

Much further.

Sarah needed to despise Tay as much as he did. She needed to learn her *fiancé* was a truly depraved man. A man with no soul.

But therein lay the dilemma.

Alex couldn't risk revealing *too* much about what had happened at Blackloch Castle in the dying days of the Rebellion, at least not until he was sure of Sarah's allegiance to him and him alone.

One thing was clear in his mind: he couldn't release Sarah from Eilean Dubh until he was absolutely sure of her loyalty. Because if he released her—or God forbid, she escaped—and she forgave Tay for his infidelity and wed him anyway, this whole plan had been for naught. Not only that, but if Sarah managed to work out he was Alexander Price or worse, the wanted Jacobite, Alexander MacIvor—which was entirely possible given the fact she was a canny lass and most definitely had the wherewithal—*he* would be ruined, not Tay. It was a thorny dilemma to say the least.

Sarah appeared in the doorway, rousing Alex from his troubled musings. As she hovered uncertainly on the threshold, he greeted her with a smile that he hoped was reassuring. The flickering fire and candlelight revealed how worn down and uncertain she looked. Her golden blond hair was disheveled, her blue gown creased, the hem mud stained. Fatigue shadowed her eyes as her gaze flicked to him then over the items he'd assembled on the table: linen bandages, a bowl of water, salve, and a washcloth.

He pulled out a heavy oak chair. "Please, come and sit down."

Sarah only hesitated a moment before crossing the room and gracefully taking her seat. "This really isn't necessary," she said, smoothing her skirts then folding her hands primly in her lap. "The burns aren't that bad." Her eyes were cast downwards; it was clear she was avoiding his gaze.

Would the lass also avoid his touch? Alex softened his voice. "Perhaps not. But at least consider applying some of the salve. Aileen makes it from the herbs at Black—" He broke off, cursing himself inwardly for his near slip of the tongue. He'd been about to say Blackloch Castle. "It's very soothing," he continued as he took a seat beside her. "Bandaging the abrasions might provide some relief as well."

Sarah's mouth twitched with the hint of a wry smile. "I'm pleased to hear those are bandages," she nodded toward the small pile of linen strips, "not restraints."

Alex smiled back. "I promise I won't tie you up again as long as you don't take it upon yourself to attack me with the fireiron or any other heavy or sharp object. Actually, I'm still grateful that you didn't try to push me down the stairs as I unlocked the door."

"It didn't cross my mind at the time but thank you for the suggestion."

A vivid image of Sarah wrestling with him in the confined space at the top of the stairs leapt into Alex's mind. Of him cornering her and trapping her up against the stone wall. Her breath catching and her body stilling as he brushed his thumb across her full lower lip... "I'd like to see you try," he murmured before he could stop himself.

Sarah must have guessed the direction of his thoughts, as she blushed and dropped her eyes. Not wanting to unsettle her further, Alex made a beckoning gesture with one hand, his manner all business again. "I'm only joking, lass. Now, let's see these burns."

Sarah sighed but nevertheless, did as he asked. She carefully pushed up the lace-trimmed cuffs of her sleeves then presented her forearms for him to see. As he took in the sight of the raw-looking abrasions marring her fair skin, guilt tore through his belly all over again. He still rued the fact he hadn't tied her bonds himself. Or used silk rope. He shouldn't have been so careless. "I'm so sorry about this, Sarah." He pushed the ointment toward her. "Use as much as you need."

Sarah took the small pot and gave the contents a delicate sniff before dipping her fingers into the pale yellow unguent. "What's in it?" she asked as she began to gingerly apply it. "It smells a little like lavender and something sweet, like honey."

"Your guess is as good as mine, I'm afraid, but you can ply Aileen with questions tomorrow." Alex picked up one of the bandages. "Shall I put this on for you? You should probably have those cut fingers rebandaged as well."

Sarah's eyes met his and for a long moment she studied him. She must have read sincerity in his expression rather than speculative lust this time, as she said, "Very well," and extended her right arm, her elbow on the table, her palm facing upward. Alex gently wrapped the linen around her delicately boned wrist. He held her hand to steady her arm and her pulse fluttered beneath his thumb. When he slid a glance at her face, he noticed her cheeks had flushed a delicate shade of rose pink.

Interesting... His touch as well as his rakish quips and stares affected her, and not in the way Alex would have supposed, given everything he'd put her through. His mind returned to their first encounter at Kenmuir House, and the time she'd permitted him to restore the circulation to her half-frozen feet. And then there'd been that highly charged moment last night at the Stag's Head, when he'd been certain she'd been thinking about kissing him just as much as he'd been thinking about kissing her.

As Alex carefully tied off the bandage then proceeded to wrap another strip of linen around Sarah's other wrist, an intriguing idea flared. What if...what if he could win Sarah's devotion? If she cared for him, then he wouldn't have to worry anymore.

It was a ruthless, deceitful tactic to be sure, but the more Alex considered it, the more he believed the plan had some merit. Despite everything he'd done, there was an undeniable, simmering attraction between him and Sarah. He'd be a fool not to exploit it.

Indeed, if circumstances were different—and if his heart were capable of any type of tender feeling—he might have courted her as a gentleman should. He might even fall in love with someone like Sarah Lambert. Someone intelligent, brave, beautiful. She certainly didn't deserve to be shackled to a devil like Tay. In fact, he'd said as much at the Stag's Head when he'd blurted out she'd never have cause to doubt him if she *was* his. She'd been surprised at his rash pronouncement but she hadn't reacted *unfavorably*.

He'd have to proceed carefully, of course. Sarah barely trusted him and he didn't blame her in the slightest. He certainly had a great deal of lost ground to make up if he had any hope of charming her and rousing her affection, but he was up for the challenge.

Besides, when all was said and done, what did he have to lose?

~

"Thank you." Sarah withdrew her hand from Black's and dipped her gaze to examine her bandages—a completely unnecessary action given he'd applied them most adeptly, but right at this moment, she'd do anything to dispel the strange intimate tension surrounding them. The air fairly crackled with electricity. Her pulse leapt about madly, and her face felt far too hot.

Black's voice was soft and low as he murmured, "It's the least I can do, Sarah," and like a besotted girl, her blush deepened. *Curse him.*

When he'd held her hand and gently, almost tenderly wound the linen about her wrists and cut fingers—he'd rebandaged those too—when his muscled legs had brushed against her own knees, she'd been plagued by a most inconvenient awareness of the man's inherent physical attractiveness. His overwhelming masculinity. It seemed a heated stare, a soft touch, and a lopsided smile were all that were needed to beguile and disarm her. It would be far easier to stay on guard around him if he regarded her with callous disdain or treated her cruelly.

But he didn't.

It made Sarah want to scream with frustration at herself for being such a weak-willed peagoose. If only she weren't so exhausted, she might have summoned the energy to rally her anger and disdain.

As she'd been silently admonishing herself, Black had begun to assemble a rudimentary supper for them—a pot of tea, oatcakes, and some type of cured meat she guessed was ham—but as her eyes traveled over Black, she decided that perhaps she should forgo supper and retire for the night before she had any more foolish thoughts.

She rose from her seat and Black cast her a quizzical look. "Can I get you anything?"

"I was thinking about going to b—" Sarah bit her lip. *There was only one bed in the bedchamber.* Apprehension unfurled in her belly as she added, "I meant to ask you, what will the sleeping arrangements be?"

Black put down the carving knife he'd been using to slice the ham and met her gaze steadily. "The bedchamber is yours, and yours alone. There's another, smaller room beyond"—he nodded toward a door on the other side of the fireplace—"which I shall use." Attired only in a loose cambric shirt, breeches and boots, and with dark stubble shadowing his lean jaw, Sarah was vividly reminded of the night before at the Stag's Head when Black had undressed for bed in front of her. *The moment they'd almost kissed...*

How stupid of her to think of such things right now. Yet again she could feel a hot blush creeping over her face.

Stop it, Sarah. You are mad. Alexander Black is a fiend and you should not be attracted to him.

She cleared her throat. "Thank you...and goodnight." Picking up a candle, she started for her room.

"Aren't you hungry?"

Sarah paused on the threshold and glanced back. Her stomach rumbled loudly in the silence, as if responding to Black's question. "Yes, but I'm too tired to eat," she murmured.

Black's forehead creased. "Aye, of course. That's understandable. If you change your mind"—he gestured toward the oak dresser on the far wall—"I'll leave a plate for you there."

"Thank you."

Sarah shut the bedchamber door and sagged against it. The room was icy and seemed even more cavernous than before. The beamed ceiling was hidden in deep shadow. Shivering with cold and fatigue, she located a tinder box, knelt before the hearth, then set about lighting a taper and coaxing a fire to life. Someone had stacked kindling and logs in the grate and for that, Sarah was thankful.

Stifling a yawn, she began to undo the buttons at the front of her riding jacket. Tomorrow, when she was rested, she would plan another escape attempt. When all was said and done, she really didn't think she could bring herself to attack Black. Just like last night, she certainly couldn't imagine striking him with a poker—or anything else for that matter—as he slept. And there was simply no way she could best him in a physical altercation when he was awake. Besides, as she'd reasoned before, where would she go if she did manage to escape from the tower? It was pitch-black and she'd never rowed a boat before. And even if she could get to the shore, what then? She still had no idea where she was, or where to go.

No, she was far better off biding her time, learning as much as she could about her new environment so she could formulate another plan, one that would actually succeed. Black had mentioned Aileen was returning on the morrow. It would be far easier to evade the older woman than Black. It also occurred to Sarah that if Aileen was returning daily, she must be staying relatively close by. Perhaps there was a village somewhere near. Indeed, Black had almost let slip where Aileen procured the herbs for her salve. Unsurprisingly, it was a place name beginning with the word "Black." *Black Brae? Blackburn? Blackmoor? Blackwater?*

Black claimed he was wealthy, so logic would dictate this isolated tower wasn't his primary place of residence. He must have another house. Of course, she wouldn't be seeking help there, but she might be able to secure a decent mount and ride away as she'd tried to do the night before.

Despite her weariness, a small spark of hope at last flickered to life inside Sarah's breast. Sitting down in one of the wingchairs, she removed her boots then loosened the buttons securing the lace cuffs of her shirt. As she unfastened her lace jabot, her gaze wandered to the large oak chest at the foot of the bed and the ornate armoire beside the silk screen.

Was there anything inside? She was still confounded by the knowledge that Black had procured such well-fitting traveling garb for her. Candle in hand and curiosity pricking along her spine, Sarah crossed to the chest. It was a beautifully carved piece of glossy oak; roses, thistles, and ornate scrollwork adorned the lid, and the lock was polished brass. The lid looked so solid and heavy, she'd have to lift it with both hands.

After placing her candle on the mantelpiece, she returned to the chest, unlatched the hasp, and hefted open the lid...and gasped.

Nestled inside the satin-lined interior lay at least half a dozen exquisitely fashioned gowns of silk and velvet, satin and lace. Garments she'd never laid eyes on before. With trembling hands, Sarah lifted out the first gown of pale blue and ivory striped satin; it was low-cut around the neckline and trimmed with tiny rosettes, elaborate bows, and very fine lace. Aside from being inordinately pretty, it looked like it would fit her perfectly.

She tossed it on the bed, and with mounting horror, rushed to the armoire. As she threw open the doors and yanked open the drawers, her bewilderment and panic only intensified. Silk and wool stockings, delicately boned stays, shifts of the finest lawn and lace, soft leather gloves, shawls, and shoes—satin-covered pumps and neat kid boots—were all neatly folded or laid out upon the velvet-lined shelves.

God in heaven. The intricacy of Black's kidnapping plot stole her breath clean away. Made her stomach pitch and her ire boil.

Snatching up a handful of items, Sarah stormed back to the main chamber.

Black's eyebrows shot up at the sight of her. Putting down his knife, his gaze moved to the garments she brandished at him like a weapon and a look of uncertainty flickered across his face. "Sarah—" he began.

"Don't you dare call me Sarah. What, in God's name, are you really up to? Explain how these"—she flung the stockings, ribbon garters, and all but transparent shifts onto the table in front of him—"and all the other clothes that seem to be tailor-made for me, came to be here. You said you weren't intending to make me your doxy, but I'm seriously beginning to wonder if you're lying."

Black's forehead creased. "Of course I'm not lying."

"Then explain these." She picked up one of the gossamer silk stockings and tossed it toward him. "Did you have them made for me?"

Black inhaled deeply then let out a long sigh. "Aye. I wanted you to be comfortable during your...stay. That's all."

"Really?" Sarah planted her hands on her hips. "You still haven't told me how everything miraculously fits. Did you bribe the information out of my lady's maid? Did you steal some of my clothes? How long have you been stalking me, Alexander Black?"

He winced. "I know it looks bad, but there's really a simple explanation."

"Enlighten me then."

"At Christmastide, you might say I procured a box of your clothing. Things you were donating to the poor."

"On Saint Stephen's Day?"

"Aye."

"But...but I was in Northumberland then. The items were from my wardrobe in Linden Hall. You followed me to Linden Hall?" demanded Sarah, voice shaking with fury. "My home?"

Black pressed his lips together as if internally debating with himself about what to say next. "I've never been to Linden Hall."

"Then how...?" Sarah's anger flared brighter and hotter. "You paid someone to spy on me? And Malcolm?"

"Aye."

"Oh, my God." Sarah's knees suddenly felt like water and she gripped the edge of the table. She raised her gaze to Black's face. "You really are diabolical," she whispered.

Did she detect a flicker of guilt in the fiend's dark gray eyes or was it a trick of the light?

"Sarah... Miss Lambert..." Black ran a hand through his dark-as-midnight hair then rubbed the back of his neck. He did indeed look uncomfortable. "I'll admit I have been planning your abduction for some time. But my intention has always been to treat you well. This is about—"

"Your revenge on Malcolm. I know," she said bitterly. "But unless and until you tell me what he did to you, you'll have to forgive me for seeing *you* as the monster. *Not* him."

Black grimaced. "I suppose now is the time I should tell you that your bedchamber and mine are connected."

"What? How? I didn't see another door."

Black crossed his arms over his wide chest and the linen of his shirt pulled tight across his heavily muscled biceps. "There's a doorway behind the hanging tapestry beside the fireplace. I assure you, I don't intend to use it. But all things considered, I'd rather you know it's there."

Resisting the insane urge to let her gaze drop to Black's impressive upper body, Sarah retorted, "Oh, how gallant of you. Thank you *so* much for letting me know." She spun on her heel to go but then turned back to add, "If you do enter my room, I *will* run you through with the poker this time. Just so we're clear on the matter."

Black's mouth twitched. "As crystal."

"Good."

Sarah flounced back to her room. She would have liked to have slammed the door but it was too heavy and cumbersome for such a dramatic display. Instead, she paced back and forth across the thick Aubusson rug, cursing beneath her breath, imagining how satisfying it would feel to whack Black over the head with something. To wipe that smug, knowing smile off his too-handsome face.

Beast.

Out of morbid curiosity, she peeked behind the floor-to-ceiling tapestry beside the fireplace. An arched doorway was indeed secreted behind it and a short passageway appeared to lead to another small bedroom. There was no way to block the entrance. She would just have to take Black at his word that he wouldn't enter her bedchamber.

Her blood still boiling, Sarah undressed quickly and flung open the doors of the armoire. Ignoring the flimsy silk and lace night rails—Black was mad if he thought she'd wear anything so indecent and impractical—she threw on a plain flannel nightgown and after snuffing the candle, climbed into the enormous bed.

The sheets were crisp and cold but the pillows and mattress were soft, and it felt like heaven to be lying in a comfortable bed at long last. Closing her eyes, Sarah dashed away an errant tear with the heel of her hand and tried to resist the overwhelming urge to cry. Tears would not help her get out of this mess. Rest and a clear mind would.

She would not think of Aunt Judith and how worried she must be. She would not think of Malcolm and what he'd done. She would not think of her brush with danger in the Stag's Head's stables last night.

And she would *not* think of Alexander Black. Not his dark gray eyes, nor his raven black hair, or stubble-clad jaw. Not his admirable physique nor his roguish smiles. Not his inexplicable acts of kindness nor his perfidy.

She especially did not want to think about why he confused her so. Why he clouded her judgment and made her think about things she shouldn't.

Only one thing was as clear as it had always been: she needed to get away.

~

Lounging in one of the window seats, gazing out across the dark expanse of Loch Rannoch, Alex sipped his second glass of whisky for the night as he mulled over his plan of attack to win over Sarah Lambert's heart.

His mouth curved with grim amusement as he recalled her berating him over her bespoke clothing. She was certainly pricklier than a hedgehog hiding in a bramble bush when she wanted to be. But underneath her pique and suspicion, he sensed reluctant attraction and a passionate nature. Even though her pretty blue eyes darted with fire every time she looked at him, in time he was sure he would succeed in seducing Sarah to his side, thus eliminating any threat she might pose to him in the future.

The days ahead would be interesting indeed.

His whisky finished, he snuffed out all but one of the candles then retired to the small bedchamber adjacent to Sarah's. After lighting the fire, he discarded his clothes, pulled the leather tie from his hair, and settled down for the night. The bed was small but comfortable enough, and it wasn't long before bone weariness tugged him toward the welcoming arms of sleep.

Until something jerked him awake. An anguished cry was followed by a soft, heart-rending sob. Then came the muffled sound of a woman weeping.

Oh, hell. Was the lass having nightmares? Considering what she'd been through—what *he* had put her through—it wasn't surprising.

Alex sat up and ran a hand down his face. He could ignore Sarah, of course. The last thing she probably wanted was for him to invade her room, especially since he'd assured her that he wouldn't. He might drive her farther away...

Then again, this could also be an opportunity for him to offer the lass comfort and perhaps gain her trust. If he approached her the right way. In an unthreatening way.

It was a risk, but as Sarah continued to cry, as his own heart clenched with sympathy and more than a small degree of guilt, Alex decided he would be a bigger heel if he just sat idly by, listening to the sounds of her distress.

Even if he were to blame.

After throwing on a clean shirt, a pair of breeches, and a velvet banyan, he quietly padded along the cold stone corridor to the tapestry where he paused to listen. Sarah had stopped crying—perhaps she'd heard him. He let out a shaky exhale.

Nothing ventured, nothing gained, Alexander MacIvor...

Drawing a deep breath, he pushed the tapestry aside. The room was only dimly lit by the fire; the tester bed was in deep shadow. "Sarah, are you all right, lass?" he whispered.

Silence greeted him. Then a soft whimper and the bedclothes rustled.

Christ. Was she still asleep?

"Sarah?" he murmured again, stepping farther into the room.

All of a sudden she thrashed against the bedclothes, before sitting bolt upright with a gasp. "Oh, God, help me," she sobbed. "Get off me. D-Don't hurt me."

"Sarah." Alex rushed to her bedside. "Wake up, lass. You're safe."

Sarah sucked in a startled breath and threw her arms about him. "Black. Oh, thank God."

Shock froze Alex for a moment as the young woman clung to him, her wet cheek pressed against his shoulder. Of their own volition, his arms rose to cradle her gently. His hand stroked her tangled hair as he attempted to soothe her. "Hush, sweetheart. No one will hurt you." He wasn't sure if she was completely awake. Whatever monster she'd been dreaming about, it clearly hadn't been him. *At least, not this time.*

"I thought... My nightmare...it seemed so real. Those men... If you hadn't noticed I'd gone last night... If you hadn't followed me..." Sarah's voice cracked on another sob.

"It's all right," Alex murmured against her temple. The incident at the Stag's Head had clearly affected Sarah more deeply than he'd initially thought. "I'm here."

As he continued to stroke her back and her hair, he desperately tried to focus his thoughts and his anger on the bastards who'd tried to rape her, and all other curs like them. Curs like the Earl of Tay, her very own *fiancé*. He shouldn't be aware of the feel of her slender body, clothed only in a night rail, beneath his hands, or the soft press of her breasts against his chest. He shouldn't savor the sweet floral scent of her hair, or the way her warm breath caressed the bare skin of his throat....

When shameful desire inevitably surged, a wave of guilt immediately washed over Alex. The last thing the lass needed was to feel his cock twitching. She was already traumatized and he didn't want to make things worse. Which was ironic, really, but what was done was done.

Ever so gently, Alex unwound her arms from his neck as he set her away. "There's only one thing I know of that will make you feel better after a bad dream."

Sarah's brows drew together and her nose wrinkled. "Not whisky, I hope."

Alex smiled. "Well, that can help too, but I have something else in mind. Why don't you take a seat by the fire and I'll bring it to you."

Sarah sniffed then dabbed at her eyes with the edge of her sleeve. "Very well. And thank you. I...I apologize if I woke you."

Alex stepped away before the temptation to haul her back into his arms became too strong. "Do not worry. I'll be back in a wee moment."

Sarah wrapped herself in a shawl then installed herself in one of the damask-covered wingchairs before the fire, a thick blanket tucked around her. It wasn't lost on her that both she and Black were in a shocking state of dishabille. Again. Not that anyone would ever find out —goodness, Aunt Judith would be *horrified*—but still, it was highly improper.

Of course, everything about this whole situation was improper, and had been from the very start.

Sarah's cheeks burned as she recalled how she'd unthinkingly thrown her arms around Black when she'd woken from her hideous nightmare. Even though she'd been distraught and not in her right mind, it was embarrassing to say the least.

She'd sought comfort from the very man who'd kidnapped her.

It was wrong and it was mad, but no matter how hard she tried, she couldn't deny that last night he'd saved her from an assault which didn't bear thinking about. More than that, he'd made her feel safe. It seemed she was beginning to accept Black's word that she wasn't in any physical danger.

What had he said earlier tonight? *I swear to you, with God as my witness, I will not hurt you.* In fact—if she overlooked the way Black had brought her here to the island—all he'd done was take care of her since the incident at the Stag's Head. Even when she'd railed at him and called him a monster, he hadn't taken umbrage. Indeed, right at this very moment, he was still taking care of her. And despite multiple opportunities to take advantage of her, Black hadn't.

It was a bizarre situation. Confusing and disconcerting. Sarah felt as though she didn't know which way was up and which way was down. She shouldn't trust Black at all, but a small part of her did. She should be furious with the man for invading her bedchamber, but she wasn't. She shouldn't find Black so fascinating, but every time he walked into the room—as he was doing right now—she couldn't take her eyes off him.

Even though her hair was a bird's nest, her eyes red-rimmed, and her nose undoubtedly pink from crying, it certainly seemed Black was attracted to her too. The smile he flashed was nothing but rakish as he placed a tray on a small oak table between the chairs and offered her a china cup with a flourish. "Hot chocolate, just for you, Miss Lambert. I hope it's to your liking."

Hot chocolate? If Black had offered her manna from heaven, Sarah would have been less surprised. She examined the cup's contents. Sure enough, rich, thick, foaming hot chocolate filled the cup to the brim. It smelled divine and her mouth watered.

"I purchase the paste from an exclusive chocolate house in London," Black explained as he sat down in the other chair. "I believe it contains vanilla and cinnamon, and I added sugar and milk. It's very good, if I do say so myself."

"I'm sure it is." Sarah took a tentative sip, then another and hummed in appreciation as the dark and delicious liquid slid smoothly down her throat. When she opened her eyes, it was to find Black openly smiling at her reaction.

"So, what do you think?" he asked lightly.

Still only clothed in breeches, a loose open-necked shirt, and a banyan, with his raven locks brushing his wide shoulders, Sarah thought Black looked just as dark and delicious as the hot chocolate. To hide her blush—between Black's smile and her wayward thoughts, it seemed she was fighting a losing battle at maintaining any semblance of composure —she took another sip then turned her gaze to the fire as she answered. "It is lovely and just the thing for dispelling nightmares. Thank you."

"You're very welcome."

Again a lingering, heated stare sent her pulse skittering and stomach fluttering. It had never been like this with Malcolm. He was an attractive man too, but she'd never felt so...so off balance around him. So aware of his physicality. But then Malcolm had never sprawled so nonchalantly in a chair before her, sans half his clothes, with such a careless disregard for propriety.

Even now she could feel the weight of Black's appreciative gaze, and instead of being affronted by it, she was at last willing to admit to herself that she quite liked it. Besides, it was not as though she owed Malcolm any loyalty anymore. He'd betrayed her most grievously. Destroyed her trust entirely.

Sarah, what is wrong with you? Stop this. You're falling under Black's spell again. You cannot trust him either. You really don't know what he has planned for you.

Sarah took one more sip of her hot chocolate then set it aside. "At the risk of ruining the temporary truce between us, Mr. Black, I must venture to ask, how long do you plan on keeping me at Eilean Dubh? You've told me Lord Tay must pay a ransom to secure my release— which leads me to believe there must be a due date for it to be paid."

"Yes..." A muscle twitched in Black's lean jaw as if he were debating with himself whether to add more. "In about a fortnight from now," he finally said. "The first of March."

"The first of...?" Sarah swallowed, her mouth suddenly dry. That was only a week before her wedding day—if she still chose to marry Malcolm. Had Black chosen that particular date for a reason? She forced herself to ask the next logical question. "What...what will happen if he doesn't pay by then?"

"Whether Lord Tay pays the ransom or not, I promise no harm will come to you."

"So you keep saying, Black. And I want to believe you. But will—" She bit back the question that hovered on her lips: *will you keep me here indefinitely if he doesn't pay?* Because that was the logical alternative, wasn't it? Could Alexander Black really risk letting her go when there was a very good chance she could find out who he actually was? He must have given his real name to the magistrate at Dunkeld. Lord and Lady Kenmuir probably knew his true identity, too. She could hunt him down and have him prosecuted if she wished. The answer Black might give to her unspoken question suddenly terrified her. "Never mind."

What if he does intend to keep you here, Sarah? Perhaps he's trying to charm you for a reason. If you're more biddable and pliant—if you fall for his charms—it makes life far easier for him, doesn't it? Despite his denials, perhaps he does *intend to make you his mistress.*

Her thoughts strayed to all the elegant clothes—and the flimsy undergarments—in the chest and armoire.

She shivered and Black noticed.

"Are you cold?" he asked.

"A little," she lied.

Black rose and threw a few more logs on the fire. "If there's nothing else, Miss Lambert, I will bid you goodnight again." He bowed and threw her a roguish smile that was no doubt calculated. "I hope you sleep well."

"Thank you." She made herself smile back. "I'm sure the hot chocolate will help. Goodnight."

As Black—*her captor*, she reminded herself—disappeared behind the tapestry, Sarah stared into the fire. *Two can play at this game, Black. Perhaps I should try to charm you into submission too.*

If he fell for her, if she could gain his trust, it would give her some power in this strange relationship. Surely it would be easier to escape if she could lull Black into...well, a false sense of security. If she could get him to share more about his life, if she could find out exactly where she was, if he let down his guard, she'd have a greater chance of succeeding, wouldn't she?

But how long would that take? And even though she'd been betrothed to Malcolm—in her heart and mind, the scoundrel had irrevocably broken their engagement—she knew next to nothing about seduction.

All she knew was that Malcolm might never pay the ransom. And if she couldn't secure her release with her own money, she'd have to rely on the only other currency she had at her disposal—her wits and her feminine wiles.

At least she now knew there was an end date—of sorts—in sight.

Two weeks...

CHAPTER 13

Sarah awoke to the sound of pans clattering, the muted murmur of female voices, and the smell of...frying bacon?

Blinking sleepily, she pushed herself up against the plump pillows of the tester bed. Pale sunlight filtered through the mullioned windows of Eilean Dubh's main bedchamber, highlighting the silver and gold thread in the sage-green embroidered counterpane. Someone had placed a vase of snowdrops on the window ledge.

It must have been Aileen. Sarah couldn't imagine that Black would cook her breakfast or bring her flowers. But then, he'd made her hot chocolate...

She slipped from the bed and after donning some slippers and a velvet robe, peered into the adjoining chamber. Aileen and a young redheaded woman looked up from where they were plating food at the table.

"Ah, good mornin', Miss Lambert," greeted Aileen in her usual brusque manner. "The master said ye would be verra hungry so my daughter and I thought ye might like a braw meal." She gestured at the young woman with her chin. "This is Isla."

"Good mornin' to ye, Miss Lambert." Isla bobbed a curtsy and offered a shy smile. "I hope ye like the flowers."

"Yes. Thank you. They are lovely." Sarah glanced toward the door that led to the chamber Black had slept in last night. "Is Mr. Black about?"

"Nae, miss," replied Isla, fiddling with her white apron. "He has returned to Bla—"

Aileen gave her daughter a poke in the ribs and finished her sentence for her. "He has business to attend to. But he will be back this evenin'."

Returned to where? Black-somewhere? Sarah would definitely make it her business to talk with Isla when she was alone. The girl seemed to have a loose tongue.

Pretending as best she could that nothing out of the ordinary had occurred, Sarah murmured, "I see," and took a seat at the table. Aileen immediately offered her a plate piled with bacon, eggs, fat sausages, and thick slices of something Sarah didn't recognize but reminded her of a coarse terrine. She touched it with a fork. "What is this?'

"Och, ye've never had haggis, miss?" replied Isla. "Lord—"

Aileen shot her daughter a sharp look and again amended what Isla had started to say. "Aye, it's haggis. And Lord above is it good. 'Tis the master's favorite dish. It's a sheep's stomach stuffed with oats and sheep's pluck. Ye ken, lungs, and liver, and heart."

"Oh, it sounds...interesting." Sarah took a tentative bite and despite her initial reservations, thought it rather tasty.

"Would ye like tea or hot chocolate, miss? Or coffee?"

"Tea thank you, Aileen." Sarah watched with bemusement as the middle-aged woman poured her a steaming cup to her specifications. Then the servant shooed her daughter into the main bedchamber where she began issuing brusque orders about making the bed and heating water. For jailers, they were both very attentive to her needs.

Sarah shook her head but decided not to dwell on how strange everything was—not when the plate of food in front of her looked and smelled so good. As she began to eat, she realized it had been a whole day since she'd last had anything substantial. She couldn't let anxiety get the better of her. She'd be more likely to succeed in escaping if she were well fed and well rested.

Which reminded her... She was completely alone right now. Had Aileen and Isla locked the door? As quietly as she could, Sarah put down her knife and fork and pushed away from the table. The legs of the chair scraped a little on the flagstone floor and she held her breath, listening. When neither Aileen nor Isla returned to the room, she rose from her seat and crossed to the heavy, iron-studded oak door. *Damn it.* It *was* locked, and there was no key to be seen anywhere. It wasn't in the lock and it wasn't hanging conveniently from a hook by the door.

Double damn. She scowled. It was probably on that blasted iron ring at Aileen's waist.

"Och, lassie. Ye're no' one to give in easily, are ye?" said Aileen from somewhere behind her. "But I wouldna bother trying to escape. Even if ye did manage to open the door, one of the master's burliest footmen, MacLagan, is guarding the stairs. He's a big laddie and ye wouldna get verra far."

Sarah sighed heavily and turned to find the woman standing in the doorway to the bedchamber, arms crossed over her ample chest and an almost sympathetic look in her eyes. However, Sarah refused to feel contrite. "You cannot blame me for trying," she said stiffly.

"Nae, I suppose not." Aileen brushed her hands down her calico apron then nodded toward Sarah's abandoned breakfast. "Is it no' to yer liking? I would be verra happy to make ye somethin' else. Toast or scones. Or porridge."

"No, what you have prepared is quite fine, Aileen. But thank you." Sarah returned to her seat. Whilst she ate and lingered over her tea, Aileen stirred something in a large pot that was suspended over the fire —it smelled like some kind of soup or stew.

At least she wasn't going to starve to death.

Eventually Isla returned to the room and offered to help Sarah with her morning toilette, and she readily agreed. The young woman had an amiable nature and a ready smile, and her inconsequential chatter provided a welcome distraction as she helped Sarah to bathe then don the provided stays and stockings, petticoats and pannier, and finally her gown.

Even though Isla prattled away, the girl didn't inadvertently divulge any more useful tidbits of information about Black or the location of Eilean Dubh; Aileen had obviously warned her daughter to speak with more care. But that didn't mean Sarah would give up. A slip of the tongue was bound to happen eventually, especially if she led Isla in the right direction with an artful question or two.

Within the space of a half hour, Sarah was attired in the blue and ivory satin *robe à la française* with her hair styled into a neat arrangement of twists and curls at the back of her head. As Isla offered her a silver-framed hand mirror, she decided that even if she didn't feel like her usual self, at least she looked presentable—if one discounted her bandages, the shadows beneath her eyes, the touches of windburn on her face, and the scrape upon her cheek. Whilst it still rankled that she must wear the garments Black had procured so deviously, if she had any hope of snaring his affections, she needed to make some effort with her appearance.

She thanked Isla for her help then drifted back to the main chamber. Aileen was busily rolling out pastry on the table and there looked like there was nothing for her to do except sit in the window seat and gaze out upon the view of loch, forested braes, and snow cloaked mountains for hours on end. The vista was stunning but dear Lord, she would surely die of boredom.

Rather than sit, she began to make a slow circuit of the room, examining the contents of the dresser, the candelabra on the mantelpiece, the enormous tapestry depicting a hunting scene—and that was when she noticed a heavy velvet curtain to the left of one of the window embrasures; it swayed slightly, as though caught in a draft.

Curiosity piqued, she twitched the curtain back. A narrow set of stairs spiraled upwards into shadow.

"The old solar is up there, miss," Aileen informed her matter-of-factly. "The master says ye are welcome to go up there if ye like. There are books and other things to keep you occupied."

"Oh. That's…" *Considerate? Wonderful? Another method Black is employing to ensure my compliance?* Sarah swallowed back her bitter retort and made herself smile. "That's useful to know."

She had, after all, been seeking some sort of diversion. Pacing around the kitchen-cum-dining room would wear thin very quickly. Picking up her voluminous skirts, she ventured up the worn stone stairs. When she reached the top, she paused to catch her breath…and gasped.

The room was lovely. Just like in the main chamber, diamond-paned windows in each wall afforded breath-taking views of the countryside in every direction. The upholstery, thick rugs, and damask curtains were all in shades of cream, ivory, primrose yellow, and gold with touches of spring green. It was like being inside a bright, sunlit flower.

A glass-fronted bookcase in golden beechwood held an array of leather-bound volumes and in one corner of the room stood an exquisite spinet. In quiet awe, Sarah ran her fingers along the gleaming parquetry lid that featured an intricate pattern of leaves, fruit, and flowers. She was not a brilliant musician by any means—at least that's what her music tutor had told her countless times—but that wouldn't stop her playing. Or singing.

An escritoire of honey-hued oak contained all manner of writing tools—swan quills, fine parchment, a crystal and brass inkwell—and inside a cherrywood box by one of the window seats she found everything she would need for sewing: dozens of skeins of jewel-colored embroidery thread, an array of needles and a silver thimble, a small pair of ornate embroidery scissors, an embroidery frame, and numerous squares of soft ivory linen.

As she sorted through the silken skeins, an idea for a project sprang into her mind. When Isla joined her an hour later, she'd already made a good start.

"Oh, ye're verra clever, Miss Lambert," Isla exclaimed as she examined Sarah's design. "Is that an iris petal? Or a crocus?"

"An iris," Sarah replied with a smile, pleased at Isla's reaction. "I'm going to embroider several cushions for the window seats. All of them will have flowers like snowdrops, daffodils, crocuses, and irises. Indeed, the snowdrops you put in my bedroom gave me the idea."

A pink blush of pleasure bloomed across Isla's cheeks. "May I help ye, miss?"

"Yes, of course. Perhaps you could wind some of the thread onto bobbins for me so it doesn't get tangled."

Isla sat beside her in the window seat and dug out the embroidery scissors from the sewing box. "'Tis a braw morning, miss," she said as she unraveled a decent length of bright purple thread and snipped it. "I was going to ask if ye wanted the fire lit but it is muckle warm here in the sun."

"Yes, it is indeed." Sarah let her gaze wander to the loch. "And the view is beautiful. Have you always lived here? By the loch?"

"Aye. Always."

Isla's smile faded but Sarah decided to risk another gentle question in the hope of finding out something useful. "And your family has always been in service to Mr. Black?"

Isla's mouth turned down and she shook her head. "I ken what you are tryin' to do, Miss Lambert. But I willna tell you anythin' of import. The master and my ma both said ye would try to wheedle information oot of me."

Sarah sighed. *So much for being artful.* She decided to try another tack. "I do not want to get you into any sort of trouble, Isla. But it is very difficult being in a situation like this—to be so far away from those I care about and who care about me. Did you know I was…I mean, I am to be married in three weeks?"

Isla's mouth tightened with displeasure. "Aye. To the Earl of Tay."

"Yes." What on earth had the girl heard about her *fiancé* to make her pull such a face? It was beginning to look like she wouldn't be able to count on Isla for any kind of sympathy or assistance after all. "Do you know him?"

"Nae. I do no'." Isla's gaze remained fixed on the purple thread she was winding neatly around a small bone bobbin.

"But you *have* heard of him," Sarah persisted, her fingers stilled. "And judging by your expression, you don't seem to think much of him…"

"Aye. I've heard of him. And that's all I'll say aboot the matter. I fear I've already said too much." Isla put down the bobbin. "If ye'll excuse me, miss, I will light the fire. The sun seems to have gone behind a cloud."

Indeed it had. An ominous bank of dark clouds had begun to pile up behind the mountains on the other side of the loch. Wind ruffled the surface of the water and the trees below the tower shivered.

When Isla took her leave—claiming her mother needed her—Sarah put aside her embroidery frame and curled up on the window seat. She suddenly felt too weary, too dispirited, too troubled to focus on such fine needlework anymore. She watched the clouds draw closer and it wasn't long before snow swirled about Eilean Dubh, turning the world to a miserable pewter gray.

What did you do, Malcolm? I'm trapped here because of you.

It had to have been a terrible act considering how negatively Isla had reacted at the mere mention of the Earl of Tay. Unless...unless the girl was only judging Malcolm based on information Black had told her. Although, logic dictated it must be dreadful, for why else would Black resort to such extreme measures to exact revenge?

The more Sarah thought about it, the more it made sense to her that Malcolm had indeed done something that must be beyond the pale.

But what?

Pinpricks of doubt needled at Sarah. As she watched the whirling snow, she examined everything she knew about Malcolm...though now it seemed she didn't know much at all.

She and her father had met him through mutual acquaintances at a private dinner party in London in June the year before—and she'd been smitten at once by the earl's charming manner and handsome looks. And of course, his title. It wasn't every day a peer of the realm paid court to the daughter of a mere shipbuilder, rich or not. Naturally, her father and Aunt Judith had been initially suspicious of the earl's interest —they'd been concerned Malcolm might be a fortune hunter—but when her father had made discreet inquiries about the earl's circumstances through their mutual friends, all accounts indicated that Lord Tay was not only well off with a vast estate in Perthshire, but well regarded by Society. Her father had also been impressed to hear that Malcolm had been lauded for his service to King and country during the Forty-five Rebellion at the age of only three-and-twenty. So of course, when Lord Tay had offered for her hand only a month after their first encounter, Sarah had readily accepted with her father's blessing.

But now...now she had to wonder if Malcolm had been hiding something—something dark and horrible. She recalled how moody he'd been over the last few weeks. She'd put it down to his impatience to wed because she'd been in mourning for her father and their marriage had been delayed by an extra five months. Indeed, even though she would have preferred to marry after Easter, Malcolm had insisted they wed a whole month earlier, even though it would still be Lent. He'd asserted that he'd waited long enough for her to become his wife.

Sarah's mouth twisted and a hollow feeling settled in her belly. In reality, Malcolm hadn't waited for her at all. He'd betrayed her in the worst possible way at Kenmuir House.

Which begged the question: *what else was he capable of besides infidelity?*

Sarah shivered, but not because of the cold permeating the now gloomy solar. Perhaps it was a blessing in disguise that she was discovering the man she'd been going to marry was not who she thought he was.

The only person who could answer her questions about Malcolm—and grant her freedom—was Alexander Black. Charming him, and somehow coaxing the truth from him, had become more important than ever.

Alex pushed open the door into the welcoming warmth of Eilean Dubh's kitchen and was unexpectedly greeted by not one, but two heavenly things: the mouth-watering smell of pastry baking and the ethereal sound of an angel's voice intermingling with the sweet tinkling notes of a spinet.

And then his collie dog, Bandit, rushed in. He shook the snow from his shaggy coat, eliciting a string of muttered curses from Aileen, and the magical spell was broken.

Alex removed his tricorn and greatcoat and stamped the snow off his boots. "My apologies, Aileen. I know you and Isla are about to leave but I wouldn't worry about a wee bit of melted snow on the floor."

"Aye, sir. If ye say so." Aileen gestured at the scrubbed oak table where Isla was laying out plates, silverware, and wine glasses for two. "There's a beef pie for ye and Miss High-and-mighty on the hearthstone, and a dish of neeps and carrots. The bread and butter are on the table and I took the liberty of decantin' some of the wine from the cask by the dresser."

"Excellent. May I venture to ask how the day has gone?" Alex tilted his head meaningfully toward the stairs leading to the solar before pouring himself a glass of claret.

Aileen's brow furrowed. "As well as can be expected, sir." She shot a scowl Isla's way and lowered her voice to a harsh whisper. "Although this one needs to watch her tongue. She nearly mentioned the castle and almost called ye by yer title."

A bright red blush stained Isla's cheeks. "I'm verra sorry, sir. I didna mean to. I have been verra careful around Miss Lambert ever since."

"That's good to hear, Isla. Miss Lambert is certainly a canny young lady so you must always be on your guard."

Isla threw him a shy smile as she dipped into a curtsy. "Aye, sir. I will be, sir."

"Good. MacLagan is waiting to row you and your mother back to shore. I shall see you both on the morrow, weather permitting." The snowfall had grown heavier throughout the day and a storm seemed likely. Fortunately, Blackloch Castle—where both he and his servants resided when not at Eilean Dubh—was but a mile from the island. Farther along the shore of Loch Rannoch, tucked away behind a thickly forested bend, there was no way that Sarah could see his ancestral home from here. If she *had* been able to, no doubt she'd be asking him all sorts of inconvenient questions that he wasn't ready to answer. Worse still, she might mount another genuine escape attempt if she thought help might be close at hand...

Hopefully Isla wouldn't have another accidental slip of the tongue. For that matter, he must be on his guard around Sarah too given his own near miss the night before.

Once the door closed after Aileen and Isla, Alex stood by the fire drinking in its warmth as he sipped his claret. Sarah had begun to play a melancholy tune which reminded him of the old Scots ballad *O Waly Waly*. Her lovely voice floated down the stairs as she sang.

> *"The seas are deep and I cannot wade them,*
> *Neither have I wings to fly,*
> *I wish I had some little boat,*
> *To carry over my love and I."*

Alex's mouth curved into a sardonic smile. Sarah's song choice was not only apt but ironic, given her circumstances. He put down his glass of wine then ruffled Bandit's scruffy black and tan mane. "Why don't we go upstairs and I'll introduce you to Miss Lambert, my lad?"

Bandit stood and cocked his head.

"And just a word of warning, you must be on your best, gentlemanly behavior. Miss Lambert is a fine lady, so no jumping under any circumstances." Bandit's tongue darted out so Alex added with a mock frown, "And no sniffing her person, or licking either."

Bandit whined but stayed at heel as Alex climbed the stairs to the solar. On entering the room, Sarah immediately ceased singing and lifted her fingers from the spinet's keys.

"Oh, you're back," she said with a soft smile that was wholly unexpected. A smile that suffused Alex's blood with more warmth than the fire or his discarded claret could. Her gaze settled on Bandit. "And you've brought a handsome friend, I see."

"Aye," Alex replied, ruffling the collie's fur. "This is Bandit. But do not stop singing or playing on our account. We were enjoying your performance immensely." *And the splendid view.* Sarah in a blue and ivory silk gown featuring a rounded, low-cut neckline was a sight to behold.

"Oh...thank you." The flickering candlelight from the gilded candelabra atop the spinet revealed a wash of bright color flooding Sarah's cheeks.

Alex wasn't sure if it was his compliment or the appreciative look he'd raked over her that put her to the blush. Either way, he was encouraged that his plan to woo her might just work. As Alex flipped out his coattails and took a seat on a silk-upholstered chair by the fire, she took up the ballad where she'd left off.

> *"I set my back against an oak,*
> *I thought it was a trusty tree.*
> *But first it bent, and then it broke,*
> *And so did my false love to me—"*

Sarah's voice cracked on the last word and her fingers stumbled over the ivory keys. "Heavens." She blinked rapidly as though clearing tears from her vision. "Perhaps I should have chosen another song."

Alex sat forward, unable to hold himself back. "Perhaps. But it was lovely all the same. Might I suggest we repair to the kitchen for dinner? Aileen has baked a wonderful beef pie for us and it smells divine."

Sarah rose from her seat at the spinet and Alex's gaze was drawn to the sway of her skirts about her hips as she crossed the floor toward him. "I think that is a very good idea. My appetite has quite returned."

"I will admit, I'm particularly famished myself." *But not for food.* It was such a very long time since Alex had deliberately set out to win a woman's affection. Since Maggie, all of his liaisons over the years had been impersonal affairs with experienced women—widows, bored wives seeking sexual gratification, or paid courtesans. Courting a virginal young lady was not *de rigueur* for him, by any means, and he reminded himself to flirt with care.

Nevertheless, the rogue within him couldn't resist teasing Sarah as he offered her his arm to escort her to the stairs. When he dipped his gaze to her mouth, her breath caught and he was rewarded with the sight of her luscious breasts swelling above the tight bodice of her gown.

Considering his thoughts were rapidly running toward lustful, Alex decided it would be prudent to return to playing the part of the perfect gentleman for a little while. After all, he didn't want to scare Sarah by showering her with too much rakish attention too soon.

However, as he pulled out a chair for her at the dining table, Alex was more than a wee bit surprised when she gifted him with a decidedly coquettish glance from beneath her eyelashes before taking her seat. She was certainly more at ease tonight. Indeed, her defiance and anger seemed to have melted away like the snow on Rannoch Moor beneath a warm spring sun. While he didn't want to be suspicious of her more amiable attitude, he couldn't help but wonder what had prompted the change.

Pushing aside his apprehension—he really shouldn't complain about Sarah's genial, bordering-on-flirtatious manner—Alex played servant and plated the pie and vegetables before pouring both of them generous glasses of claret. Bandit, who'd followed them downstairs, flopped on the flagstones in front of the hearth. He knew better than to beg for food; Alex would feed him the rest of the pie later.

As Sarah ate, Alex's gaze fell to her bandaged wrists below the cascading white lace at her sleeves. "How are your rope burns?"

"Improving." She put down her fork, her expression suddenly apprehensive and a little shy as she added, "I... It may sound odd, but I want to thank you, Mr. Black. I had not expected to be treated so well during my...confinement. The solar and all the lovely things you've provided to keep me entertained, my luxurious bedchamber, the care Aileen and Isla have shown me..."—her cheeks pinkened as she touched a wrist—"the way you tended to my injuries and offered me comfort last night after I woke from a bad dream...I am most grateful to you. If you were another sort of man..." She inhaled deeply as though gathering her nerve. "Well, for a kidnapper, you *are* being very civilized about everything. If I am to be deprived of my liberty, I'd much rather be here than locked up in a freezing dank dungeon."

To say Alex was astonished at Sarah's pronouncement would have been an understatement. "I... Thank you. I am aware how hard this must be for you. And I want you to know that I appreciate your exceptional courage and your graciousness in such trying conditions. As I've said before, I truly believe Lord Tay doesn't deserve you."

A shadow of sadness crossed Sarah's face. "I'm beginning to wonder if you might be right, Mr. Black." She picked up her claret and took a delicate sip before her blue eyes returned to his face. "I have wondered... It bothers me that you seem to know so much more about Malcolm than I. I cannot help but dwell on the fact you won't tell me what it is he did to you. It must be terrible. Perhaps even unspeakable. Truth to tell, that worries me more than I can say."

Alex frowned. Although this was exactly the topic he'd wanted to discuss with Sarah, he needed to tread carefully. "There is much you do not know, but it is difficult for me to talk about, Sarah. Suffice it to say, Lord Tay is not... He is not an honorable man."

Sarah fiddled with the bandage about one of her cut fingers. "It is abundantly clear to me that you do not need Malcolm's money, Mr. Black. Or mine. Malcolm is wealthy too, so demanding a ransom for my safe return will surely be nothing more than an inconvenience to him rather than a punishment. *If* he still wishes to marry me, of course." Her features slid into an expression that was heartbreakingly sad. "I'm all but ruined now. I doubt Malcolm, or anyone else for that matter, would want to marry me after this."

"Sarah, he'd be mad not to want to marry you," Alex asserted. Dare he ask her his next question? How she responded was critical. He caught Sarah's gaze and when the corners of her lovely mouth turned up into a slight smile, he decided to dive in. "The real question is, do *you* want to marry him?'

She shook her head and the look in her eyes grew haunted. "I really don't know any more," she murmured thickly. "I'm so...confused. Whichever way I look at any of this—my situation, how I feel about Malcolm, what is to become of me—my thoughts seem to keep going round and round and tripping over themselves. I just..." She sighed heavily. "I just wish I knew more. About him. Then I could make a fully informed decision about my future."

Alex drew a fortifying breath. Now was the moment to share a little of the truth. *But how much? And would Sarah believe him?* "Perhaps it will make more sense to you if you consider what it is that I'm trying to put a stop to. In a few weeks' time..."

Sarah frowned. Last night, Black told her that the due date for the ransom was a fortnight away. A mere week before her wedding day. The realization jolted her to her very bones. "You...you're trying to stop our marriage from taking place? You don't want Malcolm to marry me?"

"Precisely."

"But...but why?"

Black stroked the stem of his wine glass, as though weighing his words before he spoke. When he did, it was with a slow, steady tone. "This may come as a shock to you, Sarah, but did you know that your Lord Tay is on the brink of financial ruin?"

"Wh-What?" Sarah picked up her wine with trembling fingers then put her glass down again on the oak table, untasted. "That cannot be true. I'm sure my father would never have agreed to our betrothal if that were the case. Never."

Black shrugged a wide shoulder and twisted the onyx and gold ring he always wore on his right ring finger. "I cannot speak for your father, but what I'm telling you is true. Tay is desperate to wed you, Sarah. He's desperate to get his hands on your fortune. But I won't let him."

Sarah pushed her plate of half-eaten food away. Nausea roiled as things she'd noticed but had politely dismissed during her stay at Tay House sprang into the forefront of her mind. The shabbiness of some of the furnishings. The dark patch on the green flock wallpaper in the upstairs gallery where a painting had once hung. The stray cobwebs and dust upon the furniture in some of the rooms. The scarcity of servants... Aunt Judith had mentioned these things, but she'd refused to listen. She'd fancied herself in love and that Malcolm was falling in love with her too. *What a fool I've been.*

"If this is indeed the case, there's no possibility he will ever to be able to pay the ransom," she whispered.

Black's gray eyes narrowed and an emotion akin to sympathy crossed his features. "Probably not. He'll try to raise the funds though. Make no mistake, he does want you for his wife, Sarah. But not for the reasons you thought, I'm afraid."

"Yes..." The fact that Malcolm had been with another woman didn't seem all that strange anymore.

He doesn't love me. He's never loved me... He never will. The knowledge stung far more than it should. Hot tears welled and Sarah dashed them away roughly. *He's not worth crying over. Not now. Not ever.*

"I'm so sorry, Sarah," murmured Black, his voice soft with compassion.

Sarah inhaled a breath and raised her chin to meet Black's gaze across the table. "You...you could have just told me all this. In Edinburgh. You could have come to me at Linden Hall, months ago for that matter. I would certainly have reconsidered the union if I'd known the full facts. Why—why kidnap me?"

Black's features tightened with anger. "Because I want Lord Tay to suffer like he never has before. I want—" His fist clenched on the table, his knuckles bone white beneath the skin. His eyes closed and, on a ragged exhale, he relaxed his hand. "I'm sorry for my display of temper, Sarah," he said at length. "I don't wish to frighten you."

Sarah nodded, acknowledging his apology. "I can see how strongly you feel about Malcolm. But you still haven't told me *why* you want him to suffer so. Please, I *need* to know. I want to understand."

"Lord Tay and I have a long history..." Black paused, clearly measuring his words again. His anger had dissipated but deep lines of tension bracketed his wide mouth. "He hurt those I loved, Sarah," he said at last, his voice rough with emotion. "Grievously. I will never be able to forgive him nor forget. And I will make him pay if it's the last thing I do. I will not say more."

The bitter determination in Black's voice, the turbulence in his gray eyes, made Sarah shiver. And she was more than a little afraid. She wanted Black to tell her everything, but she could see he was in no mood to make further disclosures. Instead, she reached for his hand. The onyx ring was cold beneath her palm. "I believe you," she said softly. "I don't know why, but I do."

Black nodded. "Thank you," he said. His mouth suddenly quirked into a wry smile. "Who would have thought you would be offering me comfort, Sarah Lambert?"

A blush scorched Sarah's face and she withdrew her hand. "Yes... Well," she muttered. She took a sip of her wine and then another. When she chanced another glance at Black, he was smiling.

"I know you said your wrists were improving, but are you sure you wouldn't like me to change your bandages?"

Sarah's first instinct was to say no. But if she were to gain Black's complete trust and her freedom, she needed to continue to court his favor. He'd let down his guard more than she'd anticipated so she'd be foolish not to take things further. Her heart beating faster, she extended her arm. "Why yes. Thank you."

Black pulled his chair closer until his muscled thigh, clad in figure-hugging buckskin breeches, brushed against hers. She didn't pull away —didn't want to pull away—and brazenly leaned closer. When Black's gaze grazed the tops of her breasts, her nipples tightened and her breath quickened. She was playing with fire, but for better or for worse, she wasn't going to stop.

After all, she owed Malcolm nothing. Not one deuced thing. And so far, turning Black around her finger seemed to be working.

Black very carefully unwrapped one bandage, exposing the abrasions beneath. Wherever his fingers brushed, her skin burned, and heat coursed through her veins.

"You are right. Your wrists are much better," he murmured. His thumb brushed over the heel of her hand, raising gooseflesh along her arm.

"Aileen's salve has worked well," said Sarah, her voice low and more than a touch breathy. "I-I don't think I need fresh bandages."

"Aye. I agree."

Sarah let her wrist linger in Black's warm grasp. He didn't seem in any hurry to relinquish his hold on her either. His long fingers stroked the underside of her forearm, and when she leaned forward a fraction, his gaze caressed her lips. From beneath his black lashes, she could see his gray eyes were dark with desire. No, it was more than that. It was hunger.

Oh my goodness. She knew that look. Black wanted to kiss her. And in her heart of hearts, Sarah knew she wanted to kiss him too. But if she let him, where would it end? They were totally alone. Anything could happen...

A potent combination of sharp want and trepidation catapulted her heart into a wild gallop. "Alexander," she whispered, not sure if she was uttering an invitation or a warning.

At the sound of her voice, Black gently released her hand and sat back in his chair, breaking the spell. "I... Ah... Perhaps... Applying a little more ointment wouldn't hurt, Miss Lambert." He stood and went to the dresser, dug around in one of the drawers, then placed the pot of Aileen's salve on the table. Bandit abandoned his spot beside the fire and nudged Black's leg with his nose. "All right, lad," Black said as he snagged the remains of the beef pie off the table. "Let's go outside so you can have your dinner."

Sarah closed her eyes as the door shut and the key scraped in the lock. Her heartbeat slowed and her breathing returned to a regular pace, but her mind was in turmoil. Feverish, unfulfilled desire warred with disappointment and an overwhelming sense of relief.

What on earth am I doing?

Tempting Black, winning his trust, this was a dangerous game indeed. The question was: how far was she willing to go? What price was she willing to pay for her freedom? Did she really want to give herself to Black completely? Because if they kissed, it wouldn't end there.

Aside from finally acknowledging she no longer wished to have anything to do with Malcolm, that was the only other thing Sarah was sure of.

~

Sweet Jesus, he needed some fresh air.

With Bandit at his heels, Alex all but bolted down the stairs of Eilean Dubh to the ruined courtyard below. Once he'd deposited the remains of the pie onto the snow-covered flagstones, he took up a position behind one of the crumbling walls. A howling, bitter wind flung flurries of snow through a yawning gap, and he welcomed the shock of it. Inhaling a great lungful of frigid air, he closed his eyes and slowly but surely, the rampant lust surging through his veins began to subside.

Things were careening out of control and he had to slow down. Stealing a kiss from Sarah was one thing, but he couldn't afford to scare her away with the strength of his ardor. God help him, when she'd leaned toward him, her breasts rising and falling with each breath she took, her luscious pink lips slightly parted as though inviting him to drink his fill, his cock had thickened and he knew that if he did kiss her, he'd be hard pressed not to try for more. And she didn't deserve that, to be ravished like a common doxy. Not when the poor lass was already plagued by nightmares of cold-blooded men who'd tried to take her against her will.

Yes, if he wanted Sarah to care for him, he had to woo her slowly. But slow wasn't what he was capable of right now. She was a decent young woman, and she was alone and completely at his mercy. It would be wrong of him to take complete advantage of her in this situation, just as he would never force her to do anything against her will. No matter how much he desired her.

He wasn't like Tay. He was better than Tay.

He had to be.

CHAPTER 14

The Office of Mr. Charles Swindon, Solicitor
Newcastle, Northumberland, England
February 19, 1757

"Something's not right, Mr. Swindon," said Judith Lambert, trying but failing to keep the note of panic from her voice. "Something has happened to Sarah. Do not tell me it has not, because I know it."

Charles Swindon eyed her over the top of his brass-rimmed eyeglasses with a look that could only be described as skeptical. *Curses.* Judith didn't want to come across as an anxious, bird-witted woman, but it seemed that she had.

"Surely not, Miss Lambert," the elderly solicitor said in a voice as dusty as the ledgers and leather-bound tomes on the shelves behind him. He put down his quill, pushed the papers he was working on to one side, and folded his gnarled hands together on the leather blotter. "From what you've told me, the letter Sarah wrote more or less stated that she's only suffering from the usual nerves that plague most young women before they wed. If Lord Tay is not concerned—"

"If Lord Tay is behind Sarah's disappearance—and I suspect he is—then of course he's not going to show any concern," rejoined Judith in a firmer tone. "I'm completely certain that letter he showed me is a forgery."

Beneath his gray periwig, Mr. Swindon's grizzled brows plunged into a deep frown. "You really *are* that sure, Miss Lambert?"

"Yes, I am," asserted Judith with a decided nod. "I suspect Lord Tay's vixen of a sister, Lady Glenleven, forged Sarah's handwriting."

"How so? Why not Lord Tay or someone he hired for such a task?"

"Because," said Judith firmly, "I once overheard Lady Glenleven bragging about how clever she was at that sort of thing at a soiree we all attended. How she often forged her late husband's signature on bank notes when he refused to foot her bills. As though it was all some sort of high-spirited lark, not out-and-out theft." She gave a disapproving sniff. "Not only that, but I noticed the woman poking about Sarah's bedchamber the day before I left Tay House. She claimed she was looking for a jeweled comb that Sarah supposedly borrowed, but I didn't believe her for a minute. She was probably trying to pilfer something of value."

Judith, who was presently perched upon an Adams-style wooden chair in front of the solicitor's wide mahogany desk, sat up even straighter as her decidedness increased. "And furthermore, when I announced I was leaving to check if Sarah was at Linden Hall, Lord Tay suggested I leave all of Sarah's things behind in case she returned in my absence. But because I don't think she will, and I don't trust Lord Tay or his sister, I took Sarah's jewelry box in case they try to sell its contents. Unfortunately, the earl has Sarah's pearl and sapphire parure secreted somewhere, so I'm especially worried about that. I also took Sarah's private papers. I didn't think it wise to leave any of her personal stationery or blank bank notes lying about. Not when Lady Glenleven might try to forge her handwriting again."

Mr. Swindon's eyebrows shot up into his wig. "You—you think Lord Tay would try to pawn Sarah's jewels and withdraw her money? Why would he do that? After all, her fortune will be his in only a matter of weeks." The solicitor shook his head and his jowls quivered. "This makes no sense, Miss Lambert."

Judith raised a brow. "It does make sense if Lord Tay is on the verge of ruin. Which I think he is."

"Surely not!"

"I know a run-down household when I see one, Mr. Swindon," said Judith. "Lord Tay's Edinburgh residence is woefully understaffed. The furnishings are shabby. At first I thought he'd let things go so Sarah could refurbish the townhouse to her liking once they were married. Some men are considerate like that. But as the weeks passed, I began to suspect the earl might be short of funds."

Mr. Swindon's brow furrowed in thought. "But Edwin had me investigate Lord Tay's financial situation last year when he suspected the earl might propose to Sarah. He'd sold off some of his unentailed land in recent years, but as the Taymoor Castle estate is huge, it hardly mattered. Nothing else untoward turned up."

"But how deep did you really dig?" asked Judith.

Mr. Swindon's mouth flattened into a grim line. "From what you've told me, clearly not deep enough."

"And then there are other things that don't sit well with me." Even though the solicitor had not dismissed her cares out of hand, Judith couldn't stop herself from wringing her hands as she added, "Lord Tay drinks far too much and has quite a temper. And his sister, Lady Glenleven... Well, I recently saw fresh bruises on her chin—as though she'd been grabbed—after I'd overheard harsh words being spoken between the pair. I didn't want to upset Sarah by saying anything, but now I honestly wish I had."

"Right then," said Mr. Swindon, his eyes clouded with concern, "I shall write straightaway to Campbell & Coutts in London to look out for any suspicious attempts to withdraw any of Sarah's money. Would that help, do you think?"

Judith's nod was adamant. "Yes. Yes it would."

"Have you been back to Linden Hall, by the way? Have you spoken with any of Sarah's friends?"

"Yes I have. On both counts. She is not anywhere to be found. It's like she's disappeared into thin air." Tears misted Judith's vision. "I'm sorry to get so emotional, Mr. Swindon, but Sarah is so very dear to me. I love her like a daughter. If anything terrible has happened..." She couldn't go on. More than that, she would not voice her worst fear of all.

That her kind, sweet, beautiful niece might have been killed...

As Judith rummaged in her reticule for a handkerchief, Swindon steepled his fingers beneath his ample chin. "Would it also ease your mind if I hired an inquiry agent, Miss Lambert? To look into Sarah's whereabouts? Someone must have seen her leave the ball at Kenmuir House. The agent can also look into Lord Tay's affairs. Ordinarily I wouldn't offer to take such action, but you've convinced me that something very odd indeed is going on. I'm sure if Edwin were still alive, he'd concur."

Judith dabbed her eyes. "Thank you, Charles," she murmured thickly. "And I know Sarah—wherever she is—would thank you too."

~

Tay House, Edinburgh

"What have you unearthed so far, Mr. MacNab?" Malcolm drummed his fingers upon the gray marble mantelpiece in the library of Tay House, then swore beneath his breath when he noticed his claret-hued brocade sleeve was covered in dust.

The rusty-haired inquiry agent cleared his throat as he withdrew several sheets of parchment from a battered leather satchel, then crossed the threadbare Turkish hearthrug to hand them to Malcolm. "Milord, as ye suggested, I began my inquiries at Kenmuir House. Withoot too much trouble, I managed to procure the Saint Valentine's Day ball guest list from the housekeeper."

"Excellent, MacNab." With a mounting sense of excitement, Malcolm ran his eyes over the extensive list. Even though more than two hundred guests had been in attendance that night, his gut told him his nemesis Janus must have been one of them.

Many of the names were indeed familiar, but only one leapt out at him.

Mr. Alexander Price, Esquire.

Price, by all accounts, was a filthy rich dog of dubious origin who'd not only purchased the estate that bordered Malcom's in Perthshire— the forfeited Rannoch estate—but over the last five years, he'd also snapped up huge parcels of Malcolm's own unentailed land. Land he'd been forced to put on the market to cover some of his mounting debts. By now, the bastard probably owned half of bloody Perthshire.

Malcolm had never met Price in person, but from what he'd heard, he was ruthless when it came to business. Amongst other enterprises, he apparently owned a logging company, mills, and a highly successful mercantile and insurance company that operated out of Edinburgh, Glasgow, Liverpool, and London. Rumor also had it that he was having Blackloch Castle on the shores of Loch Rannoch rebuilt. Malcolm smirked. The common upstart probably fancied himself as the next laird.

However, considering Price had more money than Croesus, it didn't seem likely that he'd bother kidnapping an heiress in exchange for a ransom.

No, Malcolm was looking for someone as desperate as himself. There *had* to be another name on this list that fit the bill. One thing was clear: he needed more information.

MacNab cleared his throat again. "I dinna ken if ye've noticed it yet, milord, but the young woman you had a liaison with, Nell ye said, she isna on the guest list. Of course, another guest may have escorted her in without an invitation..."

"Yes..." Malcolm frowned. *Nell*. He'd never come across her at any Society events before. And it wasn't likely that he'd forget a woman with such bountiful tits. The fact that she'd been more than eager to fuck him in every way imaginable after only a chance encounter now seemed rather odd. She'd been up for anything... Just like a whore...

The more Malcolm thought about it, the more the timing of his encounter with Nell bothered him. Whilst he'd been occupied, Sarah had disappeared. Of course, Sarah simply could have run off if she'd seen him with Nell and had then, unwittingly, met with misadventure. But he didn't think it likely. No, Janus had clearly planned Sarah's kidnapping meticulously—and perhaps Nell had been part of that plan. He didn't know why he hadn't thought of the possibility earlier.

"MacNab, I want you to start scouring the brothels for pretty, fair-haired whores with big tits," he said. "The woman in question may have used a false name as well."

"Aye, milord. However, I should say that might take me a wee bit of time."

Malcolm thumped his fist on the mantelpiece. "For Christ's sake, MacNab, I'm not asking you to sample the wares."

MacNab winced but held his ground. "I'm sorry, milord," he said with an obstinate lift of his chin, "but I'm sure there's many a buxom blond whore in Edinburgh. Perhaps ye could give me a wee bit more information to go on...?"

Malcolm sighed and wished to God he had a glass of whisky at hand. "The woman I met with was slender, of middling height, with good teeth. Her hair was her own and blond, not dyed. Paps as red as raspberries too and her mound was bare. I don't think she was more than five-and-twenty."

"Aye, milord. That should narrow the search down." MacNab shuffled his feet. "Ye've paid me handsomely, milord. However, I'm afraid I will need extra funds. To loosen the tongues of the brothel owners, ye ken."

Fucking hell. Malcolm gritted his teeth. The man was right. He ordered the inquiry agent to wait before he went through the interconnecting door to his private study. After unlocking the compartment secreted behind a false section of the bookcase, he withdrew one of his few remaining bags of gold coins and measured out a half-dozen guineas. Sarah's sapphire and pearl parure had netted him a decent amount, but he had nowhere near as much money as he'd hoped. Her bloody bitch of an aunt had absconded with all of Sarah's private papers and the rest of her jewelry, even though he'd ordered her not to. Judith Lambert was clearly suspicious of him, but that was a problem he'd deal with another day.

At least Damaris had delivered. The diamond and ruby bracelet Lord Arbelour had lavished upon her winked at Malcolm from a dark corner of the compartment. He'd get his man of business to pawn it tomorrow. But he still wouldn't have anywhere near the ten thousand pounds he needed to secure Sarah's release.

And time was running out.

"I want another report first thing tomorrow morning," Malcolm growled on his return to the library as he handed the guineas over to

MacNab. It wouldn't be long before Janus sent him another letter of demand providing further instructions on where and when the ransom was to be paid. But if MacNab found out something useful about the blond whore...

His cock began to swell at the thought of questioning the bitch before he used her again. Roughly. "Or as soon as you have any news about Nell."

CHAPTER 15

Eilean Dubh
February 21, 1757

Although the sky was a deep brilliant blue, it was icy-cold in the walled garden of Eilean Dubh. As Sarah wandered aimlessly along the gritted path, the late afternoon sun turned the marchpane-like snow cresting the top of the western facing wall and the gnarled bare branches of an ancient oak to a blinding white.

"Look out, miss!"

Sarah ducked to the side and for the first time in days, smiled as Bandit bounded past her in pursuit of a snowball pitched by MacLagan, the young footman who was technically one of her guards. Apparently before Black had departed the area on 'business' three days ago, he'd decreed that she could take walks in the walled garden around the tower as long as she was accompanied by a male guard like MacLagan, and either Aileen or Isla. Today, Isla was with Sarah, trailing behind her by several yards; Aileen was reportedly unwell with the ague.

And of course, there was Sarah's newfound friend, Bandit.

The collie, his brown eyes dancing and long black muzzle covered in snow, came racing back heading straight for MacLagan, and Sarah was obliged to make another sidestep. Black had left Bandit behind with her and Sarah appreciated the dog's simple yet cheerful company. She was especially grateful at night as she sat by the fire in the solar or her room, endeavoring to read or sew. She didn't feel so alone, not when he pressed his comforting weight up against her legs or pushed his elegant head onto her lap, demanding an ear rub.

For the most part, it really did seem Bandit was her only genuine companion. She wasn't sure why, but Isla had become as taciturn as her mother since Black's departure. And she could hardly talk to MacLagan or Dobson, not when they took turns to dutifully guard the entrance to the tower both day and night, effectively destroying any hope she harbored of escape.

Escape. It still seemed like an impossible feat and as the days marched on, Sarah's uneasiness grew. On her fourth circuit of the garden, she paused at the locked wrought-iron gate, and her longing gaze traveled where she couldn't, through the short stretch of woodland where snowdrops and purple crocuses nodded, down to the dark loch beyond. She couldn't even see the shore from here, but to the east, a sharp, snow-blanketed peak jutted above the trees into the cold blue sky.

She was trapped in the middle of a beautiful but desolate landscape. With no way out.

Gripping the bars of the gate with glove-clad fingers, Sarah leaned her forehead against the unyielding iron and failed to quell a wave of rising frustration and perversely, humiliation. Her plan to charm Black had gone completely awry. How could she possibly succeed if he wasn't even here? Indeed, she hadn't seen him since the night he'd rejected her hesitant offer of a kiss.

Of course, it was nonsensical to feel slighted, but she did. When Black had deposited Aileen's ointment in front of her then all but fled the tower like the hounds of hell, rather than Bandit, were at his heels, a dark, weighty blanket of disappointment had settled over her and had not shifted. Especially when she learned the next morning that Black had gone.

She'd tried to convince herself that she felt this way simply because her plan had been thwarted. Though deep down inside, she knew her feminine pride had been crushed. Even more bizarre was the startling and altogether unsettling realization that she...missed him.

Yes, she missed her captor. The smoky rasp of his voice, his storm-cloud eyes, their verbal sparring. She missed how he made her feel when he smiled at her. Even more telling was the fact that she didn't miss Malcolm. Not one little bit.

God in heaven, I am not in my right mind.

Black had been gone three days, and she had no idea when he would return. Or *if* he would return.

And it was now less than two weeks until the ransom was due...

With a heavy sigh, Sarah pushed away from the gate and resumed her walk. Isla continued to shadow her like a dark cloud, but the girl's sullen mood was the least of Sarah's concerns right now. As she'd told herself a thousand times, there was no point dwelling on things she could not control. It made perfect sense in the cold light of day, but not so much when she lay alone in a wide, unfamiliar bed, unable to sleep, listening to the wind hurtle about the tower and rattle her bedchamber's windowpanes.

She hadn't gone far before Bandit flashed past again, a blur of tan, black, and white.

When he trotted back, he headed straight for her, tail wagging, pink tongue lolling, and a look of expectation in his bright eyes.

"It looks like the furry rascal wants you to throw a snowball, Miss Lambert," called MacLagan.

"Yes, I think you might be right." Sarah bent down, scooped up a ball of snow, then turned on her heel and hurled it as hard as she could in the direction from whence she'd come.

And it hit Black square in the face as he pushed through the gate.

"Oh, my God. I am so sorry," cried Sarah, her gloved hands flying to her mouth.

Black shook his head and brushed the snow from his face and the wing of raven black hair that flopped over his brow. "I probably deserved that, Miss Lambert," he said, a faint smile playing about his lips as he approached her. "At least it wasn't a heavy, blunt object."

"I suppose so." Sarah's cheeks grew so hot, her face probably matched the scarlet gown she wore beneath her black wool cloak. Then she frowned. "How did you get here, by the way? It's clear you didn't swim. Unless you really *are* Lucifer, like I've always suspected, and you're hiding your devil's wings beneath your greatcoat..."

Black laughed, eyes dancing wickedly. "No, Miss Lambert, I didn't fly over. I paddled over in a coracle that I barely fit into."

Isla, her cheeks awash with bright color too, released a girlish giggle as she bobbed a curtsy. "Welcome back, sir."

"Thank you." A joyously prancing Bandit claimed Black's attention but when he'd finished ruffling the dog's coat, his gaze returned to Sarah. "I trust he's been keeping you company, Miss Lambert?"

"Yes. Yes he has." Even though Sarah tried to suppress any reaction to the unexpected interest in Black's eyes, warmth bloomed inside her and flooded through her chest. "He's a delightful companion. Thank you for leaving him here."

Black inclined his head and smiled. "You're most welcome. Shall we go in? Before it gets dark?"

He offered Sarah his arm and as she took it, she was taken aback when Isla threw her a hard glare. She wouldn't be surprised if the girl thought she had become Black's mistress. It was an obvious conclusion to draw, given Black had already spent two nights at Eilean Dubh alone with her. Her lavish gowns, just like the one she wore now, were cut low at the neckline and Isla knew very well what the armoire contained.

Sarah almost laughed. Isla wouldn't be so disapproving if she'd seen how Black had run a mile at the mere suggestion of a kiss the other evening. But now he was back, would he dismiss the servants and stay the whole night again at Eilean Dubh?

Black's thoughts appeared to be running in a similar direction, for when they arrived back at the tower's ruined courtyard, he paused to bid MacLagan and Isla farewell with instructions to return on the morrow. "Take the rowboat. I'll take the coracle back in the morning."

As the two servants took their leave, a flurry of nerves assailed Sarah. Tonight she would indeed have the opportunity to try and charm Black again. Despite her wounded pride, despite all her reservations, she must be brave and try to flirt with him. To tempt him.

To make him care.

She mustn't listen to the voice inside her head whispering her plan was flawed. That he might reject her again, or worse, he could take the bait she offered, use her, then discard her without a second thought. Just like Malcolm had so easily discarded her.

But Black does care a little, Sarah. You know he does, she reminded herself as he led her across the courtyard toward the stairs. Why would he leave Bandit here to keep her company if he didn't care about her wellbeing? Why would he bother to make her hot chocolate to comfort her after a bad dream? Why else would he have just placed his hand at her back to steady her as she climbed the stairs to Eilean Dubh's kitchen? Why would his eyes glow with warm appreciation as she removed her cloak, revealing the red velvet gown beneath?

Suddenly feeling breathless with nervous anticipation, Sarah moved away from Black who was in the process of removing his own coat. The sight of his tall, muscular physique attired in black boots, tight buff riding breeches, and a form-fitting frockcoat of midnight blue velvet, vividly reminded her that the man she sought to bewitch could just as easily bewitch her.

"Isla has made cock-a-leekie soup for supper," she remarked to dispel the enchantment he was effortlessly casting over her. Picking up a ladle, she concentrated on stirring the fragrant contents of a large cast-iron pot that hung over the fire. "She mentioned it was one of your favorite dishes."

"It is." Black poured himself a tankard of small beer from the cask standing on the oak dresser. "May I offer you something to drink, Miss Lambert? I believe I have some elderberry wine somewhere, or claret, if beer is not to your liking."

"Elderberry wine would be lovely, thank you." *And perhaps it will lend me some much-needed courage so I can do what I need to do—play the unfamiliar role of a coquette.*

Sarah took her wine glass from Black with a murmured thanks and made a show of taking a seat by the window. Spreading her velvet skirts about her, she nonchalantly tossed her loose curls over one shoulder so they caught the light of the setting sun and gleamed like guinea gold. After she took a sip of her wine, she ran her tongue along her lower lip then inhaled deeply so her breasts rose and strained against the tight bodice of her gown.

Black joined her in the window seat and, judging by the heat in his eyes, her preening had achieved the desired effect. His gaze locked with hers over the rim of his tankard as he drank, and despite her outward display of boldness, Sarah found herself blushing again. She couldn't help but wonder what he was thinking. *Did he know what she was up to?*

Not able to hold his gaze, Sarah turned to examine the view outside. Above the distant mountains, the sky was awash with glorious shades of crimson, orange, and gold. "I know you cannot reveal too much about Eilean Dubh, or where we are for that matter, but I would be interested to learn more about this place. It is clearly very old, much older than my home, Linden Hall. Do you know much of the tower's history?"

Amusement danced in Black's eyes. "A little."

Sarah raised an eyebrow. "And would you care to share any of it?"

Black rubbed his chin in apparent contemplation and Sarah's attention was drawn to the shadow of dark stubble on his sharply cut jaw. "Not really."

"Then what are we to talk about, Mr. Black?"

"Why do you feel the need to talk?"

"Well, it's what civilized people do."

Black's gray eyes grew imperceptibly darker. "Perhaps I'm not that civilized."

Sarah swallowed. At long last she'd roused the predator in Black, though she wasn't sure if she was happy about it or terrified. "Is that a warning?" she asked in a voice that was noticeably husky.

"Perhaps, Miss Lambert." Black's gaze dipped to her mouth before he took another sip of his beer.

Knowing full well she was treading along a dangerous path, Sarah toyed with the black satin ribbon adorning the neckline of her gown. "Well, what do you propose we do instead of talk, Mr. Black?"

When Black put down his tankard and leaned closer, his eyes alight with avid male hunger, Sarah's breath caught. *Oh, heavens above. What have I started?*

However, the man merely bared his even white teeth in a wolfish grin and in a low voice murmured, "Eat," before heading for the dresser to gather bowls and silverware.

Breathing a sigh of relief—she clearly needed more elderberry wine to bolster her wavering bravado—Sarah followed Black's lead. Perhaps after she'd eaten, and after imbibing a little more liquid courage, she would at last be brave enough to do what needed to be done. These half-hearted measures at seduction were not going to get her very far.

Nerves harnessed and resolve restored, she surreptitiously downed the contents of her glass—Black was still busy at the dresser—then moved to the fireside to stir the soup again. Bandit, who'd been lying in his customary spot by the hearth, got up and wagged his tail, a hopeful look in his brown eyes, but Black shooed him to the side with a gentle nudge and a muttered curse of, "Begone, dog. You shall have your fill later."

Sarah began to ladle the soup into the bowl Black handed her. "He's quite well behaved for such a large dog," she said in Bandit's defense.

Black grunted. "Aye, I suppose so." He drew closer, his arm brushing her shoulder. "May I help you with that, Miss Lambert?"

"No. I think I can manage," she replied as she tried to focus on what she was doing rather than Black's distracting presence. Truth to tell, the hastily drunk wine seemed to be going to her head a little too. With care, she passed the brimming bowl to Black. "I don't mind playing servant."

He took it with a smile and a polite "thank you," and when he retreated to the table, she filled another bowl for herself. Turning around, she took a step forward, only to find herself tripping over something—*Bandit.*

The dog yelped, Sarah stumbled, and her entire bowl of hot soup slopped down the front of her velvet dress before crashing onto the floor.

"Bandit!" Black thundered, chasing the dog away from the mess of spilled soup and smashed porcelain. In the next instant he was at Sarah's side, gripping her by the elbows. "Lass, are you all right? Are you burned?"

Burned? Only by your touch...

But Sarah wasn't brave enough to say that. "I'm fine," she managed then grimaced at the sight of her ruined gown. "Aside from being hideously embarrassed and covered in soup, that is." *Oh, Lord.* How could she possibly try to seduce Black now?

"You still look delicious to me, Miss Lambert," Black said with a gentle smile. "But I expect you would like to change."

"Yes." Face aflame with mortification, Sarah beat a hasty retreat to her bedchamber. This evening was turning out to be another monumental disaster. Somehow she had to salvage things. With shaking hands and tears prickling in her eyes, she opened the chest containing all the gowns Black had bought for her and pulled out one of embroidered apricot silk. It would do.

She retreated behind the silk Chinoiserie screen but in the fading light, she struggled with all the clasps and fiddly ribbons and ties of the ruined red velvet gown. The satin brocade stays beneath were soiled too. *Damn and blast. If only Isla or Aileen were here.*

Then Sarah froze, her heart beating hard and fast as inspiration struck. Isla and Aileen were *not* here.

But Black was...

Dare she ask him to help?

❧

Still cursing Bandit to Hades for trying to break Sarah's neck, Alex picked up the broken pieces of porcelain and dumped them in an empty bucket by the hearth. Velvet darkness was rapidly cloaking the tower so he began to light the candles and restoke the fire, all the while attempting to ignore the fact Sarah was undressing in the next room.

The saucy minx. She'd been deliberately flirting with him earlier, he was certain of it. Since he'd left Eilean Dubh, he'd spent a great deal of time re-examining the last evening he'd spent here. The more he'd thought about it, the more he'd been convinced Sarah had attempted to play the part of a seductress, even if she wasn't entirely comfortable in the role.

The only conclusion he could draw was that the lass was trying to court his favor, just as he'd determined that he must try to court hers. It would be amusing, but for the fact it reminded him how desperate Sarah had become: that she'd do anything to escape.

And that was a sobering thought indeed.

For the past three days and nights he'd stayed at Blackloch Castle.

Aside from arranging delivery of the final ransom note to Tay House in Edinburgh, he'd busied himself with estate matters and had checked with the mason in the village of Kinloch on the final plans for the almost complete reconstruction of the castle's east wing. He'd only returned this afternoon because he believed that he'd be able to keep a tight rein on his lust for the wily lass, whatever provocation she threw at him.

But God help him, right now, he didn't know if he could. He wanted her, more than he'd ever wanted any other woman before. Living in such close confines was proving to be pure torture.

"Excuse me...Mr. Black?"

Alex swore beneath his breath before calling back, "Aye? What is it, Miss Lambert?"

"Would you mind bringing me a candle? It's terribly dark in here and I'm having a spot of trouble with... Well, never mind. If you could just bring a candle, I would be most grateful."

Hell. Alex closed his eyes for a moment and tried to think of anything but a half-naked Sarah Lambert. He thought about the spilled soup that Bandit was in the process of cleaning up. He thought about all the ledgers he needed to go through with his factor and all the tenant issues he must deal with. He thought of the expression on Tay's face when he opened the next ransom note...

Promising himself he wouldn't flirt with Sarah anymore, nor try to sneak a peek at her in a state of dishabille—and heaven help him, he wanted to, badly—Alex picked up one of the wrought-iron candelabras and headed for the bedchamber. As he entered, he exhaled a ragged sigh of relief when he discovered she was behind the silk screen.

"Thank you," she called. "Now if you could just— Oh, for goodness sake..."

The silk screen rocked and Alex grimaced. Sarah was clearly struggling with her gown. He'd undressed enough women to know how damned complicated the process could be. "I'll leave the candelabra right here on the bedside table," he said, trying to ignore another mumbled curse from Sarah and the twitch in his breeches. Before he could stop himself he added, "If you need anything else—"

"Yes. Yes I do."

Damn. Why had he opened his mouth? *You know exactly why, Alexander MacIvor. You've seen her before in nothing but her shift and stays and it's a sight worth beholding again.* "I'd be happy to light more candles or—"

Sarah's face, framed by disheveled blond curls, poked around the side of the screen. "I cannot undo my stays, Mr. Black. The laces are at the back and Isla tied them too tightly. I need your help." She disappeared again.

"Very well." Alexander blew out a breath and rolled his shoulders. He could do this. Provide the assistance Sarah needed without pawing her like some savage beast.

He crossed the short distance to the screen and stepped behind it—then knitted his fingers together behind his head to stop himself hauling Sarah into his arms.

Sweet Jesus and all his saints.

Sarah had divested herself of everything except for her white silk stockings, thin linen shift, and the stubborn stays. Her back to him, she pulled her tumbling curls to one side and cast him a glance over one slender shoulder. "If you could help loosen the knot, I'd be most grateful, Mr. Black."

"Alex," he corrected, dropping his arms and stepping closer. "If I'm going to help you undress, Sarah, I think we can dispense with formalities, don't you?"

She turned her head away. "Yes. I suppose you are right," she said softly.

Alex released a shaky sigh. *Right, MacIvor. Get this over with before your cockstand gets any bigger.* His pulse galloping, he raised his hands and focused his attention on the tightly tied laces between Sarah's delicate shoulder blades. When his fumbling fingers accidently brushed her smooth-as-cream skin, she sucked in a startled breath. Despite her brazen request, it seemed she was as skittish as he was.

"Easy, lass," he murmured as he plucked at the stubborn knot.

Sarah's shoulders stiffened. "I'm not your horse, Mr. Black."

"Alex," he reminded her. "And you're right, you're not." *You're a gorgeous goddess and I wish you were mine...*

Christ where had *that* mad thought come from?

The knot gave at last, and Alex began to loosen the laces down the length of Sarah's back.

"I'm still not even sure that actually *is* your name," murmured Sarah. Her soft breathy voice felt like an intimate caress across Alex's skin.

"What?" he asked, his tone gruffer than he meant it to be. "Which, Alex or Black?" He was so disconcerted, he wasn't sure what he was saying. He sure as hell couldn't control his voice. Not when Sarah shrugged off her stays and tossed the garment onto the floor. Not when her shift slid off her shoulder and she looked back at him again from beneath her lashes.

"Both names," she whispered huskily. "You have so many secrets."

"Aye." He was about to step away, but Sarah suddenly turned and pressed herself against him. Beneath his coat, her palms slid restlessly along the satin of his waistcoat.

"Sarah," he cautioned, but it seemed his own body wasn't inclined to heed the warning either. His hands clasped her upper arms but instead of setting her away, he gathered her closer. He could feel the rapid rise and fall of her chest, the impudent jut of her nipples, as hard as pearls, through all the layers of his clothes. His nostrils flared as he drew in her intoxicating scent—something floral like roses and her own feminine essence. With every beat of his heart, wild lust pounded straight to his groin. "You and I... We shouldn't..."

Sarah's tongue darted out to moisten her soft lips and her blue eyes, dark with longing, locked with his. "Yes, we should."

"Aye." With a groan, Alex gave into temptation. Sarah Lambert had awoken the wolf inside him, and he intended to feast. He tilted Sarah's small chin up then ruthlessly plundered her sweet willing mouth with reckless abandon. Tasting. Caressing. Devouring.

When her tongue dueled with his, fire licked through his veins. When her fingers speared into his clubbed hair, pulling it free from its leather tie, he shrugged out of his frockcoat. It seemed the shy maid he'd first encountered in the library at Kenmuir House had gone and a woman who knew what she wanted, who wanted *him*, had taken her place.

Like a starving man presented with a banquet, he couldn't get enough of her. The taste of her. The feel of her pliant, slender body beneath his questing hands. Her soft moans and whimpers.

Mindless with passion, Alex pushed her against the rough stone wall at her back and ground his hips against hers. Burying his face in her neck, he lavished her with hot, hungry kisses. When she ripped his shirt from his breeches and splayed her hand against his naked torso, he growled his appreciation.

Her shift slipped even farther down her arm, and with nothing more than a gentle pull, he exposed one of her high, proud breasts.

Dear God, she was delectable. He drew back to take in the glorious sight of Sarah, dazed with desire. Panting, chest heaving, her pale rose-pink nipple puckered beneath his gaze. He had to taste her there.

Cradling the tender weight of her breast with one hand, he lowered his head and laved the tight bud. She arched into him, her fingers twisting in his hair. "Alex."

Christ, his name on her tongue was the sweetest thing he'd ever heard.

Sarah suddenly lifted her leg, wrapping it around one of his, and while Alex continued to lavish attention upon her breast, he also took the opportunity to slide his hand beneath her rucked-up shift, his fingers seeking the hot, wet sleekness between her thighs.

She gasped.

He froze. *What, in God's name, am I doing? This is wrong... So wrong.*

"I'm sorry, I've never done this before. But keep going." Sarah pressed her hand against his throbbing cock. "I know you want me," she breathed in a husky whisper that did nothing to quell the fire raging within him. "Take me."

"Aye, I want you." Alex reluctantly lifted his head and searched her face. "But the question is, Sarah Lambert, do you truly want me? Want this?" He pushed himself into her hand. "Because this stops right here, right now, if this isn't honest and true."

"Yes." A shadow flickered in her eyes, belying her declaration. "I do want this."

Alex dropped his hands and clenched his fists. The truth was, he did want this woman, so very desperately. *But not this way.* Something akin to suspicion twisted inside him like a viper. "Why are you really doing this, Sarah?" he gritted out. "Tell me."

Her brow furrowed. "I told you. I wa—"

"I don't believe you." Alex levered himself away from her.

With a small cry, Sarah snatched up his hand and placed it over her naked breast. "What do you feel, Alexander Black?" she demanded hotly. "These past few days, all the hours you've been away, I've thought of no one but *you*. My heart is racing. For *you*. I do not care for Malcolm, and I do not wish to wed him. You must believe me. It's *you* I want to be with."

With a tremendous effort, Alex removed his hand from her breast and gently tugged her shift back into place. Bitter self-recrimination burned like acid in his gut. "The problem is, you have no real choice in the matter, Sarah. I sense desperation within you. God knows, I've driven you to it. You...you don't have to prostitute yourself in exchange for your safety or your freedom. Because that's what you're doing, isn't it? You cannot deny it."

Sarah's eyes flashed with bright blue fire and tears. When she spoke, her voice quivered with anger. "God damn you, Alexander Black. How dare you? Get out."

Alex gave one short sharp nod and strode from the room, closing the door behind him. She was angry with him, but it was no less than he deserved. If she had taken a fireiron to him right now, he'd have welcomed the blow.

What an arrogant, selfish, stupid bastard I am. How could she ever possibly care for me?

Heading straight for the dresser, he snagged a bottle of whisky, pulled out the cork with his teeth and took a large swig. A heart-rending sob crashed into the silence.

Bloody hell. Sarah was crying.

But it was better this way. She pretended she wanted him, but she didn't really. How could she? He was holding her prisoner, for God's sake. Seducing and deflowering her under duress was no better than raping her.

Fuck, fuck, fuck. Everything was a mess. Alex gulped down another mouthful of whisky, welcoming the hot sting at the back his throat.

He'd promised himself he would *not* be like Tay. A cold-blooded, murderous animal who took whatever he wanted. A brute who fucked and destroyed lives with impunity.

But you're destroying Sarah's life, MacIvor. What the hell are you going to do now?

Alex put down the whisky and wiped a shaking hand across his mouth. One thing was clear: he needed to calm down because right at this moment, he felt as though he was being ravaged by a fever. His heart hammered, his cock throbbed, and in his head spun a tempest, a whirling storm of too many contradictory thoughts and emotions—a potent mixture of impotent rage, and utter despair, and rampaging desire. Worst of all was the clawing guilt, ripping him apart. He'd made Sarah feel so desperate and worthless, she'd been prepared to pay any price. But he wouldn't let her.

Another sob reached his ears and right at that moment, Alex hated himself. He couldn't stay here tonight. He had to get away. Even though night had fully descended, he'd take the coracle and then walk the mile back to Blackloch in the freezing darkness.

With savage movements, Alex yanked on his gloves and threw on his greatcoat, and after snatching up the whisky bottle again, he slammed out the door, not bothering to lock it. Sarah would be safe enough. He'd leave Bandit with her, and Isla and MacLagan would be back just after sunrise.

And only when he felt sane again would he return to say he was so very sorry.

CHAPTER 16

Eilean Dubh
February 22, 1757

The creak of her bedchamber door pulled Sarah from sleep. Rolling over, she opened her eyes, blinked, and watched Isla creep into the room. Bandit, who'd spent the night in Sarah's bedchamber, greeted the maid with a thump of his tail on the hearthrug, but Isla ignored him as she stirred up the coals and threw a few logs into the grate.

As Sarah pushed herself up against the fat, feather-down pillows, she swept her tangled hair from her eyes. Judging by how cold and dark the room was, she guessed it was either early, or the weather was inclement, or both. When Isla pulled back the curtains, weak gray light filtered in through the diamond panes. The morning appeared to be perfectly matched to Sarah's desolate mood.

"Is Black here?" she asked in a voice hoarse with sleep and too much weeping. She didn't expect him to be. After their disastrous tryst, she'd heard him slam the door when he left.

Isla approached the tester bed. "Nae, miss. He took the coracle back and spent the night at Black—I mean, he isna here." Her gaze wandered over Sarah and her brow knitted. "Are ye all right, miss? Can I get ye anythin'?"

Sarah tugged up her sagging, crumpled shift. She hadn't bothered to change into a night rail last night. She'd been too upset and really, what would have been the point? "Just some hot water and a robe to begin with," she said. "And then maybe a little breakfast."

"Aye, miss."

When Sarah slipped from the bed and crossed to the washstand, she caught sight of her face in the looking glass and grimaced. No wonder Isla had looked concerned; her eyes were puffy with exhaustion and tears, her cheeks as pale as milk. Thankfully, Isla helped her with her toilette without further comment and it wasn't long before Sarah was ensconced before the blazing fire in her room with a plate of freshly buttered toast and a cup of tea.

As she fed the crusts of her toast to Bandit, Isla emerged from behind the silk screen with a bundle of clothes—her ruined red velvet gown and to her horror, Black's dark blue velvet frockcoat.

A furious blush scalded Sarah's cheeks. She'd completely forgotten that Black had discarded it last night. *What must Isla think?*

Clearly the worst, judging by the girl's severe expression. Her mouth had flattened into a disapproving line and the look she shot Sarah was nothing short of accusatory as she crossed the chamber.

"Isla—"

"'Tis none of my business, miss." Isla disappeared into the kitchen and Sarah let out a shaky sigh. It seemed the rest of her day was going to be filled with uncomfortable drawn-out silences and censorious glances.

"At least I have you, Bandit," she murmured, caressing the unruly mane around the dog's neck. "Perhaps you can help me come up with another way to escape."

With a soft snuffle, the collie subsided onto the hearthrug and Sarah twisted the ribbon ties of her velvet robe as she stared into the leaping flames of the fire. Her plan to make Black care for her had failed, dismally. Not only had he worked out what she'd been up to, he'd all but called her a whore.

Closing her eyes against the prick of tears, a wave of shame and anguish washed over her as she recalled Black's words and the anger in his eyes. The harsh bitterness in his voice as he'd rejected her yet again.

It made the memory of his glorious kisses and caresses hurt all the more. Yes, to her shame, she'd enjoyed everything they'd done. Black might want her in a physical sense—he'd definitely been aroused when she'd boldly cupped his manhood—but it was also abundantly clear that he despised her for how she'd debased herself and attempted to manipulate him.

But then, wasn't it his fault that he'd pushed her into such an intolerable position? He'd said as much himself. However, when all was said and done, dwelling on who was to blame wasn't going to help Sarah get away from Eilean Dubh. And considering the due date for the ransom was drawing ever closer, the imperative to escape was more urgent than ever.

But how?

The answer to Sarah's seemingly insurmountable problem came from an unexpected quarter but an hour later.

After she'd dressed, Sarah retired to the solar, looking for something to do besides sitting in her bedchamber and fretting the day away. Sewing was not sufficiently engaging—it gave her too much time to brood—and she was not in the mood to play the spinet, so she perused the titles in the glass-fronted bookcase as she'd done a thousand times before. But this time, a thick book covered in tooled, dark green leather with distinctive gold lettering caught her eye: *Architectural Antiquities of Scotland* by J.M. Arbuthnot.

How odd she hadn't noticed it before. Though it was not the sort of book she was usually drawn to, it might be sufficiently diverting to take her mind off her troubled thoughts, at least for an hour or two.

Pulling it from the shelf, Sarah took it to the window seat and began to peruse the musty, yellowed pages. There were fine, detailed etchings of many of the former royal residences of the deposed Scottish monarchy—the Royal Palace of Holyroodhouse, Edinburgh Castle, Linlithgow Palace, Falkland Palace, and Stirling Castle—as well as lesser-known manor houses and castles.

And that's when she saw it, a few pages past a section on the tower house of Balmoral...a small lithograph entitled *Blackloch Castle on the*

Shores of Loch Rannoch, Perthshire. Above the forest, behind the castle, a distinctive sharp peak jutted into the sky. It was the very same peak that could be viewed from all of Eilean Dubh's west facing windows.

Heart pounding, Sarah rushed over to the window to compare the vista to the one in the book. And her breath froze in her chest.

Oh, my God. I know where I am.

With trembling fingers, Sarah turned the page and read a short paragraph on the history of Blackloch Castle. Phrases jumped out at her: the Lairds of Blackloch... Seat of the Chief of Clan MacIvor... Baron Rannoch... Vast holdings in and around Loch Rannoch and Rannoch Moor.

And farther on: Eilean Dubh, a ruined medieval tower house situated on an island at the western end of Loch Rannoch... Sacked by Fergus Campbell, the first Earl of Tay, in the fourteenth century...

Taymoor Castle, Malcolm's ancestral seat was in Perthshire too.

Her knees like water, Sarah collapsed onto the window seat. Alexander Black was really Alexander MacIvor, she'd stake her life on it. Perhaps he was even Baron Rannoch. Hadn't Isla called him "lord" on Sarah's first morning here?

The MacIvors and the Campbells of Tay had apparently been feuding for centuries, but that didn't explain why Alexander had such a personal grudge against Malcolm. It was the one last piece of the puzzle Sarah was burning to discover.

She stared at the picture of Blackloch Castle again for another full minute to make sure she wasn't dreaming. Then, with the book in one hand and her skirts in the other, she rushed down the stairs to question Isla.

The maid was in the kitchen, kneading a large mound of soft, white dough on the oak table. She didn't even look up when Sarah entered the room, just kept on pushing and folding and pummeling the dough as if her life depended on it. Perhaps Isla imagined she was pummeling her master's Sassenach prisoner.

Sarah cleared her throat. "Isla, I need to speak with you about something most urgent."

Isla turned the dough over and dusted it with a handful of flour. "What is it?" she asked in a tone as sour as the weather outside.

Sarah thrust the book in front of the maid's nose and pointed to the picture of Blackloch Castle. "I found this. Your master is Alexander MacIvor, the Laird of Blackloch, isn't he, Isla? Or should I call him Lord Rannoch? Eilean Dubh belongs to him too, doesn't it?"

Isla's cheeks turned bright red and she immediately stopped kneading the dough. "Where did you find that, miss?" she whispered.

"In the bookcase upstairs."

"Och, no." The maid closed her eyes and shook her head. "I...I dinna ken what to say."

"Just tell me, Isla," Sarah demanded, pulse pounding. "Am I correct?" Her voice cracked as she added, "Please. I have to know."

Isla's thin shoulders rose and fell with a shaky sigh as she sank onto a chair. "Aye, miss. Ye are. Aboot everything."

The relief that washed over Sarah was so great, she nearly burst into tears. At long last she'd found out the true name of her captor and where she was. She dropped into a chair beside the maid and took one of her flour-dusted hands in hers. "Thank you."

Isla shook her head. "I shouldna have said anythin', miss. Lord Rannoch will be most displeased. But I canna..."

"You can't what, Isla?"

"I canna do this anymore. Watch the master keep ye here, knowin' that in less than two weeks he's going to—" Isla bit her lip and twisted her apron with white-knuckled fingers. Fear flickered in her eyes before she looked away.

A sharp spike of alarm shot through Sarah. "What is Lord Rannoch going to do in two weeks, Isla?"

The maid lifted her gaze to Sarah's face. "When Lord Tay doesna pay the ransom, and we know he willna because he canna, Lord Rannoch is going to..." Isla's face crumpled. "Ye are not safe here, miss. And now that ye ken who the master really is, things are even worse. If he finds out ye know the truth aboot him..." Isla reached out and gripped Sarah's hand. "I'm verra scared he will try to silence you."

"Silence me? Do you mean he would...he would do me harm? Perhaps even—" Sarah halted. She couldn't complete the terrifying thought.

"Aye, miss," whispered Isla, her face pale with fear. "I think that's exactly what he plans to do. But...but I ken where he keeps his flask of laudanum. And he kens ye canna swim... 'Twould be easy enough for him to...' The maid's throat convulsed before she all but wailed, "Oh, dinna make me say it!"

Oh, dear God. Ice-cold terror gripped Sarah's heart. Would Alexander really render her unconscious then drown her? He'd promised over and over again that he'd never hurt her. Despite his harsh words and rejection last night, Sarah had even come to believe he cared for her a little.

But that was before I knew his true identity...

Sarah swallowed past a throat tight with fear. She must not panic. Whether she believed Alexander MacIvor really was a wolf in sheep's clothing who was capable of murder was almost immaterial at this point. Because now she had an ally. And an opportunity.

"Isla, please help me escape." Sarah squeezed the maid's hand. "I promise not to tell anyone what I have learned about your master. I do not want retribution either. Just my freedom."

Beneath her linen and lace cap, Isla's brow furrowed with uncertainty. "What aboot yer Lord Tay? He is a powerful man."

"I can assure you, I do not wish to marry Lord Tay anymore and I will never divulge who was behind my kidnapping. I know the earl is not a good man. In fact, I never want to see him again. I just want to return to Linden Hall, my home in Northumberland. I can pay you—"

Isla shook her head. "Och, I dinna want yer money, miss. But aye, I will help ye."

Oh, thank God. Unbidden tears welled in Sarah's eyes, blurring her vision. "Thank you.'

"Och, dinna cry, miss. Ye dinna have time for that." Isla stood and dusted off her hands. "I have a canny plan and the sooner we begin, the better. First, we must get ye into more suitable clothes. Ye have a long way to travel."

"Of course." Fear and excitement thrumming through her veins, Sarah returned to her bedchamber where Isla helped her change out of the apricot silk gown and matching embroidered pumps into her blue woolen riding habit, thick woolen stockings, and sturdy black boots. Black kid gloves and her black hooded cloak completed the ensemble.

"Now, miss. Ye must take something to eat with ye," said Isla, ushering her back into the kitchen. "There's bread and cheese on the table. And apples in the bowl on the dresser. And while ye are readyin' that, I need to take care of MacLagan."

Sarah took a clean linen napkin from the dresser to wrap up the food. "What do you mean?"

"Well, he willna let ye go, so I'm thinkin' he might be needin' a wee nap." Isla disappeared into the small chamber Black—or rather, Lord Rannoch—slept in, and emerged a minute later with a silver flask.

Sarah recognized it at once and shivered. "You're going to dose him with laudanum?"

"Aye." Isla filled up a tankard with small beer then measured out a large spoonful before stirring it into the ale.

"That seems like rather a lot." Aunt Judith sometimes took laudanum for her megrims but never more than a teaspoonful.

Isla shrugged. "MacLagan is a fair-sized man and we want to make sure he goes to sleep quick, and for a while. Ye need to be well away from here before Lord Rannoch returns. MacLagan is supposed to row over to the mainland at noon and pick him up."

Noon? Sarah's gaze darted to the mantel clock. That was only two hours away. Good Lord. Isla was right, about everything. She needed to make haste.

Sarah quickly cut off a hunk of bread and wrapped it up in the napkin. "I take it you'll row me over to the shore?"

But Isla shook her head. "Nae, ye will have to row yerself."

Sarah's stomach tumbled over with panic. "But...I don't know how to."

"I'll show ye." Tankard in hand, Isla unlocked the door with the key she kept at her waist. "'Tis not verra hard. Ye will manage, miss."

The door closed and Sarah looked about the room. Bandit sat by the fire, watching her with sad brown eyes. *Did he sense she was leaving?* "I'm afraid it's time for us to say goodbye, my friend."

The collie whined and sidled over to her, his bushy tail swishing back and forth. Tears in her eyes and a hard lump in her throat, Sarah ruffled his soft fur. "Thank you for keeping me company. I will never forget you."

When Isla appeared in the doorway again, Sarah was ready. She'd packed her rations into a small willow basket, along with a number of items she hoped to barter in exchange for a horse somewhere along the way: the silver-backed mirror and matching brush; the ornate embroidery scissors and thimble from the sewing box; and a pretty comb decorated with seed pearls. Small, easily portable, and precious. Black—or should she say Lord Rannoch?—would hardly miss them.

"MacLagan was beginnin' to nod off when I left him, miss." Isla beckoned her over to the door. "So it's best ye leave now."

Her pulse racing, Sarah followed the maid down the stairs and sure enough, the footman was slumped on the ground in a relatively sheltered alcove in one of the courtyards ruined walls, empty tankard in hand and his chin on his chest, snoring away. Nevertheless, they both tiptoed across the flagstones, heading for the garden gate.

"Do you have the gate key, too?" murmured Sarah as they drew close.

The maid nodded. "Aye."

Within seconds, the gate was unlocked and Sarah was outside, following Isla along the barely discernible pathway toward the stony shore. But trepidation quickly replaced exhilaration when Sarah saw how far she needed to row.

"I don't know if I can do this, Isla," she said, staring with longing at the far bank. A bitterly cold wind carrying the scent of rain ruffled the surface of the loch's dark waters. "Won't you reconsider and come with me?"

Isla shook her head. "Nae, I canna. It needs to look like ye escaped withoot any help. If I take ye, I will be on the wrong side."

"But couldn't you row back?"

"Aye, but then the boat would be on Eilean Dubh, which means Lord Rannoch will know I helped ye. I dinna want him to suspect I was involved in yer scheme."

Sarah frowned. Isla spoke sense and of course she didn't want the girl to get into any trouble. But why did a prickle of apprehension suddenly creep down her spine? Isla had clearly put some thought into all of this.

Sarah studied the serving girl's face. She *seemed* earnest enough.

Perhaps she simply wanted Black all to herself and that was why she was helping. It was clear the lass had developed a *tendre* for her handsome master. Regardless of Isla's motive, this was Sarah's first, perhaps only real chance to escape and she'd be foolish to throw away the opportunity.

"Very well," she said. "But before you show me what to do, you must tell me where to go once I get to the other side."

Isla pointed to the east. "Blackloch Castle is that way, miss, and farther on is the village of Kinloch. The folk there are loyal to the master so dinna head that way, whatever ye do. Ye must head west, in the other direction. Go into the woods and follow the shore until ye get to the end of the loch. Then just go straight across Rannoch Moor. There's a small river that flows west so if ye follow it, ye canna go wrong. Ye only need to travel aboot three or four miles to get to the next village. There's an inn where I'm sure ye will be able to borrow a horse and get directions that will take ye back to Edinburgh."

"Are...are Lord Tay's lands that way?"

Isla shook her head. "Nae, miss. 'Tis Clan Robertson land. The Earl of Tay's lands are over twenty miles away or more. Over the mountains to the south-east."

Isla showed her how to work the oars and after Sarah placed her wicker basket in the boat, they both pushed it down the shingle into the water. Picking up her skirts and cloak so they wouldn't get soaked, Sarah climbed in and once she was seated, Isla gave the boat another hard shove—and she was away.

The icy water lapped at the sides of the boat and Sarah had to close her eyes for a moment to tamp down a surge of panic. *You won't fall in. You're not going to drown. The shore is not far. You can do this, Sarah Lambert.*

Sarah gripped the oars tightly, leaned forward, then pulled them back toward her chest. The boat moved forward and she released the tight breath she'd been holding. The going was slow and more than once, one of the oars slipped and splashed in the water ineffectually, but within the space of a quarter hour, she'd reached the other side. When the prow of the boat slid onto the shingle, she almost cried with relief.

At long last, she was free.

As Sarah turned back to take one last look at Eilean Dubh, a squall of freezing rain hit so she dashed into the trees to take cover. It was only after she'd reached the end of the wood and gazed out upon the vast stretch of desolate moorland that she realized the strange gripping ache in her chest was…loss. She'd never see Alexander MacIvor again.

Pulling her cloak tightly about her body, she trudged along the rough ground along the river's edge, her vision blurred by mizzling rain.

Not tears.

At least, that's what she tried to tell herself anyway.

Alex cracked open his eyes and groaned when his valet, Gordon, drew back the heavy damask curtains, revealing a miserable day.

"Forgive me, milord, but you said ye did no' wish to sleep away the whole day. That ye wanted to rise by eleven o'clock."

"Aye, I did." Alex dragged himself upright out of the tangled sheets and burgundy silk quilt, ruing the fact he'd drunk far too much whisky last night. His right temple throbbed dully and his mouth was as dry as the Sahara. However, the guilt roiling in his gut was the worst sensation of all. "Might I have some coffee, Gordon?"

"Of course, milord. I hope ye dinna mind, but I took the liberty of bringing up a tray already."

"Excellent, man. Thank you."

As Alex washed down his hearty breakfast of eggs, haggis, and toast with bitter black coffee, he mulled over how he would approach Sarah. He'd pushed her to the brink of desperation and had then grievously insulted her by suggesting she was prostituting herself. She had very good reason to hate him.

He prayed she didn't.

He hadn't wanted to admit it to himself—in fact, he hadn't been able to for days—but he had truly begun to care for Sarah Lambert. Deeply. Perhaps it was wishful thinking on his part, but his gut told him that despite everything he'd done, she had begun to develop feelings for him too. Feelings that went beyond mere physical attraction. During the dark hours of the night, as he'd steadily worked his way through the bottle of whisky, he'd gone over everything she'd said to him during those fraught, passionate minutes in her bedchamber. Hadn't she told him her heart raced just for him...? That she no longer cared for Tay?

He hadn't believed her last night because his own guilt had made him blind to everything else. But oh, he did so want to believe her.

He had to make things right between them.

He had to say he was truly sorry.

He had to take a leap of faith and tell her the truth.

Those three thoughts were uppermost in his mind an hour later as Alex rode the short mile from Blackloch to Eilean Dubh. After he'd tethered his mount to an ancient pine, he made his way through the trees to the shore. MacLagan was supposed to meet him here at noon and ferry him back across to the island.

And then Alex frowned in confusion for there, on the shingle, was the rowboat...but there was no sign of MacLagan who'd always been reliable as clockwork.

What the hell? The skin at Alex's nape prickled. Something was wrong. He could feel it in his bones.

He frantically scanned the surrounding shoreline—the coracle was still in the boatshed where he'd left it last night—then he retreated into the woods from whence he'd come, but there was no sign of the footman or Isla for that matter. Alex hadn't seen either of them on the route from the castle to Eilean Dubh.

So why, in God's name, was the rowboat on the wrong side of the loch?

Alex examined the ground at the edge of the woods—even though sleet and rain had been falling on and off all morning, there were still large patches of snow lying between the trees—and within the space of a few minutes, he found what he'd been looking for. A footprint in the muddy snow.

A small woman's footprint made by a boot. And there were several more farther on.

Devil take him. They had to be Sarah's footprints and she was heading west, straight toward Rannoch Moor. Alex's chest tightened while a volley of questions slammed into his mind thick and fast.

How had she managed to escape? And how long had she been gone? She couldn't have run off last night—she hadn't a key to the garden gate and no boat to row across. And surely MacLagan and Isla would have come back to the castle early this morning to raise the alarm if they'd discovered that Sarah was missing.

But the rowboat was definitely here on the wrong side...

His heart in his mouth, Alex pushed the rowboat out, leapt in, and rowed himself across to the island. Sprinting through the trees he spotted that the gate was open, and on entering the courtyard he discovered MacLagan, out cold and virtually insensible. An empty tankard lay beside him.

Bloody hell.

Alex bolted up the stairs and as he'd expected, the door was wide open. Isla lay slumped on the table, a half-drunk cup of small beer beside her. He took a sip and grimaced. There was a distinct bitter aftertaste. *Laudanum.* Christ, Sarah must have got her hands on his silver flask and laced the beer.

"Isla, wake up, lass." Alex shook her gently. She moaned a little and her eyelids flickered but that was all.

Damn. He couldn't waste time trying to rouse her and MacLagan. Or fetch extra help from Blackloch Castle.

Bandit nudged his leg with his nose, his tail wagging. "You're going to have to help me find Sarah, lad." Alex started for the door. "Come."

Another freezing shower of rain gusted across the loch as Alex rowed with all his might for the shore. As soon as he mounted his horse, he kicked it into a canter. Bandit would keep up. He had no idea how much of a head start Sarah had on him, but he had to find her, and soon. Rannoch Moor was treacherous even in high summer. In this kind of weather, it was deadly.

If anything happened to Sarah Lambert, Alex would never be able to live with himself.

CHAPTER 17

She was in deep trouble.

Sarah had been traversing the bleak moor for well over an hour, perhaps longer, when she came to that heart-sinking realization. Soaked to the bone, shivering with cold, she stood on a small hillock with her arms wrapped around herself, uncertain which way to go.

To her right was a rushing stream, the one Isla had mentioned surely. The water boiled violently between sharp granite rocks. Less than ten yards to her left was nothing but a vast peat bog, which she'd only discovered by accident when her boot had sunk below the spongy ground into a pool of sucking, freezing mud. Born and raised in Northumberland, she knew enough about bogs to realize how perilous they could be, so heading south was clearly out.

Before her was nothing but a great stretch of snow-crusted sedge grass, and in the far distance lay another nameless range of mountains, their peaks obscured by a heavy gray shroud of low-lying cloud. The village Isla had spoken of was nowhere in sight.

Had she taken a wrong turn? Sarah very much doubted it. She'd done exactly as Isla had instructed. At the end of the loch, she'd headed westward in the straightest line she could manage across the rugged ground. The going was slow but she estimated she must have traveled at least three miles by now. Yet nothing indicated the presence of another living soul, let alone a village, anywhere close by. Not even a crofter's cottage. Not even a deer or a bird wheeling on high.

The place was...deserted.

A chill that had nothing to do with the weather snaked its way down Sarah's spine. Had...had Isla deliberately sent her out here in the hope she would get lost? But why would she do that?

She recalled the girl's sullen, judgmental attitude over the last few days, how the young maid always blushed and smiled and stammered in her master's presence. Yes, Isla was clearly smitten with Alexander MacIvor, but would the maid really try to put her, Sarah, in harm's way out of mere spite and jealousy?

Mulling over the reasons why Isla may or may not have given her ill advice wasn't going to help Sarah get out of this situation. And the weather was rapidly deteriorating. The ice-cold rain, which had been falling steadily since she'd set out, had turned to sleet, and Sarah could no longer feel her feet or her fingers. Every breath she exhaled emerged as a frozen white puff of mist. She needed to make a decision about what she would do—whether to keep going forward, or turn back toward Loch Rannoch. Isla had mentioned another village, Kinloch. If she turned back now, she'd hopefully reach it before dark.

But she might also encounter Alexander... Fear knotted Sarah's belly at the thought. He'd taken great pains to convince her that he meant her no harm. And she'd begun to trust him. But what if she'd been wrong? Isla had been adamant he'd been planning to get rid of her. She didn't know who to believe or what to do.

One thing was clear: she couldn't continue standing here in the middle of the moor in the sleeting rain. She'd freeze to death, especially if she didn't reach any kind of shelter before nightfall.

Perhaps if she crossed the stream, the ground on the other side would be firmer. It was nigh impossible to tell without investigating. Telling herself she'd be fine—although the waters were turbulent, the stream was shallow—Sarah carefully picked her way along the rocky edge of the bank until she reached a narrower section. The opposite side was only a few feet away and there was a high, flattish rock in the middle she could use as a stepping-stone.

Picking up her skirts, she drew in a steadying breath and stepped forward. The rock was slick and for a heart-stopping moment she teetered on the edge before regaining her balance. To reach the other bank, she would have to jump. Not wanting to risk falling again, she tossed her sodden basket over and it rolled onto its side, the contents scattering between the rocks and the tussocks of sedge grass beyond. She cursed aloud but at least everything hadn't fallen into the water.

Bending her knees slightly, Sarah counted to three then launched forward, aiming for a flat patch of snowy grass—but as she landed her right foot slipped and with a startled cry she toppled toward the rocks—

Alex wiped the rain from his eyes and halted his horse on the fringes of a peat bog. Bandit, sopping wet and looking for all the world like a giant half-drowned rat, trotted back toward him and barked.

"Please don't tell me she went in that direction, lad." They'd been steadily making their way west across the moor for an hour in an almost dead straight line and with each passing minute, Alex's dread had grown. He knew this countryside as well as the lines and scars on his own hand. If Sarah had strayed into any one of the innumerable bogs or deep crevices of rushing water hidden by the snow... Dear God in heaven, it didn't bear thinking about.

Alex squinted at the barren, frozen wasteland ahead, scanning the near distance, middle ground, then the horizon for any flash of color that wasn't dun brown, gray or white, for any flicker of movement. But he saw nothing and no one. At least he had several more hours of decent light left. Though, as time marched on, the less likely it would be that he would find Sarah before something terrible happened.

Please God, keep her safe.

Bandit snuffled the wet sedge grass a few feet away then barked again.

"All right, lad. I trust you."

Head down and tail up, Bandit started off again, skirting the edge of the bog, heading slightly north-west toward a rocky burn. Alex urged his horse forward, following the dog but at a slower pace, picking the way carefully. He was determined not to miss anything, nor did he want his horse to end up in the bog.

Bandit had gone less than a hundred yards when he stopped at the edge of the burn; tail wagging madly, he barked frantically. And then Alex's heart lurched. Behind an outcrop of rocks on the opposite bank, he glimpsed a patch of bright blue. A streak of dark gold.

Sarah.

Oh, no. Dear Lord, no.

Alex slid from his horse and bolted to the burn. His Sarah lay face down and motionless in a crumpled heap of sodden black and blue wool. An upturned basket lay beside her.

His gut clenching in fear, he leapt to the other side and dropped to his knees. With gentle hands he turned Sarah over and didn't know whether to curse or thank the heavens. She was alive but unconscious; a fair-sized bump and angry red cut marred her forehead, near her temple. The blood had already started to clot. Just as concerning was how cold she was; her face was deathly pale, almost as white as the snow, and her lips and eyelids were blue.

He needed to rouse her and get her warm and dry as fast as possible.

"Sarah. Sarah, lass," Alex called squeezing one of her gloved hands. He gently stroked her cheek with the back of his fingers. "Please wake up."

Her eyelids fluttered and a soft moan escaped from between her bloodless lips. "Black?" Her voice emerged as a mere thread of sound.

"Aye," he smiled. *Black would do.* "I'm here."

"Wh-What happened?" Before he could respond, Sarah's eyes flew open and she stiffened and pushed a hand against his chest as though warding him off. "P-Please. Don't hurt me."

Alex frowned. "Hurt you? Why would I hurt you?"

"Isla said... She t-told me you'd be angry... That I sh-should run...b-because I f-found out..." She grimaced and touched her forehead. "I slipped and fell."

"Yes, you did. And I don't care what Isla told you, I would never hurt you, Sarah. You have no idea how relieved I am that I found you. Can you sit up?"

Sarah's eyes grew bright with tears and her bottom lip trembled. "You've come to take me b-back to Eilean Dubh, haven't you?"

"Not quite but somewhere safe." With an arm around her shoulders, Alex helped Sarah to a sitting position. Then he removed her wet cloak and replaced it with his thicker greatcoat which was still relatively dry inside. Sarah's teeth were chattering and her body quaked with violent shivers.

He was about to ask her if she thought she'd be able to stand when she pulled away from him. "I'm—I'm going to be sick."

Poor lass. As she cast up the meager contents of her stomach, Alex held back her tangled wet hair.

"I'm sorry," she whispered eventually.

"Och, don't be sorry. You've taken a fair knock on the head. It's to be expected." Alex helped Sarah to her feet then he carefully slipped into the burn. Even though it was fast flowing, it was shallow and if he was careful, he wouldn't lose his footing. He beckoned to Sarah. "Come here, lass."

"Wh-What are you doing?" Sarah eyed him doubtfully.

"I'm going to carry you across. Jumping clearly isn't an option."

"I d-don't know."

Alex cocked an eyebrow. "You're really going to argue with me now, Sarah Lambert? I'm standing in a freezing cold burn that's almost up to my knees."

She began to scowl but then winced. "My head hurts t-too much to b-be cross with you."

"Well, that's a consolation of sorts. Come now." He reached out his arms. "I promise I won't drop you."

Holding onto a nearby boulder for support, Sarah took a small step toward the edge of the bank. Heeding his instructions, she then sat down to make it easier for him to scoop her into his arms; he didn't think she'd appreciate being tipped upside-down over his shoulder, not with a head injury at any rate.

When they were both safely on the other side, Sarah's gaze locked with his. "Thank you f-for helping me," she said softly. "You seem to have a gift for getting me out of d-dire scrapes."

Alex smiled. "How could I not? Although I should say Bandit's the real hero. He found you faster than I could have done alone."

The collie had been dancing around their legs, begging for attention, and Sarah bent down to lavish him with a warm hug about the neck.

Lucky wee bastard, thought Alex enviously. When Sarah stood upright again, she clutched Alex's shoulder.

Alarm spiked through him. "Are you all right, lass?"

Sarah put a hand to her head. "J-Just a little d-dizzy...that's all."

"Hmmm. I think it's best if we share my horse. I don't want you falling off." Not waiting for her to respond, Alex lifted her onto the saddle then climbed up behind her. Lashing an arm around her waist to keep her steady, he kicked his horse into a trot. "We'll be back before you know it, Sarah."

She turned her head slightly, her wet curls brushing his cheek. "Back where?"

"I'm going to take you home." Enough was enough. Alex didn't want any more secrets between them. "My *real* home. Blackloch Castle."

~

She was safe. And it was Alexander who'd saved her.

Again.

The relief enveloping Sarah warmed her heart even if the rest of her was half frozen. With Alex's strong arms around her, she at last truly believed she could trust him. He could have left her to die out on Rannoch Moor, but he hadn't. Indeed, in setting out on a search for her, he'd risked his own life.

It made her wonder if he actually was developing some sort of tender regard for her. Perhaps more than she'd ever anticipated.

It also made her wonder what Isla's true agenda was... It was abundantly clear that the young woman had deliberately sent her into the middle of a dangerous wilderness on a wild goose chase. There was no village on Rannoch Moor, Sarah was sure of it.

So many questions and confused thoughts tumbled around in her mind, it made Sarah's head ache all the more. Alex had obviously returned to Eilean Dubh around noon, just as Isla had told her he would. Thank God that he had, otherwise he wouldn't have discovered she'd escaped.

Alex would have seen that MacLagan had been drugged. But what about Isla? She supposed the maid had confessed to her master that she'd run off, but had Isla mentioned her direction was Rannoch Moor? That hardly seemed likely, if Isla bore her ill will.

Thank God Bandit had been able to find her.

A frisson of fear passed through Sarah at the thought of what her fate would have been if Alex hadn't returned to Eilean Dubh when he had. If he'd had second thoughts and changed his mind. If he hadn't searched for her...

Alex must have noticed her shivering again as he tightened his hold about her and murmured against her ear, "Hold on, lass. It won't be long before you're tucked up in bed with a hot chocolate."

Too exhausted to speak, Sarah nodded and leaned back against his wide chest. Isla must have also told him she'd discovered his real identity. Why else would he take her to his home, Blackloch Castle, rather than back to Eilean Dubh? It obviously didn't matter to him that she knew the truth. Instead of being perturbed, he only seemed to be concerned about her comfort and safety.

If she could ever discount the fact he'd kidnapped her, she might be tempted to fall in love with him...

The sleet turned to snow, and as the world turned darker and grayer, Sarah eventually gave up trying to sort out everything in her mind. By the time they reached the main gates to Blackloch Castle, she was shivering uncontrollably and her head throbbed. It took all of her concentration just to stay alert and upright. Thank God Alex held her securely on his mount.

She was barely aware of the castle's well-manicured grounds as Alex steered his horse down a winding oak-lined gravel drive. When they emerged from the trees onto a forecourt, Sarah's breath caught at the sight of Blackloch. It was massive. And beautiful. Through the swirling snow, she caught a brief glimpse of gray brickwork covered in ivy, towering turrets, and crenelated walls. Before she could blink, they were passing through an arched barbican passage into a large courtyard.

Alex gave a shout for assistance as he reined in his horse, and almost immediately a gaggle of servants emerged from various directions—stablehands, a pair of liveried footmen, several maids.

And Aileen.

The woman gave her a brusque nod but Sarah didn't have time to acknowledge her greeting, such as it was, because Alex dismounted and carefully lifted her down from the horse. As soon as Sarah's feet touched the ground, a great wave of dizziness assailed her. Dark spots danced before her eyes and her knees buckled.

In a flash, Alex swept her up into his arms. "You need to stop giving me frights like this, lass," he admonished as he carried her across the flagged courtyard toward a wide-open door. "You'll be the death of me."

Sarah closed her eyes and rested her cheek against Alex's shoulder. Even though his tone was light, she detected an underlying current of tension in his voice. "S-S-Sorry," she whispered, her teeth chattering so much she could hardly speak.

To her surprise, she felt the brush of Alex's lips on her temple. "Don't be. Just be well, that's all I ask of you."

I'll try. With each passing moment, fatigue pulled Sarah toward sleep. Even forming words seemed an effort. She had a brief impression of Alex carrying her up a wide set of stairs then into a vast bedchamber with heavy oak furniture and dark red curtains. Then darkness claimed her.

~

Christ. Sarah had lapsed into unconsciousness. Except for the angry red gash on her temple, her face was as white as the fine linen sheets on his tester bed.

Fighting a rising wave of panic, Alex called for Aileen who'd been hovering near the doorway of his bedchamber with two of the housemaids. "We need to get Miss Lambert undressed."

He placed Sarah gently on the bed and began tugging off her muddy leather boots.

"Sir," protested Aileen, rushing forward. "Ye canna be doing this. 'Tis not proper."

"I don't give a fig about what's proper, woman." Alex gently rolled Sarah over and eased his sopping wet greatcoat off her. "Not when Miss Lambert's life hangs in the balance."

Aileen planted her hands on her hips. "Fiona, Moira, and I will manage. In fact, we will work faster if ye will just step oot of the way. A man isna much help in a sickroom. Besides, ye need to get warm and dry yerself."

Alex couldn't argue with that. Reluctantly he stepped away and the women descended like a flock of mother hens. "I want warming pans in that bed," he called over his shoulder, heading for the adjoining dressing room. "She'll need dry towels—and you can dress Miss Lambert in one of my nightshirts for now."

A short time later, Alex—attired in a quilted silk banyan—returned to find Sarah had been tucked up in his bed, the covers pulled up to her chin. The housemaid, Fiona, had just pushed a warming pan beneath the burgundy silk counterpane and sheets, and Aileen was wringing out a washcloth in a basin of water on the bedside table.

"The lass's heid needs attending to," she murmured, gently dabbing around Sarah's wound; it had started to bleed again but whilst the cut was about an inch long, it was shallow. A purple bruise had begun to flower around the area.

"I'll do that."

Aileen scowled as he took the cloth from her, but she didn't argue with him. "If ye dinna mind my asking, sir, what happened?"

Alex lowered his voice so the other maids wouldn't hear. Only his most trusted servants at Blackloch—Aileen, Isla, MacLagan, and Dobson—knew who Sarah was and the situation on Eilean Dubh. "Sarah escaped but took a wrong turn and ended up lost on Rannoch Moor."

"What? Is Isla all right? And MacLagan?"

"They are both fine, but send Dobson out to get them. The rowboat is on the Blackloch side. And get Isla to bring some of Miss Lambert's clothes." He didn't want to go into details right now. "I need some linen bandages. And something hot to drink. Coffee for me.

Perhaps hot chocolate for the lass." *If she wakes up.* Sarah hadn't stirred at all since she'd fainted in his arms. And now her breathing was unnaturally shallow and rapid. He didn't like it. Not one little bit.

"Aye, sir." Aileen touched his arm in an uncharacteristic display of tenderness. "She will recover, milord," she whispered.

"I hope you are right, Aileen."

Fiona and Moira soon finished their fussing and disappeared, and after Aileen delivered the bandages and drinks he'd requested, the door closed and he was left alone with Sarah.

With great care, Alex wound a linen bandage around her head before he collapsed into a bedside wingchair. As he quietly sipped his coffee, he watched Sarah; her pallor and the blueness around her lips persisted even though she was tucked up tightly. She'd stopped shivering but that didn't ease his fear. In fact, she seemed *too* still.

Putting down his cup, he reached out and touched her cheek. Dear God, she was cold.

This wasn't good. Somehow, he had to do something else to warm her up.

But what? Short of moving her closer to the fire, which was already roaring, he couldn't think of a single thing.

Unless...

Praying silently to Sarah for forgiveness for what he was about to do, Alex crossed to the other side of the bed and slipped beneath the covers. His silk banyan was cool to the touch so he opened it and very carefully drew Sarah into his arms until her back was against his bare torso with his leg draped over hers.

Pressing his face into her tangled, damp hair, he whispered another prayer, this time to heaven. If anything happened to her... His throat constricted and he closed his eyes and hugged Sarah tighter.

Because for the very first time in such a long time, his heart remembered and welcomed the bittersweet pain that came with being in love. And that something—that *someone*—was more important to him now than revenge.

CHAPTER 18

She was warm. Deliciously warm.

And comfortable. Swathed in soft fabrics. Her head cradled by a down pillow.

With a sigh, Sarah turned over and a flash of pain in her forehead made her wince. And then reality crashed through the haze of sleep. Her eyes flew open. She wasn't alone.

Oh, my goodness... She was lying in Alexander's arms in a strange bed.

His bed at Blackloch Castle.

A vague memory of Alex carrying her into this room emerged from the cloud of confusion in her mind. She'd been so very cold and her head ached because of her fall on Rannoch Moor.

She reached up to touch her forehead. Someone had bandaged the wound. And someone had dressed her in a man's cambric nightshirt and put her to bed.

Alex?

The light in the room was muted and gray, as though snow fell outside, but there was enough for her to see Alex's face. Sleep softened his harshly handsome features and she only just resisted the urge to trace her fingertips along the blade of his nose, his slashing eyebrows as dark as charcoal, his high cheekbones. To brush the tousled black wing of hair away from his eyelids. Once again, he reminded her of a fallen angel. Beautiful yet dangerous. It didn't help that her body was pressed against his. His hot, hard, practically naked body. Aside from a silk robe that was splayed wide open, he wore nothing but linen smallclothes.

It made Sarah think of all manner of sinful things that a young, unwed woman most definitely shouldn't. Like touching the wide planes of his chest with its intriguing scattering of dark hair. Or kissing the strong line of his neck where his pulse beat. The sharp line of his jaw, shadowed with dark stubble.

His mouth.

Her lips tingled at the memory of his kisses last night. On her own mouth. Her bared breast. When Malcolm had kissed her, it had never felt like that. So intense. So arousing.

So right.

Shocked at the waywardness of her thoughts, she silently berated herself. *Stop it, Sarah. You should not be entertaining such wanton notions. It's not as though you need to try and seduce Alex any longer. It's not as though he wants to seduce you either. He's had ample opportunity, but so far he has refused you.*

What did he say last night? That what you offered wasn't honest and true?

In a way, he'd been right. But it didn't lessen the sting of his words.

So why *was* she in Alexander MacIvor's bed? Whatever his reason, it must be a sound one.

A gilded clock upon the mantelpiece softly chimed the hour—four o'clock in the afternoon. Sarah carefully slid from the bed and held onto the bedpost for a moment. Her body felt sore and bruised in odd places but her light-headedness seemed to have abated, so she tiptoed across the Turkish rug in search of Alex's dressing room. Once inside, she found the necessary stool behind a silk screen and because the room was chilly, she borrowed one of Alex's banyans—a dark blue velvet robe. Wrapping it around herself, she hoped he wouldn't mind. But then, wasn't she already wearing one of his nightshirts?

Before she returned to the main chamber, she caught sight of herself

Sarah blinked as though emerging from a dream. "Sorry. What did you say? I still can't quite believe you just said you'd let me go."

"Well, I did and I mean it." *Poor lass.* Alex didn't blame her for not quite believing her ears. He slid from the bed, pulled his banyan closed, and went to the door. After issuing directions to a footman lurking outside, he returned to Sarah. "I promised you hot chocolate on our way back to Blackloch and you haven't had any yet."

Sarah's eyes shone with warmth. "That's very true."

"Well, I'm a man of my word."

She caught his hand and smiled. "Yes, I'm beginning to see that."

Alex's chest swelled. If he weren't about to bare his soul to Sarah, he would be tempted to kiss her. Her thoughts must have run the same way as her gaze dipped to his mouth, but he knew if they started kissing he wouldn't want to stop.

No, there would be no more kisses until Sarah truly wanted him for all the right reasons. He wouldn't take what she couldn't freely give.

Instead, he dropped a gentle buss on her forehead then retreated to the fireside and threw a few more logs into the grate. Sparks flew and the flames leapt high reminding him of that devastating day, almost eleven years ago, when he'd watched Blackloch burn. When he'd watched his dreams and everything and everyone he'd held dear turn to ashes.

His fingers curled into his palm and he felt the ridge of the scar he'd made years before when he'd vowed bloody vengeance on Tay. Curling his fist tighter, the band of the gold and onyx ring cut into his ring finger. He'd never shared his story with anyone. He'd never trusted anyone enough.

Until now.

Christ, he was going to need a drink or ten to get through this.

With that in mind, he crossed the plush Turkish rug to an oak cabinet and with a shaking hand, poured a sizable dram of whisky into a cut-glass tumbler. He downed it then poured another.

Lost in his thoughts, he didn't realize Sarah had drawn close until he heard the creak of a floorboard and the soft rustle of fabric. Turning his head, he found she'd moved to one of the brocade-upholstered settees by the fireside. She'd curled her legs beneath her and his blue velvet robe covered everything except her ankle and one pale slender foot. The nightshirt she wore gaped at the neck and the creamy swell of one of her breasts taunted him.

Alex gulped at his whisky again. Sweet Jesus, she was temptation itself. He'd be hard pressed to string a coherent sentence together, let alone tell his story with her looking so utterly delectable. Despite his resolve not to seduce her, his desire was as acute as ever. Although it was entirely wrong of him, part of him wasn't the least bit sorry for stealing Sarah away from Tay. "Can I get you something? A sherry perhaps?" he asked in a voice that was far from smooth. "Or a blanket?"

She shook her head. "No, thank you. I'm quite warm enough. And I'm happy to wait for the hot chocolate."

At that moment, there was a knock at the bedroom door. To save Sarah further scrutiny from his understandably curious staff, Alex put down his whisky glass and went to answer it. As he took the silver tray from the housemaid Fiona, she bobbed a curtsy. "Will that be all, Mr. Price?"

"Yes. Thank you."

He felt the weight of Sarah's curious stare even before he turned around.

"Price? You're also known as Alexander *Price*?"

Alex returned to the fireside and placed the tray on a low, polished table in front of the settee and the wingback chairs. He raised his eyes to Sarah's as he passed her a steaming cup of hot chocolate. "Yes."

"My goodness, you're a complicated man." She arched a brow. "So what should I call you? Lord Rannoch or Mr. Price? Certainly not Mr. Black. Although, I must say, it does suit you."

He took a seat in a brown leather wingchair and retrieved his whisky. "I like it when you call me Alex. But in the presence of everyone else, it's probably best if you refer to me as Mr. Price. For now."

"Mr. Price it is." Sarah studied him over the rim of her cup as she took a delicate sip of her hot chocolate. "I suppose you're going to tell me why you do not wish to be addressed as Lord Rannoch?"

"Aye, I am." Alex contemplated his whisky before swallowing another mouthful. His heart had begun to thud uncomfortably. His mouth was dry. It was not like him to be nervous, but he couldn't help but wonder how Sarah would react to everything he was about to tell her. Not only was he about to entrust her with his deepest secrets, but he was also going to shock her.

Nothing would be the same for either of them after this conversation.

He drew a steadying breath and looked Sarah in the eye. "Did you know Lord Tay fought in the Rebellion? The Forty-five? For King George."

"Yes I did. Father told me he commanded one of the Campbell regiments." Sarah frowned at him. "Did you fight as well?"

"Yes" Alex held her gaze. "But not for George. For James Stuart. I followed his son Charles, the Young Pretender into battle."

Comprehension lit Sarah's eyes. "You're a Jacobite," she whispered.

"Aye."

"Heavens..." Sarah put down her cup very carefully. "And now you are using a false name which means..." Her frown deepened. "You haven't been pardoned yet, have you? You're a wanted man. Wanted for treason."

It sounded even worse, said softly in her dulcet tones. Alex tapped his nose. "You're a canny lass."

"If you are still wanted, then how...?" Sarah gestured around the room. "Blackloch Castle is your home and somehow you've managed to become the laird again. You're a veritable phoenix. I cannot imagine how you've achieved such a thing."

"How I was able to reinvent myself is...rather a long story. But I have. Now most of Society, both in Scotland and farther afield, know me as Alexander Price, the new Laird of Blackloch. Only a handful of people—people I trust implicitly—know who I really am. Know my past."

Sarah inclined her head. "Then I am honored you are taking me into your confidence."

"I have debated with myself long and hard about sharing my history with you, and my history with Lord Tay—" He broke off and took another sip of his whisky to fortify himself for his next disclosure. "Are you sure you don't want something stronger to drink than hot chocolate, Sarah?"

Her eyebrows drew together. "I don't think I like the sound of that. But I'll have a sherry, if you think it will help."

"I do."

Alex poured a decent amount of Spanish sherry into a crystal glass, and after taking a sip, Sarah fastened him with a look that was both determined and grave. "What happened, Alex? Tell me everything. I'm dying to know."

CHAPTER 19

Alex took a seat beside Sarah on the settee and she tried to calm her frantically beating heart as he began his tale.

"The MacIvors of Rannoch and Campbells of Tays have long been rivals," he said, his expression wry. "Reiving each other's cattle. The odd skirmish here and there over adjacent territory. My father and Malcolm's, Angus, the former Earl of Tay, were involved in a legal dispute over a parcel of land about seventeen years ago. And I'd had the dubious pleasure of meeting Malcolm, about a year before the Rebellion broke out. We played several rounds of faro at a club in Edinburgh, and he was none too pleased when I trounced him." A sardonic smile twisted Alex's mouth. "In fact, he threatened to call me out for cheating, but I didn't take the bait. I had better things to do than fight a preening coxcomb like him. He'd recently inherited his father's title and was full of bluster and bravado. I suppose it was inevitable that we would be on opposite sides of the Rebellion."

"Did you fight against Malcolm?" Sarah asked quietly.

"No, I never met him on the battlefield. Although I wished to God I had. Then he wouldn't have..." Alex swallowed and pinched the bridge of his nose

The anguish in his voice sent a frisson of apprehension through Sarah. "Then he wouldn't have what?"

Alex raised his head and met her gaze. "Have you heard about the Battle of Culloden? On Drumossie Moor."

"Yes. Your side was defeated."

"We were slaughtered," said Alex, his tone rough with both anger and grief.

Sarah touched a hand to her throat. "You were there?" she whispered.

"Aye."

"I can't even begin to fathom what that must have been like." From what she'd heard, it was a miracle anyone had survived. The English, under the command of "Butcher" Cumberland, had crushed the Jacobite army in the space of an hour. It wasn't a battle. It was a massacre.

Alex wiped a hand down his face before continuing. "My father, Lachlan MacIvor, the sixth Baron Rannoch and our chief, led out the clan after Charles Edward Stuart raised the standard at Glenfinnan. Two hundred and ten men strong we were. We joined the Jacobite army on the eve of the Battle of Gladsmuir. By the time the Jacobite forces gathered to fight at Drumossie Moor, our contingent of Clan MacIvor men had been reduced to less than half that. After Culloden, I was the only man from our clan left standing."

"Oh, my God, Alex. All those men... And your father, he was killed too?"

"Aye. He was shot... And so was I. In the thigh." Alex rubbed his right leg and stared off into the fire. A muscle worked in his jaw. "I really don't know how I managed to get away, but somehow I did... God, it was awful."

Sarah wanted to reach out and touch him, to offer comfort, but he seemed so tense and withdrawn, she wasn't sure how he would respond. Instead, she waited, sipping her sherry, trying to ignore the knots in her belly and the odd flutter of her heart.

Eventually Alex continued. "As I mentioned, I didn't meet Malcolm Campbell on the battlefield, but I knew the Campbells of Tay were present at Culloden. At any rate, after I escaped the horrors of Drumossie Moor, I made my way back here to Blackloch. You see, my mother, my younger sister, and my *fiancée* were here. I thought they might need me. With most of the clansmen gone, they'd been left to fend for themselves."

"You...you were engaged?" whispered Sarah. "To be married?"

"Aye." Alex's mouth curved into a bittersweet smile. "To a sweet lass named Maggie Stewart. She came to live at Blackloch when she was sixteen and I was eighteen. She was pretty and lively and I was thoroughly enchanted by her. Her father, Lord Comyn, was a distant cousin on my father's side. When Lord Comyn passed away, she became my father's ward. I proposed to her right before we left to join the Jacobite army. If I hadn't gone..." He shook his head as though lanced by so much unspeakable pain he couldn't go on.

"You weren't to know the Jacobite cause would fail. Or that Culloden would be a rout. And how could you not support your father?"

"Aye. You speak sense but it doesn't ease the guilt." Alex sighed and rubbed his thigh again as though it still pained him. "My leg injury slowed me down so it took me well over a week to ride the ninety miles from Culloden to Blackloch. There were times when I'd had to lie low to avoid being captured by patrolling dragoons, or make a detour through remote countryside. There were times when I could barely sit in the saddle. To be honest, most of that period is a nightmarish blur. But somehow, I made it back home. Only...only when I got here, it was to discover that Lord Tay and his men, en route to Taymoor Castle, had arrived first."

Oh, no. Oh, dear God no.

Alex's eyes met hers. "Sarah, I don't know if you've heard much about the reprisals disloyal clans suffered after Culloden, but Cumberland encouraged his men and those clans loyal to King George to give no quarter to any Jacobite, or to any folk who'd supported the cause. The abuses were widespread. The acts committed, reprehensible...barbaric. And I'm afraid Lord Tay was more than happy to lend a hand."

"What did he do?" Sarah's voice was little more than a whisper.

"Aileen has told me that she was with my mother when Lord Tay and his men arrived to subdue the 'traitorous and troublesome MacIvors' once and for all. She'd been settling a dispute between two clanswomen in the Great Hall. Apparently my ten-year-old sister, Anne, was with Maggie in the garden behind the castle, picking roses. My mother believed she could reason with Lord Tay—after all, she was Lady Rannoch, a baroness."

"She sounds like a remarkable woman," murmured Sarah.

Alex gave a decided nod. "Aye, she was indeed. Fearless and intelligent, she'd been acting as clan chief and managing the estate in my father's absence. She...she was selfless to the very last. Before Tay entered the Hall, she ordered the clanswomen and Aileen, who was Blackloch's housekeeper, to take Isla—only nine years old at the time—to hide in the priest hole below the main staircase. She sent one of the male servants out to the gardens to find Anne and Maggie."

"I had no idea Aileen had been in your service for such a long time."

"Dobson too. He and Aileen are married. Isla is his daughter."

Sarah blinked in genuine surprise. "Oh, I didn't know that either," she said. "But, please go on. I've interrupted you."

Alex reached for her hand and the sense of foreboding that gripped Sarah made the hair rise on the back of her neck.

"Aileen said that my mother..." Alex paused and blew out a breath. "My mother ordered Lord Tay to leave but he merely laughed. And then Aileen heard her scream and beg for mercy. But he didn't heed her. He—" Alex wiped a tear from the corner of his eye. "He raped my mother. And when he was done with her, he ran her through with his sword."

"Oh, my God." A wave of horror washed through Sarah. Her stomach roiled as her hand fluttered to her face. "How could he? That's...that's appalling. Abominable."

Alex's mouth twisted. "Aye."

Sarah's eyes swam with tears. *What could one say to such a horrifying yet heartbreaking tale?* "Oh, Alex. I am so, so sorry."

"'Tis not your fault, lass. The problem with blood lust is that once it rampages through a man's veins, it's hard to stem the flow. I cannot say for sure, but I think Tay got a taste for inflicting pain and killing on the battlefield, and once he was given permission by Cumberland to run amuck, he couldn't stop."

Not wanting to hear the rest, but knowing she would not be satisfied until she knew everything, Sarah asked in a shaky whisper, "What else did he do, Alex? If you can bear to tell me. This must be so difficult for you. To talk about this."

Alex's mouth twisted with a grim smile. "I can stand it, Sarah. The telling is not as bad as living through it."

Sarah nodded, but her heart clenched with anguish all the same.

"So..." Alex threw back the rest of his whisky and wiped his mouth with the back of his hand. A hand that shook. "Aileen tells me she hid in the priest hole for well over an hour, perhaps two, covering Isla's ears. Although, poor woman, she heard everything that went on. Apparently, Tay gave his men carte blanche to do whatever they wanted to with the servants, both men and women. And then eventually, she smelled smoke. She thinks it was about that time I stumbled upon the scene."

"Oh, Alex."

"Before I even saw Blackloch, I knew something was wrong because I smelled smoke in the air too. Tay had set the castle on fire. The east wing. I dismounted in the woods not far from the edge of the loch and skirted the edge of the trees. My injured leg slowed me down but there wasn't much I could do about it. As I approached, I could hear screams and cries. But worse than that, the sound of men laughing and shouting as...as if they were making merry. It was the sound of hell."

Sarah held her breath. While she dreaded to hear the rest, she would listen to whatever Alex disclosed. "I can't even imagine what you witnessed," she murmured. "Or how you managed to survive."

Alex bent his head as though the weight of his nightmarish memories was too much. "I don't know either. I still have no idea how many of Tay's men were there. Too many, at any rate. And I was just one man. A wounded man. But the blood lust took hold of me too. I'd lost my musket on the battlefield but I still had my sword and my dirk. I cut my way through as many bastards as I could until I reached the Great Hall and...and my mother."

Alex closed his eyes. His shoulders heaved with emotion and Sarah watched his furious expression bleed into grief. "When I saw her...just lying there on the flagstones with her eyes open but unseeing...the gaping wound in her belly, I couldn't move, Sarah. And then like the Devil himself, Tay appeared out of the smoke, heading for the door. Heading toward *me*. Blackloch's main wing was also burning by then, and he was coughing, but as soon as he laid eyes on me, despite my putrid state, he knew me. I lunged toward him, but I hadn't seen the pistol in his hand. And he shot me. In the shoulder. I don't remember much after that... When I fell, I hit my head on the flagstones and was knocked out cold."

Tears misted Sarah's eyes. How could she have ever fancied herself in love with Malcolm? He was an evil, depraved man. "You're lucky you weren't killed," she whispered.

Alex nodded. "Aileen told me later that she'd recognized my voice—apparently I'd shouted at Tay, though I have no memory of it. After she heard the shot, then nothing else, she waited another five, perhaps ten minutes before emerging from the priest's hole. Tay and his men had gone so she was able to get Isla out safely, and then she and the clanswomen pulled me out of the Great Hall before it began to burn."

"Blackloch still stands, though. How was it saved?"

"Heaven must have taken pity at long last," said Alex, "as rain began to pour down, extinguishing most of the blaze so some of the castle was spared. The west wing and some sections of the main keep. After I had established myself as Alexander Price, I was able to purchase the forfeited estate. Over the past five years, I've had the castle rebuilt."

Sarah's throat tightened with a surge of overwhelming emotion—a potent mixture of sorrow and admiration and aching tenderness. "You've accomplished so much in the face of such tragedy and terrible loss, Alex. I'm in awe."

His mouth twitched with the ghost of a smile. "Thank you. Although, I will not lie, lass. It hasn't been easy."

Drawing a shaky breath, Sarah asked the question she knew would perhaps give this remarkable man the most pain. But she had to know. "At the risk of upsetting you further, may I ask what became of your sister...and Maggie, your *fiancée*?"

With an abruptness that startled her, Alex stood and strode over to the drinks cabinet to pour himself another measure of whisky.

Guilt cramped Sarah's heart. "I'm sorry. I ask too much of you."

"No. It's all right." Alex returned to his seat. "You have a right to know all this, too. I hesitate because of the pain you must feel, Sarah. It must be harrowing indeed to hear the man you were to wed is capable of such horrific things."

"It...it is. But I think it's important I learn the truth," said Sarah. She clenched her fists, bracing herself to hear the rest of Alex's horrifying, heartbreaking history. "No matter how terrible."

"Aye." A crease appeared between Alex's brows and his gray eyes glistened. "My poor little sister, my bonnie Anne, she'd been run through too. Dobson—he'd been conducting business in the village of Kinloch, about ten miles away, when everything happened—he found her in the rose garden later on. Alone."

Sarah could hardly make her lips move. "And Maggie?"

Alex's throat worked in an audible swallow. "Tay's men had dragged her into a copse of trees and had...had used her. I don't know how many, or if Tay participated in her brutalization, but when they were done with her, someone slit her throat."

"Oh, dear God." Bile rose in Sarah's throat; horror and grief and anger coursed through her veins, made her heart pound so hard, she could hear the beat of it in her ears. *How could I not have known... Could I not have seen Malcolm for who he truly is?*

A monster in truth.

The Devil himself.

Those hands that had touched her, they had committed acts too foul and unjust to think of. Those lips that had whispered sweet words of wooing, lips that had kissed her, had issued depraved orders, commanding men to defile and murder innocents.

She reached out and clasped Alex's hand. "Words cannot express what I feel right now," she whispered in a voice choked with tears. "No wonder you hate him so. I hate him too."

Alex cupped her cheek and gently brushed her tears away with his thumb. "I know I could have come to you at Linden Hall months ago to tell you all this, instead of kidnapping you, and ransoming you to hurt Tay. But I didn't know if you would believe me. Not only that, because I'm a wanted man, I couldn't risk sharing my past with you—not until I knew you'd understand what was at stake."

Sarah covered his hand with hers. "You can trust me, Alex. I won't betray your secrets."

His gaze grew dark. Troubled. He withdrew his hand. "You have every right to condemn me, Sarah. I've been consumed with dark, bloody anger for so long, I'm afraid I've become that which I despise."

"No." Sarah shook her head in denial. "No, you are not like Malcolm. Don't you dare think it. Not for a minute."

Anguish flashed in Alex's eyes. "But in the process of exacting my pound of flesh, I've hurt you."

"I will heal. And I completely understand your need to avenge those you loved. I forgive you, Alexander MacIvor," said Sarah, her voice firm with conviction. "With all my heart, I forgive you."

Alex's wide mouth curved into a soft smile. "God knows, I don't deserve your forgiveness, but I thank you."

Sarah's pulse began to race. Perhaps it was the effect of Alex's smile. Perhaps it was because his firm leg was pressed against hers and they were both barely dressed. Perhaps it was because his warm gaze made her feel cherished. Whatever the reason, she couldn't deny what was in her heart any longer. Not to herself, and most definitely not to him. "You said earlier that once I'd heard the truth, you'd set me free and I could choose what would happen next."

"Yes, I did." Alex focused his attention on her mouth before his gaze returned to meet hers. "And what is that, Sarah Lambert? What do you choose?"

The flare of heat in his eyes gave Sarah courage. His invitation was clear. Raising her hand, she brushed her fingertips along Alex's strong jaw before leaning closer. Her mouth hovered a breath away from his. "I choose this," she whispered. "I choose you." And then she kissed him.

As her lips touched Alex's, he growled deep in his throat and captured Sarah's face with his hands. Tilting her head, he angled his mouth over hers, claiming her as his own. His hot, hungry tongue swept over her lips and she opened for him, inviting him to delve inside with a beckoning flicker of her own tongue.

With a groan, Alex tasted her completely and the flavor of whisky filled her mouth, intoxicating her, scattering all thought. Nothing existed, nothing except the silken slide of Alex's lips and the velvet, swirling caress of his tongue. Desire heated her blood, made her bold, and Sarah slipped her hands inside Alex's robe seeking the sleek, hard flesh beneath. Her fingers splayed over his heavy pectoral muscles and she felt his nipples pebble beneath her palms. A maddening pulse, low in her belly, had her shifting uneasily in her seat.

Perhaps sensing her need, Alex slid her onto his lap and she felt the welcome evidence of his own arousal; his silk robe had fallen open and the press of his thick member against her thigh couldn't be concealed by his linen smallclothes. Curious, she boldly slid her hand downwards to cup the hot, hard length of him, and he sucked in a breath, breaking the kiss.

"You are not at all shy, my sweet," he murmured thickly.

She bit her lip, suddenly uncertain that she'd gone too far, that she'd shocked him. "Does that bother you?'

Alex's smile was pure lust. "Not at all. I love how fearless you are. How wild. I have another secret to confess." He pressed his lips to her ear. "You are driving me wild too."

He pushed the blue velvet robe off her shoulders then buried his face in her neck, his mouth nuzzling and nipping, his rough stubble grazing her flesh. Hot shivers danced over Sarah's skin as his tongue traced along the line of her collarbone. When his lips fastened around one of her nipples and he suckled her through the cambric of his night-shirt, molten pleasure blasted through her.

Breathless with want, barely able to speak, Sarah tugged on the silky black tresses of his unbound hair. "Alex."

He mistook her desperate plea for more as uncertainty, immediately raising his head. "How far do you want to take this, Sarah?" he said, his voice low and rough as his eyes, a dark burning gray, searched hers. "We can stop at any time."

"No. I don't want to stop." She swallowed, her mouth suddenly dry. Her bravado was faltering. "I want..." Dare she admit what she truly wanted? How she really felt? What if he didn't believe her? What if he thought her feelings weren't genuine? They'd been at this point before and he'd rejected her. She didn't think she could bear it if he did so again; not when her heart pounded for him. Not when her body ached for him.

Alex seemed to recognize the reason for her hesitation. "I've made you doubt me." He stroked the hair back from her face. "And I'm to blame." He tilted her chin up, trapping her gaze. "Would it help if I told you I'm mad for you? That I think I have been since the moment I first saw you at Kenmuir House? But what I feel now, it's more than lust. Being the blind fool that I am, I didn't realize it until I almost lost you today. I've...I've fallen hopelessly in love with you, Sarah. And even though it's unlikely that you could possibly feel the same—"

Sarah pressed a finger to his lips. Tears filled her eyes and joy flooded her heart. "But I do. I love you too."

Alex's voice was a shocked whisper. "Truly?"

Sarah smiled through her tears. *This is what love is meant to feel like.* "Yes. Truly."

"Say you'll be mine, Sarah Lambert."

"Alexander MacIvor, I'm yours."

With a triumphant growl, Alex lifted her and crossed the room to the bed. After laying her on the pillows, he swiftly shed his robe and undergarments and stood before her in all his naked glory.

Sarah's gaze traveled over him, noting the pucker of angry red scars on his left shoulder and on his right thigh—but they did nothing to mar his rampant male beauty. He was lean and well-muscled, and her fingers itched to explore every inch of his hard flesh —including his impressively erect member rising proudly from a tangled nest of black hair. She supposed she should have found the sight of his fearsome cockstand intimidating, but she didn't. If anything, the heavy ache to have him between her thighs, filling her, intensified.

She reached out a hand. "Come to bed," she whispered but Alex shook his head.

"Not until you are naked too, my sweet."

A strange nervous thrill skittered through Sarah as she rose to her knees and shrugged off Alex's robe. She'd never been naked in front of a man before, but whilst the maidenly part of her quailed, the reckless, wanton part of her wanted to do this. As she grasped the hem of the nightshirt, and lifted it to her waist, she could have sworn Alex held his breath. And then she closed her eyes and wrenched it off.

When Sarah ventured a glance at Alex again, this time she felt nothing but a deep thrill of satisfaction. His eyes, heavy-lidded and dark with need, raked over her, devouring her. Such a heady sensation, to feel so desired, so treasured.

Before she could utter a word, Alex pushed her onto the bed and slid over her, hovering on his forearms, the thick cords of muscles in his arms tense and bulging. The furnace like heat of his body set her own skin aflame. The hard heavy length of his manhood pressing against her lower belly sent her need spiraling.

"I want to touch you." Sarah's hands grasped his biceps and wrapped around the bunched muscles. Her fingertips traveled over the hard planes of his chest, exploring the light whorls of dark hair. His tight bronze nipples. She ventured lower, tracing along the line of a rib. The ridges of muscle along his abdomen.

Alex watched her the whole time she played, an indulgent yet hungry wolf. Until her fingers curled around the rigid yet velvet smooth shaft of his cockstand...then a sharp hiss escaped him. "Careful, lass. If you keep touching me like that, you'll make me come off too soon."

"I'm sorry. I didn't mean—"

He hushed her with a searing kiss. "It's all right. I just want to pleasure you first, before seeking my release."

"Pleasure me? That sounds positively wonderful and wicked at the same time."

His mouth kicked into a sinful smile as his hand found one of her breasts. "Aye. It is. Just you wait and see."

Alex lowered his head and flicked his tongue over her nipple, and she gasped, arching into him. His mouth curved into a smile before he swirled his tongue around and around the tight peak then gently surrounded it with his lips, suckling delicately. All the while, he plucked and rolled her other nipple with his fingers. Delicious tremors shot through her, all the way to her most secret place—the place that now throbbed with sharp arousal and was slick with desire.

Brimming with restless energy, Sarah parted her legs beneath Alex and instinctively tilted her hips so her sex brushed against his shaft. A low growl vibrated in Alex's throat and he transferred his mouth to her other breast. His wicked ministrations were maddening and it wasn't long before Sarah was writhing beneath him.

"Please," she whispered, as she scraped her nails down Alex's strong back. She didn't know what she wanted exactly but she was sure Alex could give her what she craved.

He kissed her mouth again and rolled alongside her. At the same time, his hand skimmed down her belly and ruffled the curls hiding her mound before slipping between her thighs. "Is this want you want, Sarah?" he whispered as one of his long fingers caressed the damp seam of her sex. "Do you want me to touch you here?"

"Yes." She parted her legs and pushed against his questing finger. "Yes please." Desperation made her bold.

"Your wish is my command, sweetheart." Alex slid his finger between her wet folds and pressed against something—a small nub she'd barely ever noticed—that made her gasp with pleasure.

"Oh," she whispered, head spinning.

"Oh indeed." Alex lay on his side, his weight on one elbow, watching her face. His finger teased the same exquisitely sensitive spot, circling, stroking, mercilessly flicking, fanning the flames of her desire. Closing her eyes, she clutched at Alex's shoulder and rocked against his hand, panting, craving, wanting something wonderful that just lay out of reach.

Alex's mouth covered hers and as he kissed her, everything inside her pulled tight...and a bright burst of pulsating pleasure swept through her, carrying her away on a glorious wave to a place of blissful satisfaction the like of which she'd never known before.

When she opened her eyes, Alex was smiling down at her, his gray eyes soft and warm. "So, was it both wonderful and wicked?'

Sarah smiled back. "Yes. You know it was."

"Good." Alex moved over her. Taking his weight on his forearms, he settled himself between her parted thighs. "Let's see if we can find pleasure together."

～

Sarah brushed the tousled hair back from his brow. "I would love that," she whispered.

A surge of tenderness flooded Alex's heart. Even though his cock pulsated with need, and he would like nothing more than to bury himself to the balls in Sarah's liquid heat, he wanted to make sure her first time was enjoyable. "I'm afraid this will hurt at first, lass," he warned as he used one hand to position himself between her drenched folds.

"I can bear it. I want you inside me. I want to be yours in truth."

Alex groaned. Dear God, her words would have him spending before he'd even entered her. He dropped a kiss on her sweet lips. "I want that too, my love. I will be as gentle as I can."

A small crease appeared between Sarah's brows as the head of his cock pressed against her entrance. She closed her eyes as he tilted his hips forward and pushed farther in. She was so very tight, and hot and wet. As he rocked forward again, her breath caught and her frown deepened. Her fingernails dug into his back.

"I'm sorry," Alex whispered, withdrawing a fraction.

She opened her eyes and offered a reassuring smile. "I'm fine. It's not pain as such. I...I just felt a burning pinch and then...very full."

"Are you sure?"

"Yes."

"All right then." Gritting his teeth against the overwhelming urge to pound into her mindlessly, Alex surged forward again then groaned with pleasure as the satiny heat of Sarah's sex completely enveloped him. Beneath him, Sarah's body tensed, but as he rained gentle kisses across her brow and her cheeks, she released a soft sigh.

"Ready for more, lass?"

She slid her hands to his tightly bunched buttocks. "Yes please."

Alex slid out ever so slowly then on a smooth glide, thrust back into her welcoming warmth. The tight clasp of her inner sheath about his throbbing length was indescribable. Lowering his head, he plundered her mouth with a ravenous kiss.

A delicious moan slipped from Sarah as he set up a gentle rhythm. Her legs wrapped around his and she began to rock her pelvis, meeting him thrust for thrust, and it wasn't long before he succumbed to the urge to increase the pace. The pressure, the need for release was piling up inside him like an approaching storm. But he wanted to make sure Sarah achieved satisfaction again.

Taking his weight on one arm, he slid his hand between them and caressed the sensitive nub at the apex of her quim. Almost immediately she cried out and clutched his shoulders, her sex clenching and rippling around him, her body quaking with the force of her climax.

He couldn't hold on. His blood roaring, his control fraying, Alex frantically pounded into Sarah, losing himself in her lusciously tight warmth, hurtling headlong toward beautiful oblivion. With an almighty groan of elation, his balls tightened, his body bucked, and a cataclysmic release threw him heavenward.

Sweet Jesus. Had sexual congress ever felt so sublime?

He didn't think so. His breath sawing, his heart pounding, he pushed himself up and gazed down at the beautiful angel in his arms.

His voice was no more than a hoarse whisper when he was able to speak. "My beautiful, Sarah. God, how I love you." Knowing he was being a brute for demanding more of her, but unable to resist temptation, he swooped down and seized her mouth in an ardent kiss.

Sarah's fingers speared into his hair and she kissed him back with equal ferocity. "I love you too, Alexander," she whispered when he drew back.

"You know, under Scots law, we're as good as wed now."

Sarah's eyebrows rose. "Really?"

"Yes, really. We've exchanged vows of commitment and consummated our union. Now we're handfasted."

She pouted prettily. "Well, you might have warned me."

"What?" Alex couldn't help but laugh. "You don't wish to be wed to me?"

Mirth sparkled in her blue eyes. "A proposal would have been nice. And a wedding before God in a church."

"You're right." Buried deep inside her, his body humming with pleasure, Alex couldn't think of a more perfect way to offer for her hand. "Sarah Lambert, would you do me the untold honor of consenting to be my wife?"

"And who shall I be marrying?" She arched an elegant brow but her eyes twinkled with mischief. "Mr. Price or Lord Rannoch?"

Alex frowned. She was right. "Does it matter?" He held his breath, waiting for her answer.

"Of course not," she said, stroking his cheek. "Not to me. Only it might matter when we have children."

"Yes..." *Children.* In his heart of hearts, Alex had always longed to be a father. And he would love nothing more than to create a family with Sarah. But she was right...

"I've made you upset," she murmured.

"No. Don't even think it." Alex kissed her again before adding, "I know someone who might be able to help me reclaim my title."

"You do?" A smile lit Sarah's eyes. "That's wonderful."

"Yes. Only..." How to tell her the next part, the woman he loved. "There's always the risk that I might not be granted a pardon. That things might go wrong." *Such as being arrested and tried for treason... Being executed...*

"Oh..." A deep furrow appeared between Sarah's brows.

"Do not fret, my love. I'm sure everything will work out." God, Alex hoped so.

"I believe you. And whatever you decide, I'll be there by your side, as Sarah Price, Sarah MacIvor, or even Sarah Black."

"So is that an unqualified yes?"

Sarah's smile was a balm for his blighted soul. "Yes, Alexander. Indeed it is."

"Thank you, my love." Alex cupped her face and brushed his lips across hers, savoring her sweetness. "You've made me happier than you'll ever know."

Gathering her into his arms, he tucked her head beneath his chin. "Sleep now, my sweet, Sarah," he whispered. "We shall work out where we go from here tomorrow."

CHAPTER 20

Red Velvet House, The Cowgate, Edinburgh
February 22, 1757

"Good sir, what can we do for ye this fine evenin'?" simpered Mrs. MacLean, the Red Velvet's middle-aged madam. Her brightly rouged cheeks were as plump as apples as she beamed a gap-toothed grin at Malcolm.

Malcolm eyed the garish reception room—its faux-gilt candelabra and smoky wall sconces, the blood-red velvet settees and the lopsided chandelier overhead—along with the equally garish woman before him, with distaste. Her tightly cinched corset did nothing to enhance her doughy figure. Indeed, her ample breasts spilling from her puce silk bodice reminded Malcolm of deflated choux pastries. Dragging his gaze from her sagging cleavage, he looked down his nose at her. "I want to engage one of your tarts. A certain Miss Nell."

"Och. Ye have verra good taste, sir." Mrs. MacLean winked at him. "She has the best titties in this whole establishment."

"I don't doubt it." Malcolm withdrew his pocket watch and consulted the time. "I want her for an hour. And I want your best private room."

"Aye. Of course." The madam's gaze traveled over his brocade and velvet frockcoat and black satin breeches. She was clearly assessing how much he'd be willing to pay. "For you, that will be a guinea."

Malcolm snorted. "I don't care how good her tits are, I won't pay more than two crowns." The girl probably was worth a guinea but he didn't want to waste what coin he had left. MacNab, the inquiry agent, had already spent far too much hunting down the buxom Nell.

"Hmmm." Mrs. MacLean tapped a finger beside the tiny heart-shaped patch beside her rouged lips. "I'll let ye have her for three, and I'll throw in a decanter of my verra best brandywine."

"Forget the brandywine." It was probably watered down horse piss. "But I agree on the price."

"Excellent." The madam held out a beringed hand for the money. "If ye just take a seat and wait here a few more minutes, sir," she added as she tucked the coins into her bodice, "I shall make sure Miss Nell is ready to receive ye."

Flipping out his coattails, Malcolm took a seat on a settee and twirled the end of his silver-topped cane on a Persian rug that had seen better days. A few minutes turned into a quarter of an hour. With nothing better to do than take a pinch of snuff, and watch a few other men skulk in before being escorted away by other scantily clad whores, Malcolm was seething by the time Mrs. MacLean returned.

"About bloody time," he said, rising to his feet. "I don't have all night, you know." Which was true considering he wasn't absolutely certain that the 'Nell' of Red Velvet House was the woman he was looking for. He was running out of time to raise the ransom and he needed to know who Janus was.

The madam frowned and planted her fisted hands on her ample hips. "Now, now, sir. I ken ye are a fine gent, but we'll have none of that sort of language. Or I might need to rethink our arrangement."

Malcolm took a menacing step forward. His fingers itched to unsheathe the sword concealed within his walking cane and prick the madam in the jowls. "Don't you know who I am?"

The cursed woman didn't budge an inch, just cocked a painted brow at him. "Nae, I dinna ken who ye are. Do ye *really* want me to?"

Malcolm eyed Mrs. MacLean narrowly. She did have a valid point.

He didn't really want anyone at this brothel to know he was the Earl of Tay. Aside from that, there was a rather burly guard in the nearby entry hall. Even though Malcolm had a weapon, he couldn't afford to make a fuss. Avoiding any kind of scandal was still uppermost in his mind. "Very well," he conceded sourly. He adjusted his lace cuffs. "Just take me to her."

"Aye, sir. This way, if ye please."

The woman ushered Malcolm through to a dimly lit hallway that smelled oddly of rising damp, burnt toast, and a heavy musk-like scent, before leading him up a narrow flight of stairs. The sounds of enthusiastic fucking—rhythmic grunts, moans, and the occasional squeal of laughter—filled the air and he felt his prick begin to harden.

At the end of the corridor, the madam pushed open a wooden door with a tarnished brass handle. "Here ye go, sir. I'll be back in an hour."

Malcolm brushed past her, impatience turning to sharp anticipation as he entered the chamber. The claret-red velvet curtains were drawn but there was enough light from the fire and several branches of candles to reveal an overly ornate bed, the headboard decorated with paintings of fat cupids frolicking in a rose bower...and hallelujah, the woman he'd been searching for.

Nell, attired in an almost transparent rose-colored peignoir, was reclining upon a pink and red striped chaise longue—but as soon as she laid eyes on Malcolm, she leapt to her feet.

"Och... milord..." she said, her hand fluttering to her slender throat. "Fancy meeting ye here."

"Aye, fancy that." Malcolm advanced toward her, unsheathing his rapier before pushing the point between her bountiful breasts. Through the peignoir he watched her nipples harden and his cock swelled, tenting his breeches.

Nell's eyes widened in alarm. "Wh-What can I do for ye, milord? I dinna mind things to get a wee bit rough but no' like this."

Malcolm traced the tip of the rapier up to Nell's throat. "I want to know who hired you to distract me at Kenmuir House. Don't even think about lying, or your pretty throat is as good as slit."

Nell swallowed, but to her credit, she held his gaze. "Och, is that all ye wish to ken? 'Twas a verra handsome black-haired gentleman by the name of Mr. Alexander Price. And verra generous he was too. Hired me for the whole night."

Triumph flared inside Malcolm's chest. *Price.* Price was Janus. He had to be.

But why the fuck had Price kidnapped Sarah?

It didn't make sense. Unless the dog wasn't as rich as everyone thought...

Malcolm narrowed his gaze. "Did he tell you *why* he hired you?"

Nell frowned. "All he asked me to do was keep ye entertained for an hour or so. I was to take ye to a private parlor he'd picked out and make sure the curtains were left open. I assumed he wanted to watch us. Some men like that, ye ken. To watch."

Bastard. The fucking bastard. This Alexander Price must have taken Sarah out to the terrace, then whilst she was reeling from what she'd seen, he'd somehow spirited her away. Probably through the nearby garden gate to the lane beyond. MacNab, during his discreet inquiries at Kenmuir House, had discovered the gate's lock had been broken.

As Malcolm had puzzled over Nell's revelation, she'd slid off her peignoir and now stood before him stark naked. Her puckered raspberry nipples had his mouth watering and the sight of her bare mons made his balls throb.

She must have noticed the flash of lust in his gaze as she arched a brow and twirled a flaxen curl around one of her fingers. "Ye seem displeased, milord. If ye wish to punish me for being a verra bad lass at the ball, perhaps I could suggest a spanking..."

Malcolm lowered his rapier and sheathed it. "Right after you use your mouth on me," he said, unbuttoning his breeches. As much as he'd like to throttle Nell, he may as well get his money's worth while he was here. And the idea of spanking that lovely round arse of hers until it was as red as her nipples was certainly appealing.

Nell grinned and sank to her knees. "Och, aye. With pleasure, milord."

～

Janus's—or Alexander Price's—next letter of demand arrived on the doorstep of Tay House some time before dawn the following morning.

As the only remaining Boulle clock in the entire house struck seven, Drysdale shuffled into Malcolm's bedroom with the letter and Malcolm, still abed, snatched it up and tore it open with alacrity rather than trepidation. The note contained brief instructions about where he should deposit the ten thousand pounds in order to reclaim Sarah, on the first of March.

The location was an isolated spot, a cairn at the foot of the mountain Schiehallion—the Maiden's Pap—on the south-eastern side, not far from a stretch of dense woodland. Of course, Malcolm knew the area well. After all, it was only ten miles from Taymoor Castle. Interestingly enough, on the other side of the mountain was Price's land—the old MacIvor estate that the Crown had seized following the Rebellion. It made perfect sense and only confirmed that Price must be Janus.

Malcolm cast the letter onto the rumpled bedclothes and for once, he smiled rather than cursed at his ancient butler. "I want coffee, my good man. And after I've dressed, brush down my greatcoat then pack my trunk. I also want the carriage brought round by nine. Send one of the footmen to engage a couple of hacks from the Whitehorse Inn. I'm returning to Taymoor Castle."

"Aye, milord."

Malcolm rubbed the morning's bristles on his chin. "Is Lady Glenleven in?" He hadn't seen Damaris since early yesterday afternoon and wanted to share the good news.

Drysdale shifted his weight from side to side as he studied the bedroom floor. "Nae, milord. I dinna think she is…"

Malcolm snorted. She was probably still at Arbelour House, screwing more jewels out of the old earl. He threw back the covers and reached for the chamber pot beneath the bedside table. "If she arrives whilst I'm getting ready, tell her to come and speak with me. At once."

"Of course, milord."

Malcolm picked up Janus's ransom note again as he relieved himself.

Fuck you, Price. His mouth curled into a smile. He couldn't wait to confront the prick and have him thrown in jail. To watch him swing at the end of a hangman's noose. But even better than that, he'd have Sarah back.

Ruined or not, he was going to make her his wife.

CHAPTER 21

Blackloch Castle, Perthshire
February 23, 1757

"Ye wanted to see me, sir?"

"Yes, Isla. I did." Alex swept the young serving woman with an assessing look as she stood before his oak desk. The early morning sunlight filtering through the library window revealed that her red hair was disheveled beneath her lace cap, and her face was pale and pinched. Lines of tension bracketed her mouth.

Her gaze stayed fixed on the Turkish rug beneath her feet and her hands twisted her apron as she waited for him to say something else. Alex rubbed his chin, anger warring with heartfelt regret. He didn't like seeing the lass so cowed. He'd known her since she was a wee babe. Indeed, Aileen had given birth to her at Blackloch and the lass had grown up at the castle whilst Aileen had served as Blackloch's house-keeper and Dobson filled the role of first footman.

After Alex had purchased Blackloch five years ago, Isla had served him faithfully and well in the capacity of a maidservant. But he just couldn't condone what she'd done to Sarah.

There must be consequences. But he was willing to let the lass have her say first.

"When Miss Lambert discovered the book about Eilean Dubh and Blackloch Castle—I'm also suspicious as to how such a title ended up in the solar, mind you—why didn't you tell me about it, Isla, instead of taking it upon yourself to get rid of the threat you thought Miss Lambert posed? You gave her wrong directions, didn't you? So she'd meet with an accident on the moor perhaps?"

"I..." Isla shuffled her feet, still studying her toes, and her face became as flushed as the ruby-red curtains behind her. "I didna do such a terrible thing, milord. I do no' remember much after Miss Lambert took her breakfast. I had a cup of small beer and then—"

Alex slammed his hands flat on the desk and the maid jumped. "Don't you dare lie to me, Isla. It was you who fished out the laudanum and laced the small beer both you and MacLagan drank. We both know it was in a locked casket in my bedchamber at Eilean Dubh. Your mother and I were the only ones with a key and Aileen tells me that her key has gone missing." His gaze flitted to the iron key ring at her waist. "But something tells me I won't have to look far to find it."

At last Isla looked up. Her green eyes were glazed with tears. "I was only trying to help, milord. Ye've taken such pains to hide who ye really are. And with Miss Lambert being a Sassenach and all, I thought ye would be happy if she just disappeared..."

"Disappeared?" Alex snorted. "You mean *died*. And you were wrong, Isla. Very wrong in the way you acted. And very wrong about how I feel about Miss Lambert." Alex rounded the desk and leaned on the edge closest to Isla. He crossed his arms and drew a deep breath in an attempt to tamp down his anger and disappointment. "Miss Lambert has become very dear to me. In fact, I have asked her to be my wife. And she has consented."

A flicker of strong emotion—pain, or was it resentment?—flashed in Isla's eyes before she dropped her gaze again. "Then may I offer my sincere congratulations to ye both, milord?" she whispered.

Alex sighed. "The problem is, Isla, I don't think you are being sincere."

The maid didn't contradict him. She just continued to stare at the floor, her fingers crushing her apron.

"Miss Lambert will soon be the new mistress of Blackloch. And I cannot see how I can possibly keep you on here when you bear her such ill will."

"Milord." Isla clasped her hands together and dropped to her knees. Tears streamed down her face. "Please, dinna send me away. This is my home. I ken what I did was no' right, but I did it to protect ye. Truly I did. I will serve yer new lady faithfully. I swear—"

Alex held up a hand. "Enough, Isla. Please, get up. Begging will do you no good."

The maid bit her lip and did as he'd asked. "What...what will become of me?" she whispered.

Alex had already given the matter some thought, wrestling with justice and kindness. Isla might not like his plan, but it was the fairest solution he could come up with. "I'm sending you to one of the inns I own, the Boar's Head in Aberfeldy, to take up a chambermaid's position. It is only twenty or so miles from here, so it's not like I'm banishing you to the ends of the earth. I want you to pack what you can take with you on horseback. Your mother can pack a trunk for you and I will send it to the Boar's Head later on. Your father will escort you. You will leave within the hour."

Isla's face crumpled and tears slipped from her eyes again. "I canna believe ye're sending me away straightaway, milord."

"It's for the best, Isla. I shall give you some money for the journey too."

Isla dabbed at her tears with the corner of her abused apron. "Aye, milord," she said with a sniff. "Thank ye."

"Very good. It's sad to part on such terms but I'm glad that you understand."

Isla nodded. "Would you please tell Miss Lambert that...that I'm verra sorry, milord?"

"I will." Alex pushed away from the desk and ushered the maid to the door. Sadness tugged at his heart as he watched her trudge along the gallery toward the servants' stairs. He knew deep down that Isla had been harboring a secret *tendre* for him for at least the last year or so.

He'd never done anything to encourage it and he'd hoped her feelings would abate with time, that a stablehand or footman would catch her eye. Clearly, none had.

Yes, as much as it pained Isla, it was best that she left Blackloch for good.

~

An hour later, as directed, Isla and her father, Dobson, spurred their horses down Blackloch's drive, heading toward Loch Rannoch and eventually the road that would lead them south-east to Aberfeldy.

"She's in love with you, you know," murmured Sarah.

"I know." As Alex watched Isla disappear from view, he wrapped his arms around Sarah and rested his chin on her shoulder. Her curls tickled his cheek and he turned his head to breathe in her delicious scent. After Isla had quit the library, he'd taken Sarah on a tour of the castle and they'd eventually ended up on the battlements so he could show her the magnificent views.

"I'm sorry it had to end this way." Sadness laced Sarah's tone. "Isla seemed like such a sweet girl at first."

"She used to be. Perhaps what happened, all those years ago, affected her in ways I had not seen. Despite everything, I wish her well."

"I do too."

Alex shook his head. "You are an amazing woman. Not many could forgive such perfidy."

Beneath her wool cloak, Sarah shrugged a slender shoulder. "I have you. And you love me. That's all that matters." She turned in his arms, pushing her hands beneath his black wool redingote and gifted him with a sweet kiss on the mouth. "So, Lord Rannoch," she whispered against his lips, "tell me more about your kingdom."

Alex groaned. "I'd rather show you my bedchamber again."

She smiled and withdrew her hands. "Later."

"Very well," he sighed, and after threading his fingers through Sarah's, he led her carefully across the ramparts to the east-facing parapet. There were still blocks of stone, a few discarded tools, and small piles of rubble lying about that the masons hadn't yet removed, so they needed to pick their way.

Alex drew her into his arms again and pointed out the distinctive sharp peak toward the eastern edge of the loch. "Can you see Schiehallion? It's Gaelic for Fairy Hill of the Caledonians."

It was a cold but relatively calm day. High clouds drifted across a pale, ice-blue sky and only a gentle breeze ruffled their hair and the snow-white fichu and lace sleeves of Sarah's rose-pink gown.

"Or some call it the Maiden's Pap," he added in whisper-soft voice. "It's rather an apt name, don't you think?" Sarah's quiet huff of embarrassed laughter had him grinning.

"Yes. I can see it," she answered lightly. "But I think I shall refer to it as Fairy Hill. There's something simply romantical about the sound of it."

"Romantical? You mean fanciful?"

She playfully swatted at his hand. "What's wrong with romance?"

"Nothing at all, my sweet." As Sarah gazed out upon the vista he loved so well—the still, mirror-like lake, the wooded braes, and the snow-capped mountains—he gently nuzzled Sarah's neck.

At length she observed, "The village of Kinloch mustn't be far. Isla told me there is a dragoon barracks there."

"Aye."

Sarah turned her head and threw him a curious look. "You don't seem nervous at all that the King's men are virtually on your doorstep. Considering you are a wanted man, *my lord*, I'm curious as to why that should be the case."

"One thing I've learned over the past ten years, my sweet Sarah, is there isn't much money cannot buy." His eyes held hers. "Except love, that is."

Sarah's cheeks pinked, matching the hue of her gown perfectly. "Well, I agree. Nevertheless, I'm dying to know how you have achieved all that you have. You had nothing at all after Culloden, yet you've created yourself anew. Not only have you reclaimed your land and castle, but you've also rebuilt Blackloch. It's nothing short of miraculous."

"Aye, it is indeed." Alex had shown Sarah every wing and turret of Blackloch, including the east wing; repairs to the ornate brickwork and parapets had not yet been completed and some of the scaffolding still stood at the rear.

He knew he should feel proud of all he'd accomplished but deep down, he didn't. Not when he'd all but stolen a casket of Jacobite gold. Not when he'd been consumed by the dark desire for vengeance for well over ten long years and counting. A dark desire that had ended up hurting Sarah. Every time he looked at her and saw her smiling back at him with love, every time she kissed him, he almost had to pinch himself to make sure he wasn't dreaming. Surely he didn't deserve such bliss.

Ever perceptive, Sarah touched his arm. "What's wrong, Alex? You look so...grim."

He sighed. "I'm afraid you will see me differently when I tell you how my change of fortune came about."

She smiled and gave his hand an encouraging squeeze. "Surely not."

"We shall see." He leaned back against the parapet and drew Sarah into the shelter of his arms. "After my shoulder and wounded leg had been patched up by Aileen, and my poor mother, Anne, and Maggie had been laid to rest along with all the other servants, I left Blackloch. I thought never to return. Even though Tay must have believed I'd been killed when he'd shot me, I knew that if word got out I was still alive, more marauding clansmen loyal to King George or patrolling dragoons would be sure to capture or kill me. I didn't want anyone else from Clan MacIvor to suffer if they were caught harboring a fugitive."

"Where did you go?" asked Sarah, her voice soft with compassion.

"Nowhere and everywhere. For weeks on end, I lived hand to mouth in the remotest parts of the Highlands I could find, places where dragoons would not even think to venture. I was lucky to still have my horse, but with my leg such a mess, it was hard to sit in the saddle for long periods. I tended to rest during the day and travel at night. Thank God it wasn't the dead of winter, for I surely would have perished."

Alex closed his eyes for a moment as memories of that terrible time suddenly invaded his mind. How he'd dragged himself through endless days and nights, mad with grief and impotent rage, exhausted and in constant pain. Of the nightmares rampaging through his head...until Sarah's hand tightened in his, pulling him back.

Drawing a shaky breath, he resumed his tale. "Then, late one day when I'd risen from sleep and was about to go in search of food, I stumbled across something which can only be described as amazing. I'd been camping out in a cave above Loch Arkaig—it's about seventy miles north-west of here, well past the other side of Rannoch Moor, heading toward the sea. Clan Cameron land--they were also supporters of the Pretender. Anyway, whilst I was foraging in the woods above the loch, I heard voices. Cameron men. They were in the process of burying seven large wooden caskets lower down the slope."

Sarah's blue eyes gleamed with interest. "And what exactly did the caskets contain?"

"Gold. Jacobite gold. Thousands upon thousands of Louis D'or. Gold for the Pretender to support the cause to pay for troops, weapons, and supplies. I learned later the two French frigates that delivered the stash, the *Mars* and *Bellona*, arrived too late. The Jacobite force had already been crushed at Culloden so they simply unloaded the money and left. Apparently the Chief of Clan Cameron had been charged with keeping the treasure safe."

"Oh, my God," breathed Sarah. "That's incredible."

"It is indeed," agreed Alex.

"I gather you managed to claim some of the coin?"

"Aye." Alex grinned. "I certainly did."

When he'd finished recounting how he'd recovered one of the caskets and had stashed the gold in a cave, high above Loch Arkaig, Sarah cast him a dubious look. "Only one casket?"

Alex shrugged a shoulder. "Aye, it might be hard to believe, but it seems I'm not a greedy man. It was more than enough. In a blink of an eye, I'd gone from being completely lost and desperate, with nothing to live for, to being a very rich man." By force of habit, he rubbed his scarred left palm as memories of that long ago dawn when relief, anger, and bitterness all assailed him. "And that was when I vowed to punish the Earl of Tay for everything he'd done. To avenge those he'd hurt and killed. No matter how long it took me."

Sarah took his hand and traced along the faint line of his scar. A furrow appeared between her brows. "I've noticed you do that sometimes. Rub your palm as if it still pains you." She raised her gaze to his. "Did you make a blood vow?"

"Aye. I did."

Her gaze hardened as it met his. "I would have done the same."

"It's a dark place to be, Sarah. Hating someone this much, for so long." He lifted her chin with gentle fingers. "But now I have you, some of that darkness is receding. You've brought joy and hope back into my life."

Sarah's eyes glowed. "It warms my heart to hear you say that, Alex." He slanted his head to kiss her but she pressed a finger to his lips. "You haven't finished telling me about your rise from the ashes."

Minx. "Ah, yes. I suppose you're right," he conceded. Talking wasn't precisely what was on his mind right now, but then he did have the rest of the day and night, indeed forever, to make love to Sarah. To show her how much she meant to him. Sliding his hands to her waist, he gently turned her around so they were both facing the battlements again and the view beyond. "I dreamt of reclaiming Blackloch, my title and my heritage. Stepping into the place of my father, of all my ancestors. Of supporting my clan. I knew they'd be suffering too. And they were. Without the leadership of my father, with many of the clansmen killed, the families who were left fell victim to the predations of other leaderless clans—the Robertsons and the Menzies, the bastards, and Tay's men on and off. Aileen, Dobson, and Isla took refuge with some of Aileen's kin to the east in Kinross—her sister's family had not participated in the Rebellion so at least they had a safe haven until I returned a few years later. I would have sent them money, but I didn't know where they were for some time."

Curiosity sparked in Sarah's bonnie blue eyes. "I'm interested to learn how you became Alexander Price."

"As I said before, money can buy you almost anything. Including a new name. With my pockets full of gold, I was able to secure forged papers from a magistrate in Fort William who was rumored to be a Jacobite sympathizer. From there, I secured passage on a merchant ship and embarked on a journey to the New World—the Caribbean and the Americas, particularly New England and New France."

"Why so far away?"

"To start anew and establish myself as a successful man of business —a magnate if you will—in a place where no one would know me. To make the money I had, work for me. I invested in several commercial ventures revolving around shipping, banking, and maritime insurance. Although, my longing for Scotland—along with the desire to execute my plan for vengeance—grew so strong, in the end, I couldn't stay away. I returned to Glasgow and established several profitable business enterprises at home too. I acquired large parcels of agricultural land and local businesses—coaching inns like the Stag's Head and Boar's Head—and founded a logging company. Of course, I couldn't do any of this using my real name, so I continued to use the identity I'd adopted in the New World."

"Mr. Alexander Price?"

"Aye. I styled myself as a gentleman with English paternity but a lowlander Scot for a mother. I'd already learned to soften my Scots burr years before so no one would suspect I was a Highlander born and bred."

Sarah turned her head and cast him a wry smile. "You are quite the chameleon."

He shrugged. "I suppose so. Whilst I didn't intend to mix in the same circles as the Earl of Tay, I needed to be careful all the same."

"So when did you reclaim your estate and Blackloch?"

"The estate was forfeit and had gone to rack and ruin. But eventually—five years ago, to be exact—the forfeited estate's commission put it up for sale. And one Alexander Price, owner of the Price Logging Company and the Price Mercantile and Insurance Company in Glasgow, Edinburgh, and Liverpool, purchased it."

"My word, Alex," Sarah whispered. "That's incredible."

"I think so too." He laid a gentle kiss on the edge of Sarah's temple, taking care not to brush her wounded forehead. "As I mentioned, gangs of clansmen had wrought havoc in the area. And that couldn't continue. A dragoon barracks had been established at Kinloch at the eastern end of the loch and whilst the soldiers had done their best to stop the outlaws—mainly men from Clan Robertson—from conducting raids on the innocent folk of Clan MacIvor still left in the area, more needed to be done. And that's when I also seized my first opportunity to get back at the Earl of Tay."

"What did you do?"

"I paid the dragoon captain in charge of the barracks to turn a blind eye to certain 'activities.' Which essentially meant I employed a number of the remaining bands of outlaws to conduct raids on the Earl of Tay's lands instead. To reive as much cattle from that bastard as they possibly could. I knew Tay was already in financial trouble. I'd had men spying on him for some time. It was reported he liked to drink and had lost considerable sums at the gaming tables. He'd already sold off some of his unentailed land to me. Of course, he had no idea that his neighbor, Price, was really his old nemesis, Alexander MacIvor."

"Oh, my goodness."

Alex couldn't see Sarah's face but she'd shivered beneath his hands. "I've shocked you," he said. *How could he not?* It was dark deeds he spoke of in this quiet morning.

"A little. But I understand your need to be ruthless. To give Malcolm no quarter. I agree that ruination is no less than he deserves."

Alex exhaled a shaky sigh of relief. "You astound me, Sarah."

"I do?"

"Yes. To think you could love a beast of a man like me—"

She spun around and pressed her fingers to his lips. "Stop right there, Alexander MacIvor. Despite what you think, you are a good man. You deserve to be happy and to be loved. Never doubt that. And never doubt me."

Heart humming, he smiled and kissed her fingertips. "With you here, Sarah, Blackloch is beginning to feel like home again." All the ghosts and horrors that had tormented him for so long were starting to recede.

"Strange, I feel like I've come home too." She looked up at him from beneath her eyelashes. It was a look that he loved. A look that heated his blood and made his pulse quicken. "You said before that you wanted to show me your bedchamber again."

"Aye, but I have a better idea. I want to make some new memories, right here."

"Here? On the ramparts?"

Beneath the folds of her cloak, Alex skimmed his hands up Sarah's slender torso and gently cupped her breasts. Even through the silk brocade of her gown, and her undergarments, he could feel the eager jut of her nipples against his palms. "Yes. And later on, on my desk in the library. And then there's the Turkish hearthrug in the drawing room. And the window seat in the morning room…"

Sarah splayed her hands against his chest as though she meant to push him away. Although, if anything, she seemed to lean closer. "Stop, you wicked man," she murmured, her voice husky with barely suppressed merriment and desire. "You're making me blush."

"Oh, I want to do more than make you blush, my love. I want to make you scream."

～

Oh my.

Sarah bit her lip as a deliciously dark thrill shot through her. "Now that sounds entirely wicked," she whispered.

"It is," Alex said with a grin. "But in a good way."

"Wicked, yet good? That doesn't make sense."

Alex cocked a dark brow. "Says the woman who remarked yesterday that our lovemaking was both wicked and wonderful?"

The man had a point. "Oh, yes. I did say that, didn't I?"

"You most certainly did." Alex dropped to his knees and splayed his hands across her hips. "Lift your skirts, my love."

"I-I beg your pardon? What?" Sarah clutched the silk brocade of her skirts, intrigued yet uncertain. Surely he didn't really want her to do something so wanton. *It was the morning, after all. And they were out in the open air.* "What are you doing down there anyway? You'll get all wet and dirty." There was snow and masonry grit everywhere—and Alex was wearing fine breeches and highly polished boots.

He looked up at her through his dark lashes. The glint in his eyes was purely sinful and his smile was the most rakish she'd ever seen. "Oh, I intend to get *very* dirty," he murmured in a voice graveled with lust. "And so will you. In fact, we are going to be so dirty and wicked together, you're going to come off like you never have before. So please, my sweet Sarah, lift your skirts."

"Goodness. All right…" Her heart racing, Sarah conceded. Closing her eyes, she pulled up her voluminous skirt and petticoats, and her chemise. Cool air drifted over her skin and she shivered.

"Lovely." Alex ran his fingers through her curls then blew across the wet seam of her sex, making her shiver again, this time with nervous anticipation.

She dared to crack an eyelid. She couldn't see Alex's face anymore but she could feel his warm breath against her most intimate parts. While she trusted him—and she truly wanted to share herself with him—she couldn't quite quell a sudden flutter of shyness. "Wh-What if someone sees us?"

"Then they are going to be green with envy." His fingertips grazed over her upper thigh. "Put your foot up on this block of stone, my love."

Her face burning, Sarah complied. Suddenly, without warning, Alex slipped his fingers through her dew-slick folds, parting them.

"What on earth are you doing down there?" she gasped.

'I'm savoring the view. Your pretty pink quim is the most delectable thing I've ever seen. And if you consent, I want to savor how you taste..."

Alex shifted on his haunches and peered up at her, waiting for her response. All the while one of his wicked fingertips pleasured her most sensitive spot, circling and rubbing with light, teasing, thoroughly maddening strokes.

"I..." Sarah swallowed. She'd never imagined a man would want to *do* such a strange thing. But Alex's searing gaze was enough to convince her that he really did. She also couldn't deny there was a curious, wanton part of her that wanted to experience whatever sensual delights the man she loved was offering. "Very well..."

Leaning back against the parapet for support, Sarah closed her eyes and surrendered herself to Alex's decadent caresses. His tongue, warm and wet, pushed into the furrow of her sex then lazily licked a path along each lip to the bud where her pleasure was centered. He swirled the tip around and around before deploying a volley of delicate flickers, setting her body aflame.

Knees trembling, Sarah moaned and lifted her skirts higher, opened her legs wider, pushed her hips forward. One of Alex's hands gripped her naked thigh above her silk stocking, holding her steady, whilst he slid one finger then two inside her, rhythmically thrusting them in and out, creating delicious friction, the perfect counterpoint to what he was doing to her with his wickedly lapping tongue.

She couldn't believe she was letting him do this, *encouraging* him to do this, something so totally abandoned and wild. Yet she couldn't deny she loved every little thing he did with his fingers, and tongue, and now his lips. He'd captured her nub and was suckling her without mercy, pumping his fingers faster and faster, relentlessly driving her closer and closer toward the peak of pleasure.

Panting, oblivious to anything but the sublime sensations building inside her, Sarah brazenly ground herself against Alex. His tongue rapidly flicked and fluttered against her painfully tight bud and then with a cry of joy, she plunged into ecstasy. Her knees gave way and as she crumpled, Alex caught her against him.

Through the haze of her blissful delirium, she felt the rumble of a chuckle deep in Alex's chest, right before he captured her mouth in a fervent kiss.

"I told you I'd make you scream, didn't I?" he said when he released her mouth.

Sarah clutched the lapels of his coat. "Be that as it may, you are looking entirely too smug for my liking." She tried to look severe but failed miserably. Her cheeks were awash with a hot flush and she couldn't suppress her own satisfied smile.

Alex's smile lit his eyes. "The woman I love more than anything is glowing with pleasure. How could I not be self-satisfied?"

Sarah's heart, indeed, her whole body sang with the knowledge that the man she adored was so happy. Nevertheless, she said, "Just you wait until we retire to your bedchamber. I intend to make you scream as well."

Alex kissed her again, his thumbs caressing her cheeks. "I cannot wait, dear heart," he said, and judging by the fire in his eyes and the press of his arousal through her skirts, Sarah believed him.

～

Much later, as Sarah lay spent and deliciously naked in his bed, Alex gazed with tenderness at her lovely face. She'd finally fallen asleep after their enthusiastic bout of bed sport. And whilst he hadn't screamed, he'd certainly groaned with gusto, on at least two occasions.

He was so physically replete, the urge to drift into slumber too was strong, but his mind was atumble with plans for the future—a bright future with Sarah. A future he'd never thought he would have—one that involved happiness, and laughter, and children. Lots of children...

But he wanted their children—his and Sarah's—to bear his name, MacIvor, without fear or shame. He wanted the son he might have with Sarah to inherit his title, Baron Rannoch. To take his place in the long list of lairds who had served their people and this land.

He didn't want that bastard, Tay, to have the potential to hurt him or those he loved, ever again. Which meant he was going to have to clear his name sooner rather than later.

Sarah stirred in his arms. Her eyelids fluttered and she blinked sleepily at him. Her beautiful blue eyes, all hazy with satisfaction and love, sought his.

Alex kissed her. "I'm going to have to go away tomorrow, my lovely, but only for two or three days."

A small crease appeared between her brows. "Oh... Is this to do with Malcolm?"

"Yes and no. I mentioned I know someone who may be able to help me secure a royal pardon. And I want to sort the matter out now. When we marry, I want you to be Sarah MacIvor, Lady Rannoch. The woman I love deserves nothing less."

Sarah stroked his face and he turned his head to kiss her palm. It seemed in such a short space of time, he'd become addicted to kissing her.

"I understand," she said simply. "You must do what you have to." Her mouth lifted into a soft smile. "I shall miss you. Hurry back."

"I will. You'll be safe here."

"I know."

After they made love again, this time with exquisite languor, Alex at last found himself drifting asleep, a smile on his lips. For once in his life, he counted himself blessed.

CHAPTER 22

Tay House, Edinburgh
February 24, 1757

"Thank you, Mr. Weston. You have been most kind." Judith Lambert smiled up at the tall, gray-haired inquiry agent as he helped her alight from Sarah's carriage in front of Tay House. He'd traveled with her all the way from Newcastle and she'd been grateful for his congenial company and quiet confidence. Whilst she was still deeply anxious about Sarah, the man was a reassuring presence. With him at her side, she wouldn't have to question Lord Tay alone. She was certain he would be able to find out things she couldn't.

"You are very welcome, Miss Lambert," Mr. Weston said in that deep smooth voice of his that sometimes made her blush like a giddy girl. "Would you like me to accompany you inside?"

Judith glanced up the gray-stone townhouse and its black front door with its tarnished brass handle. Although his offer had great appeal, she shook her head. "I think I should investigate the lay of the land first. See what I can discover without arousing Lord Tay's suspicions that I may be working against him. And who knows"—Judith tried to summon a smile—"perhaps my niece has already returned."

Mr. Weston's thin, distinguished face broke into a smile as well. "That would be very good news indeed. I shall bid you adieu then, Miss Lambert. I intend to take rooms at the Whitehorse Inn. It isn't far."

"I shall have one of Lord Tay's footmen deliver your luggage to you shortly."

"Thank you." Mr. Weston bowed over her hand. "Perhaps I will see you later this afternoon? To discuss 'the lay of the land'?"

"Yes, of course."

The distinguished inquiry agent secured his black tricorn on top of his head and bowed once more. "Very good. I look forward to it."

For a brief moment, Judith watched Mr. Weston's long-legged stride as he walked toward the Royal Mile. Despite the ever-present knot of worry inside her, a small smile played about her lips as she ascended the stairs to the townhouse and rapped on the door. *What a lovely man.*

Unlike Lord Tay.

Drysdale, Lord Tay's ancient butler, greeted her. "It's verra lovely to see ye back, ma'am, but if ye wish to see his lordship, I'm afraid he is no longer here. He left early yesterday morning, bound for Taymoor Castle."

"I see." *Thank heaven for small mercies.* Judith removed her leather gloves and crushed traveling cloak and handed them to the butler. "Is Lady Glenleven in residence?" She doubted Sarah had returned to Tay House during her absence but nonetheless, she felt compelled to add, "Or my niece?"

"Aye, her ladyship is here, but I'm sorry to say, no' Miss Lambert."

Judith sighed shakily, swallowing back a wave of tears as cruel reality hit her once again. Sarah had been missing for ten days now and as time marched on, she sometimes despaired that her darling niece had indeed met with foul play. Possibly at the hands of Lord Tay. Of course, he may not be complicit—but there was something about the man that did not sit well with her. Then again, whilst she was relieved the earl wasn't here, it also meant neither she, nor Mr. Weston, would be able to question him about Sarah's disappearance.

And she wouldn't be able to ask him about the whereabouts of Sarah's pearl and sapphire parure.

No, she didn't trust the Earl of Tay as far as she could throw him.

But perhaps Lady Glenleven knew something... After all, she'd probably forged the letter that had been purportedly penned by Sarah.

"Might I have a pot of tea and something light to eat sent to my room, Drysdale?" The journey from Newcastle had been long and tedious and she would need sustenance and a small rest before tackling Lady Glenleven.

Drysdale shuffled his feet, drawing attention to the abysmal state of his scuffed leather shoes. "I'll see what Cook can drum up. There might be a wee bit o' shortbread or a scone left ..."

Good God. Was Lord Tay so short of funds he couldn't even afford to keep his kitchen stocked with food in his absence? Minding her tongue—it certainly wasn't poor Drysdale's fault—Judith simply offered her thanks and crossed the muddy parquetry floor of the entry hall, heading for the stairs.

She'd reached the landing that led to her room when Lady Glenleven appeared in the doorway of her sitting room. Her terrier, Bonnie, was in her arms.

"Oh, Miss Lambert. I thought I heard your voice. Won't you come in?" The young widowed countess stepped back from the door, the rumpled skirts of her sack-back dress swaying with the movement of her slender hips.

"I... Of course." Crushing down a weary sigh—she really wasn't ready for this conversation—Judith followed Lord Tay's sister into the room. It was cold. The fire had long burnt out and only ashes and dead black coals lay in the grate. Trays covered in half-drunk cups of tea, smeared glasses, and dirty plates littered nearly every flat surface in the room, and through the half-open doorway leading into the countess's bedroom, Judith could see her bed was unmade.

Where on earth were all the servants?

Lady Glenleven waved a thin, pale hand toward a settee covered in a worn and faded floral brocade. "Please, take a seat."

Judith gingerly moved a crumpled sheaf of papers and a discarded shawl to the side then perched on the edge of the chair. Lady Glenleven, her dog still in her arms, gracefully subsided onto a chaise longue on the opposite side of the hearthrug.

Her slender shoulders lifted and fell with a dramatic sigh. "My brother isn't here."

"I know, Drysdale told me."

"I'm not sure when he'll be back. Sarah's desertion has struck him hard."

Judith huffed. "Lady Glenleven, I think it's about time you stopped playing games with me. I know Sarah never penned that letter your brother showed me." She narrowed her eyes. "You wrote it, didn't you?"

The countess's auburn eyebrows shot up. "How...how did you know?" she breathed.

"Considering I taught my niece to write, I'd know her penmanship anywhere. And that handwriting was not hers. Aside from that, I once overheard you boasting about how clever you were at forging your late husband's signature."

"Oh..." Lady Glenleven's mouth turned down and she plucked at her skirts. Her brow was furrowed—whether in thought or displeasure, Judith wasn't sure. Perhaps both.

She decided to venture another question. "Do you know where Sarah is, my lady? I love her with all my heart. Indeed, she is like a daughter to me. If anything terrible has happened to her, I really do not think I could bear it."

The countess lifted her gaze, and there was a degree of sincerity in her expression that Judith had never seen before. "Miss Lambert, I honestly do not know where your niece is. As far as I know, neither does my brother. I'm sorry I gave you false hope by penning that letter but Malcolm was so set on avoiding any scandal. He didn't want you going to the Town Guard and stirring up a fuss."

"Thank you for your honesty, my lady." Judith looked about the room then brought her gaze back to Lady Glenleven's. "I'd appreciate it if you could also be frank about your brother's financial situation. It seems to me that he is rather short of money."

The countess pushed a lank, undressed curl away from her face. Her cheeks reddened. "Yes. He is."

"Sarah's disappearance must be quite an ordeal for him then. And for you. You cannot be happy here... With the way things are..."

In the ensuing silence, the only sounds were the ticking of the plain wooden mantel clock and a faint snuffle from Bonnie as she snuggled into her mistress's lap. As Judith watched Lady Glenleven, her topaz eyes grew unusually bright, and when she attempted a smile, her lips trembled.

"I m-must confess, things have been...better." The countess dropped her gaze and stroked Bonnie's silky ears.

"If you no longer wish to stay here—"

Lady Glenleven looked up. "I've just received an offer of marriage from the Earl of Arbelour. I'm thinking of accepting. He's a good deal older than me, but he's kind. And I think he loves me."

"He sounds lovely."

Lady Glenleven's smile was less fragile this time. "He is."

"I'm happy for you, then."

"Thank you."

Judith got to her feet. There was really nothing else left to be said. "If you don't mind, my lady, I should like to retire to my rooms. The journey from Newcastle is a long one."

"Of course." Lady Glenleven put Bonnie aside and rose also. Then, to Judith's astonishment, the countess took her hands in hers.

"Thank you again, Miss Lambert, for your understanding," she said, her expression earnest. "I hope you find your niece. As I said before, I truly do not know where she is, and neither does Malcolm. He is desperate to find her of course, but—" She broke off then her gaze firmed as if she'd made a decision. "I rather think Sarah should think twice about marrying him when...when she returns."

It was Judith's eyes that brimmed with tears this time. "Do you think she will?"

"I pray that she does." The countess squeezed her hands. "In the meantime, I think you might like to visit the Grassmarket as soon as you feel able to. There's a shop there by the name of Dunmore's. Hopefully you will still find something of Sarah's there. Something that is no doubt dear to her."

Judith's breath caught. "Thank you, my lady."

"I would've suggested that you take my sedan chair, but Malcolm recently sold it... But have Drysdale hail a public chair for you. I trust you have the funds?"

Judith knew the countess was referring to the money she would need to secure Sarah's stolen parure, not the fee to hire the sedan chair. "I think I will be able to scrape something together."

The countess nodded. "Good."

"God bless you, Lady Glenleven." As Judith took her leave, she decided that her pot of tea and plate of shortbread could wait until later. She'd call on the capable Mr. Weston and ask him to accompany her to the Grassmarket. When Sarah returned, her mother's jewelry would be waiting for her.

CHAPTER 23

Lochrose Castle, near Grantown, the Highlands
February 25, 1757

Alex's gut was a ball of tight knots as he waited in the elegantly appointed library of Lochrose Castle. It had been well over a year since he'd last seen his friend, Robert Grant, Viscount Lochrose, in Kingston, Jamaica. Although, at that particular time, he'd gone by the name of Robert Burnley.

Alex trusted he would receive a warm reception. But would Robert's welcoming attitude change when he asked him for a favor, one that might very well place *him* at risk? Would he be willing to put his name and reputation on the line for another Jacobite-on-the-run?

Of course, it couldn't hurt to ask...

At least that's what Alex tried to tell himself as he paced back and forth across the richly patterned Turkish rug in front of a magnificent mahogany desk. The longcase clock in the corner marked the hour, noon, and he was horribly aware of how filthy he was. Since he'd left Blackloch yesterday morning, he'd ridden all day and half the night, only stopping to change horses and grab the occasional meal. His boots were mud-caked, his buckskin breeches and cambric shirt stank of horse and sweat, and he desperately needed a shave.

But then he reminded himself that he was doing this for Sarah. Sarah and the children they would have.

Every other care paled into insignificance.

He'd just twitched back the plush velvet curtains to study the sweeping vista of picturesque loch and wooded braes through one of the tall, mullion-paned windows, when the polished oak doors swung open.

"Alex!" Robert Grant strode into the room, a wide grin curving his mouth. He grasped Alex in a warm hug, slapping him on the back before releasing him to study his face. "It's been too long, my friend."

"Indeed it has." Despite his qualms, Alex found himself grinning too. "You look well. Actually, damn well. Living the life of a landed nobleman who's happily wed clearly agrees with you."

"Aye, it certainly does." Robert crossed to a carved mahogany sideboard and held up a crystal decanter. "Care to share a wee dram for old times' sake?"

"You need to ask?"

Armed with tumblers of whisky redolent of peat smoke and honey, Alex and Robert took seats before the crackling fire.

Ever perceptive and forthright, Robert got straight to the point. "So, what brings you to Lochrose? Something tells me this isn't just a social call."

Alex took a fortifying sip of his whisky then grimaced. "Aye. You're not wrong at all."

His friend reclined in his brown leather wingchair and sipped his own whisky, waiting for Alex to elaborate.

"It's..." Alex sat forward, rolling his tumbler between his hands as he contemplated how best to broach the sensitive subject on his mind. "Oh, hell. I've met a woman. The most amazing, beautiful, and delightfully sweet woman. And I want to make her my wife."

"Well, that's superb news, Alex." Robert leaned over and clapped him on the shoulder. "Congratulations are in order, then."

Alex sighed. "Not quite."

"You mean, you haven't proposed to her yet?"

"Aye, I have—and you could have knocked me over with a feather when she accepted. Only..."

Robert's dark blue eyes narrowed. "Only you wish she could take your name, MacIvor."

"Exactly."

Alex's friend inclined his head. "I understand completely. So—"

"Robert, I've just come back from the village, and ye'll never guess which crofter's wife had her wee babe last night..."

Alex stood up as the most breathtaking redheaded lass he'd ever laid eyes upon entered the room. Dressed in a burgundy wool riding habit, her red-gold curls spilled over her shoulders as she pulled off then tossed a jaunty hat, decorated with pheasant quills, onto a nearby chair. "Och, I'm so verra sorry for interrupting, Robert," she said as soon as her gaze fell on the interloper in her home. Her honey-brown eyes darted back to her husband. "If I'd known ye had company, I would have knocked."

"It's quite all right, Jessie. Alex and I are old friends." Robert, who'd risen from his chair as well, turned to him. "Alex, may I introduce my lovely wife to you? Jessie, Lady Lochrose."

"My lady." Alex stepped forward and bowed over her gloved hand.

"And Jessie, this is Alexander MacIvor, Baron Rannoch," continued Robert. "Although outside of this room, it's probably best if you refer to him as Mr. Alexander Price."

Alex smiled at Lady Lochrose. "Or you may call me Alex. That's what my friends do."

Jessie smiled at him. "Alex. Of course."

Robert touched his wife's arm claiming her attention. "Alex and I... we have some past history in common, if you take my meaning. And we are both in similar lines of business in the New World."

Understanding flashed in Jessie's clear brown eyes. "Ah, I see."

"Alex is also getting married. To..." Robert cocked a dark eyebrow at him.

"Miss Sarah Lambert," finished Alex.

"Och, that's wonderful," said Jessie with a dazzling smile. "Congratulations! I hope I shall have the opportunity to meet Miss Lambert one day."

Alex tilted his head. "Thank you, my lady. And I think that it is entirely likely. May I offer my sincere congratulations to you and Robert as well? I can see how happy you both are."

"Thank you. We are indeed." Jessie's cheeks became suffused with color as she cast a soft look her husband's way. "Verra much."

Robert caught Jessie's hand and brought it to his lips. "I haven't spoken to Father yet but I'm sure he will lend his unreserved support in assisting Alex to secure a pardon."

Jessie beamed. "I'm sure he will too."

Tension slowly melted away from Alex's shoulders. Robert had once been estranged from his father, the Earl of Strathburn, but clearly that was no longer the case. To see his friend so damn content and secure gave Alex hope that maybe such a fate was within his reach too. After all, the issuing of royal pardons for Jacobites was not unheard of. Aside from Robert attaining one, Ranald the Younger of Clan Ranald who'd been living in exile in France after the Rebellion had also been allowed to return to Scotland three years ago.

Yes, there was definitely hope.

Robert and Jessie kindly invited Alex to stay the night at Lochrose rather than rushing off to Blackloch straightaway. When he politely but regretfully declined, his heart already longing to be back in Sarah's arms, there was much consternation. However, in the end, they reached a compromise, and Alex agreed to stay for luncheon. The charming Lord Strathburn joined them too. Although physically frail, he was both jovial and sharp-witted and by the end of their repast, he'd pledged to Alex that he would do everything in his power to secure an unreserved royal pardon for him. Fortuitously, in a fortnight's time, the earl was due in Edinburgh to meet with his solicitor and the Lord Advocate, the King's representative in Scotland. And now, at Lord Strathburn's urging, Alex would join him for the latter meeting too.

When it came time for Alex to quit Lochrose Castle—he was reluctant to leave Sarah alone at Blackloch for too long—he did so with a considerably lighter spirit.

By God's grace, within the space of a month he would be known as Alexander MacIvor again, and the title of Baron Rannoch would no longer be attainted. Then there would be nothing in the world to stop him from marrying Sarah.

CHAPTER 24

Taymoor Castle, Perthshire
February 26, 1757

"Milord, I'm sorry to disturb ye during breakfast, but there's a young lady here to see ye."

Malcolm frowned at the young footman—he couldn't remember the lad's name—hovering in the doorway to the morning room at Taymoor Castle.

A young woman? What the deuce? He put down his cup of coffee and anticipation spiked as another thought occurred to him. "Well, did she give her name?" *It couldn't be Sarah, could it?*

"Nae, milord." The footman's cheeks turned pink and he nervously pulled at the grimy frayed cuffs of his liveried jacket. "But she said ye would want to see her. That the matter she wanted to speak to ye aboot was verra important. Something to do with some letters ye've received recently... aboot another young lady...?"

"Christ, man! Why didn't you say so?" Malcolm threw down his napkin and pushed away from the table with such force, the china and silverware rattled. "Show her to the library. Now. I'll be along directly."

"Aye, milord."

Malcolm ran a hand through his hair as he strode down the icy-cold denuded corridor—the carpets, curtains, paintings, marble busts, and occasional chairs had all been sold months ago—heading toward his almost-as-bare library. He hadn't bothered dressing properly this morning. He badly needed a shave and he hadn't bathed for several days. Not having a valet was becoming increasingly annoying. But then, why should he be bothered about a strange, presumptuous lass's opinion of him?

His attire of breeches, stained boots, loose shirt, and rumpled striped-silk banyan would have to do.

The nameless lass—a young redhead—was waiting by the empty fireplace, her arms wrapped around herself to ward off the cold. As soon as she saw him, she dropped into a curtsy. "Milord, thank ye for seeing me at such short notice."

Malcolm crossed his arms and slowly, deliberately raked his gaze over her, from the top of her bright orange-red curls to the hem of her mud-splattered, nondescript brown wool gown. Despite the plainness of her garb, she was a pretty thing with bright green eyes, good-sized tits, and a nice trim waist. "You'd better not be wasting my time, Miss..."

"Isla Dobson," she said with a proud lift of her small pointed chin. "And I'm not."

"Humph. I'll be the judge of that." Malcolm gestured toward the worn leather wingchair and matching settee behind them. "Won't you take a seat, Miss Dobson?"

"I'd prefer to stand."

"Very well." *Obstinate chit.* Malcolm pinned her with a narrow-eyed stare. "My footman tells me you have information about some of my private correspondence. Correspondence related to a very sensitive matter..."

"Aye." Her gaze didn't waver. "I know all aboot your betrothed's kidnapping, milord. But more importantly, I know exactly where ye can find her."

Could the lass really be telling the truth? Malcolm tapped a finger against his stubble-rough chin. "How could you possibly know that?"

"I know, because I've been helpin' to care for Miss Lambert whilst she's been held captive."

This sounded too good to be true. Could this be another elaborate trap of Price's? A trick? "Really? Pray, Miss Dobson, how did you know where to find me? I've only just arrived here from Edinburgh." It bothered him that no sooner had he returned to Taymoor Castle, this girl turned up on his doorstep. It was highly suspicious to say the least.

The wench regarded him steadily. "Until recently, I worked as a housemaid for Mr. Alexander Price, the Laird of Blackloch Castle, milord. However, I now work at the Boar's Head Inn at Aberfeldy. Ye made a brief stop there on yer way here. I saw ye as ye were leavin' yesterday evening."

At least the whore, Nell, had been telling him the truth about Price then. But Malcolm still didn't know about Isla. "Hmmm. How do I know this isn't an elaborate ruse? That you and Alexander Price aren't playing me for a fool? For instance, why have you suddenly decided to betray your master and help me instead?"

The chit raised her chin. "It is no' a ruse, milord, I swear it."

"Prove it."

The lass swallowed and her cheeks grew pink. "I dinna wish any harm to come to Mr. Price but...but I do want Miss Lambert gone. And judging by the state of Taymoor Castle"—Isla Dobson cast a pointed look about the dusty, half-empty bookcases and the curtainless, grimy windows—"ye need Miss Lambert's coin. Badly. So I'd suggest ye trust me."

"Why, you little bitch—" Hot anger flared and Malcolm lunged for Isla Dobson, gripping her about the throat. "Who do you think you are, to insult me so?" he thundered. "Tell me everything you know, right fucking now, or I'll wring your scrawny neck."

Isla's green eyes bulged and she clawed at his hands. Malcolm loosened his grip a little and she gasped. "Milord!"

"Sit." Malcolm released her so abruptly Isla stumbled over to the settee.

He waited for a minute for the girl to catch her breath before advancing forward to loom over her, his feet planted wide, his hands on his hips. "Where is she?" he demanded.

"It isna going to work like that, milord," croaked Isla. "I-I need ye to promise that ye will no' harm Mr. Price."

Malcolm's knuckles cracked as he pushed down the urge to beat the truth from the obstinate chit. "I'll make no such promise yet," he growled. "Tell me, why do you wish Miss Lambert gone?"

"Because Mr. Price intends to wed her."

What the fuck? What the actual fuck? Malcolm scrubbed a hand through his hair. Of all the things Isla Dobson could have said, all the things he could have guessed, it had never been that. It meant that Price probably didn't need the ransom money at all.

It also meant he had to get Sarah back. *Immediately.*

"When? When does he plan to marry her?"

"I canna be sure, but soon."

"Tell me where she is. Is she at Blackloch Castle?"

"I am no' a fool, milord, and neither is Mr. Price. I willna confirm her precise whereabouts until ye agree to my terms."

"Where is she?" Malcolm bellowed in her face, but it made no difference. The stubborn bitch clamped her eyes shut and pressed her lips together.

Only when he stepped back did Isla open her eyes again. "Ye can shout all ye like, Lord Tay," she said through gritted teeth—but I willna tell ye anything more until ye give me yer word—if ye swear—that no harm will come to Mr. Price."

Malcolm snorted. "Don't tell me you're in love with the bastard."

The lass's green eyes sparked with defiance. "Aye. I am."

"Jesus Christ."

Isla said nothing, just stared at him. There was such fire in her eyes, Malcolm had the inkling that even torturing her wouldn't wring the truth from her.

He retreated to one of the windows and stared out at the ill-kept grounds of Taymoor: the all-but invisible garden paths; the tussocks of dead, overgrown grass between the patches of snow; the brambles that caught at one's clothes; the rampant ivy that was crumbling the brickwork.

He needed Sarah, it was that simple. If Price intended to marry her, that meant he'd probably fucked her by now—not that it really mattered to him at this point. He'd already decided days ago that he wasn't in a position to be particular about another man's leavings. As long as Sarah's fortune was his, he didn't much care if she bore him a bastard.

He turned back to face the room and uttered the lie Isla Dobson needed to hear. "All right," he said grimly. "We have a deal. You take me straight to Miss Lambert, and once I have her, your master will have nothing to fear. I will not retaliate."

"Ye swear?" Isla gave him a narrow-eyed glare as though that would be enough to sway him.

"I swear." *Stupid chit.*

CHAPTER 25

Kinloch, Loch Rannoch, Perthshire
February 26, 1757

"Mind the dung, miss," instructed Aileen as she handed the reins of her horse to MacLagan. "Ye dinna want yer boots and riding habit to get mucky."

"Thank you." Sarah, who'd already dismounted with MacLagan's assistance, neatly sidestepped the fresh pile in the middle of the half-frozen muddy square that was most probably the village green—at least, in the summer.

When Sarah had heard that Blackloch's resident housekeeper was going to visit the village to make a few purchases for the castle's cook, she'd asked to come along, too. Alex had been away from Blackloch for two whole days, and to take her mind off missing him—not only did she yearn for his company, but quite shockingly, his lovemaking—she'd thought a tour of Kinloch would be just the diversion she needed.

It would also help her to stop worrying about Aunt Judith who must be sick with worrying about her...

Now that she was free, Sarah was eager to send word to her aunt explaining she was safe, along with an invitation to join both her and

Alex at Blackloch Castle. Alex had promised that upon his return, he would dispatch a courier to both Linden Hall and to Charles Swindon's office in Newcastle to make sure Judith learned of her whereabouts. Even though Alex had been fairly certain Malcolm would no longer be at Tay House, he was quite understandably reluctant to send a message there.

Home. Sarah still couldn't quite believe Blackloch and the village of Kinloch would indeed be that place rather than Tay House or Taymoor Castle. How remarkable it was that her life had completely changed course in such a short space of time.

Trying to ignore the curious glances of a pair of red-coated dragoons riding past, and a dour-faced woman tending a small patch of garden in front of her cottage, Sarah picked up her red wool skirts and followed Aileen toward a cluster of neat, gray stone buildings with thatched roofs set against the imposing backdrop of a towering craggy hill. It was an overcast, frosty day and the hill's peak was lost in a blanket of dark cloud. Sarah hoped it wouldn't rain on the return journey to Blackloch.

"The master has worked miracles here, Miss Lambert," said Aileen when she caught up to the servant. Her mouth had lifted at one corner into a rare smile, and her gray-green eyes shone with pride. They'd paused by the window of a small building that looked like a shop for general purchases. "Och, only a few years ago, this place was as wild as could be, despite the dragoons' barracks. The master has worked verra hard with the dragoon captain, the factor of the forfeited Robertson estate, and the new pastor and his wife, to make the countryside a wee bit more civilized. Over there"—Aileen pointed with one gnarled finger across the green to a larger building with wide wooden doors—"is the blacksmith's and the wheelwright's. Next door is the mason's. And behind the trees, closer to the river, is a schoolhouse. The pastor's wife has also been teaching the crofters' wives to spin and weave. One day the master hopes there'll even be a mill, a tailor, dressmaker, and shoemaker here. He also has plans underway to build a better bridge across the Tummel and a fine new kirk on the other side. All for the villagers."

"That is indeed wonderful," agreed Sarah with a smile. Her chest swelled with pride to think the man she loved had such a great sense of philanthropy and social responsibility. Unlike Malcolm...

She pushed thoughts of the blackguard and the havoc he'd wrought aside as she followed Aileen into the small shop. The housekeeper was greeted warmly by the stooped, gray-bearded shopkeeper. He stood behind a long wooden counter piled high with all manner of odds and ends including jars of sweetmeats, several large wheels of cheese, and a wooden crate of vegetables. Aileen introduced him as Mr. Reid.

The elderly Mr. Reid studied Sarah with interest. "We dinna get ladies as bonnie as you visiting Kinloch verra often," he remarked in a voice cracked with age. He suddenly winked. "Are ye staying up at the castle then? As a guest of Mr. Price?"

Sarah blushed but before she could respond, Aileen shot a sharp glare at him.

"Mr. Reid!" she admonished. "Where are yer manners, man?"

"Och, I'm sorry, lass. It's just that many of us from around these parts have been hopin' our laird will settle down with a wife. 'Twould be a braw thing indeed to see some wee bairns at Blackloch." He winked again, but this time at Aileen. "Just like in the old days, eh, Mrs. Dobson?"

"Aye, it would indeed," agreed Aileen. Quite unexpectedly, she cast a rather knowing but friendly smile Sarah's way, and Sarah felt her blush deepen. It seemed her erstwhile jailer was warming to the idea that an Englishwoman, one formerly betrothed to her master's nemesis, was going to be the next mistress of Blackloch Castle. Considering that her daughter Isla had clearly resented her, Sarah was both grateful and relieved to discover Aileen bore her no ill will.

Aileen made her purchases—a cone of sugar, a small quantity of soft soap, and two dozen fat beeswax candles—and once she'd arranged for the delivery of several sacks of oats, barley, and flour to the castle, they returned to where MacLagan waited with their horses on the edge of the green.

The weather had changed whilst they'd been inside Mr. Reid's shop. Although it was only early afternoon, a freezing fog had rolled in, obscuring the view of the loch and completely hiding the peak of Fairy Hill. As they clattered across the bridge at the southern edge of Loch Rannoch, heading toward the Black Wood with its massive ancient pines and birches, Sarah really wished she'd thought to wear her cloak.

The distance from Kinloch to Blackloch Castle was seven miles, so it would take them almost an hour to trot all the way back, especially in thick fog. With any luck, the inclement weather wouldn't delay Alex's return. She rather hoped he might be home by nightfall.

Sarah was lost in deep thought, dreaming of Alex to take her mind off how cold she was, when Aileen—ahead of her on the woodland path—suddenly reined in her horse.

"Isla?" the older woman exclaimed. "What on earth are you doing back here, lassie?"

Sarah and MacLagan halted their mounts too. Sure enough, a few yards away beneath a towering pine was Isla. Sitting atop a horse, she ignored her mother's question and stared straight past her.

Straight at Sarah.

The back of Sarah's neck prickled at the hardness of the girl's glare. "What do you want, Isla?" she asked. Even to her own ears, her voice sounded thin and anxious.

"You. Gone," Isla said. And then there was a deafening crack and MacLagan slumped over in his saddle.

A scream spilled from Sarah's throat as her horse skittered off the path and Aileen's mount reared, unseating her.

"Ye said no one would get hurt," Isla cried into the thick gray miasma behind her. "Ye promised—"

"I lied."

Oh, God. Sarah froze as a bolt of awareness struck her.

She knew that voice.

At that same moment, Malcolm materialized out of the fog, drawing alongside Isla. Attired in black, sitting astride an equally dark horse, he looked like the Devil himself. Before Sarah could even think to kick her horse into action, he'd grabbed Isla. There was a flash as a long knife—a dirk—was pressed against the girl's throat.

Aileen screamed and scuttled to her feet. "Dinna hurt my wee bairn," she cried. "Please. I beg you—"

"Now, now, old woman. There's no need for histrionics," drawled Malcolm. "If you do as I say, both of you"—Malcolm's attention briefly shifted to Sarah before returning to Aileen— "nothing will happen to Isla."

Aileen nodded furiously. "Aye, sir, anything. Anything at all."

"And what say you, *my love*?" Malcolm's gaze skewered Sarah and her heart stumbled in terror.

"What do you want, Malcolm?" she whispered, even though she knew the answer.

"You."

Sarah swallowed. Her gaze darted to Isla. The girl's green eyes were round with fear. Her chest rose and fell rapidly with each frantic breath she took. Malcolm had already shot, and possibly killed, poor MacLagan. Even though ice-cold dread gripped her, Sarah wouldn't let anyone else get hurt. Not even Isla. Not even after the girl had betrayed her, yet again.

"Very well." Sarah flicked her horse's reins, urging it forward, but Malcolm pressed the blade against Isla's throat and blood welled.

"Not so fast," he growled and Sarah stopped. "You, old woman," he called to Aileen. "I want you to get the ropes hanging from my saddle and tie one of Miss Lambert's ankles to her stirrup. Then tie another rope to the bridle."

"Aye, m-milord."

"That really isn't necessary, Malcolm. I'll go with you willingly," said Sarah as Aileen fetched the rope. "Just do not hurt—"

"Shut it, Sarah. You'll do as I say, or this chit *and* the woman will die."

Sarah bit her lip, willing herself not to cry as Aileen firmly lashed her ankle to the stirrup. "I'm sorry, lass," the housekeeper whispered, "but Isla's my daughter."

Sarah didn't dare reply but in her heart she understood Aileen had no choice. After all, the poor woman had witnessed Malcolm's depredations ten years ago, and knew better than anyone exactly what the man was capable of.

"Now lead Miss Lambert's horse over to me," barked Malcolm.

Aileen nodded, her eyes darting between her mistress and the blade at her daughter's throat. "Aye, m-milord."

After the housekeeper had tied Sarah's mount to Malcolm's, he at last relinquished his deadly hold on Isla.

The young woman immediately kicked her horse and sidled away from him. "Ye evil bastard! Ye killed MacLagan," she shrieked.

Malcolm shrugged, his mouth curled in a sneer. "You're lucky it wasn't your precious Mr. Price. Where is he, by the way?"

The brute leveled a hard, glittering glare straight at Sarah and she straightened in her saddle, despite the icy tendrils of fear curling through her. "Away. I know not where."

And thank God for that. If Malcolm had come across Alex... Whilst Sarah's heart ached for poor MacLagan, just the thought of Alex being hurt filled her with unspeakable dread and numbing despair.

Malcolm's eyes narrowed, but he must have believed her as he simply said, "Come, *dearest*. We have better places to be."

He quickly checked Aileen's knots before kicking his horse and turning it away from the path, heading for the deeper woods. There was nothing Sarah could do but follow.

"Where are we going?" she asked as they eventually turned east, doubling back toward the trail through the Black Wood. They seemed to be heading toward Kinloch again. She recalled Isla's words from a few days ago that Malcolm's lands were to the south-east, beyond the mountains.

"Taymoor," he said over his shoulder, confirming her suspicion. His tone was gruff. "Where you belong."

Not anymore. Sarah kept the sharp thought to herself. She would do whatever she could to get away from Malcolm, this terrible beast she'd once believed she'd loved. How blind and foolish she'd been. And how ironic that she'd now been kidnapped by the very man she'd been stolen from.

Their wedding in Taymoor Castle's private chapel had been scheduled for the seventh of March so she still had nine days to work out how to get away. Again.

Although, in that time, Alex might very well try to rescue her. Aileen would be sure to tell him what had happened on his return to Blackloch and she couldn't imagine that he wouldn't attempt to save her. After all, his initial plot for revenge was dependent upon Malcolm *not* marrying her.

Moreover, Alex loved her and now wanted to make her his wife. But when he came for her, he would be in danger too.

Fear twisted Sarah's insides into knots as Malcolm led her through the dark woods at a canter. Within no time they'd reached the fork in the rough road that would take them back to Kinloch. However, Malcolm veered to the right, away from the loch and the River Tummel, heading toward Schiehallion and Taymoor Castle—a place she never, ever wished to call home.

~

They'd been traveling for over an hour when Malcolm decided to stop in a small copse of wind-blasted Scots pines by the banks of a small lochan. The fog had cleared once they'd reached higher ground and a brisk wind tore at Sarah's riding habit and hair.

"We need to water the horses," he said tersely, before dismounting and leading his gelding and her mare to the water's edge. Then he drew a pistol from the folds of his greatcoat and aimed it at her. "Just in case you decide to make a run for it," he said.

"You need me alive to marry me, Malcolm."

He shrugged. "I don't need to kill you, just disable you," he said with such cold casualness, Sarah shivered.

Every now and again she risked a glance his way as they waited for the horses to drink their fill. His face was thinner and haggard, as though he hadn't eaten or slept enough lately, and he badly needed a shave. His boots were in a terrible state and his clothes were not only travel-stained but in need of repair—Sarah spied a torn and grimy cuff poking out from the braided edge of his coat sleeve, and there were at least two buttons missing from the front of his greatcoat. If she didn't know he was the Earl of Tay, he could easily be mistaken for a ruffian.

Malcolm caught her studying him and he clearly didn't warm to her expression as his top lip curled. "What's the matter, dear Sarah? I thought you'd be happy to see me. Your chivalrous knight. Your one true love."

She kept her lips pressed together and looked away, crushing down the urge to react to his goading. She wouldn't show how much he

239

disgusted her, or how terrified she really was, or how much he'd hurt her.

However, ignoring him had the opposite effect as he took a few steps closer and placed one of his large gloved hands along her thigh. "Isla Dobson tells me you are betrothed to Price," he said in a low voice, full of menace. "He only wants you so I can't have you. Fucked you already, has he?"

The dam holding back Sarah's emotions broke. "What choice did I have but to agree to his proposal?" she countered angrily. She instinctively knew she should not admit that she'd fallen in love with Alex and that he loved her too. Such a confession would probably enrage Malcolm further. "He kidnapped me," she continued. "I was ruined anyway. And you are one to talk. You betrayed *me*, Malcolm. Why would I want to marry you after witnessing what you did with that woman at the ball?"

"A woman Alexander Price hired for me to fuck, Sarah. A prostitute. A trap. She was bait, nothing more."

"What?"

"Aha! You didn't know that, did you?"

"No..." Tears pricked Sarah's eyes, misting her vision, but she blinked them away. She supposed Alex had done such a thing to keep Malcolm 'occupied' whilst he kidnapped her. And to make sure she didn't want to marry the despicable man. She understood why, but the fresh knowledge still stung.

She didn't have time to dwell on her bruised feelings as Malcolm began to needle her again with sharp, hateful words. "And I wonder why you were out on the terrace, Sarah. Clearly Price was with you—"

"How dare you!" Sarah cried. "I was looking for you! I did nothing wrong whereas you... You had a choice, Malcolm. You could have ignored that woman's invitation. But you didn't. You went with her and you—" She bit her lip unable to finish.

Malcolm snorted, nostrils flaring. "If you hadn't been so bloody frigid, Sarah, I wouldn't have had to look elsewhere. Except...maybe you're not so cold after all." He stroked her thigh again. "According to Miss Dobson, you willingly spread your legs for Alexander Price."

"You're vile," Sarah spat. "Considering what you did to Alex's family. His poor mother—" *Oh, no.* Sarah's hand flew to her mouth, but it was too late. *Oh, no, no, no.*

"Whose family?" demanded Malcolm. "Whose mother? Alexander Price's? But I never..." His brow plunged into a deep frown and his brown eyes blazed with bright sparks of anger. "*Fuck.* I knew it." His grip tightened on Sarah's leg, bruising her. "Bloody Alexander MacIvor's behind your kidnapping, isn't he? I knew I should have gone back inside Blackloch after it had finished burning to make sure the bastard was dead... Shit." He slammed his pistol against his thigh. "Fuck."

Sarah's stomach pitched and nausea writhed inside her. "Who is Alexander MacIvor?" she whispered. It was useless to pretend what she'd said wasn't true, but she felt compelled to at least try and cast doubt.

"Don't lie to me, Sarah." Malcolm grabbed one of her wrists and squeezed hard enough that tears welled in her eyes. "Don't you dare fucking lie."

"What will you do? Shoot me?"

He squeezed her wrist harder and with such crushing force she cried out. "I could always break your wrist and then your fingers one by one," he growled. "Then take you so hard you wouldn't be able to sit on that horse for a week." He eased up his grip a fraction so she could breathe again. "So what's it to be, Sarah? The truth? Or shall we explore the alternative option? Is Alexander Price really Alexander MacIvor?"

Her heart had all but stopped beating. *God forgive her for what she was about to say.* "Yes," she whispered. "Yes he is."

The rest of the journey passed by in a blur. Guilt tore at Sarah's heart and all she could hear in her head, in time to the beat of her horse's hooves was: *I betrayed Alex. I betrayed Alex. I betrayed Alex.*

It must have been late afternoon by the time Malcolm slowed their pace again. Sarah emerged from her daze as they entered a small village, not unlike Kinloch, on the edge of a picturesque loch.

"Welcome to Balloch," Malcolm said, a note of pride evident in his voice. "Taymoor Castle is only two miles farther."

If the circumstances had been different, Sarah might have commented on how lovely the village was, how beautiful the scenery. But the words wouldn't come. No matter how hard she tried, she couldn't quite swallow down the hard lump of despair lodged in her throat or draw enough breath.

Only two miles to Taymoor. Oh, heaven help me.

What would Malcolm do to her once they got there? Dark spots danced before Sarah's eyes and she closed them, willing herself not to faint. As dire as her situation was right now, she really didn't want to break her neck.

Then, quite unexpectedly, they stopped.

Sarah dared to open her eyes again. A neat gray stone kirk that was flanked by a pair of ancient yew trees stood before them.

Malcolm dismounted then tethered his horse and hers to a ring by the lychgate.

"You have business with the kirkman?" Sarah couldn't hide the tremor in her voice or the note of incredulity.

"*We* have business, *my love.*" Malcolm jerked at the knot securing her ankle to the stirrup.

"What sort of business?"

"Good God, Sarah. You can really be quite stupid sometimes." Malcolm lifted her down and for a moment, Sarah's stiff legs buckled beneath her. Her brutish former *fiancé* caught her beneath the arms. "Christ, don't tell me I have to carry you," he sniped.

"No." Her gaze darted to the gravel path and the snow-shrouded gravestones either side of it. A few stray daffodils poked through the snow but they failed to brighten Sarah's mood. The impending sense of doom settling over her was so heavy, it forced the air from her lungs, made her heart beat so loudly she could hear it pounding in her ears like a drum. She was caught in a quagmire and there was no possible way to escape. "N-No. I cannot do this. Not today, Malcolm." *Not ever.*

Malcolm grabbed her by one arm and propelled her forward, underneath the gate and down the path, toward the kirk's front door. The blade of his dirk pressed against her ribs the entire way. "You are my betrothed, Sarah Lambert. And you will marry me. Right, fucking, now."

CHAPTER 26

The interior of the kirk was chill and dark, save for the glimmer of several altar candles at the end of the aisle and the muted light filtering in through several arched windows of stained glass. The dank, stale air was overlaid with the faintest hint of incense as Sarah drew a ragged breath, trying to ignore the fact her 'groom' was holding a lethal weapon in the vicinity of her heart.

Malcolm called out to the kirkman, his voice echoing around the stone chamber as he forced Sarah to walk down the aisle, past the empty wooden pews and fluted stone columns.

In reply, a wooden door—perhaps leading to the vestry—scraped across the flagstone floor and a rotund, balding man of middle age in a black frockcoat with a high white clerical stock around his fleshy throat, emerged. He was clearly the minister. He tipped his spectacles down his nose and peered at them.

"Oh, my word. 'Tis you, my Lord Tay," the man said with a deferential bow. His gaze shifted to Sarah. "And who might this young lady be, my lord?"

"My bride."

"Oh, Miss Lambert." The clergyman gave another solemn bow. "'Tis an absolute pleasure to meet you. My name is Reverend Lennox."

Sarah bobbed her head in acknowledgment, conscious of the blade pressing into her side. Surely Malcolm wasn't going to force her to wed him under duress? The folds of his greatcoat and the way they were standing—Malcolm had pulled her firmly against him—obviously hid his dirk as the reverend continued to smile at them both as if nothing in the world were amiss.

Dare she scream? Try to run? There had to be a way to get out of this nightmare.

She had to, not only for herself, but for Alex.

Perhaps guessing her train of thought, Malcolm's grip on her arm grew tighter and the sharp press of the steel blade beneath her breast became more insistent. "Reverend, Miss Lambert and I wish to wed. At once."

"But, my lord," protested the clergyman. His eyebrows shot up and his gnarled hands flew to his chest. "Not all the banns have been posted yet. You're not due to wed until the seventh—"

"I don't care, Lennox."

"But, this is highly irregular, my lord. I'm already overlooking the fact that your scheduled ceremony is taking place during Lent—"

Malcolm's brows crashed together. "Who helped pay for the repairs on the steeple, Reverend Lennox?" he shouted, his voice vibrating like thunder off the stone columns and in the vaulted ceiling above them. "Whose family owns this land and established this very church? Who pays your wages? Who provides the very roof that keeps you dry?"

"Why...why you. And your family, my lord," whispered Lennox. His face had turned as white as his collar.

"Good. Now we have that established," snapped Malcolm, "why don't you go and get your prayer book and change into your robes and we'll begin."

"Aye, milord," the cowed clergyman bowed. "I'll also need to summon the sexton, as a witness. He's outside tending one of the new graves."

Sarah found her voice. "Wait..."

Lennox turned back, a concerned frown creasing his brow. He peered at her over his spectacles. "Yes, my child?"

"I... I..."

Malcolm's brown eyes bore into Sarah's and he jammed the knife against her side with even greater force.

"I-I need to use the necessary," she whispered. It was a lie, but she'd say or do anything if it meant she could get away from Malcolm.

"Oh." A dark red blush spread across the reverend's face. "I can show you to the vest—"

"I'll take her," growled Malcolm, tugging her toward the open door of the minister's office.

"My lord, I-I must protest," spluttered Reverend Lennox. "You are not wed yet!"

Malcolm paused on the threshold. He clenched his jaw so hard, Sarah swore she could hear his teeth crack. "Very well." He pressed his mouth against her ear as though bestowing a kiss and whispered, "Do not try to run, *my love*. I will be very, very angry if you do." He twisted the dirk so the tip of the blade pierced the red wool of her riding habit. "You already have an ugly wound on your forehead and I'm not afraid to add to your collection of facial scars. I don't mind marrying a bride who isn't quite so pretty. The only thing I care about is the contents of your bank account."

His threat was abundantly clear. He would think nothing of disfiguring her if she failed to comply.

Sarah gave a jerky nod. "I won't run," she whispered.

Malcolm released her and once she'd stumbled through to the vestry, he closed the door...but not all the way. It was still slightly ajar by an inch.

Damn. Hopefully Malcolm wasn't going to spy on her the whole time she was in the reverend's office. Regardless of the risk, she had to do something to try and save herself.

Her gaze darted frantically about the room, looking for a way out or a weapon. The vestry was relatively small and sparsely furnished: there was a desk, a pair of wooden chairs before it, a glass-fronted bookcase, a wooden screen with the reverend's black cassock draped across it, a small window...and between two carved cabinets at the back of the shadowy room was what she'd been looking for—a door that appeared to lead outside. Even if Malcolm peeked through the gap in the door to the chapel, he wouldn't be able to see her.

Sarah dashed over and grasped the door's handle but damn it, it was locked and the key was nowhere to be seen. Tears scalded her eyes.

"What are you doing in there, my *sweet*?" called Malcolm.

Her voice tight with terror, Sarah called back, "I...I bumped a chair." *Dear God, I hope he believes me.*

She hadn't much time. Any minute now Malcolm would demand that she come out or he would come in to get her. Breaking the window clearly wasn't an option. She needed a weapon.

She rushed over to the desk. There was a letter opener but that would be a poor match against Malcolm's wicked-looking dirk. Besides, Malcolm would best her in a knife fight. No, she needed to use the element of surprise as a weapon as much as anything else.

Then she spied them—a pair of heavy brass candlesticks stood on the mantel shelf. Praying both God and Reverend Lennox would forgive her for what she was about to do, she removed one of the candles and slipped the candlestick through the slit of her skirt into the deep embroidered pocket concealed beneath. The very end of it poked out a little but hopefully Malcolm wouldn't notice.

"Sarah!" he barked, making her jump.

"I'm coming," she called then slipped behind the wooden screen which hid the necessary.

When Malcolm entered the room a moment later, she stepped out, pretending to smooth her skirts. The candlestick was a comforting weight against her leg.

"You're taking too long," he growled, taking her arm in a firm grip. To Sarah's relief, she noticed that he'd hidden his dirk. "The reverend and sexton are waiting."

"My apologies," she murmured.

Malcolm shot her a sharp glance as they emerged from the vestry, but she was careful to keep her gaze trained on the floor and her expression demure.

"Lord Tay, Miss Lambert, everything is ready," announced Reverend Lennox. He stood before the altar, the *Scottish Book of Common Prayer* in his hands.

"What...what about your robes?" Sarah asked as she and Malcolm took up their positions facing the clergyman. She'd do anything to delay what was about to happen. She also needed to find an opportunity to strike Malcolm.

Somehow, she had to distract him.

"I think we can dispense with all of the formalities on this particular occasion," replied the reverend with a strained smile.

The sexton, a tall thin man who stood to the side of the altar, gave a single nod. Sarah supposed it was only natural that he too was unwilling to gainsay the powerful Earl of Tay.

Reverend Lennox began to speak but Sarah barely listened as her mind buzzed with various plans. When he asked if either of them knew of any impediment that would prevent them from being lawfully joined together in matrimony, she briefly contemplated then discarded the idea of stating she was already handfasted to Alex. With no way to prove her claim, Malcolm would probably just accuse her of lying. She also couldn't see the reverend supporting her in the face of Malcolm's blistering ire.

Besides, there was the very real and ever-present threat that Malcolm might physically injure her in some way. *Disfigure her.*

An icy tremor shivered through Sarah as she recalled his earlier words: *I don't mind marrying a bride who isn't quite so pretty.* He might have put his dirk away, but she had no doubt he would use it on her if she refused to wed him. Even now, his right hand rested on something at his hip—probably the hilt of the knife.

Sarah slid her left hand into her own pocket and wrapped her fingers about the cold brass candlestick. If she were going to use it, she'd best do so soon, before it was too late.

At that moment, Reverend Lennox asked Malcolm, "Wilt thou have this woman to thy wedded wife, to live together after God's ordinance in the holy estate of matrimony? Wilt thou love her, comfort her, honor, and keep her in sickness and in health, and, forsaking all other, keep thee only unto her, so long as ye both shall live?"

Sarah held her breath as Malcolm raised her hand to his lips and then murmured, "I will." The glint in his dark eyes terrified her.

She didn't believe him. It was all a lie.

Reverend Lennox's gaze shifted to her and he proceeded to ask the same series of questions. "Wilt thou have this man to thy wedded husband," he began. "To live together…"

Sarah couldn't speak. Couldn't move. How could she possibly say "I will" and agree to be tied forever to such an abominable excuse for a man?

Malcolm's eyes narrowed and he squeezed her right hand when it was time for her to respond. "Sarah," he prompted through gritted teeth.

She swallowed, the sound audible in the silence, a silence that pulsed with tension and palpable menace.

"Oh, for God's sake," Malcolm snapped. He glowered at the reverend. "Her answer is yes, she will."

"My lord," spluttered Reverend Lennox. "You cannot answer for—"

"Don't try me, Lennox," barked Malcolm. "For everyone's sake, I recommend you keep going. Skip to the blessing of the ring."

The threat in Malcolm's voice was clear and the reverend nodded. With a shaking hand, he held out his prayer book to receive the ring. "My lord…"

Malcolm reached into his greatcoat and pulled out a slender gold band. When Sarah gasped—she hadn't expected him to be this prepared—he made a scoffing sound. "I'm not totally lacking in decorum, my dear," he said with a smirk. "I want the world to know that you are mine."

He placed the ring on the open pages of the prayer book but the reverend's hands shook so much, the ring slipped to the stone floor with a faint metallic clatter.

"Christ, man." Malcolm sniped. He bent low near Sarah's skirts to retrieve the ring. "Clearly, if you want a thing done well—"

Oh, God. Now, Sarah!

She pulled her weapon from her pocket and as Malcolm began to straighten, she swung with all her might. The heavy brass candlestick connected with the back of his head and with a grunt, he crumpled to the floor.

She dropped the candelabrum and jumped back, her hands flying to her face. *Oh, dear Lord, forgive me. I've killed him. In a church.*

But then Malcolm groaned and his eyelids fluttered.

Reverend Lennox grasped her arm. "Run, dear child," he urged. "Just run."

Sarah didn't need any further encouragement. Picking up her skirts, she turned and fled down the aisle, heading for the door.

It wasn't until she was flying along the road on her mare at full gallop, heading north again, that she dared a backward glance. The village of Balloch was receding. No one was in pursuit.

At least not yet. And she had well over twenty miles of unfamiliar ground to cover on her own.

She prayed she would find the way.

As evening descended, it seemed heaven had decided to answer her prayers. In the distance, Fairy Hill appeared. The rising moon illuminated the snowy peak, guiding her back toward Loch Rannoch and the husband of her heart.

Alex.

If only Malcolm would not follow. That would be a miracle indeed.

CHAPTER 27

It was several hours past nightfall when Alex dismounted from his tired, sweating horse in the courtyard of Blackloch. The journey to Lochrose Castle and back had been long, but well worth it as far as he was concerned. Within a few short weeks, unless anything untoward occurred, he would truly be a free man.

He threw the reins to one of the young grooms who appeared, and with a smile tugging at the corner of his mouth, he headed for the Great Hall. Bandit bounded out from the stables, tail wagging madly, but he only gave the collie a quick pat. He couldn't wait to hold Sarah in his arms again.

However, as soon as he pushed through the double oak doors, he sensed something was wrong. For one thing, the flickering light of the wall sconces and the blazing fire in the large stone fireplace revealed a long dark smear—perhaps blood—on the threshold.

When Dobson approached him from the shadows by the door, a grim expression on his face and a sword at his hip, panic flared.

"What's going on?" Alex demanded. "Has someone been hurt?"

Dobson bowed. "I'm verra sorry, sir." His gaze shifted to the back of the Hall and he added, "Isla had best explain."

Isla? What the Devil was she *doing here?*

Sure enough, Isla was seated on a padded wooden bench beneath the display of mounted weapons at the back of the Hall. There was something white about her neck—good Lord, surely it wasn't a bandage?—and the way she sat that made the hairs rise on Alex's nape. Her shoulders were hunched and her gaze touched everywhere but him. She had the look of someone who was defeated...and guilty.

"Where is Miss Lambert?" he demanded, glancing between Dobson and Isla. There was a snap in his voice but he couldn't help it.

Dobson nodded his daughter's way again. "Isla. Stand up, lass, and answer the master."

"Tell me." Alex approached the girl as she rose on shaky legs. "What's happened?"

"'Tis all my fault," whispered Isla and a tear slipped down her cheek. "MacLagan is grievously injured and..." She swallowed. "Miss Lambert... She's gone."

Alex grasped her by the upper arms. "What do you mean, Sarah's gone? Gone where? What happened to MacLagan?"

Isla's hand shook as she brushed another tear from her cheek. "I-I saw Lord Tay pass through Aberfeldy. And I..."

"You what?" A muscle twitched furiously in Alex's jaw as he fought against the impulse to shake the information out of the girl. "What did you do?"

She swallowed again. "I went to him and told him Miss Lambert was here. At Blackloch."

Alex's next words snapped like a lash. "*What?* Please, for the love of God, tell me you're lying."

Isla's tears flowed in earnest now. "I know what I did was verra wrong, sir, but ye see, I love you and she's a Sassenach. Ye deserve—"

Alex shook his head as a great wave of horrified fury crashed through him. "Don't tell me Lord Tay took her. Please don't say that, Isla."

The maid wrung her hands. "I'm sorry, but, aye...he did."

Oh, dear God, no. My poor love.

Alex had to get her back.

He dropped his hands from Isla. He didn't want to touch her anymore. "When? How?" he barked, not caring how angry he sounded.

"Early this afternoon," answered Dobson. "Aileen, Miss Lambert, and MacLagan were on their way back from Kinloch. Isla stopped by here first, found out where they were by questioning one of the young chambermaids who didna ken any better, then she helped Tay waylay them in the Black Wood."

Alex shot Isla a withering glare. *The little turncoat.* "Is Aileen all right?"

"Aye, sir," answered Dobson. "Shaken but muckle well enough, thank God. MacLagan took a nasty shot courtesy of Lord Tay—a graze to the temple—and he's a wee bit dazed, but he'll live. Aileen's tendin' to him. Tay also held a dirk to Isla's throat, to coerce Miss Lambert into going with him."

Sweet Jesus. Tay was clearly unhinged. Terror twisted Alex's guts, but he couldn't give into the fear. He needed to keep a clear head in order to rescue Sarah. "Isla, do you know where Lord Tay was going to take Miss Lambert?"

"Back to Taymoor Castle, sir," she whispered, her face ashen. "I think he still wishes to wed her. Verra much."

"The problem is, Isla," growled Alex, "I love her and want to marry her too. You *knew* that. And you had no right to interfere."

With that, he spun on his heel, heading for the courtyard and the stables again. If he rode like the wind, he'd be at Taymoor in a matter of a few hours, perhaps even before midnight, to free Sarah from that cur's filthy clutches. She was smart and courageous and capable, but even so, she must be petrified. *And if the bastard had hurt her...* Alex lengthened his stride.

"Sir!"

It was Isla. Alex paused at the door and shot her an icy glare. "What is it?" he ground out.

"I didna betray you. Lord Tay doesna ken who ye truly are, if ye take my meaning. I also made him swear no' to hurt you."

Alex shook his head in disgust. "Then you are just as foolish as you are selfish, Isla. The man is not to be trusted."

The sharp clatter of horse's hooves echoed off Blackloch's stone walls, claiming Alex's attention, and he spun around, heart pounding a ragged rhythm.

"Sarah!" Shock and joy reverberated through him at the sight of the woman he loved cantering up to Blackloch's open door.

She reined in her shaking mare and he rushed to her, sweeping her off the saddle into his arms. As Sarah sagged against him, Alex hugged her with all his might.

He kissed her temple. "You got away. I just got back and Dobson told me everything."

"Yes," she murmured, her voice choked with tears and emotion. "I did."

Alex drew back and framed her beautiful face with his hands. In the light emanating from the doorway, he could see she was pale, but otherwise appeared physically unharmed. But after an encounter with a mongrel like Tay, he couldn't be certain. "I hate to ask, my love, but are you hurt?"

She offered a tremulous smile. "Only shaken and saddle-sore. I cannot say the same for Malcolm. I...I brained him with a brass candlestick and knocked him unconscious."

Alex laughed, panic melting into a rough chuckle. "My clever brave lass. I shouldn't say it, but I suppose all those times you thought about doing the same thing to me came in handy."

"I suppose so," she returned with a rueful smile. "Although the difference is, I never *had* to with you."

Alex bent his head and claimed his beloved's mouth in a brief ardent kiss. "I don't deserve you," he whispered. "But I thank God you are mine."

Tears suddenly filled Sarah's eyes. "You shouldn't though. Thank God, I mean."

Alex frowned down at her as he brushed a tear from her cheek with his thumb. "What's wrong, my love?"

"I..." Sarah swallowed and a look of anguish washed over her face. "In the heat of the moment, when I was arguing with Malcolm, I let slip that I knew all about the terrible things he'd done in the past. And of course he worked out straightaway who you really are. I'm so, so sorry." Her voice cracked. "I've betrayed you—"

"Shhhh." Alex pressed a finger to her lips. "It's not your fault. None of this is your fault."

Sarah shook her head. "But you're in danger. *I've* put you in danger."

"I've been in danger for years. It will be all right. Come." Alex threaded his fingers through Sarah's and tugged her into the Great Hall.

Once inside, he paused and spoke with Dobson to issue instructions that would increase security about the castle; the portcullis was to be lowered and he wanted a pair of armed guards posted at each entrance. Isla had disappeared from the Hall. Alex supposed she'd retired to her old room. But he didn't want to think about her now.

He just needed to be with Sarah.

As soon as Alex took her hand, Sarah knew where they were headed—to his bedchamber—and she concurred with her whole heart. To have his hands on her, in her hair, cupping her breasts, to feel the warm rasp of his tongue plundering her mouth was exactly what she wanted too.

To feel loved and safe.

Cherished.

She'd given herself heart and soul to Alex—she'd give her life for Alex—and to feel that he needed her just as much as she needed him was intoxicating. Exhilarating.

The fact that Alex had immediately forgiven her for accidentally divulging his true identity to Malcolm spoke volumes about how he felt about her. If she'd ever doubted that Alex truly loved her, she didn't now.

There was no holding back for either of them when the bedchamber door clicked shut. Impatient to touch his naked skin, Sarah tugged frantically at all the layers of Alex's clothes, pushing off his navy-blue coat and tearing at the buttons of his waistcoat before ripping his shirt from his buckskin breeches.

Alex was possessed by the same sense of desperation. After yanking off his own shirt, he jerked the jacket of her riding habit open, scattering buttons. Her lace jabot and silk shirt quickly joined the pile of garments on the floor before he backed her toward the bed. All the while he devoured her mouth, his hot passionate kisses so long and so deep, Sarah was soon panting and quivering with need.

Pushing her down onto the bed, Alex deftly unlaced her stays before pulling her chemise down, exposing her breasts. He hovered above her on straightened arms, gaze searing as it traced over her body, making her nipples tighten to hard, aching points.

Sarah arched her back and gripped the tightly bunched muscles of his upper arms. "Kiss me," she whispered. Desire had rendered her breathless and without shame.

"I want to look at you." The dancing firelight threw Alex's handsome features into sharp relief, highlighting his high cheekbones and strong jaw, his chiseled mouth. His gaze dipped to her breasts before returning to her face. "You are so beautiful."

"So are you." She splayed her hands against his hard pectoral muscles and reveled in the strong beat of his heart against her palm. "I don't wish to spoil your perusal, but wouldn't it be better if I had less clothing on? And you too, for that matter."

He smiled his wolf's smile. "Ah, you see, that's my dilemma. I can't decide whether I want to undress you to look my fill, slide my fingers underneath your skirts to see how wet you are for me, or use my mouth on you straightaway."

"Oh." Sarah bit her lip. Her lower belly ached with pulsing arousal at his wicked yet wholly welcome words. "My my, that is a dilemma. I suppose you could always put yourself inside me so you can take your pleasure too. But I'm sure you'll let me know your decision soon enough."

"Why don't I show you?" He bestowed a swift yet searching kiss on her mouth, gently kissed the tip of each breast then slid off the bed. In the next moment, her skirts had been pushed up and his hands were on her thighs, gently nudging them apart.

Sarah closed her eyes then gasped as Alex blew across the damp furrow of her sex before spreading her apart. She was soaked with desire and her whole body burned as she waited for him to pleasure her.

Alex had turned her into a wanton. And she loved it.

When his tongue began to lave her intimate folds and the entrance to her sex, her fingers curled into the burgundy silk counterpane and she writhed, circling her hips, spreading herself wider. What Alex was doing felt glorious, but she needed more.

She reached past the voluminous folds of her wool skirts and petticoats to clutch his thick silky hair and he chuckled. "I know what you want," he said, his warm breath tickling her inner thigh. "But all in good time, my sweet."

Sarah lightly tugged on his hair again. "A good time would be right now, you cruel man," she replied, voice husky with need.

"Cruel?" He flicked her most sensitive spot with the tip of his tongue then returned to teasing her inner thigh with whisper-soft kisses.

She mewled in frustration and with another soft laugh he capitulated, sliding two fingers inside her. At the same time he lightly suckled her throbbing peak.

Oh, sweet heaven. Oh, yes...

A moan tumbled from her and at last Alex applied himself to the task of ravishing her sex with the unfettered abandon she craved. His long fingers rhythmically stroked inside her and he gorged on her tight, throbbing bud, licking and sucking. As an exquisite coil of tension began to spiral tighter and tighter, Sarah's blood raced, her heart pounded, her breath came in short, sharp pants. She writhed and thrashed and just when she thought she couldn't bear a moment more of Alex's sweet torture, pleasure took her. It rushed over and through her and she clung to Alex as the pulsating waves of bliss carried her away to paradise.

This is love. This is how things should be, she thought as she opened her eyes to find Alex staring down at her, his own gaze filled with burning adoration.

He'd released his manhood from his breeches, and with perfect precision, positioned himself at her entrance. On one smooth glide, he seated himself fully inside her.

Her inner muscles rippled, welcoming the powerful, rigid length of him and he groaned.

"Sweet Jesus, Sarah. You feel so good."

She curled her hands around his granite-hard shoulders. "Love me, Alex."

"Always."

~

Alex bent his head and tenderly claimed Sarah's mouth, hoping his kiss would clearly demonstrate all the love he felt for her, deep in his heart. She kissed him back, threading her fingers through his hair, pressing her naked breasts against his chest, stoking his need and setting every nerve alight until his entire body was ablaze with desire.

Sarah's fresh need must have been acute too. Moaning into his mouth, she tilted her hips, rocking against him, and he was overwhelmed by the urge to move, to take his pleasure as she had invited him to earlier.

He sank into a slow, steady rhythm, sliding in and out of her with long, sure strokes, holding her gaze, loving her with his eyes. Even when he increased the tempo, thrusting harder and faster, steadily driving them both toward release, she kept up with him. She gripped his shoulders, her rhythmic pants and moans pure music to his ears.

When the warm sleek satin of Sarah's inner passage clenched around him and she cried out, Alex knew she'd found ecstasy again. His heart swelled and his own orgasm began to gather, the pressure building deep in his spine and his balls. He pumped harder, his cock thickening, his blood pounding until he couldn't hold back any longer. With a hoarse cry he let go and blinding pleasure crashed through him. His body quaking, his chest heaving, he collapsed onto Sarah, boneless with a satisfaction that bordered on profound.

Dear God, he was the most fortunate man alive to have Sarah. And to think she loved him back, that was the true miracle.

Reluctantly, he pulled away from his love. As much as he wanted to undress her slowly and make love to her again, they had to make plans for the morrow and the coming days. And they needed to use the bed for its second purpose and get some sleep.

He called for hot water and supper, and once they were washed and their hunger sated—Alex couldn't remember the last time he'd eaten— they snuggled together on the settee before the fire. Sarah, wearing his dark blue velvet banyan with a cup of hot chocolate in hand, looked utterly content as she leaned against his chest. With a sigh—he hardly wanted to dispel the peace surrounding them—he asked Sarah to go through the events of the afternoon and evening in greater detail so he could better assess the situation.

When she described how Tay had threatened to disfigure her, he tightened his grip on his tumbler of whisky so much, he was surprised the glass didn't shatter in his hand. The fact that Sarah had been able to think so clearly and cleverly, then take decisive action to extricate herself from such a terrifying situation, made his chest swell with admiration.

Alex kissed the top of her head when she'd finished her tale. "We will need to leave Blackloch in the morning and make ourselves scarce for a little while, just to be safe."

"I know I knocked Malcolm out, but I'm still worried about what he will do. He wants me back. And I'm sure he wants to punish you."

"I agree, we do need to be careful. But I believe we are safe for tonight. And I have the support of the dragoon captain here. Malcolm cannot do much to hurt us at the moment."

Sarah put down her hot chocolate and frowned. "But the dragoon captain doesn't know you're Alexander MacIvor. What if Malcolm goes to him come morning and tells him who you really are?"

"Ah, but you see Captain Hamilton does know who I am, my love. And he doesn't care."

"Is that part of your 'arrangement' with him?"

"More or less. As I mentioned, he's very grateful that I've been working with him to end the lawlessness that had been plaguing Kinloch and the whole area. Tay would have to convince another dragoon commander much farther afield to come and arrest me. So, for tonight, I trust we are not in any danger. I'll send word to Captain Hamilton at first light, letting him know he may receive a visit from the irate Earl of Tay."

Sarah smiled and rested her head against his shoulder again. "That is a relief to know." She curled her fingers around his. It was a simple gesture that spoke of how close they'd grown in such a short space of time. He put aside his whisky, intending to kiss her but she spoke again. "You haven't told me how your visit to your friend went. You said he might be able to help you gain a royal pardon."

Alex grimaced with guilt. "I'm sorry. In all the excitement of having you back here safe and sound, I have neglected to tell you the good news. I have the support of another nobleman, one who is highly connected, the Earl of Strathburn. I'll be meeting with him and the Lord Advocate of Scotland in Edinburgh in just under a fortnight. All going well, I will be granted clemency."

"You will?" Sarah turned in his arms. Her blue eyes were alight with hope, and her smile was the brightest he'd ever seen. "Why, that's wonderful."

"Aye, it is," he murmured huskily. "Very soon you will be Sarah MacIvor, Lady Rannoch. And on that day, when I see you walking down the aisle, I will be the happiest man alive."

CHAPTER 28

Kinloch, Loch Rannoch
The following morning...

Malcolm slowed his exhausted horse as the rising sun cast pale rays through the mist enveloping the tiny village of Kinloch and the dark loch.

The dragoon barracks wasn't hard to find. The two-story thatched stone dwelling—more a house than anything resembling a decent base for troops—lay in the deep shadow of a looming granite hill.

Malcolm dismounted inside the yard with care, holding onto his horse's saddle for a moment as bile rose in his gorge and a wave of dizziness washed over him. Thanks to his cursed runaway bride, his head pounded with the steady beat of a battle drum.

The vicious blow Sarah had struck had rendered him unconscious for a good half-hour. With the help of Reverend Lennox, he'd returned to Taymoor Castle to regroup. But between his aching head, and the writhing anger in his gut, he'd eventually given up on sleep and had decided to surrender to the overwhelming urge to wreak bloody vengeance on Alexander MacIvor. And to reclaim Sarah. As much as he despised the bitch, he needed her money.

The light-headedness passed and when Malcolm looked up it was to discover a pair of young, red-coated dragoons eyeing him with suspicion from the shelter of a covered portico. It probably didn't help he carried a sheathed sword at his waist. If he removed his greatcoat, they'd also see he carried a brace of pistols at his back. After the Rebellion, weapons had been proscribed in the Highlands, but because he was a nobleman loyal to the King, the ban had never really applied to him.

One of the lads greeted him as he approached. "Good morning, sir. May we be of assistance?"

"Aye." Malcolm wasn't fooled by the soldier's cordial tone. Not when both men had tightened their grips on their muskets. "And it's 'my lord' as far as you are concerned." He removed his tricorn hat, and after tucking it beneath one arm, pulled off his gloves and slapped them against the palm of his hand. "I want to speak with your commander. Tell him the Earl of Tay is here."

"Of course, Lord Tay." The taller, slightly older soldier—a Sassenach judging by his accent—gave a deferential bow. "Follow me."

Malcolm was ushered through the entry hall to a small but scrupulously neat office; a bright fire burning in the grate illuminated the gold-embossed print on the spines of the books in a pair of bookcases and a brass candelabrum on the matching desk of polished oak. He winced and clenched his fist when he spied the candlestick.

The soldier—a corporal—invited him to take a seat in the brown leather wingchair in front of the desk before disappearing. Within a few minutes, a connecting door at the back of the room opened and the dragoon captain emerged.

Finally, someone who would be some use to him.

Malcolm rose as the athletic-looking captain greeted him.

"Lord Tay, good morning to you. I'm Captain Hamilton. You've journeyed a fair way to see me. What can I do for you?" He indicated they should both take seats, so Malcolm reclaimed the wingchair whilst Captain Hamilton took the straight-backed Jacobean chair behind his desk.

Malcolm flicked a piece of non-existent lint off the braided cuff of his greatcoat. "I rather think it's a case of what we can do for each other." He reached into his pocket and pulled out his silver snuffbox. "Would you care for some?"

Beneath his perfectly dusted periwig, the captain raised an eyebrow. "Thank you, but no. Let me tell you something about myself, Lord Tay. I am not fond of snuff or beating about the bush. Perhaps you could speak plainly."

Malcolm bristled at the Englishman's condescending tone. The arrogance of the man! Nevertheless, he put away his snuff case and got straight to the point. He really wasn't in the mood to practice false civility either. "Alexander Price of Blackloch Castle is not who he says he is. He's really Alexander MacIvor, a wanted Jacobite. He fought in the Forty-five, as did his late father, Baron Rannoch. I want you to arrest him for treason."

Captain Hamilton's expression did not change. "I'm afraid you are mistaken, my lord," he said coolly. "I've seen Mr. Price's papers and everything is in order. The man I know is above reproach. By all local accounts, Alexander MacIvor perished in the great fire at Blackloch Castle over ten years ago. I've also heard his mother, Lady Rannoch, his younger sister, Anne MacIvor, his *fiancée*, Lady Margaret Stewart, and a good many of the castle's servants and defenseless crofters' families around Loch Rannoch were murdered...by you and your men." The captain cocked an eyebrow again. "So I think I know everything I need to."

Malcolm leapt to his feet and planted his fists on the table. "Why you puffed-up toad-eater. What's MacIvor paying you? I'll have you stripped of your rank for this. Court-martialed."

Captain Hamilton also rose and looked down his nose at him. "I rather think you won't. Do you really want everyone to know what you did, *my lord*?"

Malcolm's face was hot and his head felt like someone was pounding it with a hammer. "I was within my rights."

"Yes. Quite. Some indecent souls might believe that. But many won't. How old was young Anne MacIvor again?"

"Fuck you," snapped Malcolm.

"Not today." Hamilton's gaze shifted to the door. "Corporal Jones will see you out. I trust your journey back to Taymoor Castle will be a pleasant one."

Malcolm remounted his horse and spurred the beast into a gallop, heading toward the bridge over the Tummel River. But it wasn't Taymoor Castle he was bound for.

It was Blackloch.

CHAPTER 29

"Are you almost ready, my love?" Alex cast a glance at Sarah as he buckled the leather strap on the satchel containing documents he wanted to take to Edinburgh.

"Yes. I think so." She tucked the slim volume of poetry she'd been perusing into her own satchel and glanced toward the library window. "I'm pleased to see the weather is holding fair. How far is it to the inn at Port-na-Craig?"

"About thirty miles. I'm sorry to make you ride so far again after yesterday's ordeal..."

"No, it's all right." Sarah's face was pale and her eyes shadowed with fatigue but she managed a smile nonetheless. "It must be done. I'd rather be safe than sorry."

Alex rounded the desk and kissed her. "My brave lass. Tomorrow you will be able to luxuriate in a carriage with soft blankets and furs and warm bricks at your feet."

"And foot rubs?"

"You can have as many of those as you like. Or any other kind of caress, for that matter."

Her blue eyes danced with amusement and another emotion he rather suspected was desire. "That's very obliging of you."

His hand slipped to her lovely round bottom as he whispered, "I promise you, you won't be interested in that book of poetry for long."

A knock at the door had Alex inwardly cursing. It was Dobson who entered. "Sir, you said to let you know when the horses were ready. I have your sword here too."

"Thank you." Alex took the sheathed weapon—a basket-hilted sword—and strapped the scabbard to the leather belt at his waist. "And is the portcullis raised?"

"Aye, sir. Just now."

"Excellent."

"Sir." Dobson's brow had folded into deep furrows and his gaze had fallen to the carpet. "About Isla... If you had the time to have a quick word... She's waiting to see you outside..."

Alex frowned. Dealing with Isla right now was an added irritation he could do without. "Miss Lambert and I have given the matter some thought and we think it's best that my original plan still stands. She can work at the Boar's Head. I do not have time—"

He broke off as the sound of Bandit barking madly echoed up the stairs from the Hall. He crossed the library and fully opened the door to the Long Gallery. *What the deuce?*

That was when his blood turned to ice. There was a shout below and then a shot rang out followed by a scream.

Christ, no. "Dobson, stay here and protect Miss Lambert." Alex shrugged out of his coat and tossed it to the servant. "Get my pistol. It's in the desk. Top drawer. Load it. Don't hesitate to use it."

Dobson's expression tightened grimly. "Aye, my lord."

Fear flickered in Sarah's eyes. "Oh, God. Is it Malcolm?"

Alex gave a curt nod. "I think so."

At that moment, Tay's voice carried up the stairs. "Wherever you are, I'm coming for you, Alexander MacIvor, you bastard."

"Don't worry, Sarah." Alex turned back and gave the woman he loved with his entire being a swift kiss, refusing to believe it could be their last. "Stay here with Dobson."

Heart hammering, the lust for vengeance coursing through his blood, Alex drew his sword and stepped into the Hall as Tay reached the top of the stairs.

The disgraced earl's face was contorted with anger. In one hand he brandished an ornate basket-hilted sword. In the other he held a pistol. "You fucking arsehole!"

"My lord. Watch out!" Isla appeared as if from nowhere and launched herself at Alex at the same moment the pistol discharged.

Oh, God no. The maid's eyes widened for an instant and she slumped to the Turkish hall runner at Alex's feet, a crimson stain blooming on her back. Before he could even blink, Tay was charging toward him, red-faced, sword raised.

White-hot anger seared through Alex, stirring him to action. Praying God would forgive him for his neglect, he stepped away from Isla, sword at the ready, muscles braced for the onslaught. As much as he wanted to help the lass, he needed to draw Tay away from Sarah and dispense with the sick bastard once and for all.

The games were over. The day of reckoning had arrived.

With a roar Tay lunged, slashing wildly, but Alex easily parried his move and then drove him back toward the staircase with a series of quick thrusts. Moving down the Long Gallery in a macabre dance of advance and retreat, thrust and parry, Alex quickly ascertained that Tay might be tall and well-muscled, but he was less skilled. His reflexes were slower, his countermoves less sophisticated. The brute's unbridled anger —whilst it might lend a certain recklessness to his moves—was also likely to be a hindrance rather than a help. His offensive strokes were more aggressive, which meant he would probably tire sooner rather than later.

Clearly incensed he'd started to lose ground, Tay leapt backward then twisted with an agility that took Alex by surprise. The cur's blade sliced through the sleeve of his cambric shirt, nicking his left bicep, and Alex swore. He barely had time to suck in another breath before Tay lunged at him again. Alex ducked, the blade missing him by a whisker, and then Tay lost his balance, his forward momentum making him stumble.

He crashed into a chair but before Alex could strike, Tay spun, hurling the piece of furniture in his direction. Alex leapt out of the way but as he landed, Tay slashed out at his thigh.

Shit. The hot sting of the cut fired Alex with renewed purpose.

The clash of steel and their ragged breathing and grunts filled the air as Alex continued to drive Tay away from the library. At the bottom of the stairs leading up to the second floor, his foe pushed forward, the blade of his sword sliding down Alex's until their weapons were locked at the hilt. For several fraught moments they grappled each other for the advantage; Tay's eyes burned with murderous rage as his nostrils flared and his chest heaved. "I'm going to gut you...like a fish," he panted.

"When it's a cold day in hell, Tay." Arm and thigh muscles shaking with the strain, Alex gave an almighty push and threw Tay off.

Tay staggered back but he swiftly regained his footing and bolted up the stairs to the next floor. When Alex gave chase, Tay turned and lunged wildly again, blade flashing through the air with a hiss. Alex neatly ducked and spun low, kicking out at the bastard's knee, knocking him into the paneled wall with a crash.

Now was his chance. Launching himself forward, Alex tried to catch Tay on the defensive—but the dog darted away into the center of the corridor again.

Fucking hell. Harnessing his frustration, Alex gave chase.

Lungs burning, sword flashing, he made cutting stroke after cutting stroke, forcing Tay down the second-floor gallery, past the morning room and his private study, the guest bedchambers and his own suite. Tay's reaction time was slowing, his stamina failing, his parries growing weaker. It wouldn't be long until Alex had Tay right where he wanted him—skewered by his sword, the blackguard's heart cleaved in two.

Tay suddenly swung around but his feint failed and he tripped on the rug. As he parried Alex's next blow with an upthrust arm, their blades locked again and they crashed against each other. "Where's...Sarah?" Tay panted as they wrestled, chest to chest. "When you're dead...I'm going to fuck her...so hard. Just...like your mother...and your Lady Margaret."

Alex saw red. Blood-red.

Baring his teeth in a feral snarl, he shoved Tay away then slashed his sword downwards with all his might. The blade struck the basket-handle with such force, Tay lost his grip and his weapon went flying.

Shock flashed through Tay's widened eyes. Then he spun and fled down the last few yards of the gallery, heading for the door leading to the battlements.

Triumph flaring, Alex sprinted after him up the stairs...

~

Sarah's hands shook as she pressed a wadded-up piece of fabric—her silk fichu—against the bullet wound in Isla's right shoulder blade. The maid was unconscious, her breathing shallow and shaky; lying on her belly, her head turned to the side, the lass's face was bone-white whereas the stain upon the back of her pale gray gown was bright red.

When Alex and Malcolm had moved down the Long Gallery, away from the library, Sarah had helped Dobson to carry his daughter inside. After they'd laid her upon the damask upholstered settee before the fire, Dobson had gone to Alex's desk and had taken out his pistol. As he loaded the weapon, he asked in a shaking voice how Isla was.

"I don't know, Dobson," Sarah said with tears in her eyes. "I honestly don't know."

She'd never nursed anyone with such a grievous injury before. Kneeling beside the settee, her fingers covered in Isla's blood, she supposed they should cut the maid's dress away and examine the wound to see if the bullet was still lodged inside her, but she didn't have anything resembling a knife or scissors.

And all the while, her ears strained to hear what was going on in the Gallery.

Oh, dear God. If anything happens to Alex... If Malcolm comes for me again...

Her mouth dry, her throat tight, Sarah swallowed down her fear and tried to focus on helping Isla. There was just so much blood. Her silk fichu was totally inadequate in stemming the flow. Perhaps she could rip off some of the cushion covers and use those. Even though Isla had betrayed her, twice, she would do what she could to save the lass.

Somehow, she didn't think it would be enough.

The door flew open, and Sarah jumped whilst Dobson aimed the pistol at the unexpected intruder.

Thank the Lord, it was only Aileen.

The distraught woman's hands flew to her face. "Och, no. My poor wee bairn," she cried, before rushing to the settee and dropping to her knees beside Sarah. With shaking fingers, she pushed her daughter's red curls away from her ashen face.

The housekeeper raised her gaze to Sarah's, eyes brimming with tears. "I heard pistol fire and shoutin' in the Great Hall. And then I saw Lord Tay mounting the stairs. But I didna realize he'd shot my poor Isla."

"Yes, I'm afraid so," Sarah replied. Tears spilled from her eyes and ran down her cheeks as well. "I didn't see what happened, but I heard Isla call out right before the shot. I think she was trying to save Lord Rannoch."

"Aye, I think so too," Dobson said. Ever faithful, he now stood by the cracked open door, his gaze and his pistol trained down the Long Gallery.

"I hope the master cuts the bastard to pieces and sends him straight to where he belongs—to the devil," muttered Aileen.

"So do I." Sarah hated to ask the question but she did so anyway. "Did you see who else was injured, Aileen?"

"Aye. Lord Tay shot young Andy Stark in the arm and stabbed MacWilliam in the side. Both were on duty at the front door in the Great Hall."

Oh, no. Sarah closed her eyes. How could one man wreak so much havoc? Cause so much damage and death? She prayed Stark and MacWilliam, and even Isla, wouldn't die.

Most of all, she prayed for Alex.

At that moment, Dobson opened the door wider admitting MacLagan.

The footman's face was as white as the bandage about his head. "I heard Isla had been hurt," he began. "Moira saw it happen. She sent me with these." He nodded at the bowl of water and bundle of fresh linen bandages he carried.

Even though Lord Tay's bullet had grazed his temple the day before, Sarah was impressed the young man had risked his own safety again.

"Thank you, MacLagan." Sarah waved him over to the fireside. "Do you happen to have a dirk about you? Or what about you, Dobson? We need to cut away Isla's gown."

MacLagan retrieved something from the desk. "Here's the master's penknife, Miss Lambert. It should be sharp enough."

Sarah took it with thanks, and with Aileen's and MacLagan's assistance, they carefully repositioned Isla onto her side before cutting away her blood-soaked bodice, stays, and shift to investigate the wound beneath. The injured girl did not stir.

"It looks like the shot has gone all the way through," murmured MacLagan, gently wiping the blood away with a damp cloth.

"Is...is that a good thing?" asked Sarah, swallowing hard against a surge of queasiness. She'd never dealt with anything like this before.

MacLagan nodded and smiled. "Aye, it is, Miss Lambert. Now if we can just stop the bleedin'..."

All of a sudden, Isla's eyelids fluttered and she moaned.

Aileen squeezed her daughter's hand. "Isla, my bonnie wee lassie. It's yer mam."

Isla opened her eyes and blinked dazedly. "What...what happened?"

Alex emerged onto the battlements, all his senses on high alert and his sword arm poised to strike. Even though his chest burned and his breathing was ragged, he was ready for anything Tay cared to throw his way.

He would not be bested.

His gaze darted around the snow-dusted ramparts searching for his mark. *There.* At the eastern edge, a shadow moved. Tay was crouching behind a sizable block of stone.

As quietly and as swiftly as he could, Alex skirted the perimeter of the battlements, making his way toward Tay's hiding place. What was the bastard up to?

Alex recalled the last time he'd been up here with Sarah—a small number of masonry tools had been left behind. A chisel and a trowel, perhaps? A hammer?

To undermine Tay's confidence by disabusing him of the notion he'd have the advantage of surprise, Alex called out. "I can see where you are, Tay. What are you going to do, now? Leap out and throw stones at me?"

Tay ignored him so Alex crept closer. When he was only a few yards away from Tay's hidey-hole, he spoke again. "This is ridiculous. Why don't you come out and face your fate like a man instead of behaving like a sniveling coward?"

When Tay leapt up and hurled his spent pistol then a hammer in his direction, Alex was expecting the attack and he easily ducked out of the way.

Alex straightened and cocked an eyebrow. "What's next? The trowel or the chisel?"

"Fuck you, MacIvor," growled Tay. He adjusted his stance and that's when Alex noticed that there was indeed a chisel in his hand. "I should have made sure you were dead eleven years ago."

"Quite possibly. But it seems you have a talent for making mistakes. Of making poor choices." Alex took another few steps forward, pointing the tip of his sword straight at Tay's chest. "Whereas I have a talent for vengeance. Why don't you drop the chisel? It won't help you, you know." He lowered his voice. "Nothing will."

Tay let out a low growl and lunged, chisel raised, but Alex simply flicked his sword and neatly sliced at Tay's wrist. With a howl, Tay dropped the tool and stumbled backward into the parapet, gripping his lower arm. Blood seeped between his clenched fingers. Although his lip curled into a sneer in a display of false bravado, he was sweating. "You call me a sniveling coward, yet here we are and you won't finish this. I'm starting to think you don't have the guts—"

Alex flicked the sword tip up again and scored Tay's bristle-clad jaw with a long, fine cut. "Oh, I do have the guts, Tay. In fact, I'm just trying to decide how you'll die. What would be the most suitable punishment for someone like you, someone who despoils and takes the lives of innocents with impunity? Someone who murdered my mother, my sister, and my *fiancée*. A sorry excuse for a man who kidnapped and threatened to harm the woman I love."

Tay shot him an incensed glare. "You kidnapped Sarah first—"

"Yes, I did, but I'm not the one on trial here. You are." Alex took another step forward. "However, unlike you, I'm not without mercy. I'll let you choose. Either I run you through—" his gaze shifted to the crenellations along the parapet—"or you jump."

Tay's chest heaved and his gaze narrowed. His mouth twisted into a parody of a grin. "See you in hell then, MacIvor." He climbed up between the snow-crusted parapets, turned, and with a mocking salute, fell backward.

Alex closed his eyes as he heard the heavy crunch on the gravel path below.

Instead of triumph, all he felt was an overwhelming sense of blessed relief.

Thank God. It was over. The Earl of Tay was dead.

CHAPTER 30

A small metallic sound—the click of a latch—dragged Sarah's attention away from Isla. Her heart in her mouth, her gaze flew to the library doorway and a small cry of joy escaped her when she saw who it was.

Alex.

She leapt to her feet and heedless of her bloodstained hands and gown, rushed over and threw her arms about him. "You're all right," she breathed against his neck as relief and gratitude flooded her. "Thank God."

"Aye." He drew back a little and framed her face with his hands. His gray eyes held hers. "And Malcolm is dead."

Sarah nodded. "Good. I'm glad." It wasn't a lie. "It's a just fate for such an evil man." She slid her hands down his arms and when he winced, she noticed the bloodstained tear in the sleeve of his white shirt. "Oh, sweet heaven." She stepped back and her gaze fell to the bloodied tear across his buckskin breeches. "You've been injured too."

Alex smiled. "It's not too bad. Just a wee nick on my arm and thigh. I'll heal well enough." His gaze moved to Isla and the group clustered around the settee. "How is she?" he asked softly, his expression grim.

"Alive. It's a shoulder wound but MacLagan says the bullet has only passed through muscle and sinew, and that if the bleeding stops, she'll recover."

He nodded and swallowed. "She saved my life."

"I know." Sarah touched his face. "I think, if you have the strength for it, she would be heartened to see you."

Alex placed his hand over hers. "You are the sweetest woman alive, Sarah. Not many would be as generous and forgiving as you."

Dobson and MacLagan moved away as she and Alex approached the settee but Aileen stayed by her daughter's side; they'd dressed Isla's shoulder with linen bandages but blood had soaked through them already.

Alex touched the older woman's shoulder. "I'm so sorry all this happened, Aileen."

At the sound of his voice, Isla's eyes opened. "Milord," she whispered through pale lips. She reached out a trembling hand and Alex took it as he lowered himself to his knees.

He brushed a tendril of her hair from her clammy brow. "I'm here, Isla."

Her lips trembled. "Is...is Lord Tay dead?"

"Aye."

A sigh shivered out of her. "I'm so verra sorry...for everythin' I've done...to Miss Lambert... To you." She broke off and a tear slipped from the corner of one eye. "I've been so verra wicked... If I die—"

"You won't die." Alex squeezed her hand. "I'm going to send for the surgeon at the barracks."

He glanced at MacLagan and the young man nodded. "I'll go now, milord. I expect he'll want to see to yer wounds too, but perhaps he can also check on young Stark and MacWilliam if that is all right with ye. According to Moira, Stark's been winged and MacWilliam's side will need a few stitches but other than that, they should be fine."

Alex inclined his head. "Very good."

Isla opened her eyes again and her gaze shifted to the end of the settee where Sarah hovered. "Miss Lambert...I hope that one day ye might be able to forgive me. I thought...ye were like...Lord Tay... Selfish... And I was jealous and so verra wrong. I want..." She drew a shaky breath then tried again. "I want Lord Rannoch to be happy."

Sarah's heart clenched and she blinked away tears. "I promise I'll do my very best to make him so."

Isla's lips twitched in a weak smile. "Good."

Aileen placed a dampened washcloth over her daughter's brow. "I think she needs to rest now, until the surgeon arrives."

Sarah nodded. "I agree."

Alex relinquished Isla's hand and rose to his feet. "Dobson, thank you for standing guard whilst I was otherwise engaged. It couldn't have been easy with Isla injured so."

Dobson nodded and Sarah noticed the faithful servant's eyes were suspiciously bright. "It has always been my pleasure to serve ye and yer family, milord. I'm a Clan McIvor man. If there's anythin' else I can do..."

Alex inclined his head. "Thank you. There might be. I will let you know in due course."

Sarah gathered up some of the spare bandages from a nearby mahogany table. "As it might be a while until the surgeon arrives, I rather think it's time someone else's wounds were attended to," she said, giving Alex a pointed look. There was too much blood seeping through his shirtsleeve and his breeches as far as she was concerned. And she hadn't failed to notice his grimace as he'd risen from the floor.

"Very well, Miss Lambert." He followed her from the room, his hand at her back, and her heart tripped when he added in a velvet-soft voice, "I have something I need to speak to you about... In private."

"Is this matter related to my promise to make you happy?" she asked, suddenly feeling breathless.

"No," he replied, tugging her into the small parlor next door. "It's about my desire to make *you* happy, my love.'

With a small kick, Alex closed the parlor door and gathered the woman he adored into his arms. There were a million other things he should be doing, but right at this very moment, he could think of nothing more pressing than his need to kiss Sarah. To show her how much he loved her and how grateful he was they were both alive and free to do whatever they wanted, whenever they wanted.

Pushing his fingers into her tumbling hair, Alex lowered his head and ruthlessly ravished her mouth with lips and tongue until they were both breathless and clinging to each other.

When he raised his head, he took pleasure in watching her eyelids flutter open; her gaze was soft, her eyes a soft hazy blue reminding him of the sky above Loch Rannoch on a fine, misty morning.

"I love you," she whispered. "When I saw you fighting with *Malcolm*..." She swallowed and her eyes shimmered.

He swiped a single tear away from her cheek with his thumb. "I know. I felt the same way last night when I found out he'd taken you. But it's all over now. We have each other, and very soon, you will be my lady-wife. My Lady Rannoch."

"Yes."

They kissed again and sometime later when Alex's head was spinning, he reluctantly dragged his mouth from hers. "I'm afraid I have to sort out...certain things," he said carefully. *Like disposing of Tay's body...*

Sarah's brow dipped into a frown. "I understand," she said, fingering the silver buttons of his brocade waistcoat. "Can I help?"

Alex smiled and lifted his injured left arm. "Well, I suppose you could bandage these dashed cuts first."

Sarah grimaced, her expression rueful. "Oh, good Lord. How could I have forgotten? All this time we've been kissing, you've still been bleeding. You must be in so much pain."

"It's all right." Alex swooped down and retrieved the bandages from the Aubusson rug beneath their feet. "It's not that bad. And I *did* distract you."

"Yes, you did." Sarah made him take off his waistcoat and shirt to examine his wounded bicep.

As he'd suspected, it was a superficial cut and the bleeding had almost stopped. Nevertheless, Sarah wrapped one of the linen bandages around it and he tied one firmly around his left thigh, over the top of his breeches. He needed to go out on Rannoch Moor with Dobson in search of a convenient peat bog, so there was no point in changing clothes when he was only going to get mucky again. His riding coat and greatcoat would easily hide the bloodstain on his shirtsleeve.

"I wish you didn't have to go," Sarah said, her gaze tracing over his naked chest and torso when he reached for his shirt from the back of a nearby chair.

The desire in her gaze had his cock twitching but he had to be strong. He shrugged on his shirt and pulled on his waistcoat. "I wish I didn't either. But even though Captain Hamilton is an ally, a nobleman of some stature has just died here at Blackloch. To avoid any inconvenient questions, I think it's best the Earl of Tay's final resting place isn't here."

Sarah's trouble gaze caught his. "You're going to take his body out to Rannoch Moor, aren't you?" she murmured.

He kissed her forehead. "Yes."

Sarah's expression hardened. "Good. He deserves an ignoble burial."

"That, my love," said Alex, "is just one more thing we both agree on."

CHAPTER 31

Blackloch Castle, Loch Rannoch
March 1, 1757

The sun was high in a brilliant blue sky when Alex escorted Sarah along the gritted path toward the sundial at the center of Blackloch's formal rose garden. Even though patches of slushy snow covered the frosty ground and the rose bushes were bare, early daffodils, purple crocuses, and delicate white snowdrops brightened the neatly laid-out parterres.

Farther ahead, through the stand of ancient oaks already wearing touches of spring green, Sarah caught a glimpse of Loch Rannoch, its waters glinting with diamonds of sunlight. On such a wonderful clear morning, it was difficult for her to believe this place had been the scene of such terrible tragedy nearly eleven years ago.

They paused near the sundial where Bandit was sniffing about the sandstone pedestal, and Sarah's vision misted quite unexpectedly. Pulling a lace-trimmed linen kerchief from the pocket secreted in the skirts of her peacock-blue riding habit, she tried but failed to surreptitiously dab at her eyes.

Alex brushed her damp cheek with the back of his fingers. "Don't cry, dear heart," he murmured, his expression so grave and tender, it made Sarah's tears well all the more. "This needs to be done. It's time."

"Are you sure?" Sarah attempted a smile but all she managed was a weak tremble of her lips. Her heart ached for this man whom she loved, for all he'd lost and endured.

His wide mouth lifted into a soft half-smile. "Aye. It is."

He knelt down, and at the foot of one of the rose bushes, he dug a narrow but deep hole in the half-frozen dirt with a small trowel that he'd taken from the pocket of his black redingote. Then he slipped his onyx and gold ring from his finger and gently pushed it into the ground before covering it with dirt again. A blackbird, hidden in the boughs of a nearby oak, sang sweetly.

Alex straightened and threaded his fingers through Sarah's. "I'll always miss my family," he murmured, "but I feel like they're at peace now." Raising her hand to his lips, he captured her gaze. The light in his gray eyes was solemn yet soft. "And I'm at peace. Because of you."

Sarah, her heart swelling with love, leaned forward and gently brushed her lips against his. "Shall we pick some flowers and lay them on your family's graves before we go?" she asked. Alex had told her there was a small, rarely used chapel and a family plot on the other side of the oak copse.

He shook his head. "No. This is enough, for now." He gave her a reassuring smile. "We'd best be on our way to Edinburgh. As soon as I can openly tell the world I'm Alexander MacIvor, Blackloch will officially have a laird again, and we shall be wed."

Once more, Sarah had to blink away tears, but this time, they were of joy. "I can hardly wait for that day."

Alex drew her into the warm circle of his strong arms and rested his forehead against hers. His eyes were bright with tears as well. "Me too, my love," he whispered. "Me too."

EPILOGUE

Eilean Dubh, Loch Rannoch
June 5, 1757

Sarah slid the last of the yellow roses into the cut-crystal vase on the satinwood table in the solar, then stepped back to admire her handiwork. She'd paid a visit to Blackloch's rose garden early this morning and had filled a basket with dew-sprinkled blooms.

Crossing to the open mullion window on the southern side of the tower, she glanced over to the far shore where the boat still lay on the shingle. Dobson had rowed her out here with Bandit several hours ago and Alex had promised he would follow as soon as he could, once he'd finished with pressing estate business in the village; the Laird of Blackloch had a meeting with the factor of the Robertson estate and the dragoon captain about further plans for Kinloch.

To Sarah's delight, it hadn't taken much convincing on her part to persuade her husband they needed time completely alone this afternoon. Only yesterday, they'd bidden farewell a castle full of guests, including Aunt Judith and her sweet new husband, Mr. Henry Weston, Charles Swindon, and Lord Lochrose and his pregnant wife, the lovely

Lady Lochrose. As much as Sarah enjoyed having such entertaining company, having her husband all to herself was one of her favorite things, especially on a gorgeous summer's day like today.

With a sigh—she was impatient for Alex to arrive—she sat in the window seat and toyed with the sapphire and pearl brooch pinned to the ivory stomacher of her pale blue silk gown. Of course, while she waited, she could play the spinet or finish embroidering the last of the floral cushions she'd begun all those months ago when she'd first come to Eilean Dubh.

Strange how it seemed like it was only yesterday but also a lifetime ago.

The feeling of restlessness persisted and Sarah fell to contemplating the glorious view. At this time of year, Schiehallion was bare of snow but still majestically beautiful. The peak brought to mind so many different memories, some lovely and some troublesome; like the day she'd worked out Alex's true identity and Isla had tricked her into getting lost on Rannoch Moor. And then there was the night she'd used Fairy Hill as a beacon to guide her back to Alex after Malcolm had kidnapped her.

For several weeks after Malcolm had died, Sarah had been worried someone would suspect Alex had something to do with the Earl of Tay's demise—after all, he'd sent several ransom notes signed "Janus" to Malcolm. Even though Alex had assured her Malcolm would never be found—and no one would be able to identify him as Janus—it wasn't until Captain Hamilton had reported the Earl of Tay's horse had been discovered wandering just outside of Balloch, and that it was commonly believed he'd met with foul play at the hands of common footpads or a band of reivers, did Sarah begin to relax. In recent weeks, rumors had also been heard in Edinburgh, and as far afield in London, that the Earl of Tay had been in dire financial straits with debt collectors hounding him.

Whenever Society's curious gossipmongers asked Sarah if she knew anything about Lord Tay's whereabouts, she'd simply shrug and say they'd ended their engagement on the night of the Kenmuir's Ball in February, and having no wish to continue the association, she'd quit Edinburgh the following day.

It was telling indeed that no one seemed particularly bothered by his disappearance. Not even his sister, Lady Glenleven.

Whilst they'd sojourned in Edinburgh at the beginning of March, Sarah had learned that Damaris had become engaged to Lord Arbelour, the older gentleman she'd been flirting with over faro at the Kenmuir's Saint Valentine's Ball. By all popular accounts, Damaris was content with the match—a fact Aunt Judith had confirmed when she related the story of her last visit to Tay House when she'd been searching, not only for Sarah, but her missing parure.

As to what Damaris made of Malcolm's mysterious disappearance, Sarah had no idea, but the newlywedded Lady Arbelour certainly hadn't made a fuss about it. Perhaps she believed the theory that her brother had been murdered outside of Balloch by a person or persons unknown. According to Aunt Judith, the countess had never been terribly fond of her brutish brother. Although Sarah had never really felt any fondness for Damaris, she certainly wished her well.

Sarah touched her gold wedding band and smiled to herself. It was certainly the season for love and marriage. Shortly after she'd reunited with Aunt Judith in Edinburgh, she'd learned the inquiry agent her erstwhile guardian, Mr. Swindon, had hired had begun to delicately court her aunt with a view to marrying her. Thrilled Aunt Judith had found love at long last, Sarah had gifted her Linden Hall just before she married the affable Mr. Weston in Newcastle in April... with the proviso she and Alex could visit whenever they wanted to—a condition her aunt had readily agreed to.

Isla had also found contentment at last, with MacLagan. Sarah smiled as she recalled the footman's devotion to Isla during her convalescence, and in no time at all it seemed the maid had begun to harbor a tentative *tendre* for the young man too. The pair had been married at the kirk in Kinloch last month and Alex had set them up with a cottage in the village. Dobson and Aileen were frequent visitors, and MacLagan was due to open a cobbler's shop in the next few weeks.

And then, of course, there'd been her own wedding day—one of the most joyous days of Sarah's life. With the Earl of Strathburn acting as a sponsor, the Lord Advocate had been persuaded to grant Alex temporary clemency pending a hearing in the British Parliament, which had the power to grant him an unequivocal pardon.

And so it was on a fair morning at the end of March that Sarah had at last wed the love of her life, Alexander MacIvor—not Alexander Price nor Alexander Black—in Edinburgh's ornate St Giles Cathedral. Sarah had worn a sky-blue dress and her mother's sapphire and pearl necklace, brooch, and earrings. Whilst she was sad her father had not been alive to bear witness to her happiness, she was grateful her aunt and newfound friends—Robert and Jessie Grant, Lord and Lady Lochrose, and Robert's father, Lord Strathburn—had all been able to attend the nuptials.

The excited barks of Bandit in the walled garden below alerted Sarah to the fact her handsome husband must have arrived at last. She'd been so lost in her musings, she hadn't noticed the rowboat was missing from the far shore.

After a minute or two, she heard Alex calling her name.

"I'm up here, darling, in the solar," she called back, and within the space of a few heartbeats, he'd bounded up the stairs to join her.

They might have been married for two months, but Sarah's pulse never failed to quicken at the sight of him—especially when he grinned at her like he was grinning now.

Alex swept her up into his arms and spun her around before capturing her face in his hands and kissing her. "What are you doing all the way up here in a tower, my fair Lady Rannoch?" he asked, his gray eyes twinkling with both affection and amusement.

"It's such a glorious day, I wanted to enjoy the view."

"The only time I enjoy the view is when I'm looking at you."

She laughed. "There must be something wrong with your eyes then."

"No, I don't think so," he said, slowly and deliberately raking his gaze over her. "My eyesight is perfect."

Sarah swatted his arm playfully. "Well, when you've had your fill, there's a wonderful luncheon waiting downstairs for us. Tartlets with smoked salmon and cress, and early strawberries with clotted cream. And a lovely apple cider."

Alex lashed her close again and his mouth lifted into the wolfish grin she loved so much. "I'd much rather have my fill of you, but…" His expression altered—a slight furrow appeared between his dark brows. "I have something I want to show you first."

"Heavens, it sounds serious."

"In a way, it is."

Sarah's heart began to beat a fast tattoo as Alex reached into the pocket of his hunter green riding coat then withdrew a folded piece of parchment with a cracked, red wax seal.

"This arrived during the morning," he said gravely as he handed it to her, "after you'd left."

"What is it?" she asked in a voice breathless with nerves. Her fingers trembled as she opened the missive. Was it bad news? Dear Lord, she hoped not.

"Read it and see." Alex's mouth twitched with a smile and his gray eyes began to dance.

Dear Lord Rannoch,
Pursuant to our meeting at my offices on the seventh day of
March, in the year of our Lord, 1757, I recently petitioned
Parliament…

"It's from the Lord Advocate," she breathed.

"Yes." Alex was smiling widely now. "Read on."

… you have been granted a full pardon and your late father's titles
and lands have been fully restored to you, and your descendants,
as the rightful heir forthwith …

Sarah squealed and dropped the letter as she threw her arms around Alex. "You're pardoned! Oh, I cannot believe it!"

Alex picked her up and swung her around again until she was giddy with joy and laughter.

When her husband put her down, he lifted her chin with gentle fingers and bestowed the sweetest kiss she'd ever received, his lips tasting hers with breath-stealing tenderness. As one kiss was followed by another, then another, Sarah's toes curled in her silk shoes and she grasped Alex's firm biceps so she wouldn't melt into a puddle at his feet.

When they drew apart, Alex was smiling. "I never thought I could be this happy," he murmured, brushing his thumb along her cheek.

Sarah bit her lip and warmth flooded her face as she contemplated how her handsome husband would react to what she was about to say. "Well, my darling Alex, I have some news that I hope you will like just as much..."

Alex's breath caught in his chest as anticipation coiled tight inside him. Cradling his beautiful wife's chin, he trapped her gaze. Sarah's cheeks were flushed, her blue eyes bright with excitement. *And love.* "What are you trying to tell me, my darling?"

Her lovely mouth lifted into a shy smile. "I'm with child," she whispered. "You're going to be a father, Lord Rannoch."

Elation flared and Alex gave a whoop of joy. "Oh, my God, Sarah," he cried and he pulled her close before giving her a fierce kiss of adoration. "That's...that's wonderful!"

"I know." Tears spilled from Sarah's eyes. "I've suspected for several weeks now, but I wanted to be sure before I told you."

"Do you know how much I love you?" Alex asked fiercely, his voice thick with emotion. "Because I don't think you do."

"Why don't you show me?" Sarah whispered. Her elegant hands slid beneath the lapels of his coat and the rapid beat of his heart sent burning desire straight to his groin in response to her invitation.

"My dearest heart, I intend to."

He framed Sarah's face with his hands as though she were the most precious flower in the world and lavished her mouth with a deep and languorous kiss. Their lips tasted, their tongues caressed, their breathing melded as they drank of each other, savored each other.

Loved each other.

Impatient to touch and taste Sarah's satiny skin, Alex lifted her curling blond tresses and devoured her fragrant neck, inhaling her, unable to get enough of her.

Gripping his shoulders, she sank against him. "Undress me," she whispered.

"You read my thoughts exactly." As Alex continued to lick and kiss her delicate ear, jaw, and neck, his fingers swiftly loosened the fastenings at her bodice, and then he gently slid her gown off her shoulders. It pooled on the rug at her feet, and her petticoats quickly joined the pile.

Sarah pushed his coat down his arms. "I think you should undress too," she murmured huskily.

Alex smiled as his coat fell to the floor. "Whatever you want, my lady. I'm yours to command."

"I certainly like the sound of that." She looked up at him through her eyelashes. The boldness he adored—the spirit which had been there from the first night he'd met Sarah—was simmering under the surface. "Take off your waistcoat and shirt."

His cock swelling, Alex complied with his wife's request. How he loved the way she ran her ardent gaze over him. Traced her fingertips over his shoulders and across his pectoral muscles. Kissed his neck. Caressed his ribs and pressed her hand against his straining erection.

She was effortlessly stoking the flames of his arousal to blazing proportions.

He needed her naked. Now.

His fingers clumsy with impatience, Alex tugged at the laces of her stays and pulled off her shift until all she had on was her white silk stockings fastened with garters of pale blue ribbon and her ivory silk pumps.

Dear God in heaven, how did he get this lucky?

Sarah never failed to take his breath away. Every day he thanked God she was his, this beautiful woman who would be the mother of his child. *Their child.*

He cupped her breasts and tenderly worshipped each rosy point with his lips and tongue, all the while kicking himself for not noticing they were a little fuller and heavier. Or that Sarah's slender waist was a little thicker and her smooth belly a little rounder. "I want you like this, with your shoes and stockings on," he murmured, his voice hoarse with lust. "On the window seat."

She bit her lip as an endearing blush suffused her cheeks. "Very well."

Sarah led him to the window seat by the north-facing window with its breathtaking view of loch, braes, and sky—but nothing was as breath-stealing as the vision of his practically naked wife. A slight breeze made the gauzy white curtains flutter around her like a veil and her pink nipples tightened. Alex licked his lips.

God, how he wanted to taste her.

But Sarah apparently had other things in mind. She pushed him onto the seat and undid the buttons fastening the fall of his buff breeches. When his cock sprang out, thick and ready for her, she ran her hand up, then down, his throbbing shaft and Alex groaned. "At this rate, I'll come off in seconds, you wicked woman."

Her answering smile was purely coquettish and utterly adorable. "Oh, wicked is what I intend to be, my lord. Lie down."

Alex wasn't about to argue with her. He leaned back on his elbows and his wonderfully wicked wife straddled him. Reaching down, one of her hands circled his shaft and she unerringly guided him to her hot, slick entrance.

A deep growl of appreciation rumbled through Alex as his wife slowly lowered her body, until he was completely engulfed by her wet, satin-sleek passage. Taking his weight on one arm, he reached out and caressed the exquisitely sensitive nub at the top of her sex with the tip of one finger, exactly the way she liked it, circling and flicking her, coaxing her along the path to ultimate pleasure.

Grasping his wrist to keep his hand in place, Sarah trembled and moaned and her luscious breasts rose and fell with each breath she took. Her blue eyes were heavy-lidded and hazy with desire. Dear God, although remaining still while buried inside her was pure torture, he wondered if he'd died and gone to heaven.

Torn between his desire to take his time touching and tasting all of Sarah's lush curves and secret places, and the overwhelming need to thrust his hips, he gripped her waist. "Take your pleasure, Sarah," he urged through gritted teeth, "and I will follow.'

She smiled a siren's smile and undulated her hips, rocking and circling, teasing him, until he thought he might go mad.

"Please," Alex gasped. "I cannot bear it. Ride me hard and well, my love."

"With pleasure," Sarah whispered. Leaning forward, taking her weight on her hands, she kissed him, her tongue slipping inside his mouth and tangling with his. Her silken locks brushed his face and her hard-as-pearl nipples skimmed over his chest, making him groan.

Then, thank God she raised her hips, sliding upwards until only the head of his member remained inside her before she sank downwards, clasping him intimately again. Rippling around him. The exquisite friction, her tight inner embrace, every sensation was sublime. She repeated the action and this time he joined her, thrusting upwards.

Dear God, he was primed to come, his climax drawing steadily and inexorably closer as Sarah began to plunge up and down, over and over again. The soft wet sounds of their coupling, their gasps and pants of pleasure, filled the warm summer air. Paradise beckoned, and Alex wanted Sarah with him when he arrived. Gripping her tighter still, he locked his gaze with hers and pumped wildly, stroking in and out of her, matching her frantic pace until at last she gave an exultant cry. Her eyes closed, her brow furrowed, and he held still to watch pleasure claim her, wash through her. It was the most beautiful sight he'd ever seen and enough to send him flying skyward as well.

Alex thrust once, twice, then he climaxed, hard. His back arched and he threw his head back, calling Sarah's name as ecstasy ripped through him, carrying him away to a place beyond the clouds, into the sun, into heaven itself.

When he opened his eyes, his body still humming with bliss, it was to find Sarah looking down at him, a smile of pure contentment curving her kiss-bruised lips.

"I love you, Alexander MacIvor," she whispered, her blue eyes brighter than the sky above Loch Rannoch. "And I thank God that you love me too."

He smiled back and cradled her flushed cheek with a gentle hand. Kissed her fingertips when they brushed over his lips. "I love you too, Sarah, with my whole heart. For so long I had nothing but darkness in my life, but now I have the gift of you." His hand slid between them and caressed her belly. "And our child. And I have never felt so overjoyed. With you by my side, I will be living in the sunlight forevermore."

Sarah's answering smile made Alex's heart sing, and he drew her down for a tender kiss, his Lady Rannoch. It was a kiss meant to show her everything he felt deep down in his soul but couldn't quite put into words; a kiss of possession, a kiss of adoration, but most of all, love.

And God willing, he would kiss her, just like this every single day, until the end of his days.

Author's Note

In telling *The Laird of Blackloch*, I've used a little poetic license which I hope you, my reader, will forgive...

At the beginning of *The Laird of Blackloch*, Alex stumbles across Jacobite clansmen burying caskets of gold coins on the shores of Loch Arkaig. Legend has it there is missing Jacobite treasure hidden somewhere in the Highlands. By all accounts two French frigates, the *Bellona* and *Mars*, arrived at Loch nan Uamh on the west coast of Scotland at the end of April 1746 and delivered seven large caskets of Louis D'or gold coins donated by the Spanish to support Bonnie Prince Charlie's cause. However, the Jacobite army had already been defeated at Culloden. Apparently the Prince's former secretary, Murray of Broughton, was entrusted with looking after the treasure worth over one million livres; the money was to be used to help fugitive Jacobites. However, he was arrested by government troops in June 1746 and the treasure may have passed to the Camerons of Lochiel for safekeeping. It was reportedly buried on the shores of Loch Arkaig but may have been unearthed and reburied several times over the next few months to prevent loyalist soldiers discovering it. There are also rumors that one of the caskets was stolen by the Macdonalds of Barrisdale. Over the years, many have searched for the missing gold, but to this day its whereabouts remains an unsolved mystery.

The fictional village of Kinloch, which I describe at the eastern end of Loch Rannoch, is an amalgamation of the actual village Kinloch Rannoch and the historical hamlet of Georgetown at the western end of Loch Rannoch. I've tweaked the history of each village slightly and altered the location of certain historical landmarks. At the time *The Laird of Blackloch* is set, the dragoon barracks were actually located in Georgetown (eventually renamed Braes of Rannoch and now known as Bridge of Gaur). Following the Forty-five, there are accounts of an evangelist in the Loch Rannoch area who preached regularly to the local community, but the church at Braes of Rannoch wasn't built until 1776; the church I've mentioned in "Kinloch" and the nearby bridge are entirely fictional.

Blackloch Castle and Eilean Dubh, which I've placed toward the southwest end of Loch Rannoch, are my own inventions entirely. The Black Wood on the western edge of the loch—an ancient Caledonian pine forest—is an actual place name I drew on for inspiration. While there are several islands named Eilean Dubh in Scotland, *my* Eilean Dubh (Black Island) was inspired by Loch Rannoch's crannog—a medieval man-made island with a nineteenth century tower folly upon it—named Eilean nam Faoileag, or the "Island of Gulls." However, it is toward the middle of the loch.

Whilst Clan Robertson—also known as Clan Donnachaidh—owned much of the land around Loch Rannoch in the eighteenth century, for the purposes of my story I've chosen to feature one of the clan's septs, Clan MacIvor, instead. The hereditary title Baron Rannoch is my own invention.

At the beginning of the story, Alex says, *"Nunquam obliviscar"* when making a vow of vengeance. This Latin phrase which means "I will never forget" is Clan MacIvor's motto.

Some may question whether Alexander MacIvor, Lord Rannoch—aka Alexander Price—would have really been able to buy back his family's forfeited estate. In my story, Alexander's logging company purchases the confiscated Rannoch estate from the Crown's Forfeited Estates Commission. Whilst I've used a little poetic license, my premise isn't without historical precedent. The Forfeited Estates Commission was established in 1747 to manage the many forfeited clan estates following the Forty-five Rebellion. These estates were eventually restored to their former owners or heirs for a price in 1784, but I wanted Alexander to reclaim his estate sooner. The idea that he might be able to buy back his land—albeit on the sly—occurred to me when I came across an account of the Crown selling off a forfeited estate following the first Jacobite Rebellion. The estate of the Jacobite Earl of Callendar was apparently sold to the York Building Company in 1720, hence my idea that Alex (in the guise of Alexander Price) might be able to do the same.

O Waly Waly is an old Scottish folk song which has its origins in the seventeenth century and has a very convoluted, albeit fascinating, history. There appear to be countless variations from the eighteenth and nineteenth centuries which are related to the well-known 1906 version, *The Water is Wide*. I've included two verses from older variants which best fit the theme of my story; one comes from a ballad perhaps published in 1750 in Newcastle, England, where my heroine Sarah hails from.

THANK YOU FROM THE AUTHOR

Thank you so much for reading **The Laird of Blackloch**, Book 2 in my Highland Rogue series! If you have the time and inclination, please do consider sharing a review. I would greatly appreciate it!

Amy Rose Bennett

~

WANT TO READ MORE IN THE HIGHLAND ROGUE SERIES?
THE MASTER OF STRATHBURN
HIGHLAND ROGUE, BOOK 1

A sweeping, sexy Highland romance about a wanted Jacobite with a wounded soul, and a spirited Scottish lass on the run.

After a decade spent in exile, Robert Grant, Jacobite, has returned home to Lochrose Castle in the Highlands to reconcile with his long-estranged father, the Earl of Strathburn. Problem is, there is a price on Robert's head and his avaricious younger half-brother, Simon—pretender to the title Master of Strathburn—will do anything to stop him reclaiming his birthright. But it's not only Simon and the Redcoats who threaten to destroy Robert's plans. Perhaps the worst is yet to come, as a flame-haired complication of the feminine kind enters the scene...

Jessie Munroe is forced to flee Lochrose Castle after the dissolute Simon Grant tries to coerce her into becoming his mistress. After a fateful encounter with a mysterious and handsome hunter, Robert, in a remote Highland glen, she throws her lot in with the stranger—even though she suspects he is a fugitive. Events soon suggest that this man is dangerous, but in an entirely different way to Simon...

Despite their searing attraction, Robert and Jessie struggle to trust each other as they both seek a place to call home. The stakes are high and only one thing is certain: Simon Grant is in pursuit of them both...

DON'T MISS AMY ROSE BENNETT'S OTHER ROMANCES...

Visit Amy Rose Bennett's website at **www.amyrosebennett.com** to find out more about her books...

SCANDALOUS REGENCY WIDOWS

Lady Beauchamp's Proposal, Book 1
The Ice Duchess, Book 2
A Most Unsuitable Countess, Book 3

~

IMPROPER LIAISONS

An Improper Proposition, Book 1
An Improper Governess, Book 2
An Improper Christmas, Book 3
An Improper Duke, Book 4

~

THE BYRONIC BOOK CLUB

Up All Night with a Good Duke, Book 1
Curled Up with an Earl, Book 2
Tall, Duke, and Scandalous, Book 3

~

THE DISREPUTABLE DEBUTANTES

How to Catch a Wicked Viscount, Book 1
How to Catch an Errant Earl, Book 2
How to Catch a Sinful Marquess, Book 3
How to Catch a Devilish Duke, Book 4

~

HIGHLAND ROGUE

The Master of Strathburn, Book 1
The Laird of Blackloch, Book 2

~

WICKED WINTER NIGHTS

My Lady of Misrule, Book 1
My Lord of Misrule, Book 2
A Twelfth Night Wager, Book 3 (Out 2025)

~

STANDALONE TITLES

All She Wants for Christmas
Dashing Through the Snow

About the Author

Amy Rose Bennett is an award-winning Australian author who has a passion for penning emotion-packed historical romances and more recently, historical rom-coms with a dash of fantasy. A former speech pathologist, Amy is happily married to her very own romantic hero and has two lovely, exceedingly accomplished adult daughters. When she's not creating stories, Amy loves to cook up a storm in the kitchen, lose herself in a good book, and when she can afford it, travel to all the places she writes about.

Visit Amy's website at **www.amyrosebennett.com** to find out more.

www.ingramcontent.com/pod-product-compliance
Lightning Source LLC
Chambersburg PA
CBHW060518220726

48290CB00015B/1764